Anonymous

Hymns Ancient and Modern for the Use in the Services of the Church

Anatiposi

Anonymous

Hymns Ancient and Modern for the Use in the Services of the Church

Reprint of the original, first published in 1875.

1st Edition 2024 | ISBN: 978-3-38283-132-5

Anatiposi Verlag is an imprint of Outlook Verlagsgesellschaft mbH.

Verlag (Publisher): Outlook Verlag GmbH, Zeilweg 44, 60439 Frankfurt, Deutschland
Vertretungsberechtigt (Authorized to represent): E. Roepke, Zeilweg 44, 60439 Frankfurt, Deutschland
Druck (Print): Books on Demand GmbH, In de Tarpen 42, 22848 Norderstedt, Deutschland

HYMNS

ANCIENT AND MODERN

FOR USE IN THE

SERVICES OF THE CHURCH

WITH ACCOMPANYING TUNES

COMPILED AND ARRANGED

UNDER THE MUSICAL EDITORSHIP OF

WILLIAM HENRY MONK, Mus. Doc.,
PROFESSOR OF VOCAL MUSIC IN KING'S COLLEGE, LONDON.

Revised and Enlarged Edition.

"Young men and maidens, old men and children, praise the Name of the Lord."

LONDON:
PRINTED FOR THE PROPRIETORS BY
WILLIAM CLOWES AND SONS, Limited,
STAMFORD STREET AND CHARING CROSS.
PUBLISHING OFFICE, 13, CHARING CROSS, S.W.

LONDON:
WILLIAM CLOWES AND SONS, LIMITED, TYPE MUSIC AND GENERAL PRINTERS,
STAMFORD STREET AND CHARING CROSS.

PREFACE.

THE Compilers of *Hymns Ancient and Modern* are well aware that it is no light matter to put forth a revised and enlarged Edition of their Book. It is too widely used, and (perhaps they may add) too much loved, to allow of any change being made without good cause. But the very fact of its large circulation is their best apology for revision. It is a simple debt they owe to the Church. The fourteen years that have passed since their first copy was published have seen a great change in opinion on many points. For example, it is not necessary now, as it was thought to be then, to print an altered or shortened form of a good Hymn simply because it happened to be so used by certain congregations. No one wishes now to reprint tunes with unsatisfactory harmonies because we have been accustomed to them. The general desire is rather to have a Hymn as its author wrote it; and Compilers are expected not to make changes in it without strong reason. The best Musicians of the day are writing new Tunes and re-harmonizing old Melodies. New Hymns have been written to meet admitted needs. It would surely then have been almost a dereliction of their duty to the Church, if the Compilers of *Hymns Ancient and Modern* had not taken advantage of these altered circumstances.

They therefore now venture to offer what is not a new Book but a revised and enlarged Edition of the old. It contains nearly all the old Hymns, and most of the old Tunes; what have been omitted are such as were either seldom used, or have been replaced by better ones of a similar character. But the whole Book has been most carefully revised: in some

Hymns the original text has been more closely followed; the Translations are in some cases improved; the Tunes are often better harmonized; a more orderly arrangement has been made, according to subjects, of the "General" Hymns; and a large number of new Hymns and Tunes are added, many of them written for this Book and now printed for the first time. Among the new Hymns may be mentioned especially those on the "Seven Words," which our Lord spoke on the Cross, as being likely to meet a want which is becoming every year more widely felt; and those for the several Festivals of the Apostles and Evangelists, and for other Holy Days. Some Metrical Litanies are also given. Other improvements will be noticed; as, e.g., the type, the insertion of clefs and signatures to each line, the marks of expression added to the words, and a complete Index with the Names of Authors of Hymns as well as of Composers of Tunes.

As before, so now, they have had a large amount of kind and valuable co-operation, which they cannot too gratefully acknowledge; and that not only from old friends but from many new contributors and fellow-workers. Not to mention again those of their former contributors who now "rest from their labours" (some of whose names will long be as household words among us), the Compilers desire to offer their warmest thanks, first to Mr. Monk (now the Professor of Vocal Music in King's College, London), who has been the same kind and able coadjutor that he was at the beginning of their work, and to whose musical ability, and sound judgment, and good taste they are again so deeply indebted; and then to Dr. Stainer, the Organist of St. Paul's Cathedral, and to the Rev. J. B. Dykes, Mus. Doc., Vicar of St. Oswald's, Durham, whose patient criticisms and hearty co-operation in all the musical part of their work have been scarcely less valuable than the many beautiful Tunes which they have both contributed.

For Hymns first published in this, or former editions, and for the most part written at their request, the Compilers are under special obligation to the Rev. W. Bright, D.D., Regius Professor of Ecclesiastical History in the University of Oxford; to the Rev. John Ellerton, Vicar of Hinstock; to the Rev. W. D. Maclagan, Rector of Newington; to Mrs. Alexander (the gifted Authoress of "Hymns for Little Children"); to Mrs. William Alderson; to Miss Katherine D. Cornish; to the Rev. R. M. Benson; to the Rev. S. J. Stone; to the Rev. Henry Twells; to the Rev. Laurence Tuttiett; to the Rev. J. J. Daniell; to the Rev. J. H. Clark; to the Rev. J. W. Hewett; to the Rev. Sabine Baring-Gould; to the Rev. V. S. S. Coles; to the Rev. W. St. Hill Bourne; to the Rev. A. W. Chatfield; to the Rev. George Samuel Hodges; to Mr. William Whiting; to Mr. W. Chatterton Dix; and to Mr. D. T. Morgan.

For permission to print Hymns already published they also offer their cordial thanks to several of the fore-named writers; and to the Right Rev. the Lord Bishop of Lincoln (of whose Hymns, that on Almsgiving, No. 365, is now printed according to his own revision); to the Right Rev. the Lord Bishop of Ely; to the Earl Nelson (for the use of No. 214, from the Salisbury Hymn Book); to the Rev. Edward Hayes Plumptre, Professor of the Exegesis of the New Testament in King's College, London; to the Rev. W. Bullock, D.D., Dean of Nova Scotia; to the Rev. J. W. Irons, D.D.; to the Rev. W. Walsham How; to the Rev. Godfrey Thring; to the Rev. J. E. Millard, D.D.; to the Rev. John Henry Newman, D.D.; to the Rev. Lewis Hensley; to the Rev. Henry Downton; to the Rev. R. Hayes Robinson; to the Rev. I. Gregory Smith; to the Rev. Archer Gurney; to the Rev. G. R. Prynne; to the Rev. W. H. Bathurst; to the Rev. E. H. Bickersteth; to the Rev. Gerard Moultrie; to the Rev. R. F. Littledale, LL.D.; to the Rev. T. B. Pollock; to the Rev. J. E. Bode; to Dr. Bonar; to Mr. Albert Midlane; to Mr. Matthew Bridges; to Miss Catherine Winkworth; to Miss Frances E. Cox; to Miss Caroline M. Noel; to H. L. L., the Authoress of "Hymns from the Land of Luther" (for her Hymn, No. 357, so suitable for use by "Lay Helpers" in the work of Christ); to Miss Frances R. Havergal (for the companion Hymn to the foregoing, and for several other beautiful Hymns); to Mrs. Alford (for permission to print three more Hymns by one to whom we were from the first indebted, the late Dean of Canterbury); to Mrs. Babington (for permission to print another of Miss Charlotte Elliott's Hymns); and lastly, but with special gratitude, to the Rev. John Chandler, the Rev. J. W. Copeland, the Rev. Edward Caswall, and Mr. John David Chambers, for permitting their translations of Latin Hymns to be so freely used in this Book.

For Tunes written expressly for this Book they need not repeat their thanks to Professor Monk, Dr. Stainer, and Dr. Dykes (whose most valuable co-operation has been already acknowledged); but they must be gratefully offered to the Right Rev. Bishop Jenner; to the Rev. Sir Frederick A. Gore Ouseley, Bart., Mus. Doc., Professor of Music in the University of Oxford; to Dr. Herbert S. Oakeley, M.A., Professor of Music in the University of Edinburgh; to Sir George J. Elvey, Organist of St. George's Chapel, Windsor; to Mr. George Cooper, Organist of the Chapel Royal, St. James'; to Mr. Edward J. Hopkins, Organist of the Temple Church; to Dr. Armes, Organist of the Cathedral, Durham; to Dr. S. S. Wesley, Organist of the Cathedral, Gloucester; to Mr. John Hopkins, Organist of the Cathedral, Rochester; to Dr. Bridge, Organist of the Cathedral, Manchester; to Dr. Gauntlett; to Mr. Henry Smart; to Mr. George Alexander Macfarren; to Mr. Walter Macfarren; to Mr. E. H. Thorne; to Dr. Steggall; to Mr. Joseph Barnby; to Mr. C. A. Barry; to Mr. Frank Champneys; to Mr. J. W. Elliott; to Mr. Berthold Tours; to Mr. Henry Gadsby; to Mr. George Martin, Mus. Bac.; to Mr. Everard Hulton, Mus. Bac.; to Mr. W. H. Sangster, Mus. Bac.; to Mr. E. H. Turpin; to Mr. James Langran; to Mr. C. E. Willing; to Mr. W. S. Hoyte; to Mr. H. S. Irons; to Mr. Arthur Henry Brown; to Mr. John Heywood; to Mr. John Wilkes; to Mr. J. Hornsey Casson; to Mr. William Hurst; to Mr. James Comley; to the Rev. L. G. Hayne, Mus. Doc.; to the Rev. W. D. Maclagan; to the Rev. F. A. J. Hervey; to the Rev. W. Statham; to the Rev. Sabine Baring Gould; to the Rev. John Hampton; to the Rev. F. W. Hogan; and to Miss Maria Tiddeman.

For the use of Tunes that had been already published the Compilers desire to thank not only many of the foregoing Contributors but also Mr. Turle, Organist of Westminster Abbey; Mr. Arthur Sullivan; Mr. John Hullah; Mrs. Havergal (for a Tune by her late husband, the Rev. W. H. Havergal, whose generous aid in this work will be always gratefully remembered); Mr. Richard Redhead (for Tunes inserted with the consent of Messrs. Masters & Co., and Messrs. Metzler & Co.); Mr. Walter B. Gilbert, Mus. Bac.; Mr. A. R. Reinagle; Mr. Henry Lahee; Mr. Wilhelm Schulthes; Mr. James Watson; Mr. Frederick Westlake (for a Tune inserted with the consent of Messrs. Burns, Oates, & Co.); the Rev. R. F. Dale, Mus. Bac.; the Rev. T. R. Matthews; the Rev. R. R. Chope (for permission to insert the Tunes by Dr. Dykes to Hymns Nos. 21 (1st Tune), 99, 140 (2nd Tune), 260, 285, and 289, from his Hymn and Tune Book); the Rev. T. Darling (for permission to print from his "Hymns for the Church of England" Dr. Steggall's Tune to Hymn No. 233); Mr. Lamborn Cock (for permission to insert Dr. Steggall's Tune to Hymn No. 81); Messrs. Nisbet & Co. (for their generous permission to print Tunes which are their copyright); and the Society for Promoting Christian Knowledge.

In conclusion the Compilers venture to repeat the words of their former preface, that "they have endeavoured to do their work in the spirit of the English Prayer-book, and in dependence on the grace of God;" and they commend to Him the result of what is, in all human probability, their last revision (a revision to which, perhaps, even more anxious thought and time has been given than was spent on their first work), in deep thankfulness for the wonderful success with which He has been pleased to bless their efforts hitherto, and with the earnest prayer that they may still "promote, in some degree, His greater glory, and the good of His Church."

January 21st, 1875.

INDEX.

*The Hymns and Tunes marked thus * are copyright of the Compilers; as well as many of the Harmonies of other Tunes, and portions of the Translations.*

INDEX.

*The Hymns and Tunes marked thus * are copyright of the Compilers; as well as many of the Harmonies of other Tunes, and portions of the Translations.*

INDEX.

INDEX.

INDEX.

INDEX.

† This tune has been collated with the Original Manuscript, in the Fitzwilliam Museum; the small notes for the Organ are Handel's.

First words of Hymn.	No.	Name of Tune and Measure.	Composer of Tune.
Sing Alleluia forth	296	1. Endless Alleluia. 2. *Alleluia perenne. } 10 10 7	1. Joseph Barnby. 2. William Henry Monk.
Sing, my tongue	97	Pange Lingua. 8 7 8 7 8 7.	Ancient Plain-song.
Sing praise to God	293	Erk. 8 7 8 7, 8 8 7	German.
*Sing we the glory	39	St. Hugh. C.M.	Edward J. Hopkins.
*Sion's Daughter	100	Cassel. 7 7 7 7 7 7	German.
*Six days of labour	44	*Malmesbury Abbey. C.M.	James Comley.
Soldiers of Christ	270	*St. Ethelwald. S. M.	William Henry Monk.
*Soldiers, who are	447	Redhead, No. 45. 7 7 7 7	Ancient Melody (arr. by R. Redhead.)
Son of the Highest	459	St. Mary Magdalene. C.M.	German.
Songs of praise	297	Culbach. 7 7 7 7	German.
Songs of thankfulness	81	St. Edmund. 7 7 7 7 D.	C. Steggall, Mus. Doc.
Spirit of mercy	155	Melcombe. L.M.	Samuel Webbe.
Stars of the morning	423	*Triaagion. 10 10 10 10	Henry Smart.
Sun of my soul	24	1. Abends 2. *Keble 3. Hursley } L.M.	1. Sir. H. S. Oakeley, M.A., Mus. Doc. 2. Rev. J. B. Dykes, Mus. Doc. 3. German (?).
*Sweet flowerets	68	*Salvete Flores. L.M.	Rev. J. B. Dykes, Mus. Doc.
Sweet Saviour	28	1. *Christchurch 2. *St. Matthias 3. *In tenebris lumen } 8 8 8 8 8 8	1. Rev. Sir F. A. G. Ouseley, Bart. 2. William Henry Monk. 3. Rev. J. B. Dykes, Mus. Doc.
Sweet the moments	109	Batty. 8 7 8 7	German.
Take up thy cross	263	Breslau. L.M.	German.
Tender Shepherd	402	Meinhold. 7 8 7 8 7 7	German.
Ten thousand times	222	*Alford. 7 6 8 6 D	Rev. J. B. Dykes, Mus. Doc.
That day of wrath	206	Abbotsford. L.M.	German.
That Eastertide	126	1. *Tristes erant 2. *Easter Chant } L.M.	1. William Henry Monk. 2. Rev. J. B. Dykes, Mus. Doc.
The Advent of our	48	Franconia. S.M.	German.
*The ancient law	70	St. Michael. S.M.	From Day's Psalter.
The Apostles' hearts	126	1. *Tristes erant 2. *Easter Chant } L.M.	1. William Henry Monk. 2. Rev. J. B. Dykes, Mus. Doc.
The Church's one	215	Aurelia. 7 6 7 6 D.	S. S. Wesley, Mus. Doc.
The Day of	132	*Rotterdam. 7 6 7 6 D.	Berthold Tours.
The day is past	21	1. St. Anatolius 2. St. Anatolius } 7 6 7-6 8 8	1. Rev. J. B. Dykes, Mus. Doc. 2. Arthur H. Brown.
The earth, O Lord	354	Manchester New. C.M.	R. Wainwright, Mus. Doc.
The eternal gifts	430	Æterna Christi munera. L.M.	Ancient Plain-song.
*The fish in wave	42	St. Flavian. C.M.	Barber's Psalm Tunes, 1687.
The God, Whom	449	St. Ambrose. L.M.	Ancient Plain-song.
The great forerunner	415	Beccles. L.M.	German.
The Head that once	301	St. Magnus. C.M.	Jeremiah Clarke.
*The Heavenly Child	78	Tallis. C.M.	Thomas Tallis.
The Heavenly Word	311	1. O Salutaris. 2. St. Vincent. } L.M.	1. Ancient Plain-song. 2. J. Uglow.
*The King of love	197	*Dominus regit me. 8 7 8 7	Rev. J. B. Dykes, Mus. Doc.
The Lamb's high	128	Ad cœnam Agni. L.M.	Ancient Plain-song.
The life which God's	66	*Whitwell. C.M.	John Hopkins.
The people that	80	Dundee. C.M.	Scotch Psalter.
The radiant morn hath	19	* St. Gabriel. 8 8 8 4	Rev. Sir. F. A. G. Ouseley, Bart.
The roseate hues	229	*The roseate hues. D.C.M.	John Stainer, M.A., Mus. Doc.
The Royal Banners	96	1. Vexilla Regis 2. *St. Cecilia } L.M.	1. Ancient Plain-song. 2. Rev. John Hampton.
The Saints of God!	428	*Rest. 8 8 8 8 8 8	John Stainer, M.A., Mus. Doc.
*The Shepherd now was	405	Vulpius. 7 6 7 6	Melchior Vulpius.
The strain upraise	295	Troyte, No. 2. Irregular	Arthur H. Dyke Troyte.
The Son of God goes	439	1. Old 81st } D.C.M. 2. St. Anne } C.M.	1. From Day's Psalter. 2. "Mr. Denby" in Barber's Psalm Tunes, 1687.
*The sower went forth	386	*St. Beatrice. 7 6 7 6 7 6 7 6 7 6 7 6	J. F. Bridge, Mus. Doc.
*The strife is o'er	135	*Victory. 8 8 8	From Palestrina.
The sun is sinking fast	17	*St. Columba. 6 4 6 6	H. S. Irons.
The voice that breathed	350	St. Alphege. 7 8 7 6	H. J. Gauntlett, Mus. Doc.
The world is very evil	226	Pearsall. 7 6 7 6 D.	St. Gall. Katholische Gesangbuch.
*The year is gone	72	Tallis. C.M.	Thomas Tallis.
Thee we adore	312	1. Adoro Te devote 2. *Eucharistic Chant 3. *St. Sacrament } 10 10 10 10	1. Plain-song. 2. William Henry Monk. 3. William Henry Monk.
*There is a blessed	230	1. Annue Christe. 2. *The blessed home } 6 6 6 6 D.	1. Ancient Plain-song. 2. John Stainer, M.A., Mus. Doc.
There is a book	168	St. Flavian. C.M.	Barber's Psalm Tunes, 1687.

INDEX.

Name of Litany.	No.	Author of Hymn.	Composer of Tune.
LITANIES.			
Of the Four Last Things	463	Rev. Thomas Benson Pollock.	*1. William Henry Monk.
Of the Incarnate Word	464	Rev. Thomas Benson Pollock.	*1. Rev. J. B. Dykes, Mus. Doc. *2. Rev. F. A. J. Hervey.
Of Penitence (No. 1).	465	Rev. Thomas Benson Pollock.	*1. J. Stainer, M.A., Mus. Doc. *2. E. H. Turpin.
Of Penitence (No. 2).	466	Rev. R. F. Littledale, LL.D.	*1. ——Har. by C. Bucknall. 2. ——Har. by Arthur Sullivan.
Of the Passion	467	Committee of Clergy.	1. Rev. J. B. Dykes, Mus. Doc. 2. ——Har. by W. H. Monk.
*For the Rogation Days	468	Rev. Sir Henry W. Baker, Bart.	German.
Of Jesus Glorified	469	Rev. Thomas Benson Pollock.	*1. E. H. Turpin *2. Rev. F. A. J. Harvey.
Of the Holy Ghost	470	Compiled from Rev. T. B. Pollock, and Rev. R. F. Littledale, LL.D.	1. J. W. Elliott. *2. E. H. Turpin.
Of the Church.	471	Rev. Thomas Benson Pollock.	*1. E. H. Turpin. 2. ?
*Of the Blessed Sacrament	472	Rev. Sir Henry W. Baker, Bart.	*1. William Henry Monk. *2. Rev. Sir H. W. Baker, Bart. (Har. by W. H. Monk).
For Children	473	Committee of Clergy (chiefly).	*1. Rev. J. B. Dykes, Mus. Doc. *2. Rev. F. A. J. Hervey.

ALPHABETICAL LIST OF TUNES.

*The Tunes marked thus * are Copyright of the Compilers, as well as many of the Harmonies of other Tunes.*

TABLE OF HYMNS.

MARKS OF EXPRESSION.

The marks of expression (*p*, *mf*, *f*, *dim*, *cres*, &c.) given in this Edition, are intended chiefly for the guidance of Choir and Congregation. Such marks vary in power according to the character of the words to which they are affixed; and an Organist will of course exercise his good taste as to which of the many combinations of stops at his command he will use in accompanying.

It should be particularly noticed that each mark is intended to continue in force till another occurs.

Applications for grants of books to poor parishes (giving particulars of population, congregation, etc.), and for permission to print copyright Hymns and Tunes for Choral Festivals, should be made to the Rev. W. Pulling, *Eastnor Rectory, near Ledbury.*

Morning.

Hymn 1.

" Early in the morning will I direct my prayer unto Thee."

mf NOW that the daylight fills the sky,
We lift our héarts to God on high,
That He, in all we dó or say,
Would keep us frée from harm to-day.

May He restrain our tóngues from strife,
And shield from ánger's din our life,
And guard with watchful cáre our eyes
From earth's absórbing vanities.

O may our inmost héarts be pure,
From thoughts of fólly kept secure,
And pride of sinful flésh subdued
Through sparing úse of daily food.

So we, when this day's wórk is o'er,
And shades of níght return once more,
Our path of trial sáfely trod,
Shall give the glóry to our God.

f All praise to God the Fáther be,
All praise, Etérnal Son, to Thee,
Whom with the Spirit wé adore
For ever ánd for evermore.

Morning.

Hymn 2. (First Tune.)

To be sung in Unison.

"He that followeth Me shall not walk in darkness, but shall have the light of life."

f O JESU, Lord of light and grace,
Thou Brightness of the Father's Face,
Thou Fountain of eternal light,
True Day dispersing shades of night;

Come, Very Sun of heavenly love,
Come in Thy radiance from above,
And shed the Holy Spirit's ray
On every thought and sense to-day.

mf So we the Father's help will claim,
And sing the Father's glorious Name,
And His Almighty grace implore
That we may stand, to fall no more.

May He our actions deign to bless,
And quench the darts of wickedness;
In life's rough ways our feet defend,
And grant us patience to the end.

May faith, deep rooted in the soul,
Subdue our flesh, our minds control;
May guile depart and discord cease,
And all within be truth and peace.

So let us gladly pass the day,
Our thoughts as pure as morning ray,
Our faith as noontide glowing bright,
Our minds undimmed by shades of night.

f All praise to God the Father be,
All praise, Eternal Son, to Thee,
Whom with the Spirit we adore
For ever and for evermore.

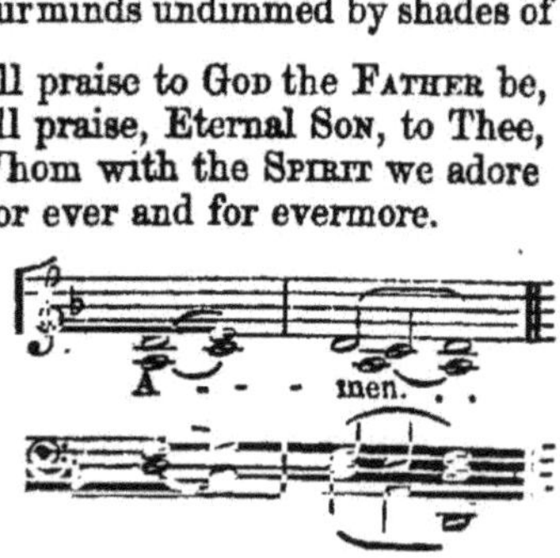

Morning.

Hymn 2. (Second Tune.)

"He that followeth Me shall not walk in darkness, but shall have the light of life."

f O JESU, Lord of light and grace,
Thou Brightness of the Father's Face,
Thou Fountain of eternal light,
True Day dispersing shades of night;

Come, Very Sun of heavenly love,
Come in Thy radiance from above,
And shed the Holy Spirit's ray
On every thought and sense to-day.

mf So we the Father's help will claim,
And sing the Father's glorious Name,
And His Almighty grace implore
That we may stand, to fall no more.

May He our actions deign to bless,
And quench the darts of wickedness;
In life's rough ways our feet defend,
And grant us patience to the end.

May faith, deep rooted in the soul,
Subdue our flesh, our minds control;
May guile depart and discord cease,
And all within be truth and peace.

So let us gladly pass the day,
Our thoughts as pure as morning ray,
Our faith as noontide glowing bright,
Our minds undimmed by shades of night.

f All praise to God the Father be,
All praise, Eternal Son, to Thee,
Whom with the Spirit we adore
For ever and for evermore.

Morning.

Hymn 3. (First Part.)

"I myself will awake right early."

f AWAKE, my soul, and with the sun
Thy daily stage of duty run,
Shake off dull sloth, and joyful rise
To pay thy morning sacrifice.

mf Redeem thy mis-spent time that's past,
And live this day as if thy last;
Improve thy talent with due care;
For the great day thyself prepare.

Let all thy converse be sincere,
Thy conscience as the noon-day clear;
Think how all-seeing God thy ways
And all thy secret thoughts surveys.

Wake, and lift up thyself, my heart,
And with the Angels bear thy part,
Who all night long unwearied sing
High praise to the Eternal King.

f Praise God, from Whom all blessings flow,
Praise Him, all creatures here below,
Praise Him above, Angelic host,
Praise Father, Son, and Holy Ghost.

Morning.

Hymn 3. (Second Part.)

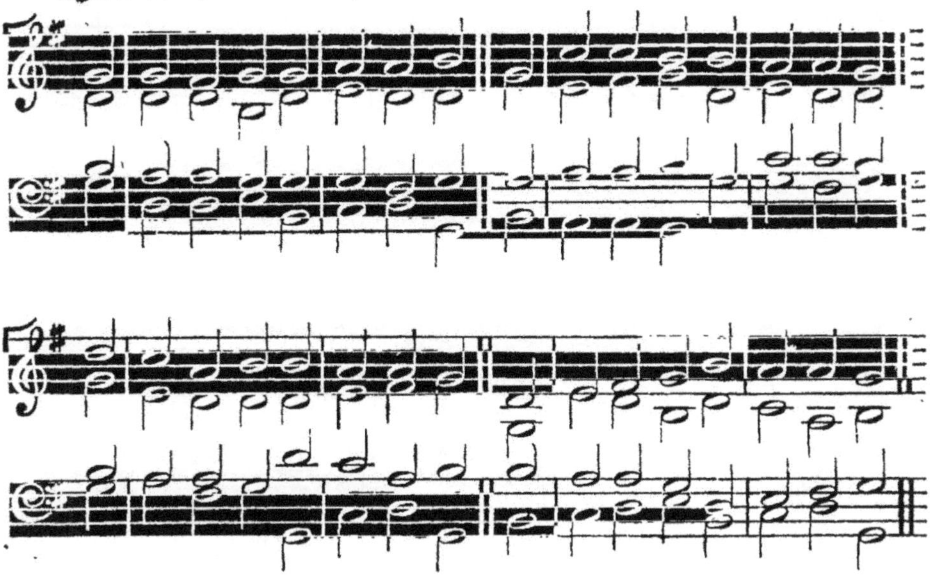

"I myself will awake right early."

Part 2.

mf Glory to Thee Who safe hast kept,
And hast refreshed me while I slept;
Grant, Lord, when I from death shall wake,
I may of endless light partake.

Direct, control, suggest, this day,
All I design, or do, or say;
That all my powers, with all their might,
In Thy sole glory may unite.

Lord, I my vows to Thee renew;
Scatter my sins as morning dew;
Guard my first springs of thought and will,
And with Thyself my spirit fill.

f Praise God, from Whom all blessings flow,
Praise Him, all creatures here below,
Praise Him above, Angelic host,
Praise Father, Son, and Holy Ghost.

Morning.

Hymn 4.

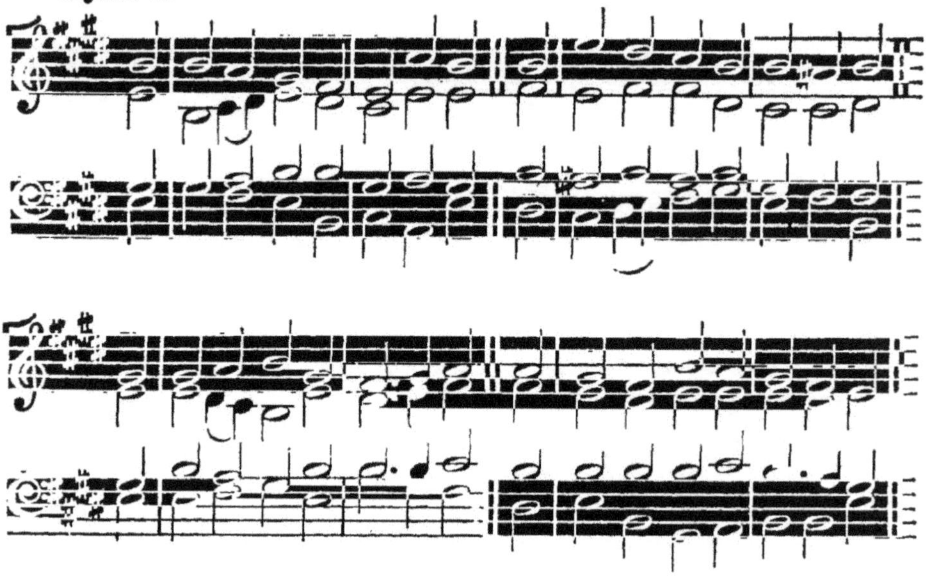

"His compassions fail not: they are new every morning."

mf NEW every morning is the love
Our wakening and uprising prove;
Through sleep and darkness safely brought,
Restored to life, and power, and thought.

New mercies, each returning day,
Hover around us while we pray;
New perils past, new sins forgiven,
New thoughts of God, new hopes of heaven.

If on our daily course our mind
Be set to hallow all we find,
New treasures still, of countless price,
God will provide for sacrifice.

The trivial round, the common task,
Will furnish all we need to ask,
Room to deny ourselves, a road
To bring us daily nearer God.

p Only, O Lord, in Thy dear love
Fit us for perfect rest above;
cr And help us, this and every day,
mf To live more nearly as we pray.

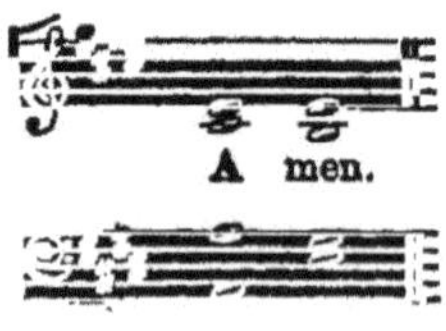

Morning.

Hymn 5.

"Whatsoever ye do, do all to the glory of God."
"Do all in the name of the Lord Jesus."

mf MY FATHER, for another night
p Of quiet sleep and rest,
cr For all the joy of morning light,
Thy Holy Name be blest.

mf Now with the new-born day I give
Myself anew to Thee,
That as Thou willest I may live,
And what Thou willest be.

Whate'er I do, things great or small,
Whate'er I speak or frame,
Thy glory may I seek in all,
p Do all in JESU'S Name.

mf My FATHER, for His sake, I pray,
Thy child accept and bless:
And lead me by Thy grace to-day
In paths of righteousness.

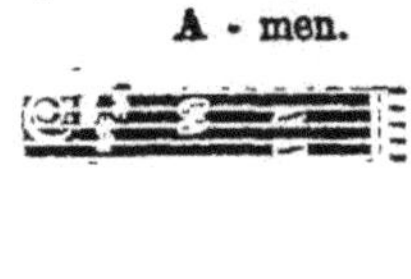

Morning.

Hymn 6.

Morning.

"Hold Thou me up, and I shall be safe: yea, my delight shall be ever in Thy statutes."

mf AT Thy feet, O CHRIST, we lay
Thine own gift of this new day:
Doubt of what it holds in store
Makes us crave Thine aid the more:
Lest it prove a time of loss,
Mark it, Saviour, with Thy Cross.

If it flow on calm and bright,
Be Thyself our chief delight;
p If it bring unknown distress,
Good is all that Thou canst bless:
cr Only, while its hours begin,
Pray we, keep them clear of sin.

mf We in part our weakness know,
And in part discern our foe;
Well for us, before Thine eyes
All our danger open lies;
p Turn not from us, while we plead
Thy compassions and our need.

mf Fain would we Thy Word embrace,
Live each moment in Thy grace,
All our selves to Thee consign,
Fold up all our wills in Thine,
Think, and speak, and do, and be
Simply that which pleases Thee.

Hear us, LORD, and that right soon;
Hear, and grant the choicest boon
That Thy love can e'er impart,
Loyal singleness of heart;
f So shall this and all our days,
CHRIST our GOD, shew forth Thy praise.

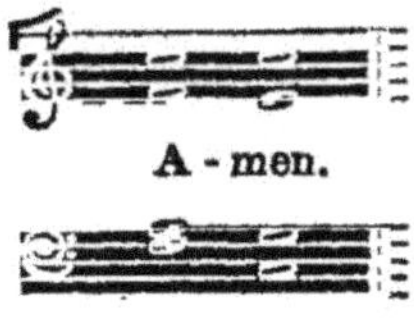

Morning.

Hymn 7.

"Unto you that fear My Name shall the Sun of Righteousness arise."

f CHRIST, Whose glory fills the skies,
  CHRIST, the true, the only Light,
Sun of Righteousness, arise,
  Triumph o'er the shades of night;
Dayspring from on high, be near;
Daystar, in my heart appear.

p Dark and cheerless is the morn
  Unaccompanied by Thee;
Joyless is the day's return
  Till Thy mercy's beams I see,
Till they inward light impart,
Glad my eyes, and warm my heart.

mf Visit then this soul of mine;
  Pierce the gloom of sin and grief;
Fill me, Radiancy Divine;
  Scatter all my unbelief;
cr More and more Thyself display,
f Shining to the perfect day.

Morning.

Hymn 8.

"I have set God always before me; for He is on my right hand, therefore I shall not fall."

mf FORTH in Thy Name, O Lord, I go,
My daily labour to pursue,
Thee, only Thee, resolved to know
In all I think, or speak, or do.

The task Thy wisdom hath assigned
O let me cheerfully fulfil;
In all my works Thy presence find,
And prove Thy good and perfect Will.

Thee may I set at my right hand,
Whose eyes my inmost substance see,
And labour on at Thy command,
And offer all my works to Thee.

p Give me to bear Thy easy yoke,
And every moment watch and pray,
And still to things eternal look,
cr And hasten to Thy glorious day;

mf For Thee delightfully employ
Whate'er Thy bounteous grace hath given,
And run my course with even joy,
And closely walk with Thee to heaven.

Morning.

Hymns 9, 10, 11. (First Tune.)

To be sung in Unison.

Hymns 9, 10, 11. (Second Tune.)

To be sung in Unison.

Morning.

Hymns 9, 10, 11. (Third Tune.)

9. The Third Hour.

"They were all filled with the Holy Ghost."

mf COME, Holy Ghost, Who ever One
Art with the Father and the Son,
Come, Holy Ghost, our souls possess
With Thy full flood of holiness.

In will and deed, by heart and tongue,
With all our powers, Thy praise be sung;
And love light up our mortal frame,
Till others catch the living flame.

p Almighty Father, hear our cry
Through Jesus Christ our Lord most High,
cr Who with the Holy Ghost and Thee
f Doth live and reign eternally.

10. The Sixth Hour.

"At noonday will I pray."

mf O GOD of truth, O Lord of might,
Who orderest time and change aright,
Brightening the morn with golden gleams,
Kindling the noonday's fiery beams;

Quench Thou in us the flames of strife,
From passion's heat preserve our life,
Our bodies keep from perils free,
And give our souls true peace in Thee.

p Almighty Father, hear our cry
Through Jesus Christ our Lord most High,
cr Who with the Holy Ghost and Thee
f Doth live and reign eternally.

11. The Ninth Hour.

"The hour of prayer, being the ninth hour."

mf O GOD, of all the Strength and Power,
Who dost, Thyself unmoved, each hour
Through all its changes guide the day,
From early morn to evening's ray;

Brighten life's eventide with light
That ne'er shall set in gloom of night,
Till we a holy death attain,
And everlasting glory gain.

p Almighty Father, hear our cry
Through Jesus Christ our Lord most High,
cr Who with the Holy Ghost and Thee
f Doth live and reign eternally.

Evening.

Hymn 14. *(To be sung in Unison.)*

"Now unto the King eternal, immortal, invisible, the only wise God, be honour and glory for ever and ever."

mf O TRINITY, most Blessèd Light,
O Unity of primal Might,
As now the fiery sun departs,
Shed Thou Thy beams within our hearts.

To Thee our morning song of praise,
To Thee our evening prayer we raise;
cr Thee may our heart and voice adore
For ever and for evermore.

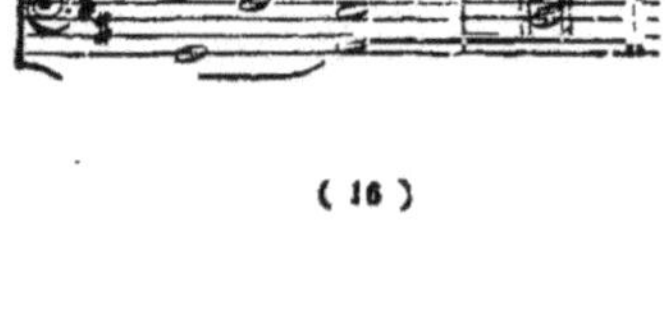

Evening.

Hymn 15.

"Thou shalt not be afraid for any terror by night."

mf BEFORE the ending of the day,
Creator of the world, we pray
That Thou with wonted love wouldst keep
Thy watch around us while we sleep.

O let no evil dreams be near,
Nor phantoms of the night appear;
Our ghostly enemy restrain,
Lest aught of sin our bodies stain.

p Almighty FATHER, hear our cry
Through JESUS CHRIST our LORD most High,
cr Who with the HOLY GHOST and Thee
f Doth live and reign eternally.

Evening.

Hymn 16.

"Thou shalt not be afraid for any terror by night."

mf NOW that the daylight dies away,
  By all Thy grace and love,
Thee, Maker of the world, we pray
  To watch our bed above.

Let dreams depart and phantoms fly,
  The offspring of the night,
p Keep us, like shrines, beneath Thine eye,
mf   Pure in our foe's despite.

This grace on Thy redeemed confer,
  FATHER, co-equal SON,
And HOLY GHOST, the Comforter,
  Eternal THREE in ONE.

Evening.

Hymn 17.

"Let the lifting up of my hands be an evening sacrifice."

p THE sun is sinking fast,
The daylight dies;
cr Let love awake, and pay
Her evening sacrifice.

p As CHRIST upon the Cross
His Head inclined,
And to His FATHER's hands
His parting Soul resigned,

mf So now herself my soul
Would wholly give
Into His sacred charge,
In Whom all spirits live;

So now beneath His eye
Would calmly rest,
Without a wish or thought
Abiding in the breast,

Save that His Will be done,
Whate'er betide,
Dead to herself, and dead
In Him to all beside.

f Thus would I live; yet now
Not I, but He
In all His power and love
Henceforth alive in me.

ONE SACRED TRINITY!
ONE LORD Divine!
May I be ever His,
And He for ever mine.

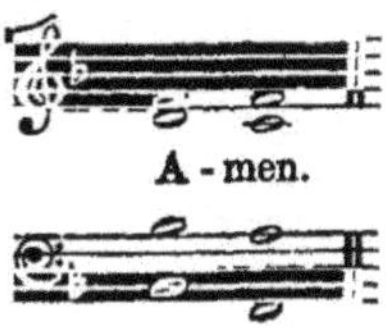

Evening.

Hymn 18. *"The true Light."*

Evening.

f
We hymn the Fa-ther, Son, and Ho-ly Spi-rit Di-vine.
mf
Worthiest art Thou at all times to be sung With un-de-fil-èd tongue,
f
cres.
Son of our God, Gi-ver of life, A-lone;
ff rall.
There-fore in all the world Thy glo-ries, Lord, they own.
A-men.

Evening.

Hymn 19.

"The Lord shall be thine everlasting light."

mf THE radiant morn hath passed away,
And spent too soon her golden store.
The shadows of departing day
p Creep on once more.

Our life is but a fading dawn,
Its glorious noon how quickly past;
cr Lead us, O Christ, when all is gone,
Safe home at last.

mf O by Thy soul-inspiring grace
Uplift our hearts to realms on high;
Help us to look to that bright place
Beyond the sky;

Where light, and life, and joy, and peace
In undivided empire reign,
And thronging Angels never cease
Their deathless strain;

f Where Saints are clothed in spotless white,
And evening shadows never fall,
Where Thou, Eternal Light of Light,
Art Lord of all.

Evening.

Hymn 20.

"And at even, when the sun did set, they brought unto Him all that were diseased, and them that were possessed with devils. And all the city was gathered together at the door."

mf AT even ere the sun was set,
The sick, O LORD, around Thee lay;
p Oh, in what divers pains they met!
f Oh, with what joy they went away!

mf Once more 'tis eventide, and we
Oppressed with various ills draw near;
What if Thy Form we cannot see?
cr We know and feel that Thou art here.

mf O Saviour CHRIST, our woes dispel;
For some are sick, and some are sad,
And some have never loved Thee well,
And some have lost the love they had;

And some have found the world is vain,
Yet from the world they break not free;
And some have friends who give them pain,
Yet have not sought a friend in Thee;

And none, O LORD, have perfect rest,
For none are wholly free from sin;
And they, who fain would serve Thee best,
Are conscious most of wrong within.

O Saviour CHRIST, Thou too art Man;
Thou hast been troubled, tempted, tried;
Thy kind but searching glance can scan
The very wounds that shame would hide;

f Thy touch has still its ancient power;
No word from Thee can fruitless fall;
p Hear, in this solemn evening hour,
cr And in Thy mercy heal us all.

Evening.

Hymn 21. (First Tune.)

" It is Thou, Lord, only, that makest me dwell in safety."

THE day is past and over;
All thanks, O LORD, to Thee;
I pray Thee now that sinless
The hours of dark may be:
O JESU, keep me in Thy sight,
And guard me through the coming night.

The joys of day are over;
I lift my heart to Thee,
And ask Thee that offenceless
The hours of dark may be:
O JESU, keep me in Thy sight,
And guard me through the coming night.

The toils of day are over;
I raise the hymn to Thee,
And ask that free from peril
The hours of dark may be:
O JESU, keep me in Thy sight,
And guard me through the coming night.

Be Thou my soul's preserver,
For Thou alone dost know
How many are the perils
Through which I have to go:
O loving JESU, hear my call,
And guard and save me from them all.

Hymn 21. (Second Tune.)

"It is Thou, Lord, only, that makest me dwell in safety."

THE day is past and over;
All thanks, O Lord, to Thee;
I pray Thee now that sinless
The hours of dark may be:
O Jesu, keep me in Thy sight,
And guard me through the coming night.

The joys of day are over;
I lift my heart to Thee,
And ask Thee that offenceless
The hours of dark may be:
O Jesu, keep me in Thy sight,
And guard me through the coming night.

The toils of day are over;
I raise the hymn to Thee,
And ask that free from peril
The hours of dark may be:
O Jesu, keep me in Thy sight,
And guard me through the coming night.

Be Thou my soul's preserver,
For Thou alone dost know
How many are the perils
Through which I have to go:
O loving Jesu, hear my call,
And guard and save me from them all.

Evening.

Hymn 22.

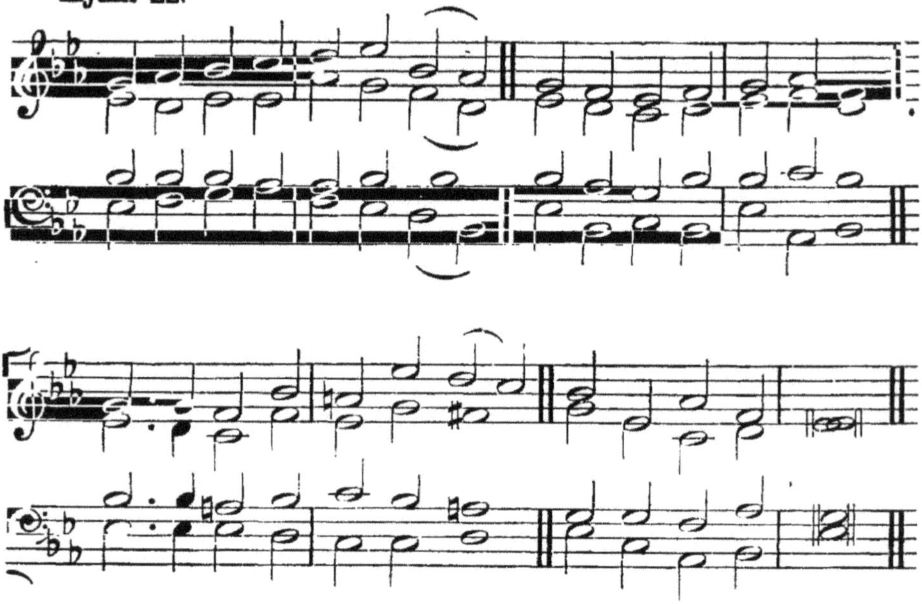

"At evening time it shall be light."

mf HOLY FATHER, cheer our way
With Thy love's perpetual ray:
Grant us every closing day
Light at evening time.

p Holy SAVIOUR, calm our fears
When earth's brightness disappears;
cr Grant us in our latter years
Light at evening time.

p Holy SPIRIT, be Thou nigh
When in mortal pains we lie;
cr Grant us, as we come to die,
Light at evening time.

mf Holy, Blessèd TRINITY!
Darkness is not dark with Thee;
Those Thou keepest always see
Light at evening time.

Evening.

Hymn 23.

"He shall defend thee under His wings."

f GLORY to Thee, my God, this night
For all the blessings of the light;
Keep me, O keep me, King of kings,
Beneath Thine own Almighty wings.

mf Forgive me, Lord, for Thy dear Son,
The ill that I this day have done,
That with the world, myself, and Thee,
I, ere I sleep, at peace may be.

Teach me to live, that I may dread
The grave as little as my bed;
p Teach me to die, that so I may
cr Rise glorious at the awful day.

p O may my soul on Thee repose,
And may sweet sleep mine eyelids close,
cr Sleep that shall me more vigorous make
To serve my God when I awake.

mf When in the night I sleepless lie,
My soul with heavenly thoughts supply;
Let no ill dreams disturb my rest,
No powers of darkness me molest.

f Praise God, from Whom all blessings flow,
Praise Him, all creatures here below,
Praise Him above, Angelic host,
Praise Father, Son, and Holy Ghost.

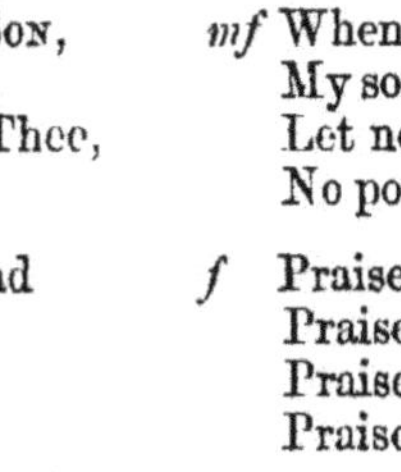

Evening.

Hymn 24. (First Tune.)

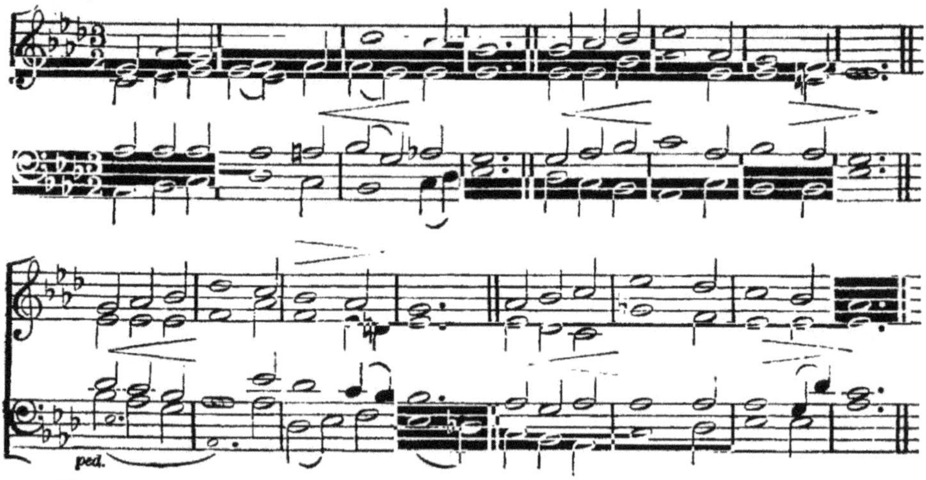

Hymn 24. (Second Tune.)

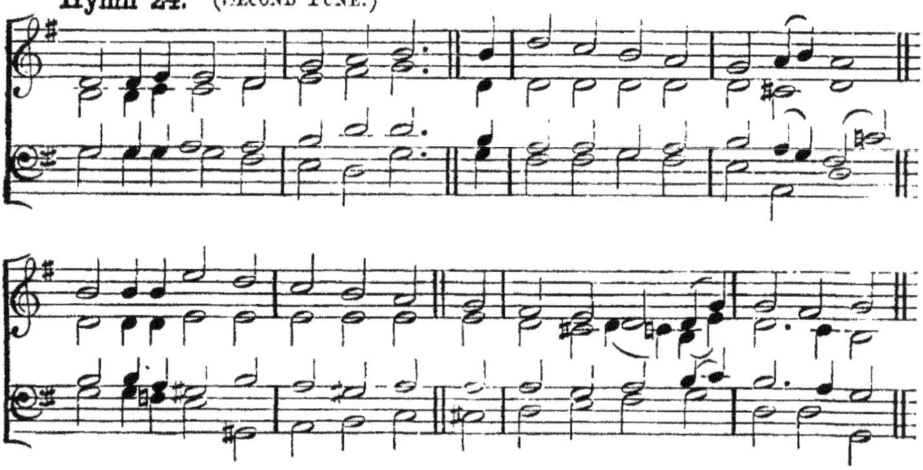

3rd verse.

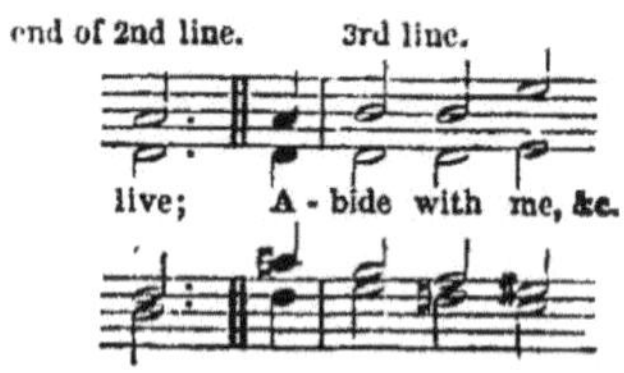

Hymn 24. (Third Tune.)

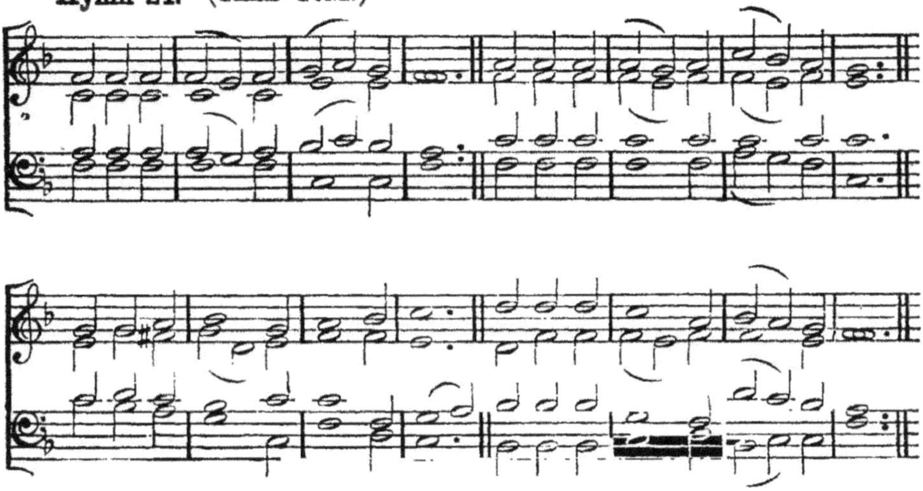

"Abide with us."

mf SUN of my soul, Thou Saviour dear,
It is not night if Thou be near:
O may no earth-born cloud arise
To hide Thee from Thy servant's eyes.

p When the soft dews of kindly sleep
My wearied eyelids gently steep,
Be my last thought, how sweet to rest
For ever on my Saviour's breast.

mf Abide with me from morn till eve,
For without Thee I cannot live;
p Abide with me when night is nigh,
For without Thee I dare not die.

mf If some poor wandering child of Thine
Have spurned to-day the voice divine,
Now, Lord, the gracious work begin;
Let him no more lie down in sin.

Watch by the sick; enrich the poor
With blessings from Thy boundless store;
Be every mourner's sleep to-night,
p Like infant's slumbers, pure and light.

cr Come near and bless us when we wake,
Ere through the world our way we take;
f Till in the ocean of Thy love
We lose ourselves in heaven above.

1.
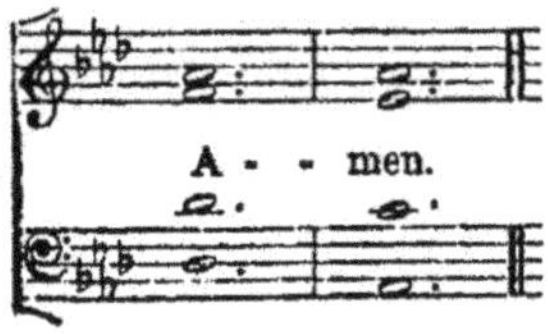

2.

3.

Evening.

Hymn 25.

"I will lay me down in peace, and take my rest."

mf THROUGH the day Thy love has spared us;
Now we lay us down to rest;
Through the silent watches guard us;
Let no foe our peace molest;
p Jesus, Thou our Guardian be;
Sweet it is to trust in Thee.

mf Pilgrims here on earth and strangers,
Dwelling in the midst of foes,
Us and ours preserve from dangers;
In Thine Arms may we repose,
And, when life's sad day is past,
p Rest with Thee in heaven at last.

Evening.

Hymn 26.

"He shall give His angels charge over thee."

mf GOD, Who madest earth and heaven,
  Darkness and light;
p Who the day for toil hast given,
  For rest the night;
May Thine Angel-guards defend us,
Slumber sweet Thy mercy send us,
Holy dreams and hopes attend us,
  This livelong night.

mf Guard us waking, guard us sleeping,
p And, when we die,
cr May we in Thy mighty keeping
p All peaceful lie:
mf When the last dread call shall wake us,
Do not Thou our GOD forsake us,
f But to reign in glory take us
  With Thee on high.

Evening.

Hymn 27.

Evening.

"Abide with us; for it is toward evening, and the day is far spent."

mf ABIDE with me; fast falls the éventide;
The darkness deepens; LORD, with mé abide;
When other helpers fail, and cómforts flee,
f Help of the helpless, *(p)* O abíde with me.

p Swift to its close ebbs out life's líttle day;
Earth's joys grow dim, its glories páss away;
Change and decay in all aróund I see;
mf O Thou Who changest not, *(p)* abíde with me.

mf I need Thy presence every pássing hour;
cr What but Thy grace can foil the témpter's power?
Who like Thyself my guide and stáy can be?
f Through cloud and sunshine, LORD, *(p)* abíde with me.

f I fear no foe with Thee at hánd to bless;
Ills have no weight, and tears no bítterness;
Where is death's sting? Where, grave, thy víctory?
I triumph still, if Thou abíde with me.

p Hold Thou Thy Cross before my clósing eyes;
cr Shine through the gloom, and point me tó the skies;
f Heaven's morning breaks, and earth's vain shádows flee;
In life, *(p)* in death, O LORD, *(cr)* abíde with me.

OR THIS CHANT.

Evening.

Hymn 28. (First Tune.)

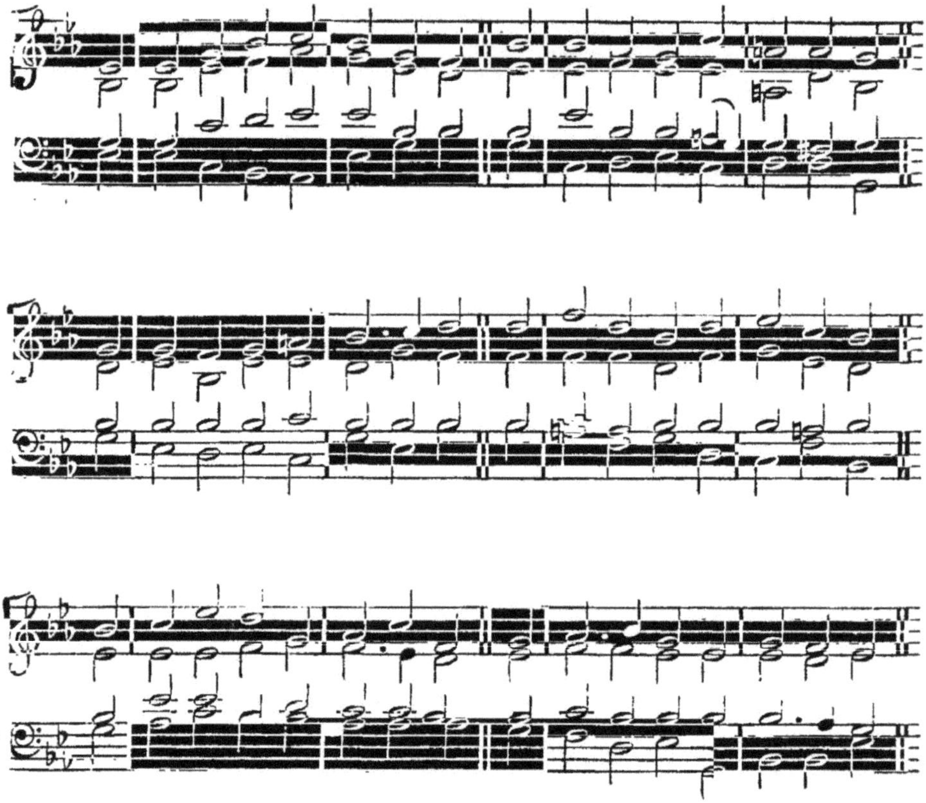

Hymn 28. (Second Tune.)

Evening.

"The Lord is my light."

SWEET Saviour, bless us ere we go;
  Thy Word into our minds instil,
And make our lukewarm hearts to glow
  With lowly love and fervent will.
Through life's long day and death's dark
O gentle JESUS, *(cr)* be our Light. [night,

The day is gone, its hours have run,
  And Thou hast taken count of all,
The scanty triumphs grace hath won,
  The broken vow, the frequent fall.
Through life's long day and death's dark
O gentle JESUS, *(cr)* be our Light. [night,

Grant us, dear LORD, from evil ways
  True absolution and release;
And bless us, more than in past days,
  With purity and inward peace.
Through life's long day and death's dark
O gentle JESUS, *(cr)* be our Light. [night,

f Do more than pardon; give us joy,
  Sweet fear, and sober liberty,
And simple hearts without alloy
  That only long to be like Thee.
Through life's long day and death's dark
p O gentle JESUS, *(cr)* be our Light. [night,

p For all we love, the poor, the sad,
  The sinful, unto Thee we call;
cr O let Thy mercy make us glad:
f   Thou art our JESUS, and our All.
Through life's long day and death's dark
p O gentle JESUS, *(cr)* be our Light. [night,

1.

2.

Evening.

Hymn 28. (Third Tune.)

Evening.

"The Lord is my light."

mf SWEET Saviour, bless us ere we go ;
 Thy Word into our minds instil,
cr And make our lukewarm hearts to glow
 With lowly love and fervent will.
f Through life's long day and death's dark night,
p O gentle Jesus, *(cr)* be our Light.

p The day is gone, its hours have run,
 And Thou hast taken count of all,
The scanty triumphs grace hath won,
 The broken vow, the frequent fall.
f Through life's long day and death's dark night,
p O gentle Jesus, *(cr)* be our Light.

mf Grant us, dear Lord, from evil ways
 True absolution and release ;
And bless us, more than in past days,
 With purity and inward peace.
f Through life's long day and death's dark night,
p O gentle Jesus, *(cr)* be our Light.

f Do more than pardon ; give us joy,
 Sweet fear, and sober liberty,
And simple hearts without alloy
 That only long to be like Thee.
Through life's long day and death's dark night,
p O gentle Jesus, *(cr)* be our Light.

p For all we love, the poor, the sad,
 The sinful, unto Thee we call ;
cr O let Thy mercy make us glad :
f Thou art our Jesus, and our All.
Through life's long day and death's dark night,
p O gentle Jesus, *(cr)* be our Light.

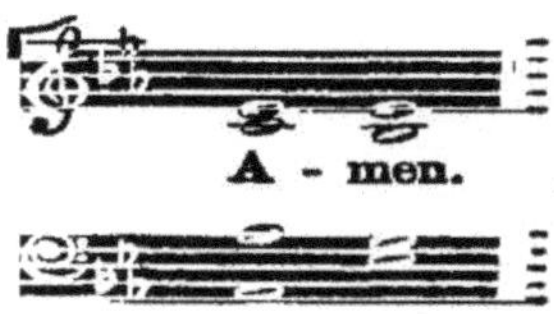

Evening.

Hymn 29.

"God, even our own God, shall give us His blessing."

mf O FATHER, Who didst all things make
That heaven and earth might do Thy [Will,
Bless us this night for JESU's sake,
And for Thy work preserve us still.

O SON, Who didst redeem mankind,
And set the captive sinner free,
Keep us this night with peaceful mind,
That we may safe abide in Thee.

O HOLY GHOST, Who by Thy power
The Church elect dost sanctify,
Seal us this night, and hour by hour
Our hearts and members purify.

f To FATHER, SON, and HOLY GHOST,
The GOD Whom heaven and earth adore,
From men and from the Angel-host
Be praise and glory evermore.

Evening.

Hymn 30.

"And all the angels stood round about the throne . . . and worshipped God."

FOR FESTIVALS.

mf OUR day of praise is done;
p The evening shadows fall;
cr But pass not from us with the sun,
True Light that lightenest all.

Around the Throne on high,
Where night can never be,
The white-robed harpers of the sky
Bring ceaseless hymns to Thee.

Too faint our anthems here;
Too soon of praise we tire:
cr But oh, the strains how full and clear
Of that eternal choir!

mf Yet, LORD, to Thy dear Will
If Thou attune the heart,
We in Thine Angels' music still
May bear our lower part.

'Tis Thine each soul to calm,
Each wayward thought reclaim,
And make our life a daily psalm
Of glory to Thy Name.

cr A little while, and then
Shall come the glorious end;
f And songs of Angels and of men
In perfect praise shall blend.

Evening.

Hymn 31.

Evening.

"The Lord shall give His people the blessing of peace."

AT THE END OF DIVINE SERVICE.

mf SAVIOUR, again to Thy dear Name we raise
With one accord our parting hymn of praise;
We stand to bless Thee ere our worship cease;
p Then, lowly kneeling, wait Thy word of peace.

Grant us Thy peace upon our homeward way;
mf With Thee began, with Thee shall end the day;
Guard Thou the lips from sin, the hearts from shame,
That in this house have called upon Thy Name.

p Grant us Thy peace, LORD, through the coming night;
cr Turn Thou for us its darkness into light;
f From harm and danger keep Thy children free,
For dark and light are both alike to Thee.

p Grant us Thy peace throughout our earthly life,
cr Our balm in sorrow, and our stay in strife;
mf Then, when Thy voice shall bid our conflict cease,
p Call us, O LORD, to Thine eternal peace.

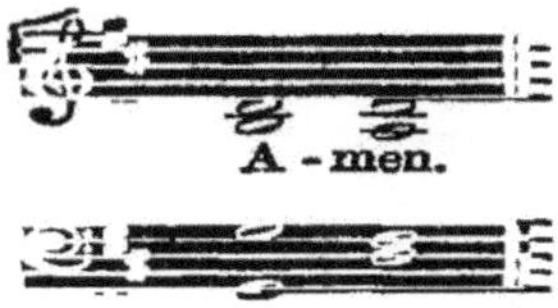

Evening.

Hymn 32.

At the End of Divine Service. *"O God, Thou art my God."*

mf AND now the wants are told, that brought
Thy children to Thy knee;
Here lingering still, we ask for nought,
But simply worship Thee.

The hope of heaven's eternal days
Absorbs not all the heart
That gives Thee glory, love, and praise,
For being what Thou art.

For Thou art God, the One, the Same,
O'er all things high and bright;
And round us, when we speak Thy Name,
There spreads a heaven of light.

O wondrous peace, in thought to dwell
On excellence Divine;
To know that nought in man can tell
How fair Thy beauties shine.

f O Thou, above all blessing blest,
O'er thanks exalted far,
dim Thy very greatness is a rest
To weaklings as we are;

mf For when we feel the praise of Thee
A task beyond our powers,
We say, "A perfect God is He,
And He is fully ours."

f All glory to the Father be,
All glory to the Son,
All glory, Holy Ghost, to Thee,
While endless ages run.

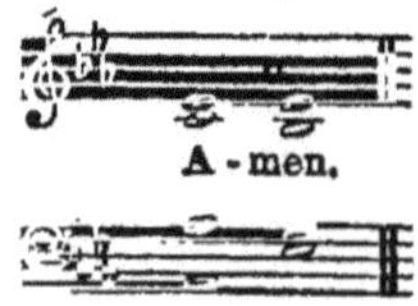

Sunday.

Hymn 33.

MORNING. *"In Thy light shall we see light."*

f MORN of morns, and day of days!
Beauteous were thy new-born rays:
Brighter yet from death's dark prison
CHRIST, the Light of lights, is risen.

He commanded, and His Word
Death and the dread chaos heard:
dim Oh, shall we, more deaf than they,
In the chains of darkness stay?

p *Nature yet in shadow lies;
cr Let the sons of light arise,
mf And prevent the morning rays
With sweet canticles of praise.

*While the dead world sleeps around,
Let the sacred temples sound
Law, and prophet, and blest psalm
Lit with holy light so calm.

Unto hearts in slumber weak
Let the heavenly trumpet speak;
And a newer walk express
Their new life to righteousness.

Grant us this, and with us be,
O Thou Fount of charity,
Thou Who dost the SPIRIT give,
Bidding the dead letter live.

f Glory to the FATHER, SON,
And to Thee, O Holy ONE,
By Whose quickening Breath Divine
Our dull spirits burn and shine.

* *These verses should be sung only at a very early Service.*

Sunday.

Hymn 34.

"*And God said, Let there be light: and there was light. . . . And the evening and the morning were the first day.*"

MORNING.

f ON this day, the first of days,
God the FATHER's Name we praise;
Who, creation's LORD and Spring,
Did the world from darkness bring.

On this day the Eternal SON
Over death His triumph won;
On this day the SPIRIT came
With His gifts of living flame.

O that fervent love to-day
May in every heart have sway,
Teaching us to praise aright
GOD the Source of life and light.

p FATHER, Who didst fashion me
Image of Thyself to be,
Fill me with Thy love Divine,
Let my every thought be Thine.

Holy JESUS, may I be
Dead and buried here with Thee;
cr And, by love inflamed, arise
Unto Thee a sacrifice.

mf Thou Who dost all gifts impart,
Shine, Sweet SPIRIT, in my heart;
Best of gifts Thyself bestow;
Make me burn Thy love to know.

GOD, the Blessèd THREE in ONE,
Dwell within my heart alone;
Thou dost give Thyself to me,
p May I give myself to Thee.

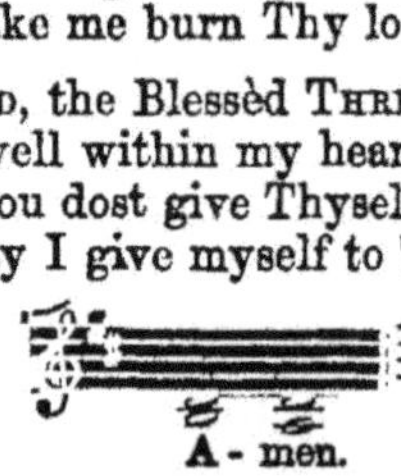

Sunday.

Hymn 35.

"This is the day which the Lord hath made."

mf AGAIN the Lord's own day is here,
The day to Christian people dear,
As, week by week, it bids them tell
p How Jesus rose from death and hell.

mf For by His flock their Lord declared
His Resurrection should be shared;
And we who trust in Him to save
p With Him are risen from the grave.

mf We, one and all, of Him possest,
Are with exceeding treasures blest;
For all He did, and all He bare,
He gives us as our own to share.

Eternal glory, rest on high,
A blessèd immortality,
True peace and gladness, and a throne,
Are all His gifts, and all our own.

f And therefore unto Thee we sing,
O Lord of peace, Eternal King;
Thy love we praise, Thy Name adore,
Both on this day and evermore.

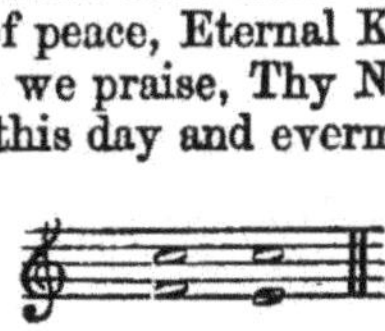

Sunday.

Hymn 36.

Sunday.

"The first day of the week."

f O DAY of rest and gladness,
  O day of joy and light,
O balm of care and sadness,
  Most beautiful, most bright;
On thee the high and lowly,
  Before the eternal Throne,
Sing Holy, Holy, Holy,
  To the great THREE in ONE.

On thee, at the creation,
  The light first had its birth;
On thee for our salvation
  CHRIST rose from depths of earth;
On thee our LORD victorious
  The SPIRIT sent from heaven;
And thus on thee most glorious
  A triple light was given.

p Thou art a cooling fountain
  In life's dry dreary sand;
From thee, like Pisgah's mountain,
  We view our promised land;
A day of sweet refection,
  A day of holy love,
cr A day of resurrection
  From earth to things above.

mf To-day on weary nations
  The heavenly Manna falls,
To holy convocations
  The silver trumpet calls,
Where Gospel-light is glowing
  With pure and radiant beams,
And living water flowing
  With soul-refreshing streams.

New graces ever gaining
  From this our day of rest,
We reach the Rest remaining
  To spirits of the blest;
f To HOLY GHOST be praises,
  To FATHER, and to SON;
The Church her voice upraises
  To Thee, Blest THREE in ONE.

Sunday.

Hymn 37.

"I was in the Spirit on the Lord's day."

mf THIS is the day of light:
Let there be light to-day;
O Day-spring, rise upon our night,
And chase its gloom away.

p This is the day of rest:
Our failing strength renew;
On weary brain and troubled breast
Shed Thou Thy freshening dew.

This is the day of peace:
Thy peace our spirits fill;
cr Bid Thou the blasts of discord cease,
dim The waves of strife be still.

p This is the day of prayer:
Let earth to heaven draw near;
cr Lift up our hearts to seek Thee there,
Come down to meet us here.

f This is the first of days:
Send forth Thy quickening Breath,
And wake dead souls to love and praise,
O Vanquisher of death.

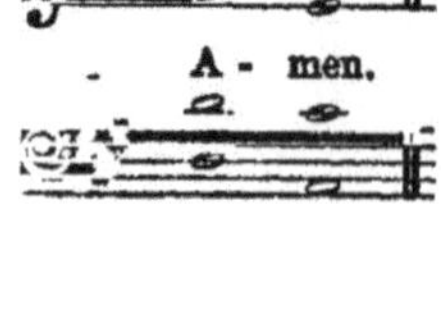

Sunday.

Hymn 38.

"The day is Thine, and the night is Thine."

EVENING.

mf BLEST Creator of the light,
Making day with radiance bright,
Thou didst o'er the forming earth
Give the golden light its birth.

Shade of eve with morning ray
Took from Thee the name of day;
Darkness now is drawing nigh;
Listen to our humble cry.

May we ne'er by guilt depressed
Lose the way to endless rest;
Nor with idle thoughts and vain
Bind our souls to earth again.

cr Rather may we heavenward rise
Where eternal treasure lies;
Purified by grace within,
Hating every deed of sin.

p Holy FATHER, hear our cry
cr Through Thy SON our LORD most High,
f Whom our thankful hearts adore
With the SPIRIT evermore.

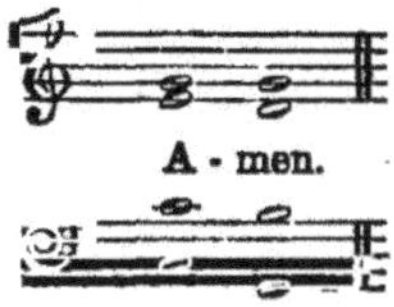

Monday.

Hymn 39.

"And God made the firmament, and divided the waters which were under the firmament from the waters which were above the firmament. . . . And the evening and the morning were the second day."

mf SING we the glory of our God,
  Who on the second day
Spread out the firmament above,
  His wonders to display.

There, floating in the blue expanse,
  The watery clouds we view,
Whence fruitful showers at His command
  The thirsty soil bedew.

How fair an image of the grace
  Which Thou, Lord, dost impart,
Like morning dew or gentle rain,
  To gladden every heart.

And when the faithful soul drinks in
  Those showers with blessings rife,
cr A well of water springeth up
  To everlasting life.

f O happy saints, on whom are poured
  Such treasures from above!
p Lord, may they ne'er forgetful be,
  But render love for love.

f To God, Who freely loved us first,
  All might, all glory be,
To Father, Son, and Holy Ghost,
  Through all eternity.

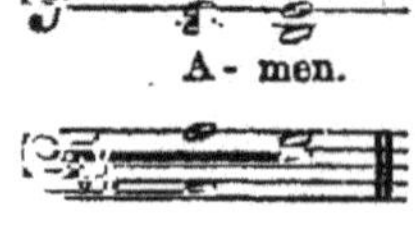

Tuesday.

Hymn 40.

"And God said, Let the waters . . . be gathered together unto one place, and let the dry land appear: and it was so. . . . And the evening and the morning were the third day."

THOU spakest, LORD, and into one
  The floods together flowed;
Freed from its watery veil, the land
  Its verdant pastures showed.

O FATHER, Who the earth hast given
  Our place of toil to be,
Knit all within its one wide bound
  In one true charity.

Strangers and pilgrims here below,
  We seek a home above,
Where Thou wilt gather in Thine own
  Who live in holy love.

Unloving souls, with deeds of ill
  And words of angry strife,
Shall never, LORD, Thy glory see,
  Nor win the heavenly life.

The earth itself from day to day
  Their burden scarce sustains,
And yearns, in travail, to be free
  From dark corruption's chains.

Yea, we too groan within ourselves,
  And that adoption wait
For which the HOLY SPIRIT's seal
  Did us predestinate.

f Eternal glory be ascribed
  To GOD, the ONE in THREE,
By Whom is poured into our hearts
  The grace of charity.

Wednesday.

Hymn 41.

"And God said, Let there be lights in the firmament of the heaven: and it was so. . . . And the evening and the morning were the fourth day."

mf NEW wonders of Thy mighty hand,
  LORD, we to-day admire,
Writ on the firmament above
  In glittering orbs of fire.

The sun is ruler of the day,
  The silver moon of night,
The starry hosts adorn the sky
  In ordered ranks of light.

But e'en that glorious sun must set,
  And knows his going down,
That silver moon must wax and wane,
  The stars their courses own.

Still in an everchanging round
  The daylight comes and goes;
f But Thou art evermore the Same,
  No change Thy mercy knows.

mf Why waver then our troubled hearts?
  Thine is a FATHER's care;
cr And they, eternal life who seek,
  Eternal life shall share.

f All praise, all glory be ascribed
  To GOD the ONE in THREE,
Who bids us cast our care on Him,
  To Him for comfort flee.

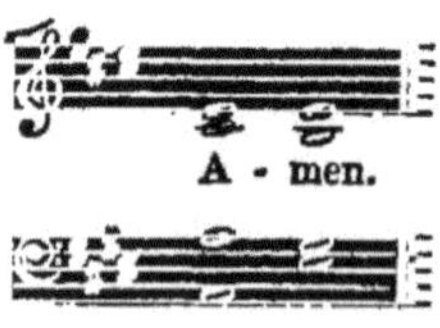

Thursday.

Hymn 42.

"And God said, Let the waters bring forth abundantly the moving creature that hath life, and fowl that may fly above the earth. . . . And the evening and the morning were the fifth day."

THE fish in wave, the bird on wing
  God bade the waters bear;
Each for our mortal body's food
  His gracious hands prepare.

But other food, of richer cost,
  The immortal spirit needs;
By faith it lives on every Word
  That from His mouth proceeds.

Faith springing from the Blood of Christ
  Has flowed o'er every land;
And sinners through the vanquished world
  Bow down to its command.

Its light the joy of heaven reveals
  To hearts made pure within;
And bids them seek by worthy deeds
  Eternal crowns to win.

f By faith the saints of old were strong
  The lion's wrath to tame; [threats,
By faith they spurned the tyrant's
  And scorned the raging flame.

p Lord, grant that we the path may tread
  Whereon its light doth shine;
cr And gather, as we onward go,
  The fruits of love Divine.

f O praise the Father; praise the Son,
  On Whose most precious Blood
Rests all our faith; and praise to Him
  Who with Them Both is God.

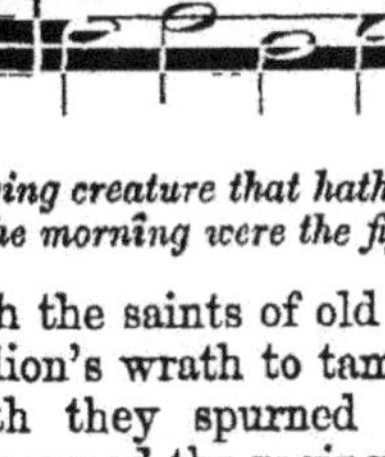

Friday.

Hymn 43.

"And God said, Let us make man in our image. . . . And the evening and the morning were the sixth day."

mf TO-DAY, O Lord, a holier work
  Thy secret counsels frame,
A king to rule Thy new-made world,
  To praise Thy glorious Name.

Thou formest man: Thy Spirit breathes
  Life into dust of earth:
Man, in Thine own true Image made,
  From Thee receives his birth.

And henceforth he dominion holds
  O'er all in earth and sea;
Yet mindful whence his being came
  Must humbly walk with Thee.

p Alas! his wilful heart rebels
  Against Thy gentle sway;
Proud dust of earth would fain be like
  The God Whom all obey.

O griefs and sorrows numberless,
  Which hence the world o'erspread;
Jesu, Thy mercy succoured us,
  Or hope itself had fled.

f O praise the Father, and the Son
  Who saved us by His death,
And Holy Ghost Who quickens us
  With His life-giving breath.

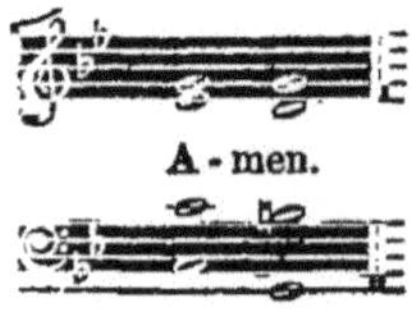

Saturday.

Hymn 44.

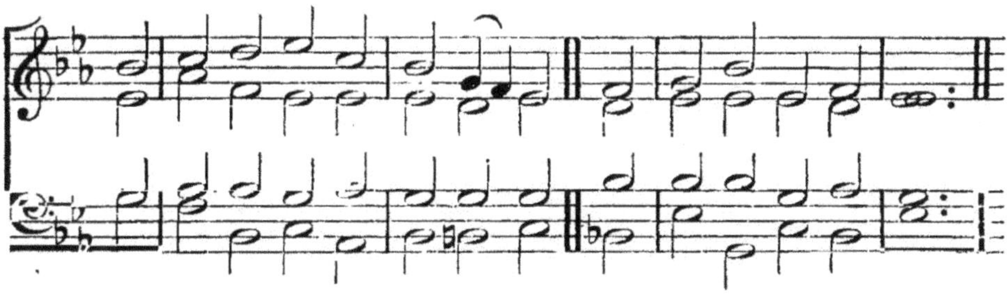

"And on the seventh day God ended His work which He had made."

SIX days of labour now are past;
  Thou restest, Holy God;
And of Thy finished work hast said
  That all is very good.

Yet while the seventh day is blessed,
  Hallowed for rest Divine,
Behold, a new creation needs
  That mighty power of Thine.

Ten thousand voices praise Thy Name
  In earth and sea and sky;
One sinner by his sin has marred
  The blissful harmony.

p O Lord, create man's heart anew,
  The heart of stone remove:
cr Then hymns of praise again shall rise,
  The fruits of holy love.

mf O for the songs that Thou wilt bless,
  Where heart and voice agree;
O for the prayers that plead aright
  With Thy dread Majesty.

f All praise to God, the Three in One,
  Who high in glory reigns;
Who by His Word hath all things made,
  And by His Word sustains.

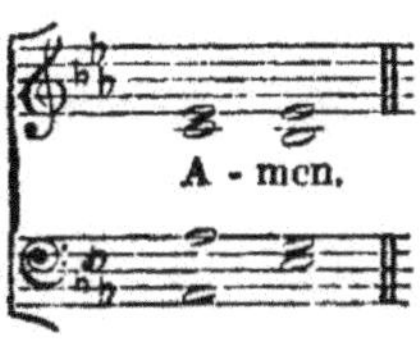

Advent.

Hymn 45.

"Which cometh forth as a bridegroom out of his chamber."

mf CREATOR of the starry height,
Thy people's everlasting Light,
Jesu, Redeemer of us all,
p Hear Thou Thy servants when they call.

Thou, sorrowing at the helpless cry
Of all creation doomed to die,
cr Didst save our lost and guilty race
By healing gifts of heavenly grace.

mf When earth was near its evening hour,
Thou didst, in love's redeeming power,
Like bridegroom from his chamber, come
Forth from a Virgin-mother's womb.

f At Thy great Name, exalted now,
All knees in lowly homage bow;
All things in heaven and earth adore,
And own Thee King for evermore.

p To Thee, O Holy One, we pray,
Our Judge in that tremendous day,
Ward off, while yet we dwell below,
The weapons of our crafty foe.

f To God the Father, God the Son,
And God the Spirit, Three in One,
Praise, honour, might, and glory be
From age to age eternally.

Advent.

Hymn 46.

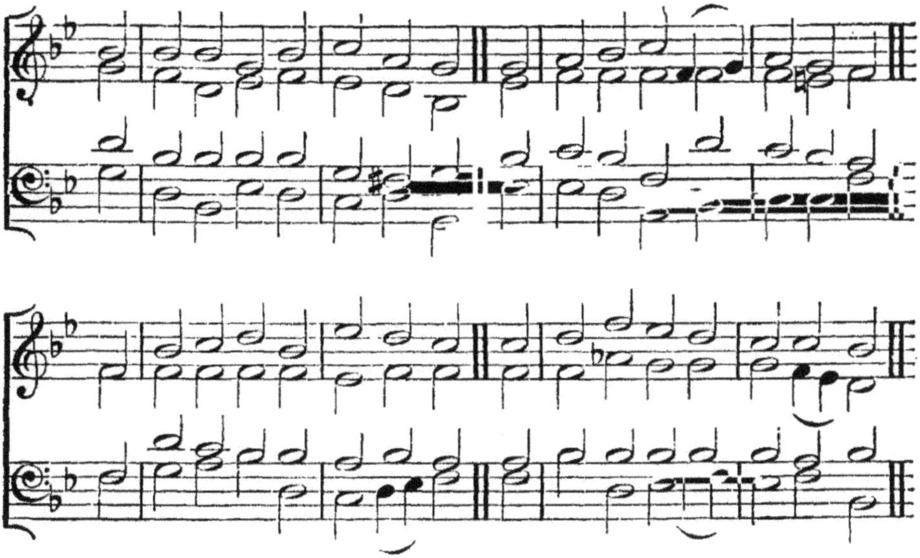

"His name is called The Word of God."

mf O HEAVENLY Word, Eternal Light,
Begotten of the Father's Might,
Who, in these latter days, art born
For succour to a world forlorn;

Our hearts enlighten from above,
And kindle with Thine own true love;
That we, who hear Thy call to-day,
May cast earth's vanities away.

And when as Judge Thou drawest nigh,
The secrets of all hearts to try;
p When sinners meet their awful doom,
cr And saints attain their heavenly home;

p O let us not, for evil past,
Be driven from Thy Face at last;
cr But with the blessèd evermore
Behold Thee, love Thee, and adore.

f To God the Father, God the Son,
And God the Spirit, Three in One,
Praise, honour, might, and glory be
From age to age eternally.

Advent.

Hymn 47.

"Now it is high time to awake out of sleep."

f HARK! a thrilling voice is sounding;
"CHRIST is nigh," it seems to say;
"Cast away the dreams of darkness,
O ye children of the day!"

Wakened by the solemn warning,
Let the earth-bound soul arise;
CHRIST, her Sun, all ill dispelling,
Shines upon the morning skies.

mf Lo! the LAMB, so long expected,
Comes with pardon down from heaven;
dim Let us haste, with tears of sorrow,
One and all to be forgiven;

mf That when next He comes with glory,
p And the world is wrapped in fear,
cr With His mercy He may shield us,
And with words of love draw near.

f Honour, glory, might, and blessing
To the FATHER and the SON,
With the Everlasting SPIRIT,
While eternal ages run.

Advent.

Hymn 48.

"Tell ye the daughter of Sion, Behold, thy King cometh unto thee."

mf THE Advent of our King
Our prayers must now employ,
And we must hymns of welcome sing
In strains of holy joy.

p The Everlasting Son
Incarnate deigns to be;
Himself a servant's form puts on,
cr To set His servants free.

mf Daughter of Sion, rise
To meet thy lowly King;
Nor let thy faithless heart despise
p The peace He comes to bring.

mf As Judge, on clouds of light,
He soon will come again,
And His true members all unite
With Him in heaven to reign.

Before the dawning day
Let sin's dark deeds be gone;
The old man all be put away,
The new man all put on.

f All glory to the Son
Who comes to set us free,
With Father, Spirit, ever One,
Through all eternity.

Advent.

Hymn 49.

To be sung in Unison.

Advent.

" The Redeemer shall come to Zion."

mf O COME, O come, Emmanuel,
And ransom captive Israel,
p That mourns in lonely exile here,
Until the SON of GOD appear.
ff Rejoice! Rejoice! Emmanuel
Shall come to thee, O Israel.

mf O come, Thou Rod of Jesse, free
Thine own from Satan's tyranny;
From depths of hell Thy people save,
cr And give them victory o'er the grave.
ff Rejoice! Rejoice! Emmanuel
Shall come to thee, O Israel.

mf O come, Thou Day-spring, come and cheer
Our spirits by Thine Advent here;
Disperse the gloomy clouds of night,
And death's dark shadows put to flight.
ff Rejoice! Rejoice! Emmanuel
Shall come to thee, O Israel.

mf O come, Thou Key of David, come,
And open wide our heavenly home;
Make safe the way that leads on high,
And close the path to misery.
ff Rejoice! Rejoice! Emmanuel
Shall come to thee, O Israel.

mf O come, O come, Thou LORD of Might,
Who to Thy tribes, on Sinai's height,
In ancient times didst give the law
In cloud, and majesty, and awe.
ff Rejoice! Rejoice! Emmanuel
Shall come to thee, O Israel.

Advent.

Hymn 50.

"The voice of one crying in the wilderness, Prepare ye the way of the Lord, make His paths straight."

f ON Jordan's bank the Baptist's cry
Announces that the Lord is nigh;
Awake, and hearken, for he brings
Glad tidings of the King of kings.

mf Then cleansed be every breast from sin;
Make straight the way for God within;
Prepare we in our hearts a home,
Where such a mighty Guest may come.

For Thou art our Salvation, Lord,
Our Refuge, and our great Reward;
dim Without Thy grace we waste away,
Like flowers that wither and decay.

p To heal the sick stretch out Thine Hand,
And bid the fallen sinner stand;
cr Shine forth, and let Thy light restore
Earth's own true loveliness once more.

f All praise, Eternal Son, to Thee
Whose Advent doth Thy people free,
Whom with the Father we adore
And Holy Ghost for evermore.

Hymn 51.

"Behold, He cometh with clouds; and every eye shall see Him, and they also which pierced Him."

mf LO! He comes with clouds descending,
Once for favoured sinners slain;
f Thousand thousand Saints attending
Swell the triumph of His train:
Alleluia!
Christ appears on earth again.

mf Every eye shall now behold Him
Robed in dreadful majesty;
p They who set at nought and sold Him,
Pierced and nailed Him to the tree,
pp Deeply wailing,
p Shall the true Messiah see.

mf Those dear tokens of His Passion
Still His dazzling Body bears,
cr Cause of endless exultation
To His ransomed worshippers;
mf With what rapture
Gaze we on those glorious scars!

f Yea, Amen, let all adore Thee,
High on Thine eternal Throne;
mf Saviour, take the power and glory;
Claim the kingdom for Thine own:
ff Alleluia!
Thou shalt reign, and Thou alone.

Advent.

Hymn 52.

Advent.

The Lord Himself shall descend from heaven with a shout, with the voice of the archangel, and with the trump of God."

mf GREAT GOD, what do I see and hear?
The end of things created:
The Judge of all men doth appear
On clouds of glory seated:
ff The trumpet sounds, the graves restore
The dead which they contained before;
p Prepare, my soul, to meet Him.

f The dead in CHRIST are first to rise
At that last trumpet's sounding;
Caught up to meet Him in the skies,
With joy their LORD surrounding:
No gloomy fears their souls dismay;
His presence sheds eternal day
On those prepared to meet Him.

p The ungodly, filled with guilty fears,
Behold His wrath prevailing;
In woe they rise, but all their tears
And sighs are unavailing:
pp The day of grace is past and gone;
Trembling they stand before His Throne,
All unprepared to meet Him.

mf Great Judge, to Thee our prayers we pour,
In deep abasement bending;
O shield us through that last dread hour,
Thy wondrous love extending:
cr May we, in this our trial day,
With faithful hearts Thy Word obey,
And thus prepare to meet Thee.

Hymn 53.

"He hath sent Me to bind up the broken-hearted, to proclaim liberty to the captives."

f HARK the glad sound! the Saviour comes,
The Saviour promised long:
Let every heart prepare a throne,
And every voice a song.

He comes, the prisoners to release
In Satan's bondage held;
The gates of brass before Him burst,
The iron fetters yield.

p He comes, the broken heart to bind,
The bleeding soul to cure,
And with the treasures of His grace
To bless the humble poor.

f Our glad hosannas, Prince of peace,
Thy welcome shall proclaim;
And heaven's eternal arches ring
With Thy belovèd Name.

Advent.

Hymn 54.

"I sleep, but my heart waketh."

FOR A LATE EVENING SERVICE.

WHEN shades of night around us close,
And weary limbs in sleep repose,
The faithful soul awake may be,
And longing sigh, O LORD, to Thee.

Thou true Desire of nations, hear,
Thou WORD of GOD, Thou Saviour dear;
In pity heed our humble cries,
And bid at length the fallen rise.

O come, Redeemer, come and free
Thine own from guilt and misery;
The gates of heaven again unfold,
Which Adam's sin had closed of old.

f All praise, Eternal SON, to Thee,
Whose Advent sets Thy people free,
Whom with the FATHER we adore
And HOLY GHOST for evermore.

The following Hymns are suitable for this season:

203 Thou art coming, O my Saviour.
204 O quickly come, dread Judge of all.
205 Thou Judge of quick and dead.
206 That day of wrath, that dreadful day.
217 Thy kingdom come, O GOD.
226 The world is very evil.
268 Ye servants of the LORD.
288 A few more years shall roll.
362 LORD, her watch Thy Church is keeping.
398 Day of Wrath! O day of mourning!
463 Litany of the Four Last Things.

Christmas.

Hymn 55.

Christmas.

"The Word was made flesh."

mf O COME, Redeemer of mankind, appear,
Thee with full hearts the Virgin-born we greet;
Let every age with rapt amazement hear
That wondrous birth which for our God is meet.

Not by the will of man, or mortal seed,
But by the Spirit's breathed mysterious grace
p The Word of God became our flesh indeed,
And grew a tender plant of human race.

Lo! Mary's virgin womb its burthen bears,
Nor less abides her virgin purity;
cr In the King's glory see our nature shares;
Here in His temple God vouchsafes to be.

mf From His bright chamber, virtue's holy shrine,
The royal Bridegroom cometh to the day;
Of twofold substance, human and Divine,
As giant swift, rejoicing on His way.

p Forth from His Father to the world He goes,
mf Back to the Father's Face His way regains,
p Far down to souls beneath His glory shows,
f Again at God's right hand victorious reigns.

With the Eternal Father equal, Thou
Girt with our flesh dost triumph evermore,
Strengthening our feeble bodies here below
With endless grace from Thine own living store.

mf How doth Thy lowly manger radiant shine!
On the sweet breath of night new splendour grows;
So may our spirits glow with faith Divine,
Where no dark cloud of sin shall interpose.

f All praise and glory to the Father be,
All praise and glory to His Only Son,
All praise and glory, Holy Ghost, to Thee,
Both now, and while eternal ages run.

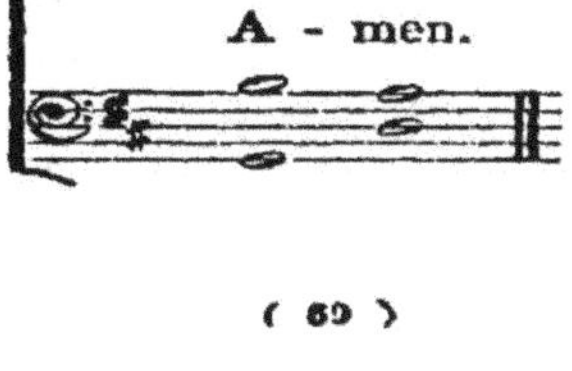

Christmas.

Hymn 56.

To be sung in Unison.

Christmas.

"God was manifest in the flesh."

mf OF the Father's Love begotten
Ere the worlds began to be,
He is Alpha and Omega,
He the source, the ending He,
Of the things that are, that have been,
And that future years shall see,
Evermore and evermore.

*At His Word the worlds were framèd;
He commanded; it was done:
Heaven and earth and depths of ocean
In their threefold order one;
All that grows beneath the shining
Of the moon and burning sun,
Evermore and evermore.

p *He is found in human fashion,
Death and sorrow here to know,
That the race of Adam's children,
Doomed by Law to endless woe,
May not henceforth die and perish
In the dreadful gulf below,
Evermore and evermore.

f O that Birth for ever blessèd!
When the Virgin, full of grace,
By the Holy Ghost conceiving,
Bare the Saviour of our race,
And the Babe, the world's Redeemer,
First revealed His sacred Face,
Evermore and evermore.

This is He Whom seers in old time
Chanted of with one accord;
Whom the voices of the Prophets
Promised in their faithful word;
Now He shines, the long-expected;
Let creation praise its Lord,
Evermore and evermore.

ff O ye heights of heaven, adore Him;
Angel-hosts, His praises sing;
All dominions, bow before Him,
And extol our God and King;
Let no tongue on earth be silent,
Every voice in concert ring,
Evermore and evermore.

p *Righteous Judge of souls departed,
Righteous King of them that live,
On the Father's Throne exalted
None in might with Thee may strive;
Who at last in vengeance coming
Sinners from Thy Face shalt drive,
Evermore and evermore.

f Thee let old men, Thee let young men,
Thee let boys in chorus sing;
Matrons, virgins, little maidens,
With glad voices answering;
Let their guileless songs re-echo,
And the heart its praises bring,
Evermore and evermore.

ff Christ, to Thee, with God the Father,
And, O Holy Ghost, to Thee, [ing,
Hymn, and chant, and high thanksgiv-
And unwearied praises be,
Honour, glory, and dominion,
And eternal victory,
Evermore and evermore.

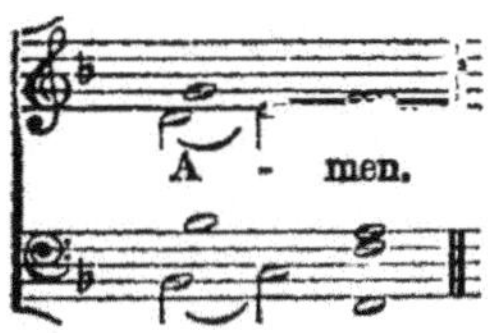

* *These verses may be omitted, if the Hymn be thought too long.*

Christmas.

Hymn 57.

"Christ Jesus came into the world to save sinners."

mf O CHRIST, Redeemer of our race,
Thou Brightness of the FATHER'S Face,
Of Him, and with Him ever ONE,
Ere times and seasons had begun;

Thou that art very Light of Light,
Unfailing Hope in sin's dark night,
Hear Thou the prayers Thy people pray,
The wide world o'er, this blessèd day.

p Remember, LORD of life and grace,
How once, to save a ruined race,
Thou didst our very flesh assume
In Mary's undefilèd womb.

mf To-day, as year by year its light
Sheds o'er the world a radiance bright,
One precious truth is echoed on,
f "'Tis Thou hast saved us, Thou alone."

mf Thou from the FATHER'S Throne didst come
To call His banished children home;
And heaven, and earth, and sea, and shore
His love Who sent Thee here adore.

And gladsome too are we to-day,
Whose guilt Thy Blood has washed away·
Redeemed the new-made song we sing;
f It is the birthday of our King.

O LORD, the Virgin-born, to Thee
Eternal praise and glory be,
Whom with the FATHER we adore
And HOLY GHOST for evermore.

Christmas.

Hymn 58.

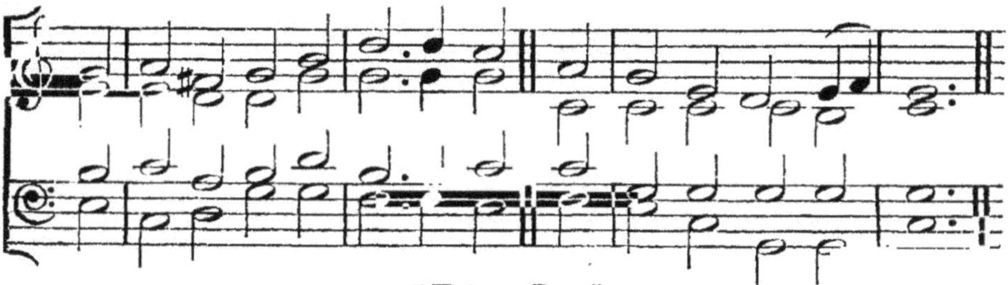

"He is our Peace."

mf GOD from on high hath heard;
Let sighs and sorrows cease;
Lo! from the opening heaven descends
To man the promised Peace.

Hark! through the silent night
Angelic voices swell;
Their joyful songs proclaim that "GOD
Is born on earth to dwell."

See how the shepherd-band
Speed on with eager feet;
Come to the hallowed cave with them
The Holy Babe to greet.

But, oh, what sight appears
Within that lowly door!
p A manger, stall, and swaddling clothes,
A Child, and Mother poor!

Art Thou the CHRIST? the SON?
The FATHER's Image bright?
And see we Him Whose Arm upholds
Earth and the starry height?

cr Yea, faith can pierce the cloud
Which veils Thy glory now;
f We hail Thee GOD, before Whose Throne
dim The Angels prostrate bow.

mf A silent Teacher, LORD,
Thou bidd'st us not refuse
To bear what flesh would have us shun,
To shun what flesh would choose.

Our sinful pride to cure
With that pure love of Thine,
cr O be Thou born within our hearts,
Most Holy Child Divine.

Christmas.

Hymn 59.

"Let us now go even unto Bethlehem."

Christmas.

p
cres.
f
O come, let us a - dore Him, O come, let us a - dore Him, O

come, let us a - dore Him, Christ . . . the Lord.

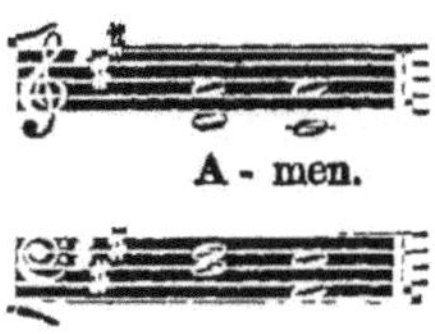
A - men.

Christmas.

Hymn 60.*

* *To be sung in Unison, except the 9th line.*

Christmas.

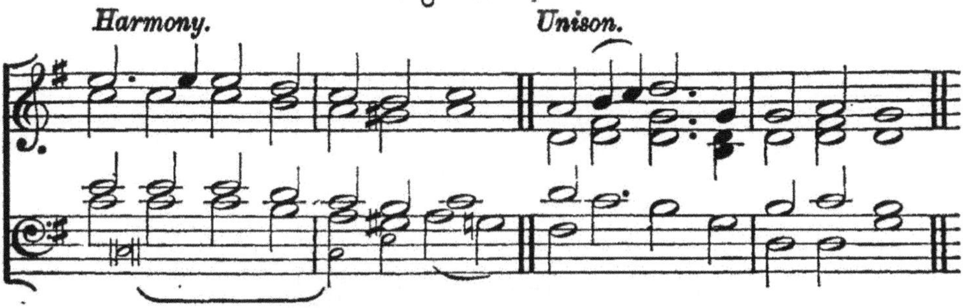

"Glory to God in the highest, and on earth peace, good will toward men."

f HARK! the herald-angels sing
Glory to the new-born King,
p Peace on earth, and mercy mild,
cr God and sinners reconciled.
f Joyful, all ye nations, rise,
Join the triumph of the skies;
With the Angelic host proclaim,
"Christ is born in Bethlehem."
ff Hark! the herald-angels sing
Glory to the new-born King.

f Christ, by highest heaven adored,
Christ, the Everlasting Lord,
dim Late in time behold Him come,
Offspring of a Virgin's womb.
p Veiled in flesh the Godhead see!
Hail, the Incarnate Deity!
Pleased as Man with man to dwell,
cr Jesus, our Emmanuel.
ff Hark! the herald-angels sing
Glory to the new-born King.

f Hail, the heaven-born Prince of peace!
Hail, the Sun of righteousness!
Light and life to all He brings,
Risen with healing in His wings.
mf Mild He lays His glory by,
Born that man no more may die,
cr Born to raise the sons of earth,
Born to give them second birth.
ff Hark! the herald-angels sing
Glory to the new-born King.

F 2

Christmas.

Hymn 61.

Christmas.

"Behold I bring you good tidings of great joy."

mf CHRISTIANS, awake, salute the happy morn,
Whereon the Saviour of the world was born;
Rise to adore the mystery of love,
Which hosts of Angels chanted from above;
With them the joyful tidings first begun
Of God Incarnate and the Virgin's Son.

Then to the watchful shepherds it was told,
Who heard the Angelic herald's voice, "Behold,
I bring good tidings of a Saviour's birth
To you and all the nations upon earth:
This day hath God fulfilled His promised Word,
This day is born a Saviour, Christ the Lord."

He spake; and straightway the celestial choir
In hymns of joy, unknown before, conspire:
The praises of redeeming love they sang,
And heaven's whole orb with Alleluias rang:
God's highest glory was their anthem still,
p Peace upon earth, and unto men good will.

mf To Bethlehem straight the enlightened shepherds ran,
To see the wonder God had wrought for man,
And found, with Joseph and the Blessèd Maid,
Her Son, the Saviour, in a manger laid:
Then to their flocks, still praising God, return,
And their glad hearts with holy rapture burn.

p O may we keep and ponder in our mind
God's wondrous love in saving lost mankind;
Trace we the Babe, Who hath retrieved our loss,
From His poor manger to His bitter Cross;
Tread in His steps, assisted by His grace,
Till man's first heavenly state again takes place.

mf Then may we hope, the Angelic hosts among,
To sing, redeemed, a glad triumphal song:
He that was born upon this joyful day
Around us all His glory shall display;
Saved by His love, incessant we shall sing
Eternal praise to heaven's Almighty King.

Christmas.

Hymn 62.

"Unto you is born this day in the city of David a Saviour which is Christ the Lord."

mf WHILE shepherds watched their
flocks by night,
All seated on the ground,
The Angel of the Lord came down,
And glory shone around.

"Fear not," said he; for mighty dread
Had seized their troubled mind;
"Glad tidings of great joy I bring
To you and all mankind.

"To you in David's town this day
Is born of David's line
A Saviour, Who is Christ the Lord;
And this shall be the sign:

"The heavenly Babe you there shall find
To human view displayed,
All meanly wrapped in swathing bands.
And in a manger laid."

Thus spake the seraph; and forthwith
Appeared a shining throng
Of Angels praising God, who thus
Addressed their joyful song:

f "All glory be to God on high,
p And on the earth be peace;
f Good will henceforth from heaven to men
Begin and never cease."

Christmas.

Hymn 63.

"The Lord is our defence."

For a Late Evening Service.

mf O SAVIOUR, Lord, to Thee we pray,
Whose love has kept us safe to-day,
Protect us through the coming night,
And ever save us by Thy might.

p Be with us now, in mercy nigh,
And spare Thy servants when they cry;
Our sins blot out, our prayers receive,
cr Thy light throughout our darkness give.

mf Let not dull sleep the soul oppress,
Nor secret foe the heart possess;
Our flesh keep chaste, that it may be
A holy temple meet for Thee.

To Thee, Who dost our hearts renew,
With fervent prayer we humbly sue,
That pure in thought and free from stain
We from our beds may rise again.

f All praise to God the Father be,
All praise, Eternal Son, to Thee,
Whom with the Spirit we adore
For ever and for evermore.

This Hymn may also be sung on Holy Days, except from Ash Wednesday to Whitsunday. Hymn 464 is suitable for this season.

St. Stephen's Day.

Hymn 64.

St. Stephen's Day.

"He, being full of the Holy Ghost, looked up steadfastly into heaven, and saw the glory of God, and Jesus standing on the right hand of God."

mf YESTERDAY, with exultation,
Joined the world in celebration
Of her promised Saviour's birth;
Yesterday the Angel-nation
Poured the strains of jubilation
O'er the Monarch born on earth;

But to-day o'er death victorious,
By his faith and actions glorious,
By his miracles renowned,
See the Deacon triumph gaining,
'Midst the faithless faith sustaining,
cr First of holy Martyrs found.

f Onward, champion, falter never,
Sure of sure reward for ever,
Holy Stephen, persevere;
Perjured witnesses confounding,
Satan's synagogue astounding
By thy doctrine true and clear.

mf Thine own Witness is in heaven,
True and faithful, to thee given,
Witness of thy blamelessness:
By thy name a crown implying,
Meet it is thou shouldst be dying
For the crown of righteousness.

For the crown that fadeth never
Bear the torturer's brief endeavour;
Victory waits to end the strife:
Death shall be thy life's beginning,
And life's losing be the winning
Of the true and better life.

Filled with God's most Holy Spirit,
See the heaven thou shalt inherit,
Stephen, gaze into the skies:
There God's glory steadfast viewing,
Thence thy victor-strength renewing,
Pant for thy eternal prize.

See, as Jewish foes invade thee,
See how Jesus stands to aid thee,
Stands at God's right hand on high:
Tell how opened heaven is shown thee,
Tell how Jesus waits to own thee,
Tell it with thy latest cry.

p As the dying Martyr kneeleth,
For his murderers he appealeth,
For their madness grieving sore;
pp Then in Christ he sleepeth sweetly,
cr And with Christ he reigneth meetly,
ff Martyr first-fruits, evermore.

St. Stephen's Day.

Hymn 65.

" Be thou faithful unto death, and I will give thee a crown of life."

mf FIRST of Martyrs, thou whose name
Doth thy golden crown proclaim,
Not of flowers that fade away
Weave we this thy crown to-day.

Bright the stones which bruise thee gleam,
Sprinkled with thy life-blood's stream;
Stars around thy sainted head
Never could such radiance shed.

Every wound upon thy brow
Sparkles with unearthly glow;
Like an Angel's is thy face
Beaming with celestial grace.

Oh, how blessèd first to be
Slain for Him Who bled for thee;
First like Him in dying hour
Witness to Almighty power;

First to follow where He trod
Through the deep Red Sea of blood;
First, but in thy footsteps press
Saints and Martyrs numberless.

f Glory to the Father be,
Glory, Virgin-born, to Thee,
Glory to the Holy Ghost,
Praised by men and heavenly host.

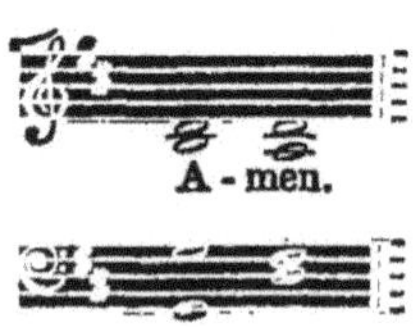

St. John the Evangelist's Day.

Hymn 66.

"That . . . which we have looked upon, and our hands have handled, of the Word of Life, . . . declare we unto you."

mf THE life, which God's Incarnate Word
Lived here below with men,
Three blest Evangelists record
With heaven-inspirèd pen :

John soars on high, beyond the three,
To God the Father's Throne ;
And shews in what deep mystery
The Word with God is One.

p Upon the Saviour's loving Breast
Invited to recline,
'Twas thence he drew, in moments blest,
Rich stores of truth Divine :

mf And thence did that angelic love
His inmost spirit fill,
Which, once enkindled from above,
Breathes in his pages still.

f Jesu, the Virgin's Holy Son,
We praise Thee and adore,
Who art with God the Father One
And Spirit evermore.

St. John the Evangelist's Day.

Hymn 67.

St. John the Evangelist's Day.

"The disciple whom Jesus loved."

mf WORD Supreme, before creation
  Born of God eternally,
Who didst will for our salvation
  To be born on earth, and die;
Well Thy saints have kept their station,
  Watching till Thine hour drew nigh.

Now 'tis come, and faith espies Thee;
  Like an eaglet in the morn,
One in steadfast worship eyes Thee,
  Thy beloved, Thy latest born:
In Thy glory he descries Thee
  Reigning from the tree of scorn.

p He upon Thy Bosom lying
  Thy true tokens learned by heart;
And Thy dearest pledge in dying,
  Lord, Thou didst to him impart;
Shew'dst him how, all grace supplying,
  Blood and water from Thee start.

He first, hoping and believing,
  Did beside the grave adore;
Latest he, the warfare leaving,
  Landed on the eternal shore;
And his witness we receiving
  Own Thee Lord for evermore.

Much he asked in loving wonder,
  On Thy Bosom leaning, Lord;
In that secret place of thunder
  Answer kind didst Thou accord,
Wisdom for Thy Church to ponder
  Till the day of dread award.

Lo! heaven's doors lift up, revealing
  How Thy judgments earthward move;
Scrolls unfolded, trumpets pealing,
  Wine cups from the wrath above;
p Yet o'er all a soft voice stealing—
  "Little children, trust and love!"

f Thee, the Almighty King Eternal,
  Father of the Eternal Word,
Thee, the Father's Word Supernal,
  Thee, of Both, the Breath adored,
Heaven, and earth, and realms infernal
  Own One glorious God and Lord.

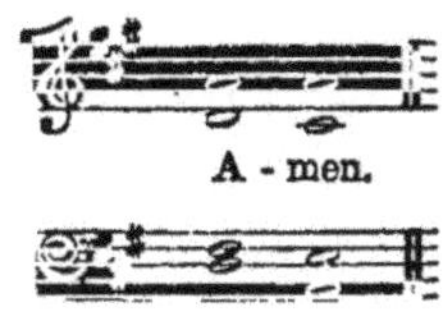

The Innocents' Day.

Hymn 68.

"The first-fruits unto God and to the Lamb."

mf SWEET flowerets of the martyr band,
So early plucked by cruel hand;
Like rosebuds by a tempest torn,
As breaks the light of summer morn;

First victims offered for the LORD,
cr Ye little knew your high reward,
mf As, at the very altar, gay
With palms and crowns ye seemed to play.

Ah! what availed King Herod's wrath?
He could not stay your Saviour's path:
cr The Child he sought alone went free;
f That Child is King eternally.

O LORD, the Virgin-born, to Thee,
Praise, honour, might, and glory be,
Whom with the FATHER we adore
And HOLY GHOST for evermore.

The Innocents' Day.

Hymn 69.

"They are without fault before the throne of God."

mf GLORY to Thee, O Lord,
Who, from this world of sin,
By cruel Herod's ruthless sword
Those precious ones didst win.

Baptized in their own blood,
Earth's untried perils o'er,
They passed unconsciously the flood,
And safely gained the shore.

Glory to Thee for all
The ransomed infant band,
Who since that hour have heard Thy call,
And reached the quiet land.

p O that our hearts within,
Like theirs, were pure and bright;
O that as free from deeds of sin
We shrank not from Thy sight.

Lord, help us every hour
Thy cleansing grace to claim;
cr In life to glorify Thy power,
In death to praise Thy Name.

Circumcision.

Hymn 70.

"When eight days were accomplished for the circumcising of the child, His name was called Jesus."

mf THE ancient law departs,
And all its terrors cease;
For JESUS makes with faithful hearts
A covenant of peace.

The Light of Light Divine,
True Brightness undefiled,
He bears for us the shame of sin,
A Holy Spotless Child.

His Infant Body now
Begins our pain to feel;
Those precious drops of Blood that flow
For death the victim seal.

mf To-day the Name is Thine
At which we bend the knee;
They call Thee JESUS, Child Divine,
Our JESUS deign to be.

f All praise, Eternal SON,
For Thy redeeming love,
With FATHER, SPIRIT, ever ONE
In glorious might above.

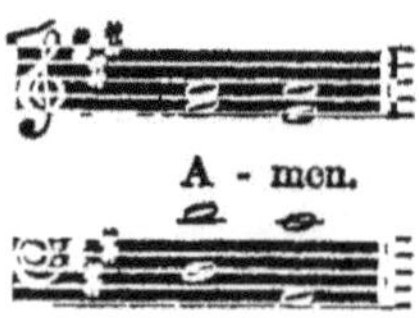

Circumcision.

Hymn 71.

"God sent forth His Son, made of a woman, made under the law, to redeem them that were under the law."

mf O BLESSÈD day, when first was poured
The Blood of our Redeeming LORD!
O blessèd day, when first began
p His sufferings borne for sinful man!

Scarce entered on this life of woe,
His Infant Blood begins to flow;
A foretaste of His death He feels,
cr An earnest of His love reveals.

mf From heaven descending to fulfil
The bidding of His FATHER's Will,
p A victim even now He lies
Before the day of sacrifice.

mf For love of us His woes begin;
The Sinless suffers for our sin;
The Law's great Maker for our aid
Obedient to the Law is made.

p The wound He through the Law endures
cr Our freedom from that Law secures;
Henceforth a holier law prevails,
The law of love which never fails.

mf LORD, circumcise our hearts, we pray,
And take what is not Thine away;
Write Thine own Name within our [hearts,
Thy law upon our inmost parts.

f O LORD, the Virgin-born, to Thee
Eternal praise and glory be,
Whom with the FATHER we adore
And HOLY GHOST for evermore.

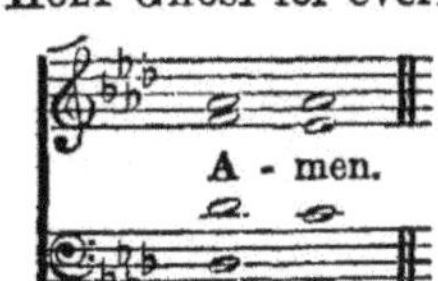

The following Hymns are suitable for this Festival:

175 Conquering kings their titles take.
179 To the Name of our Salvation.

New Year's Day.

Hymn 72.

"And now, Lord, what is my hope; truly my hope is even in Thee."

mf THE year is gone, beyond recall,
With all its hopes and fears,
With all its bright and gladdening smiles,
p With all its mourners' tears;

mf Thy thankful people praise Thee, LORD,
For countless gifts received;
And pray for grace to keep the Faith
Which saints of old believed.

To Thee we come, O gracious LORD,
The new-born year to bless;
Defend our land from pestilence;
Give peace and plenteousness;

Forgive this nation's many sins;
The growth of vice restrain;
And help us all with sin to strive,
And crowns of life to gain.

From evil deeds that stain the past
We now desire to flee;
And pray that future years may all
Be spent, good LORD, for Thee.

O FATHER, let Thy watchful Eye
Still look on us in love,
That we may praise Thee, year by year
With Angel-hosts above.

f All glory to the FATHER be,
All glory to the SON,
All glory, HOLY GHOST, to Thee,
While endless ages run.

240 Orig. Ed.

New Year's Day.

Hymn 73.

"So teach us to number our days, that we may apply our hearts unto wisdom."

nf FOR Thy mercy and Thy grace,
Faithful through another year,
Hear our song of thankfulness;
Jesu, our Redeemer, hear.

In our weakness and distress,
Rock of strength, be Thou our Stay;
In the pathless wilderness
Be our true and living Way.

Who of us death's awful road
In the coming year shall tread,
With Thy rod and staff, O God,
Comfort Thou his dying bed.

mf Keep us faithful, keep us pure,
Keep us evermore Thine own,
Help, O help us to endure,
Fit us for the promised crown.

f So within Thy palace gate
We shall praise, on golden strings,
Thee the only Potentate,
Lord of lords and King of kings.

New Year's Day.

Hymn 74.

New Year's Day.

"That God in all things may be glorified."

mf FATHER, let me dedicate
All this year to Thee,
In whatever worldly state
Thou wilt have me be:
p Not from sorrow, pain, or care,
Freedom dare I claim;
cr This alone shall be my prayer,
"Glorify Thy Name."

mf Can a child presume to choose
Where or how to live?
Can a FATHER's love refuse
All the best to give?
More Thou givest every day
Than the best can claim,
Nor withholdest aught that may
Glorify Thy Name.

If in mercy Thou wilt spare
Joys that yet are mine;
If on life, serene and fair,
Brighter rays may shine;
f Let my glad heart, while it sings,
Thee in all proclaim,
And, whate'er the future brings,
Glorify Thy Name.

p If Thou callest to the Cross,
And its shadow come,
Turning all my gain to loss,
Shrouding heart and home;
cr Let me think how Thy dear SON
To His glory came,
And in deepest woe pray on,
"Glorify Thy Name."

The following Hymns are suitable for this day or its eve:

165 O GOD, our help in ages past.
205 Thou Judge of quick and dead.
288 A few more years shall roll.
289 Days and moments quickly flying.

Epiphany.

Hymn 75.

"The Life was manifested, and we have seen it."

mf HOW vain the cruel Herod's fear,
When told that CHRIST the King is near!
He takes not earthly realms away,
Who gives the realms that ne'er decay.

The Eastern sages saw from far
And followed on His guiding star;
By light their way to Light they trod,
And by their gifts confessed their GOD.

Within the Jordan's sacred flood
The heavenly LAMB in meekness stood,
That He, to Whom no sin was known,
Might cleanse His people from their own.

And oh, what miracle Divine,
When water reddened into wine!
He spake the Word, and forth it flowed
In streams that nature ne'er bestowed.

f All glory, JESU, be to Thee
For this Thy glad Epiphany:
Whom with the FATHER we adore
And HOLY GHOST for evermore.

Epiphany.

Hymn 76.

"And thou, Bethlehem, in the land of Juda, art not the least among the princes of Juda; for out of thee shall come a governor, that shall rule My people Israel."

mf EARTH has many a noble city;
  Bethlehem, thou dost all excel:
Out of thee the LORD from heaven
  Came to rule His Israel.

Fairer than the sun at morning
  Was the star that told His birth,
To the world its GOD announcing
  Seen in fleshly form on earth

Eastern sages at His cradle
  Make oblations rich and rare;
See them give, in deep devotion,
  Gold, and frankincense, and myrrh.

Sacred gifts of mystic meaning:
  Incense doth their GOD disclose,
Gold the King of kings proclaimeth,
p Myrrh His sepulchre foreshows.

f JESU, Whom the Gentiles worshipped
  At Thy glad Epiphany,
Unto Thee, with GOD the FATHER
  And the SPIRIT, glory be.

Epiphany.

Hymn 77.

"We have seen His star in the east."

f WHAT star is this, with beams so bright,
More beauteous than the noonday
It shines to herald forth the King, [light?
And Gentiles to His cradle bring.

mf See now fulfilled what God decreed,
"From Jacob shall a star proceed;"
And eastern sages with amaze
Upon the wondrous vision gaze.

The guiding star above is bright;
Within them shines a clearer light,
Which leads them on with power benign
To seek the Giver of the sign.

True love can brook no dull delay;
Nor toil nor dangers stop their way:
Home, kindred, fatner-land, and all
They leave at their Creator's call.

p O Jesu, while the star of grace
Allures us now to seek Thy Face,
Let not our slothful hearts refuse
The guidance of that light to use.

f All glory, Jesu, be to Thee
For this Thy glad Epiphany.
Whom with the Father we adore
And Holy Ghost for evermore.

Epiphany.

Hymn 78.

"And He went down with them, and came to Nazareth, and was subject unto them."

mf THE Heavenly Child in stature grows,
p And, growing, learns to die;
And still His early training shows
His coming agony.

mf The Son of God His glory hides
With parents mean and poor;
And He, Who made the heavens, abides
p In dwelling-place obscure.

mf Those mighty Hands that rule the sky
No earthly toil refuse;
The Maker of the stars on high
p An humble trade pursues.

mf He, Whom the choirs of Angels praise
Bearing each dread decree,
His earthly parents now obeys
p In deep humility.

mf For this Thy lowliness revealed,
Jesu, we Thee adore;
f And praise to God the Father yield
And Spirit evermore.

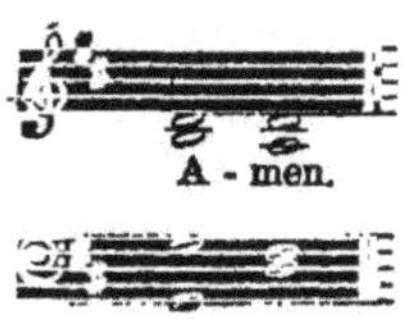

Epiphany.

Hymn 79.

"When they saw the star, they rejoiced with exceeding great joy."

f AS with gladness men of old
Did the guiding star behold,
As with joy they hailed its light,
Leading onward, beaming bright;
So, most gracious LORD, may we
Evermore be led to Thee.

mf As with joyful steps they sped,
Saviour, to Thy lowly bed,
There to bend the knee before
Thee Whom heaven and earth adore;
So may we with willing feet
Ever seek the mercy-seat.

As they offered gifts most rare
At Thy cradle rude and bare;
So may we with holy joy,
Pure and free from sin's alloy,
All our costliest treasures bring,
CHRIST, to Thee our heavenly King.

p Holy JESUS, every day
Keep us in the narrow way;
cr And, when earthly things are past,
Bring our ransomed souls at last
mf Where they need no star to guide,
Where no clouds Thy glory hide.

f In the heavenly country bright
Need they no created light;
Thou its Light, its Joy, its Crown,
Thou its Sun which goes not down;
ff There for ever may we sing
Alleluias to our King.

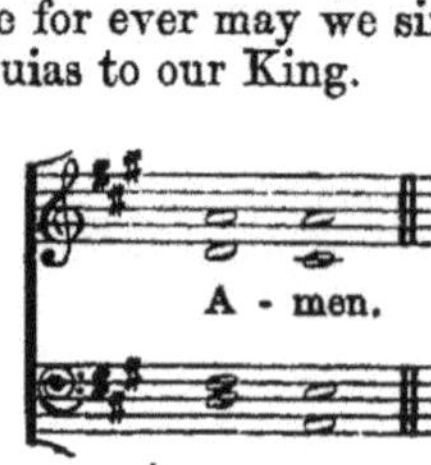

Epiphany.

Hymn 80.

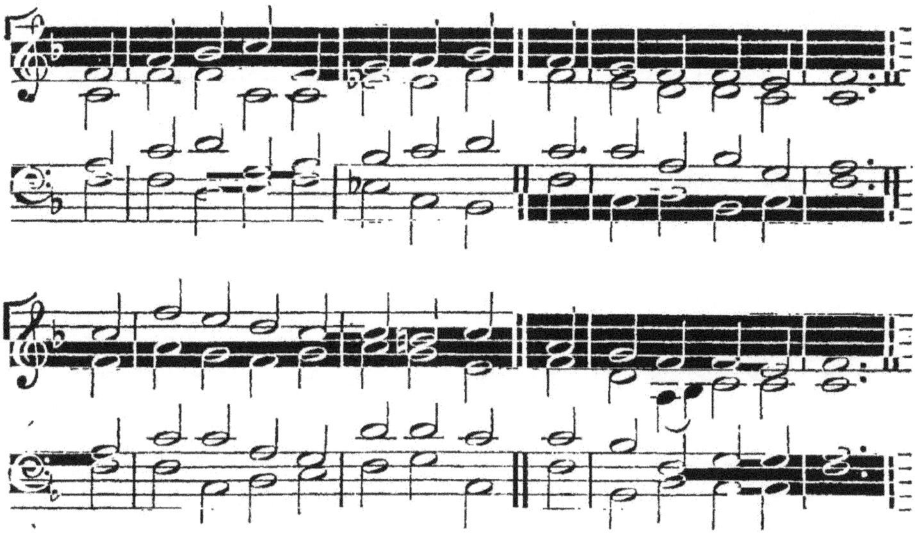

"The people which sat in darkness saw great light."

mf THE people that in darkness sat
  A glorious light have seen;
The Light has shined on them who long
  In shades of death have been.

f To hail Thee, Sun of Righteousness,
  The gathering nations come;
They joy as when the reapers bear
  Their harvest treasures home.

For Thou their burden dost remove,
  And break the tyrant's rod,
As in the day when Midian fell
  Before the sword of GOD.

For unto us a Child is born,
  To us a Son is given,
And on His Shoulder ever rests
  All power in earth and heaven.

His Name shall be the Prince of peace,
  The Everlasting LORD,
The Wonderful, the Counsellor,
  The GOD by all adored.

His righteous government and power
  Shall over all extend;
On judgment and on justice based,
  His reign shall have no end.

mf LORD JESUS, reign in us, we pray,
  And make us Thine alone,
f Who with the FATHER ever art
  And HOLY SPIRIT ONE.

Epiphany.

Hymn 81.

Epiphany.

"The Son of God was manifested."

mf SONGS of thankfulness and praise,
JESU, LORD, to Thee we raise,
Manifested by the star
To the sages from afar;
Branch of royal David's stem
In Thy birth at Bethlehem;
f Anthems be to Thee addrest,
GOD in Man made manifest.

mf Manifest at Jordan's stream,
Prophet, Priest, and King supreme;
And at Cana wedding-guest
In Thy Godhead manifest;
Manifest in power Divine,
Changing water into wine;
f Anthems be to Thee addrest,
GOD in Man made manifest.

mf Manifest in making whole
Palsied limbs and fainting soul;
Manifest in valiant fight,
Quelling all the devil's might;
Manifest in gracious Will,
Ever bringing good from ill;
f Anthems be to Thee addrest,
GOD in Man made manifest.

p Sun and Moon shall darkened be,
Stars shall fall, the heavens shall flee;
cr CHRIST will then like lightning shine,
mf All will see His glorious Sign;
All will then the trumpet hear,
All will see the Judge appear;
f Thou by all wilt be confest,
GOD in Man made manifest.

mf Grant us grace to see Thee, LORD,
Mirrored in Thy holy Word;
May we imitate Thee now,
And be pure, as pure art Thou;
That we like to Thee may be
At Thy great Epiphany;
f And may praise Thee, ever Blest,
GOD in Man made manifest.

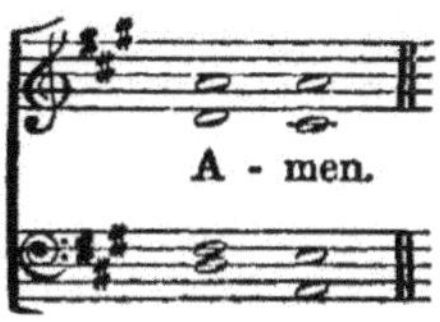

From the First Sunday after the Epiphany to Septuagesima General Hymns may be sung; especially

173 O Love, how deep! how broad! how high!
177 JESU! the very thought is sweet.
178 JESU, the very thought of Thee.
218 GOD of mercy, GOD of grace.
219 Hail to the LORD's Anointed.
220 JESUS shall reign where'er the sun.

For the Week before Septuagesima.

Hymn 82.

"And again they said, Alleluia."

f ALLELUIA, song of sweetness,
Voice of joy that cannot die;
ALLELUIA is the anthem
Ever dear to choirs on high;
In the house of GOD abiding
Thus they sing eternally.

ALLELUIA thou resoundest,
True Jerusalem and free;
ALLELUIA, joyful Mother,
All thy children sing with thee;
p But by Babylon's sad waters
Mourning exiles now are we.

ALLELUIA cannot always
Be our song while here below;
ALLELUIA our transgressions
Make us for awhile forego;
For the solemn time is coming
When our tears for sin must flow.

mf Therefore in our hymns we pray Thee,
Grant us, Blessèd TRINITY,
At the last to keep Thine Easter
In our Home beyond the sky,
f There to Thee for ever singing
ALLELUIA joyfully.

Septuagesima.

Hymn 83.

"How shall we sing the Lord's song in a strange land?"

mf CREATOR of the world, to Thee
An endless rest of joy belongs;
And heavenly choirs are ever free
To sing on high their festal songs.

p But we are fallen creatures here,
Where pain and sorrow daily come;
And how can we in exile drear
Sing out, as they, sweet songs of Home?

mf O FATHER, Who dost promise still
That they who mourn shall blessèd be,
p Grant us to weep for deeds of ill
That banish us so long from Thee:

But, weeping, grant us faith to rest
In hope upon Thy loving care;
cr Till Thou restore us, with the blest,
mf Their songs of praise in heaven to share.

f To FATHER, SON, and HOLY GHOST,
The GOD Whom heaven and earth adore
From men and from the Angel-host
Be praise and glory evermore.

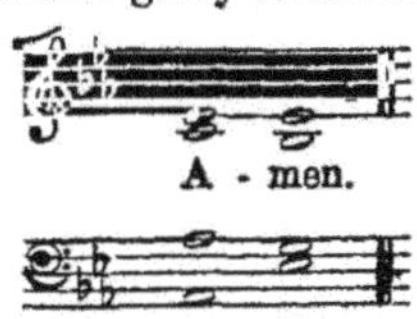

From Septuagesima Sunday to Lent the Hymns for Sunday and the other days of the week should be sung; and the following Hymns are also suitable:

162 Have mercy on us, GOD most High.
168 There is a book, who runs may read.
172 Praise to the Holiest in the height.
210 Gracious SPIRIT, HOLY GHOST.
262 Great Mover of all hearts.

Hymn 84.

"Rend your heart and not your garments, and turn unto the Lord your God."

p ONCE more the solemn season calls
  A holy fast to keep;
And now within the temple walls
  Let priest and people weep.

mf But vain all outward sign of grief,
  And vain the form of prayer,
Unless the heart implore relief,
  And penitence be there.

We smite the breast, we weep in vain,
  In vain in ashes mourn,
Unless with penitential pain
  The smitten soul be torn.

p In sorrow true then let us pray
  To our offended God,
From us to turn His wrath away,
  And stay the uplifted rod.

O God, our Judge and Father, deign
  To spare the bruisèd reed;
We pray for time to turn again,
  For grace to turn indeed.

mf Blest Three in One, to Thee we bow;
  Vouchsafe us, in Thy love,
To gather from these fasts below
  Immortal fruit above.

Lent.

Hymn 85.

"Now, saith the Lord, turn ye even to Me with all your heart, and with fasting, and with weeping, and with mourning."

mf BY precepts taught of ages past,
Now let us keep again the fast
Which, year by year, in order meet
Of forty days is made complete.

The law and seers that were of old
In divers ways this Lent foretold,
Which CHRIST Himself, the LORD and Guide
Of every season, sanctified.

More sparing therefore let us make
The words we speak, the food we take,
Deny ourselves in mirth and sleep,
In stricter watch our senses keep.

In prayer together let us fall,
And cry for mercy, one and all;
And weep before the Judge, and say,
O turn from us Thy wrath away.

Thy grace have we offended sore
By sins, O GOD, which we deplore;
Pour down upon us from above
The riches of Thy pardoning love.

Remember, LORD, though frail we be,
That yet Thine handiwork are we:
Nor let the honour of Thy Name
Be by another put to shame.

Forgive the ill that we have wrought,
Increase the good that we have sought;
That we at length, our wanderings o'er,
May please Thee now and evermore.

mf Blest THREE in ONE, and ONE in THREE,
Almighty GOD, we pray to Thee,
That Thou wouldst now vouchsafe to bless
Our fast with fruits of righteousness.

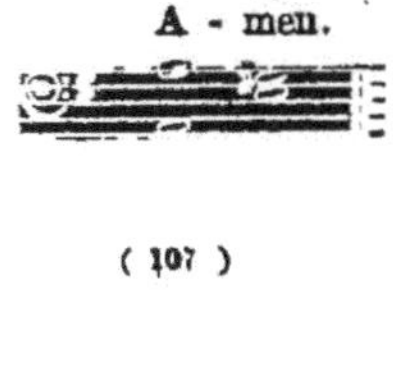

Lent.

Hymn 86.

Lent.

"In due season we shall reap, if we faint not."

mf O THOU Who dost to man accord
His highest prize, his best reward,
Thou Hope of all our race;
JESU, to Thee we now draw near,
Our earnest supplications hear,
Who humbly seek Thy Face.

p With self-accusing voice within
Our conscience tells of many a sin
In thought, and word, and deed:
cr O cleanse that conscience from all stain,
The penitent restore again,
From every burthen freed.

mf If Thou reject us, who shall give
Our fainting spirits strength to live?
'Tis Thine alone to spare;
With cleansèd hearts to pray aright,
And find acceptance in Thy sight,
Be this our lowly prayer.

'Tis Thou hast blessed this solemn fast;
So may its days by us be passed
In self-control severe,
cr That, when our Easter morn we hail,
Its mystic feast we may not fail
To keep with conscience clear.

mf O Blessèd TRINITY, bestow
Thy pardoning grace on us below,
And shield us evermore;
cr Until, within Thy courts above,
We see Thy Face, and sing Thy love,
And with Thy Saints adore.

Lent.

Hymn 87.

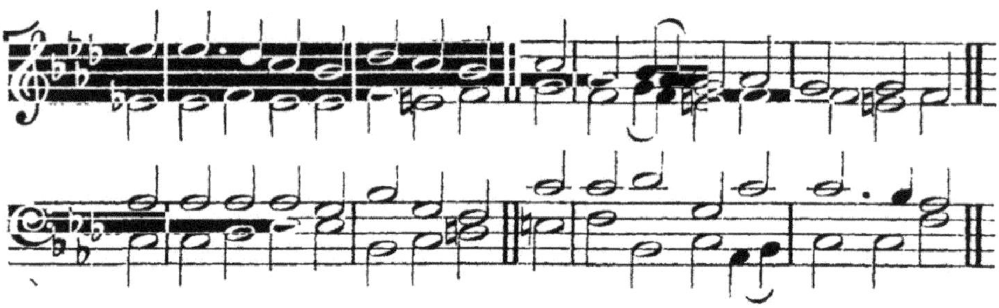

"O deliver us, and be merciful unto our sins, for Thy Name's sake."

p O MERCIFUL CREATOR, hear;
In tender pity bow Thine ear:
Accept the tearful prayer we raise
In this our fast of forty days.

Each heart is manifest to Thee;
Thou knowest our infirmity:
Repentant now we seek Thy Face;
cr Impart to us Thy pardoning grace.

p Our sins are manifold and sore,
But spare Thou them who sin deplore;
And for Thine own Name's sake make whole
The fainting and the weary soul.

Grant us to mortify each sense
By means of outward abstinence,
That so from every stain of sin
The soul may keep her fast within.

mf Blest THREE in ONE, and ONE in THREE,
Almighty GOD, we pray to Thee,
That Thou wouldst now vouchsafe to bless
Our fast with fruits of righteousness.

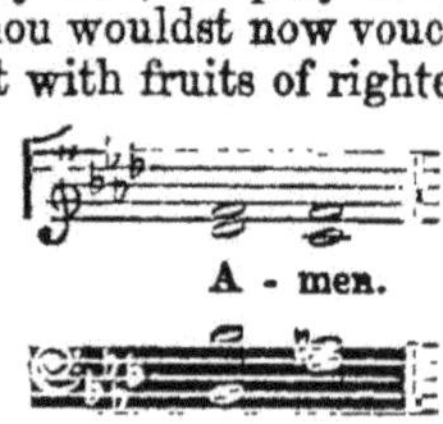

Hymn 88.

"Behold, now is the accepted time; behold, now is the day of salvation."

mf LO! now is our accepted day,
The time for purging sins away,
The sins of thought, and deed, and word,
That we have done against the LORD.

For He the Merciful and True
Hath spared His people hitherto;
Not willing that the soul should die,
Though great its past iniquity.

Then let us all with earnest care,
And contrite fast, and tear, and prayer,
And works of mercy and of love,
Entreat for pardon from above;

mf That He may all our sins efface,
Adorn us with the gifts of grace,
And join us to the Angel band
For ever in the heavenly land.

Blest THREE in ONE and ONE in THREE,
Almighty GOD, we pray to Thee, [bless
That Thou wouldst now vouchsafe to
Our fast with fruits of righteousness.

Hymn 89.

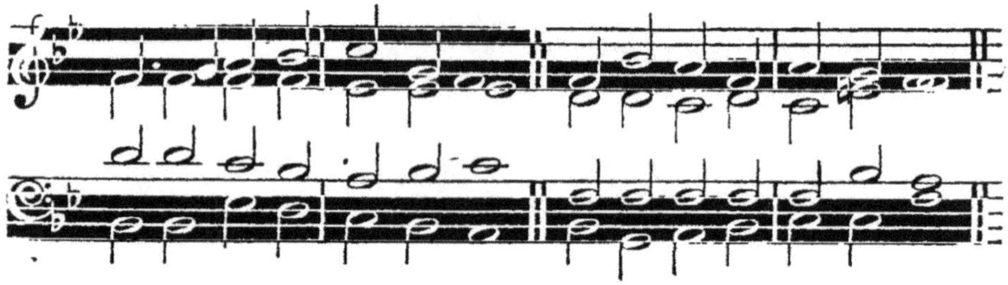

"Then shall they fast in those days."

mf GOOD it is to keep the fast
Shadowed forth in ages past,
Which our own Almighty LORD
Hallowed by His deed and word.

Moses, while he fasted, saw
GOD Who gave by him the Law;
To Elijah Angels came,
Steeds of fire and car of flame.

So was Daniel meet to gaze
On the sight of latter days,
And the Baptist to proclaim
Blessings through the Bridegroom's Name.

p Grant us, LORD, like them to be
Oft in prayer and fast with Thee;
cr Fill us with Thy heavenly might,
Be our joy and true delight.

p FATHER, hear us, through Thy SON,
And the SPIRIT, with Thee ONE,
cr Whom our thankful hearts adore
Ever and for evermore.

Lent.

Hymn 90.

"I sat down and wept, and mourned certain days, and fasted, and prayed before the God of heaven."

mf JESU, our Lenten fast of Thee
We duteous learn to keep,
A healing time, by Thy decree,
For all Thy wounded sheep.

A time in which towards Paradise,
Once lost by carnal sense,
The souls redeemed by Thee may rise
Through chastening abstinence.

Now with Thy Church be present, LORD,
In all Thy saving grace,
And hear us as with one accord,
p Mourning, we seek Thy Face.

Most Merciful, forgive the past,
The sins which we deplore;
Thy sheltering arms around us cast,
That we may sin no more.

mf To Thee our sacrifice we bring
Of Lenten fast and prayer,
cr Till, cleansed by Thee our GOD and King,
f Thy Paschal joy we share.

mf Grant this, O FATHER, through Thy SON,
And through the SPIRIT Blest,
Who art with Them for ever ONE,
Eternally confest.

Lent.

Hymn 91.

Lent.

"Whom resist, steadfast in the faith."

p CHRISTIAN, dost thou see them
On the holy ground,
cr How the troops of Midian
dim Prowl and prowl around?
ff Christian, up and smite them,
Counting gain but loss;
Smite them by the merit
Of the holy Cross.

p Christian, dost thou feel them,
How they work within,
cr Striving, tempting, luring,
Goading into sin?
f Christian, never tremble;
Never be down-cast;
Smite them by the virtue
Of the Lenten fast.

p Christian, dost thou hear them,
How they speak thee fair?
cr "Always fast and vigil?
Always watch and prayer?"
ff Christian, answer boldly,
"While I breathe I pray:"
p Peace shall follow battle,
f Night shall end in day.

mf "Well I know thy trouble,
O My servant true;
Thou art very weary,
p I was weary too;
f But that toil shall make thee
Some day all Mine own,
And the end of sorrow
ff Shall be near My Throne."

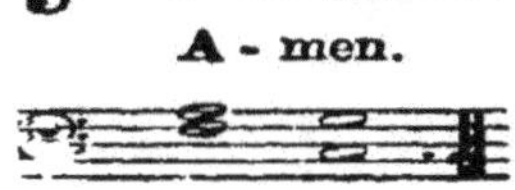

Lent.

Hymn 92.

"And Jesus . . . was led by the Spirit into the wilderness, being forty days tempted of the devil. And in those days He did eat nothing."

mf FORTY days and forty nights
Thou wast fasting in the wild;
Forty days and forty nights
Tempted, and yet undefiled.

Sunbeams scorching all the day;
Chilly dew-drops nightly shed;
Prowling beasts about Thy way;
Stones Thy pillow; earth Thy bed.

Shall not we Thy sorrow share,
And from earthly joys abstain,
Fasting with unceasing prayer,
Glad with Thee to suffer pain?

And if Satan, vexing sore,
Flesh or spirit should assail,
cr Thou, his Vanquisher before,
Grant we may not faint nor fail.

p So shall we have peace Divine;
cr Holier gladness ours shall be;
Round us too shall Angels shine,
dim Such as ministered to Thee.

mf Keep, O keep us, Saviour dear,
Ever constant by Thy side;
f That with Thee we may appear
At the eternal Eastertide.

Lent.

Hymn 93.

"Enter not into judgment with Thy servant; for in Thy sight shall no man living be justified."

O LORD, turn not Thy Face from me,
  Who lie in woeful state,
Lamenting all my sinful life
  Before Thy mercy-gate;

A gate that opens wide to those
  That do lament their sin;
Shut not that gate against me, Lord,
  But let me enter in.

And call me not to strict account
  How I have sojourned here;
For then my guilty conscience knows
  How vile I shall appear.

Mercy, Good Lord, mercy I ask;
  This is my humble prayer;
For mercy, Lord, is all my suit,
  O let Thy mercy spare.

Lent.

Hymn 94.

"My soul fleeth unto the Lord."

p LORD, in this Thy mercy's day,
Ere it pass for aye away,
On our knees we fall and pray.

Holy JESU, grant us tears,
Fill us with heart-searching fears,
Ere that awful doom appears.

mf LORD, on us Thy SPIRIT pour
Kneeling lowly at the door,
Ere it close for evermore.

pp By Thy night of agony,
By Thy supplicating cry,
By Thy willingness to die;

By Thy tears of bitter woe
For Jerusalem below,
Let us not Thy love forego.

p Grant us 'neath Thy wings a place,
cr Lest we lose this day of grace
mf Ere we shall behold Thy Face.

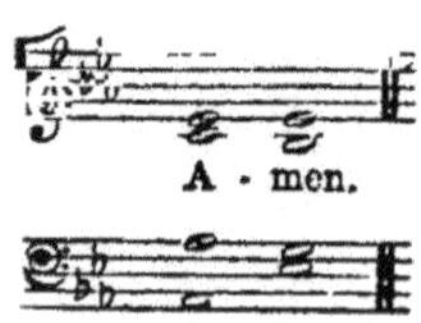

Lent.

Hymn 95.

"I am the Light of the world."

For a Late Evening Service.

f O CHRIST, Who art the Light and Day,
Thy beams chase night's dark shades [away;
The very Light of Light Thou art,
Who dost Thy blessèd Light impart.

mf All-Holy Lord, to Thee we bend,
Thy servants through this night defend,
And grant us calm repose in Thee,
A quiet night from perils free.

Let not the tempter round us creep
With thoughts of evil while we sleep,
Nor with his wiles the flesh allure
And make us in Thy sight impure.

While wearied eyes light slumber take
The heart to Thee be still awake,
And Thy right hand stretched forth above
Protect the children of Thy love.

O Lord, our strong defence, be nigh;
Bid all the powers of darkness fly;
Preserve and watch o'er us for good,
Whom Thou hast purchased with Thy Blood.

p Remember us, dear Lord, we pray,
While burdened in the flesh we stay;
cr 'Tis Thou alone our souls canst keep;
Abide with us this night in sleep.

mf Blest Three in One, and One in Three,
Almighty God, we pray to Thee, [bless
That Thou wouldst now vouchsafe to
Our fast with fruits of righteousness.

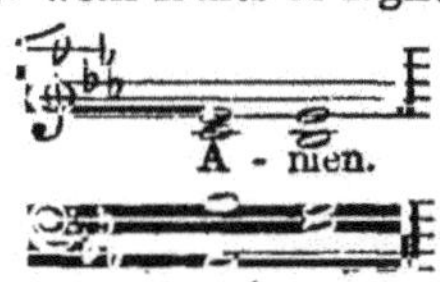

The following Hymns, and some of the Hymns on the Passion, are suitable for this season:

183 When wounded sore the stricken heart.
198 O Jesu, Thou art standing.
244 Lord, when we bend before Thy Throne.
245 When at Thy footstool, Lord, I bend.
249 Have mercy, Lord, on me.
250 Out of the deep I call.
251 Saviour, when in dust to Thee.
252 Weary of earth and laden with my sin.
253 O Jesu Christ, if aught there be.
254 Art thou weary, art thou languid.
259 Thy life was given for me.
263 Take up thy cross, the Saviour said.
288 A few more years shall roll.
465 Litany of Penitence. No. 1.
466 Litany of Penitence. No. 2.

The Fifth Sunday in Lent.

OTHERWISE CALLED PASSION SUNDAY.

Hymn 96. (FIRST TUNE.)

To be sung in Unison.

The Fifth Sunday in Lent.

OTHERWISE CALLED PASSION SUNDAY.

Hymn 96. (SECOND TUNE.)

"God forbid that I should glory, save in the cross of our Lord Jesus Christ."

f THE Royal Banners forward go,
The Cross shines forth in mystic glow;
Where He in Flesh, our flesh Who made,
Our sentence bore, our ransom paid.

mf There whilst He hung, His sacred Side
By soldier's spear was opened wide,
To cleanse us in the precious flood
Of Water mingled with His Blood.

f Fulfilled is now what David told
In true prophetic song of old,
How GOD the heathen's King should be;
ff For GOD is reigning from the Tree.

mf O Tree of glory, Tree most fair,
Ordained those Holy Limbs to bear,
How bright in purple robe it stood,
p The purple of a Saviour's Blood!

mf Upon its arms, like balance true,
He weighed the price for sinners due,
The price which none but He could pay,
f And spoiled the spoiler of his prey.

To Thee, Eternal THREE in ONE,
Let homage meet by all be done:
As by the Cross Thou dost restore,
So rule and guide us evermore.

1. 

2. 

This Hymn may be sung daily till Thursday before Easter.

The Fifth Sunday in Lent.

Hymn 97. OTHERWISE CALLED PASSION SUNDAY.

To be sung in Unison.

The Fifth Sunday in Lent.

OTHERWISE CALLED PASSION SUNDAY.

"The cross of our Lord Jesus Christ."

f SING, my tongue, the glorious battle,
Sing the last, the dread affray;
O'er the Cross, the Victor's trophy,
Sound the high triumphal lay,
p How, the pains of death enduring,
f Earth's Redeemer won the day.

mf He, our Maker, deeply grieving
That the first-made Adam fell,
When he ate the fruit forbidden
Whose reward was death and hell,
Marked e'en then this Tree the ruin
Of the first tree to dispel.

Thus the work for our salvation
He ordainèd to be done;
To the traitor's art opposing
Art yet deeper than his own;
Thence the remedy procuring
Whence the fatal wound begun.

Therefore, when at length the fulness
Of the appointed time was come,
He was sent, the world's Creator,
From the FATHER's heavenly home,
And was found in human fashion,
Offspring of the Virgin's womb.

p Lo! He lies, an Infant weeping,
Where the narrow manger stands,
While the Mother-Maid His members
Wraps in mean and lowly bands,
And the swaddling clothes is winding
Round His helpless Feet and Hands.

PART 2.

mf Now the thirty years accomplished
Which on earth He willed to see,
Born for this, He meets His Passion,
Gives Himself an offering free;
On the Cross the LAMB is lifted,
There the Sacrifice to be.

p There the nails and spear He suffers,
Vinegar, and gall, and reed;
From His sacred Body piercèd
Blood and Water both proceed;
cr Precious flood, which all creation
From the stain of sin hath freed.

f Faithful Cross, above all other
One and only noble Tree,
None in foliage, none in blossom,
None in fruit thy peer may be;
Sweetest wood, and sweetest iron;
Sweetest weight is hung on thee.

mf Bend, O lofty Tree, thy branches,
Thy too rigid sinews bend;
And awhile the stubborn hardness,
Which thy birth bestowed, suspend
And the Limbs of heaven's high Monarch
p Gently on thine arms extend.

mf Thou alone wast counted worthy
This world's ransom to sustain,
That a shipwrecked race for ever
Might a port of refuge gain,
With the sacred Blood anointed
Of the LAMB for sinners slain.

f Praise and honour to the FATHER,
Praise and honour to the SON,
Praise and honour to the SPIRIT,
Ever THREE and ever ONE,
One in might, and One in glory,
While eternal ages run.

This Hymn may be sung daily till Good Friday; and the following Hymns are suitable:

200 We sing the praise of Him Who died.

467 Litany of the Passion.

The Sunday next before Easter.

OTHERWISE CALLED PALM SUNDAY.

Hymn 98.

The Sunday next before Easter.

OTHERWISE CALLED PALM SUNDAY.

"Out of the mouth of babes and sucklings Thou hast perfected praise."

f ALL glory, laud, and honour
To Thee, Redeemer, King,
To Whom the lips of children
Made sweet Hosannas ring.

mf Thou art the King of Israel,
Thou David's Royal Son,
Who in the LORD's Name comest,
The King and Blessèd One.
f All glory, &c.

mf The company of Angels
Are praising Thee on high,
And mortal men and all things
Created make reply.
f All glory, &c.

mf The people of the Hebrews
With palms before Thee went;
Our praise and prayer and anthems
Before Thee we present.
f All glory, &c.

mf To Thee before Thy Passion
They sang their hymns of praise;
To Thee now high exalted
Our melody we raise.
f All glory, &c.

mf Thou didst accept their praises,
Accept the prayers we bring,
Who in all good delightest,
Thou good and gracious King.
f All glory, &c.

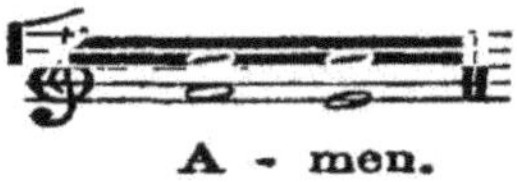

A - men.

The Sunday next before Easter.

Hymn 99. OTHERWISE CALLED PALM SUNDAY.

"And the multitudes that went before, and that followed, cried, saying, Hosanna to the Son of David."

f RIDE on! ride on in majesty!
Hark! all the tribes Hosanna cry;
p O Saviour meek, pursue Thy road
With palms and scattered garments strowed.

f Ride on! ride on in majesty!
p In lowly pomp ride on to die;
cr O CHRIST, Thy triumphs now begin
O'er captive death and conquered sin.

f Ride on! ride on in majesty!
mf The Angel armies of the sky
p Look down with sad and wondering eyes
To see the approaching Sacrifice.

f Ride on! ride on in majesty!
mf The last and fiercest strife is nigh:
The FATHER on His sapphire Throne
Awaits His own Anointed SON.

f Ride on! ride on in majesty!
p In lowly pomp ride on to die;
Bow Thy meek Head to mortal pain,
f Then take, O GOD, Thy power, and reign.

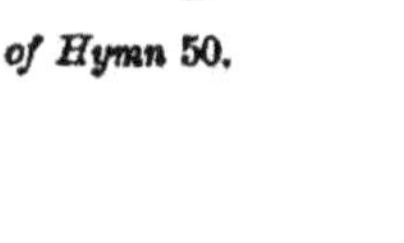

This Hymn may also be sung to the Tune of Hymn 50.

Hymns on the Passion.

Hymn 100.

"And being in an agony He prayed more earnestly."

mf SION'S Daughter, weep no more,
Though thy troubled heart be sore;
He of Whom the Psalmist sung,
He Who woke the Prophet's tongue,
CHRIST, the Mediator Blest,
Brings thee everlasting rest.

p In a garden man became
Heir of sin, and death, and shame;
cr JESUS in a garden wins
Life, and pardon for our sins·
dim Through His hour of agony
Praying in Gethsemane.

mf There for us He intercedes;
There with GOD the FATHER pleads;
Willing there for us to drain
To the dregs the cup of pain,
That in everlasting day
He may wipe our tears away.

f Therefore to His Name be given
Glory both in earth and heaven;
To the FATHER, and the SON,
And the SPIRIT, THREE in ONE,
Honour, praise, and glory be
Now and through eternity.

* *Some of these Hymns may be sung throughout the year.*

Hymn 101.

"Looking unto Jesus."

p O'ERWHELMED in depths of woe,
Upon the Tree of scorn
Hangs the Redeemer of mankind,
With racking anguish torn.

See how the nails those Hands
And Feet so tender rend;
See down His Face, and Neck, and Breast
His sacred Blood descend.

mf Oh, hear that last, loud cry
Which pierced His Mother's heart,
v As into God the Father's hands
He bade His soul depart.

mf Earth hears, and trembling quakes
Around that tree of pain;
f The rocks are rent; the graves are burst:
The veil is rent in twain.

mf Shall man alone be mute?
Have we no griefs, or fears?
Come, old and young, come, all mankind,
And bathe those Feet in tears.

p Come, fall before His Cross
Who shed for us His Blood;
Who died, the Victim of pure love,
To make us sons of God.

f Jesu, all praise to Thee,
Our Joy and endless Rest;
Be Thou our Guide while pilgrims here,
Our Crown amid the blest.

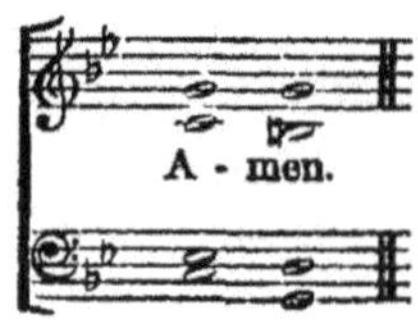

Hymns on the Passion.

Hymn 102.

"Thou wast slain, and hast redeemed us to God by Thy Blood."

HE, Who once in righteous vengeance
Whelmed the world beneath the flood,
mf Once again in mercy cleansed it
With His own most precious Blood,
v Coming from His Throne on high
On the painful Cross to die.

f O the wisdom of the Eternal!
O the depth of love Divine!
mf O the sweetness of that mercy
Which in JESUS CHRIST did shine!
dim We were sinners doomed to die;
JESUS paid the penalty.

p When before the Judge we tremble,
Conscious of His broken laws,
cr May the Blood of His atonement
Cry aloud, and plead our cause,
Bid our guilty terrors cease,
p Be our pardon and our peace.

f Prince and Author of salvation,
LORD of Majesty supreme,
JESU, praise to Thee be given
By the world Thou didst redeem;
Glory to the FATHER be
And the SPIRIT ONE with Thee.

Hymns on the Passion.

Hymn 103.

Hymns on the Passion.

"He was wounded for our transgressions."

mf NOW, my soul, thy voice upraising,
Tell in sweet and mournful strain
How the Crucified, enduring
Grief, and wounds, and dying pain,
Freely of His love was offered,
Sinless was for sinners slain.

Scourged with unrelenting fury
For the sins which we deplore,
By His livid Stripes He heals us,
Raising us to fall no more;
All our bruises gently soothing,
Binding up the bleeding sore.

p See! His Hands and Feet are fastened;
cr So He makes His people free;
Not a wound whence Blood is flowing
But a fount of grace shall be;
Yea the very nails which nail Him
Nail us also to the Tree.

p Through His Heart the spear is piercing,
Though His foes have seen Him die;
Blood and Water thence are streaming
In a tide of mystery,
cr Water from our guilt to cleanse us,
Blood to win us crowns on high.

mf JESU, may those precious fountains
Drink to thirsting souls afford:
Let them be our cup and healing,
And at length our full reward;
So a ransomed world shall ever
Praise Thee, its redeeming LORD.

Hymns on the Passion.

Hymn 104.

Hymns on the Passion.

"Behold the Man."

mf O SINNER, lift the eye of faith,
  To true repentance turning;
Bethink thee of the curse of sin,
  Its awful guilt discerning;
Upon the Crucified One look,
And thou shalt read, as in a book,
  What well is worth thy learning.

Look on His Head, that bleeding Head,
  With crown of thorns surrounded;
Look on His sacred Hands and Feet
  Which piercing nails have wounded;
See every Limb with scourges rent:
On Him, the Just, the Innocent,
  What malice hath abounded!

'Tis not alone those Limbs are racked,
  But friends too are forsaking;
And more than all, for thankless man
  That tender Heart is aching;
Oh, fearful was the pain and scorn,
By JESUS, Son of Mary, borne,
  Their peace for sinners making.

None ever knew such pain before,
  Such infinite affliction,
None ever felt a grief like His
  In that dread crucifixion:
For us He bare those bitter throes,
For us those agonizing woes,
  In oft-renewed infliction.

mf O sinner, mark, and ponder well
  Sin's awful condemnation;
Think what a sacrifice it cost
  To purchase thy salvation;
Had JESUS never bled and died,
Then what could thee and all betide
  But uttermost damnation?

LORD, give us grace to flee from sin,
  And Satan's wiles ensnaring,
And from those everlasting flames
  For evil ones preparing.
f JESU, we thank Thee, and entreat
cr To rest for ever at Thy Feet,
  Thy heavenly glory sharing.

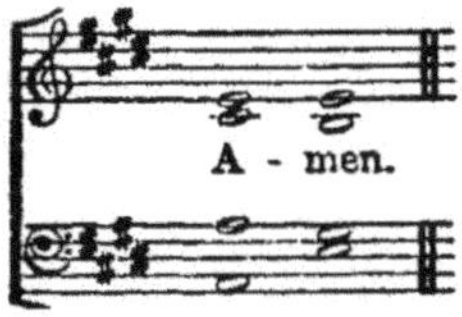

Hymns on the Passion.

Hymn 105.

"The love of Christ constraineth us."

p IN the LORD's atoning grief
Be our rest and sweet relief;
Store we deep in heart's recess
All the shame and bitterness.

Thorns, and cross, and nails, and lance,
Wounds, our treasure that enhance,
Vinegar, and gall, and reed,
And the pang His soul that freed,

cr May these all our spirits sate,
And with love inebriate;
In our souls plant virtue's root,
And mature its glorious fruit.

mf Crucified! we Thee adore,
Thee with all our hearts implore;
Us with Saintly bands unite
In the realms of heavenly light.

CHRIST, by coward hands betrayed,
CHRIST, for us a captive made,
CHRIST, upon the bitter Tree
Slain for man, be praise to Thee.

Hymns on the Passion.

Hymn 106.

"We love Him, because He first loved us."

mf MY GOD, I love Thee; *(dim)* not because
I hope for heaven thereby,
Nor yet because who love Thee not
p Are lost eternally.

Thou, O my JESUS, Thou didst me
Upon the Cross embrace;
For me didst bear the nails, and spear,
And manifold disgrace,

pp And griefs and torments numberless,
And sweat of agony;
Yea, death itself; and all for me
Who was Thine enemy.

mf Then why, O Blessèd JESU CHRIST,
Should I not love Thee well?
Not for the sake of winning heaven,
Nor of escaping hell;

Not from the hope of gaining aught,
Not seeking a reward;
f But as Thyself hast lovèd me,
O ever-loving LORD.

mf So would I love Thee, dearest LORD,
And in Thy praise will sing;
Solely because Thou art my GOD,
And my most loving King.

This Hymn may also be sung to the Tune of Hymn 272.

Hymns on the Passion.

Hymn 107.

"The precious blood of Christ."

mf GLORY be to JESUS,
  Who, in bitter pains,
Poured for me the Life-blood
  From His sacred veins.

Grace and life eternal
  In that Blood I find;
Blest be His compassion
  Infinitely kind.

Blest through endless ages
  Be the precious stream,
Which from endless torments
  Did the world redeem.

Abel's blood for vengeance
  Pleaded to the skies;
cr But the Blood of JESUS
  For our pardon cries.

p Oft as it is sprinkled
  On our guilty hearts,
mf Satan in confusion
  Terror-struck departs;

Oft as earth exulting
  Wafts its praise on high,
cr Angel-hosts rejoicing
  Make their glad reply.

f Lift ye then your voices;
cr   Swell the mighty flood;
Louder still and louder
  Praise the (*dim*) precious Blood.

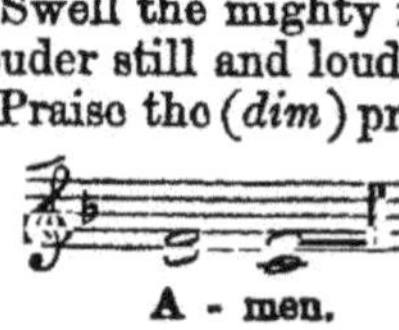

Hymns on the Passion.

Hymn 108.

"What things were gain to me, those I counted loss for Christ."

mf WHEN I survey the wondrous Cross
On which the Prince of glory died,
My richest gain I count but loss,
And pour contempt on all my pride.

Forbid it, LORD, that I should boast
Save in the Cross of CHRIST my GOD;
All the vain things that charm me most,
I sacrifice them to His Blood.

p See from His Head, His Hands, His Feet,
Sorrow and love flow mingling down;
cr Did e'er such love and sorrow meet,
Or thorns compose so rich a crown?

mf Were the whole realm of nature mine,
That were an offering far too small;
f Love so amazing, so Divine,
Demands my soul, my life, my all.

mf To CHRIST, Who won for sinners grace
p By bitter grief and anguish sore,
f Be praise from all the ransomed race
For ever and for evermore.

Hymns on the Passion.

Hymn 109.

"Unto you therefore which believe He is precious."

mf SWEET the moments, rich in blessing,
  Which before the Cross I spend,
Life, and health, and peace possessing
  From the sinner's dying Friend.

Here I rest, for ever viewing
  Mercy poured in streams of Blood;
Precious drops, my soul bedewing,
  Plead and claim my peace with God.

p Truly blessèd is the station,
  Low before His Cross to lie,
Whilst I see Divine compassion
  Beaming in His languid Eye.

mf Lord, in ceaseless contemplation
  Fix my thankful heart on Thee,
Till I taste Thy full salvation,
  And Thine unveilèd glory see.

Hymns on the Passion.

Hymn 110.

"Remembering mine affliction and my misery, the wormwood and the gall."

p GO to dark Gethsemane,
Ye that feel the tempter's power,
Your Redeemer's conflict see,
Watch with Him one bitter hour;
Turn not from His griefs away;
cr Learn of Jesus Christ to pray.

p Follow to the judgment-hall,
View the Lord of life arraigned;
Oh, the wormwood and the gall!
Oh, the pangs His soul sustained!
Shun not suffering, shame, or loss;
cr Learn of Him to bear the cross.

p Calvary's mournful mountain climb;
cr There, adoring at His Feet,
Mark that miracle of time,
God's own Sacrifice complete;
p "It is finished," hear Him cry;
cr Learn of Jesus Christ to die.

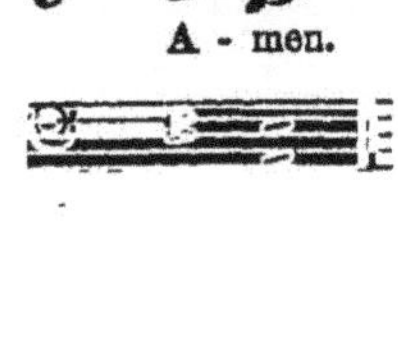

Hymns on the Passion.

Hymn 111.

Hymns on the Passion.

"Who loved me, and gave Himself for me."

mf O SACRED Head, surrounded
By crown of piercing thorn!
O bleeding Head, so wounded,
Reviled, and put to scorn!
p Death's pallid hue comes o'er Thee,
The glow of life decays,
cr Yet Angel-hosts adore Thee,
dim And tremble as they gaze.

p I see Thy strength and vigour
All fading in the strife,
And death with cruel rigour
Bereaving Thee of life;
mf O agony and dying!
O love to sinners free!
p Jesu, all grace supplying,
O turn Thy Face on me.

In this Thy bitter Passion,
Good Shepherd, think of me
With Thy most sweet compassion,
Unworthy though I be:
mf Beneath Thy Cross abiding
For ever would I rest,
In Thy dear love confiding,
And with Thy presence blest.

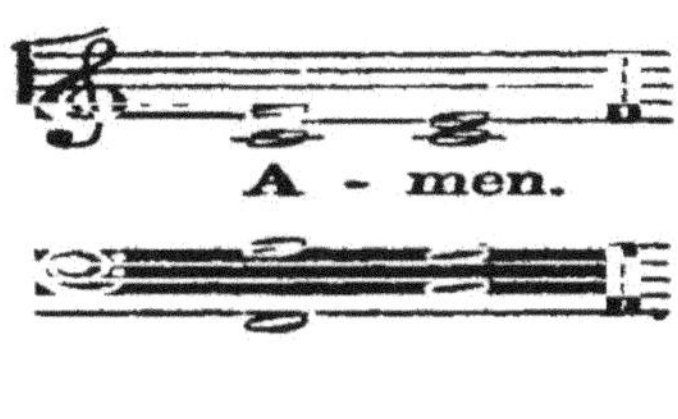

Hymns on the Passion.

Hymn 112.

"Come unto Me, all ye that labour and are heavy-laden, and I will give you rest."

mf ALL ye who seek for sure relief
In trouble and distress,
Whatever sorrow vex the mind,
Or guilt the soul oppress,

JESUS, Who gave Himself for you
p Upon the Cross to die,
cr Opens to you His sacred Heart;
O to that Heart draw nigh.

mf Ye hear how kindly He invites;
Ye hear His words so blest;
"All ye that labour come to Me,
p And I will give you rest."

mf O JESUS, Joy of Saints on high,
Thou Hope of sinners here,
Attracted by those loving words
To Thee we lift our prayer.

p Wash Thou our wounds in that dear Blood
Which from Thy Heart doth flow;
cr A new and contrite heart on all
Who cry to Thee bestow.

Hymns on the Passion.

Hymn 113.

Slow.

"Is it nothing to you, all ye that pass by? Behold and see if there be any sorrow like unto My sorrow."

mf SEE the destined day arise!
See, a willing Sacrifice,
Jesus, to redeem our loss,
Hangs upon the shameful Cross!

p Jesu, who but Thou had borne,
Lifted on that Tree of scorn,
Every pang and bitter throe,
Finishing Thy life of woe?

Who but Thou had dared to drain,
Steeped in gall, the cup of pain,
And with tender Body bear
Thorns, and nails, and piercing spear?

mf Thence the cleansing Water flowed,
Mingled from Thy Side with Blood;
Sign to all attesting eyes
Of the finished Sacrifice.

p Holy Jesu, grant us grace
In that Sacrifice to place
cr All our trust for life renewed,
Pardoned sin, and promised good.

Hymns on the Passion.

Hymn 114.

Slow.

"They crucified Him."

mf O COME and mourn with me awhile;
O come ye to the Saviour's side;
O come, together let us mourn;
pp JESUS, our LORD, is crucified.

mf Have we no tears to shed for Him,
While soldiers scoff and Jews deride?
Ah! look how patiently He hangs;
pp JESUS, our LORD, is crucified.

p How fast His Hands and Feet are nailed;
His Throat with parching thirst is dried;
His failing Eyes are dimmed with Blood;
pp JESUS, our LORD, is crucified.

p Seven times He spake, seven Words of love;
And all three hours His silence cried
For mercy on the souls of men;
pp JESUS, our LORD, is crucified.

p Come, let us stand beneath the Cross;
So may the Blood from out His Side
Fall gently on us drop by drop;
pp JESUS, our LORD, is crucified.

mf A broken heart, a fount of tears,
Ask, and they will not be denied;
LORD JESUS, may we love and weep,
Since Thou for us art crucified.

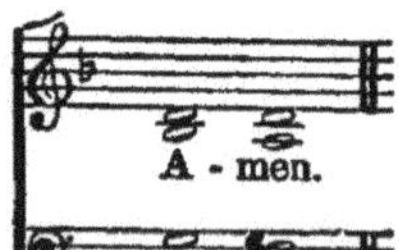

Hymns on the Passion.

Hymn 115.

"Father, forgive them, for they know not what they do."

mf "FORGIVE them, O My FATHER,
They know not what they do:"
p The Saviour spake in anguish,
As the sharp nails went through.

No pained reproaches gave He
To them that shed His Blood,
But prayer and tenderest pity
cr Large as the love of GOD.

mf For me was that compassion,
For me that tender care;
I need His wide forgiveness
As much as any there.

p It was my pride and hardness
That hung Him on the Tree;
pp Those cruel nails, O Saviour,
Were driven in by me.

p And often I have slighted
Thy gentle voice that chid;
cr Forgive me too, LORD JESUS;
I knew not what I did.

mf O depth of sweet compassion!
O Love Divine and true!
Save Thou the souls that slight Thee,
And know not what they do.

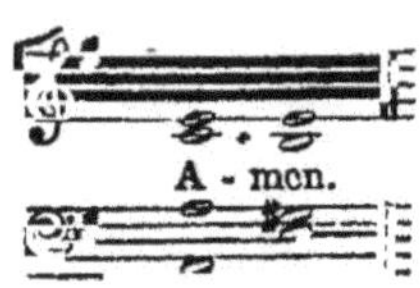

Hymns on the Passion.

Hymn 116.

Hymns on the Passion.

"Verily I say unto thee, To-day shalt thou be with Me in Paradise."

mf "LORD, when Thy Kingdom comes, remember me;"
p Thus spake the dying lips to dying Ears;
cr O faith, which in that darkest hour could see
The promised glory of the far-off years!

mf No kingly sign declares that glory now,
No ray of hope lights up that awful hour;
p A thorny crown surrounds the bleeding Brow,
The Hands are stretched in weakness, not in power.

mf Yet hear the Word the dying Saviour saith,
p rall "Thou too shalt rest in Paradise to-day;"
tempo cr O Words of love to answer words of faith!
O Words of hope for those who live to pray!

mf LORD, when with dying lips my prayer is said,
Grant that in faith Thy kingdom I may see;
And, thinking on Thy Cross and bleeding Head,
May breathe my parting words, *(p)* "Remember me."

cr Remember me, but not my shame or sin;
f Thy cleansing Blood hath washed them all away;
mf Thy precious Death for me did pardon win;
Thy Blood redeemed me in that awful day.

p Remember me; yet how canst Thou forget
What pain and anguish I have caused to Thee,
The Cross, the Agony, the Bloody Sweat,
And all the sorrow Thou didst bear for me?

cr Remember me; and, ere I pass away,
Speak Thou the assuring Word that sets us free,
And make Thy promise to my heart, *(p)* "To-day
Thou too shalt rest in Paradise with Me."

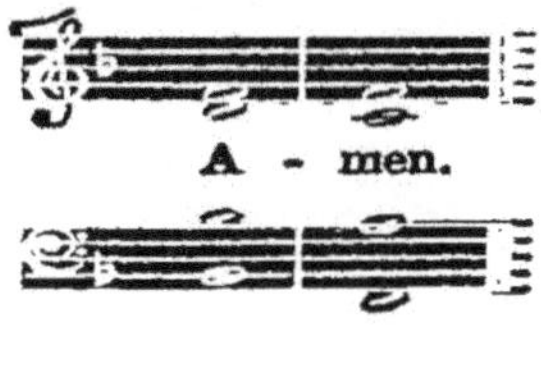

Hymns on the Passion.

Hymn 117. (First Tune.)

To be sung in Unison.

Hymn 117. (Second Tune.)

mf Slowly, and with expression.

Hymns on the Passion.

"Woman, behold thy son . . . Behold thy mother."

mf AT the Cross her station keeping
Stood the mournful Mother weeping,
Where He hung, the dying LORD;
For her soul of joy bereavèd,
Bowed with anguish, deeply grievèd,
Felt the sharp and piercing sword.

p Oh, how sad and sore distressèd
Now was she, that Mother blessèd
Of the sole-begotten One;
Deep the woe of her affliction,
When she saw the Crucifixion
cr Of her ever-glorious Son.

mf Who, on CHRIST's dear Mother gazing
Pierced by anguish so amazing,
Born of woman, would not weep?
Who, on CHRIST's dear Mother thinking
Such a cup of sorrow drinking,
Would not share her sorrows deep?

p For His people's sins chastisèd,
She beheld her Son despisèd,
Scourged, and crowned with thorn-entwined;
Saw Him then from judgment taken,
And in death by all forsaken,
Till His Spirit He resigned.

mf JESU, may her deep devotion
Stir in me the same emotion,
Fount of love, Redeemer kind,
cr That my heart fresh ardour gaining,
And a purer love attaining,
May with Thee acceptance find.

1. 

2. 

Hymns on the Passion.

Hymn 117. (Third Tune.)

"Woman, behold thy son . . . . Behold thy mother."

mf AT the Cross her station keeping
Stood the mournful Mother weeping,
Where He hung, the dying Lord;
For her soul of joy bereavèd,
Bowed with anguish, deeply grievèd,
Felt the sharp and piercing sword.

p Oh, how sad and sore distressèd
Now was she, that Mother blessèd
Of the sole-begotten One;
Deep the woe of her affliction,
When she saw the Crucifixion
cr Of her ever-glorious Son.

mf Who, on Christ's dear Mother gazing
Pierced by anguish so amazing,
Born of woman, would not weep?
Who, on Christ's dear Mother thinking
Such a cup of sorrow drinking,
Would not share her sorrows deep?

p For His people's sins chastisèd,
She beheld her Son despisèd,
Scourged, and crowned with thorns entwined;
Saw Him then from judgment taken,
And in death by all forsaken,
Till His Spirit He resigned.

mf Jesu, may her deep devotion
Stir in me the same emotion,
Fount of love, Redeemer kind,
cr That my heart fresh ardour gaining,
And a purer love attaining,
May with Thee acceptance find.

Hymns on the Passion.

Hymn 118.

"My God, My God, why hast Thou forsaken Me?"

mf THRONED upon the awful Tree,
King of grief, I watch with Thee;
dim Darkness veils Thine anguished Face,
None its lines of woe can trace,
None can tell what pangs unknown
pp Hold Thee silent and alone.

p Silent through those three dread hours,
cr Wrestling with the evil powers,
dim Left alone with human sin,
Gloom around Thee and within,
Till the appointed time is nigh,
pp Till the LAMB of GOD may die.

mf Hark that cry that peals aloud
Upward through the whelming cloud!
cr Thou, the FATHER's only SON,
Thou, His own Anointed One,
Thou dost ask Him—*(p)* can it be?—
dim "Why hast Thou forsaken Me?"

p LORD, should fear and anguish roll
Darkly o'er my sinful soul,
Thou, Who once wast thus bereft
cr That Thine own might ne'er be left,
Teach me by that bitter cry
mf In the gloom to know Thee nigh.

Hymns on the Passion.

Hymn 119.

"I thirst."

mf HIS are the thousand sparkling rills,
  That from a thousand fountains burst,
And fill with music all the hills;
p And yet He saith, "I thirst."

mf All fiery pangs on battle-fields,
On fever beds where sick men toss,
Are in that human cry He yields
p To anguish on the Cross.

mf But more than pains that racked Him then
Was the deep longing thirst Divine,
cr That thirsted for the souls of men:
p Dear LORD! and one was mine.

mf O Love most patient, give me grace;
Make all my soul athirst for Thee;
p That parched dry Lip, that fading Face,
  That Thirst were all for me.

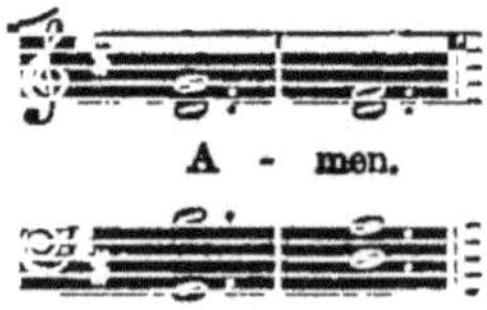

Hymns on the Passion.

Hymn 120.

"It is finished."

mf O PERFECT life of love!
All, all is finished now;
All that He left His Throne above
To do for us below.

No work is left undone
Of all the FATHER willed;
p His toil, His sorrows, one by one,
cr The Scripture have fulfilled.

p No pain that we can share
But He has felt its smart;
All forms of human grief and care
Have pierced that tender Heart.

And on His thorn-crowned Head,
And on His sinless Soul,
Our sins in all their guilt were laid,
cr That He might make us whole.

p In perfect love He dies:
For me He dies, for me:
cr O all-atoning Sacrifice,
I cling by faith to Thee.

mf In every time of need,
Before the judgment-throne,
cr Thy work, O LAMB of GOD, I'll plead,
Thy merits, *(dim)* not my own.

mf Yet work, O LORD, in me
As Thou for me hast wrought;
cr And let my love the answer be
To grace Thy love has brought.

Hymns on the Passion.

Hymn 121.

Hymns on the Passion.

"Father, into Thy hands I commend My Spirit."

p AND now, belovèd LORD, Thy Soul resigning
Into Thy FATHER's arms with conscious Will,
Calmly, with reverend grace, Thy Head inclining,
pp The throbbing Brow and labouring Breast grow still.

mf Freely Thy life Thou yieldest, meekly bending
E'en to the last beneath our sorrows' load,
cr e dim Yet strong in death, in perfect peace commending
Thy Spirit to Thy FATHER and Thy GOD.

mf Sweet Saviour, in mine hour of mortal anguish,
dim When earth grows dim, and round me falls the night,
cr e dim O breathe Thy peace, as flesh and spirit languish;
cr At that dread eventide let there be light.

p To Thy dear Cross turn Thou my eyes in dying;
Lay but my fainting head upon Thy Breast;
Those outstretched Arms receive my latest sighing;
cr And then, oh! then, Thine everlasting Rest.

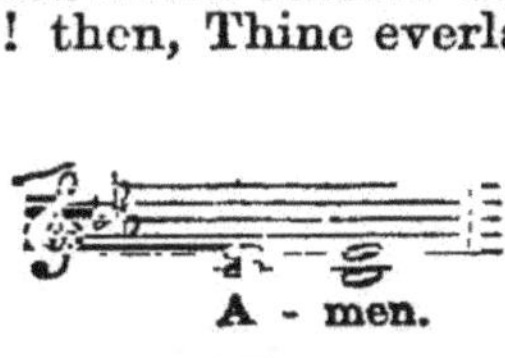

K

Hymns on the Passion.

Hymn 122.

Slowly.

"*In Paradise.*"

p IT is finished! Blessèd Jesus,
Thou hast breathed Thy latest sigh,
cr Teaching us the sons of Adam
How the Son of God *(dim)* can die.

p Lifeless lies the broken Body,
Hidden in its rocky bed,
Laid aside like folded garment:
Where is now the Spirit fled?

mf In the gloomy realms of darkness
Shines a light unknown before,
For the Lord of dead and living
Enters at the open door.

p See! He comes, a willing Victim,
Unresisting hither led;
Passing from the Cross of sorrow
To the mansions of the dead.

mf Lo! the heavenly light around Him
As He draws His people near;
cr All amazed they stand rejoicing
At the gracious Words they hear.

mf For Himself proclaims the story
Of His own Incarnate life,
And the death He died to save us,
Victor in that awful strife.

Patriarch and Priest and Prophet
Gather round Him as He stands,
cr In adoring faith and gladness,
dim Hearing of the piercèd Hands.

f Oh, the bliss to which He calls them,
Ransomed by His precious Blood,
From the gloomy realm of darkness
To the Paradise of God!

mf There in lowliest joy and wonder
Stands the robber at His side,
cr Reaping now the blessèd promise
dim Spoken by the Crucified.

p Jesus, Lord of dead and living,
Let Thy mercy rest on me;
Grant me too, when life is finished,
Rest in Paradise with Thee.

Hymns on the Passion.

Hymn 123.

"Mary Magdalene and Mary the mother of Joses beheld where He was laid."

p BY JESUS' grave on either hand,
While night is brooding o'er the land,
The sad and silent mourners stand.

At last the weary life is o'er,
The agony and conflict sore
Of Him Who all our sufferings bore.

Deep in the rock's sepulchral shade
The LORD, by Whom the worlds were made,
The Saviour of mankind, is laid.

mf O hearts bereaved and sore distressed,
Here is for you a place of rest;
p Here leave your griefs on JESUS' Breast.

Hymns on the Passion.

Hymn 124.

"And when Joseph had taken the body, he wrapped it in a clean linen cloth, and laid it in his own new tomb, which he had hewn out in the rock. . . . . And there was Mary Magdalene, and the other Mary, sitting over against the sepulchre."

mf RESTING from His work to-day
In the tomb the Saviour lay;
Still He slept, from Head to Feet
Shrouded in the winding-sheet,
Lying in the rock alone,
Hidden by the sealèd stone.

Late at even there was seen
Watching long the Magdalene;
Early, ere the break of day,
p Sorrowful she took her way
To the holy garden glade,
Where her buried Lord was laid.

mf So with Thee, till life shall end,
I would solemn vigil spend:
Let me hew Thee, Lord, a shrine
In this rocky heart of mine,
Where in pure embalmèd cell
None but Thou may ever dwell.

Myrrh and spices will I bring,
True affection's offering;
p Close the door from sight and sound
Of the busy world around;
And in patient watch remain
cr Till my Lord appear again.

Hymn 125.

"O death, where is thy sting? O grave, where is thy victory?"

f YE choirs of new Jerusalem,
  Your sweetest notes employ,
The Paschal victory to hymn
  In strains of holy joy.

For Judah's Lion bursts His chains,
  Crushing the serpent's head;
And cries aloud through death's domains
  To wake the imprisoned dead.

Devouring depths of hell their prey
  At His command restore;
His ransomed hosts pursue their way
  Where JESUS goes before.

ff Triumphant in His glory now
  To Him all power is given;
mf To Him in one communion bow
  All saints in earth and heaven.

While we, His soldiers, praise our King
dim His mercy we implore,
cr Within His palace bright to bring
  And keep us evermore.

f All glory to the FATHER be,
  All glory to the SON,
All glory, HOLY GHOST, to Thee,
  While endless ages run.

Easter.

Hymn 126. (First Tune.)

Hymn 126. (Second Tune.)

Easter.

"The Lord is King, and hath put on glorious apparel."

f * LIGHT'S glittering morn bedécks the sky;
Heaven thunders forth its víctor-cry;
The glad earth shouts her tríumph high,
And groaning hell makes wild reply;

* While He, the King, the míghty King,
Despoiling death of áll its sting,
And, trampling down the pówers of night,
Brings forth His ransomed saints to light.

mf * His tomb of late the thréefold guard
Of watch and stone and séal had barred;
f But now, in pomp and tríumph high,
He comes from death to victory.

* The pains of hell are lóosed at last;
The days of mourning nów are past;
An Angel robed in líght hath said,
ff "The Lord is risen from the dead."

PART 2.

p The Apostles' hearts were fúll of pain
For their dear Lord so látely slain,
By rebel servants dóomed to die
A death of cruel agony.

mf With gentle voice the Ángel gave
The women tidings át the grave;
"Fear not, your Master sháll ye see;
He goes before to Galilee."

cr Then, hastening on their eáger way
The joyful tidings tó convey,
Their Lord they met, their líving Lord,
dim And falling at His Feet adored.

mf Th' Eleven, when they héar, with speed
To Galilee forthwíth proceed,
That there once more they máy behold
The Lord's dear Face, as He foretold.

PART 3.

f *That Easter-tide with jóy was bright,
The sun shone out with fáirer light,
When, to their longing éyes restored,
The Apostles saw their risen Lord.

mf *He bade them see His Hánds, His Side,
Where yet the glorious Woúnds abide;
The tokens true which máde it plain
f Their Lord indeed was risen again.

mf Jesu, the King of Géntleness,
Do Thou Thyself our heárts possess,
That we may give Thee áll our days
The tribute of our grateful praise.

The following may be sung at the end of each Part.

mf O Lord of all, with ús abide
In this our joyful Éaster-tide;
From every weapon deáth can wield
Thine own redeemed for ever shield.

ff* All praise be Thine, O rísen Lord,
From death to endless lífe restored:
All praise to God the Fáther be
And Holy Ghost eternally.

1.

2.

* *When the whole Hymn is sung to the Chant, these verses may be sung in unison.*

Easter.

Hymn 127.

Easter.

"Sing ye to the Lord, for He hath triumphed gloriously."

f AT the Lamb's high feast we sing
Praise to our victorious King,
mf Who hath washed us in the tide
Flowing from His piercèd Side;
f Praise we Him, Whose love Divine
Gives His Sacred Blood for wine,
Gives His Body for the feast,
Christ the Victim, Christ the Priest.

mf Where the Paschal blood is poured,
Death's dark Angel sheathes his sword;
f Israel's hosts triumphant go
Through the wave that drowns the foe.
Praise we Christ, Whose Blood was shed,
Paschal Victim, Paschal Bread;
mf With sincerity and love
Eat we Manna from above.

f Mighty Victim from the sky,
Hell's fierce powers beneath Thee lie;
Thou hast conquered in the fight,
Thou hast brought us life and light;
Now no more can death appal,
Now no more the grave enthral;
Thou hast opened Paradise,
And in Thee Thy saints shall rise.

Easter triumph, Easter joy,
mf Sin alone can this destroy;
From sin's power do Thou set free
Souls new-born, O Lord, in Thee.
f Hymns of glory and of praise,
Risen Lord, to Thee we raise;
Holy Father, praise to Thee,
With the Spirit, ever be.

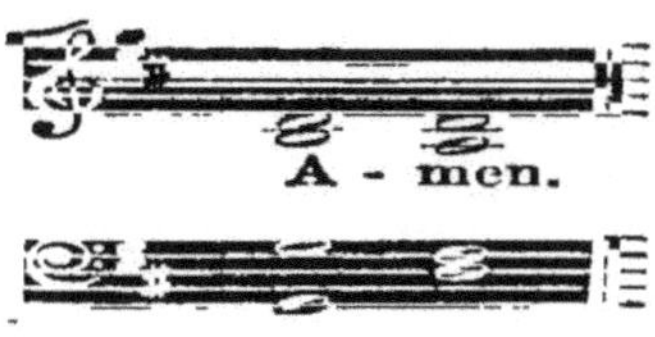

Easter.

Hymn 128.

To be sung in Unison.

"Christ our Passover is sacrificed for us; therefore let us keep the feast."

THE LAMB's high banquet called to share,
Arrayed in garments white and fair,
The Red Sea past, we fain would sing
To JESUS our triumphant King.

f Upon the altar of the Cross
His Body hath redeemed our loss;
And, tasting of His precious Blood,
Our life is hid with Him in GOD.

Protected in the Paschal night
From the destroying Angel's might,
In triumph went the ransomed free
From Pharaoh's cruel tyranny.

Now CHRIST our Passover is slain,
The LAMB of GOD without a stain;
His Flesh, the true unleavened Bread,
Is freely offered in our stead.

O all-sufficient Sacrifice,
Beneath Thee hell defeated lies;
Thy captive people are set free,
And crowns of life restored by Thee.

f We hymn Thee rising from the grave,
From death returning, strong to save;
Thine own Right Hand the tyrant chains,
And Paradise for man regains.

ff All praise be Thine, O risen LORD,
From death to endless life restored;
All praise to GOD the FATHER be
And HOLY GHOST eternally.

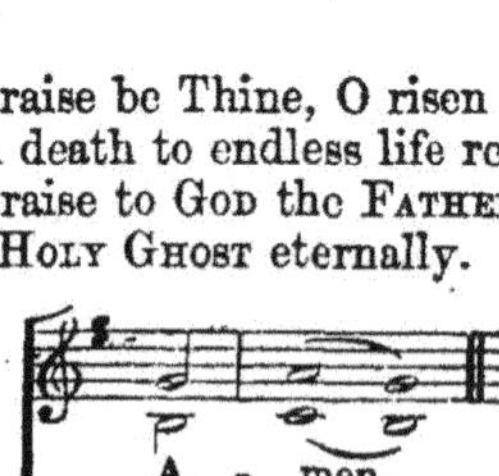

Easter.

Hymn 129.

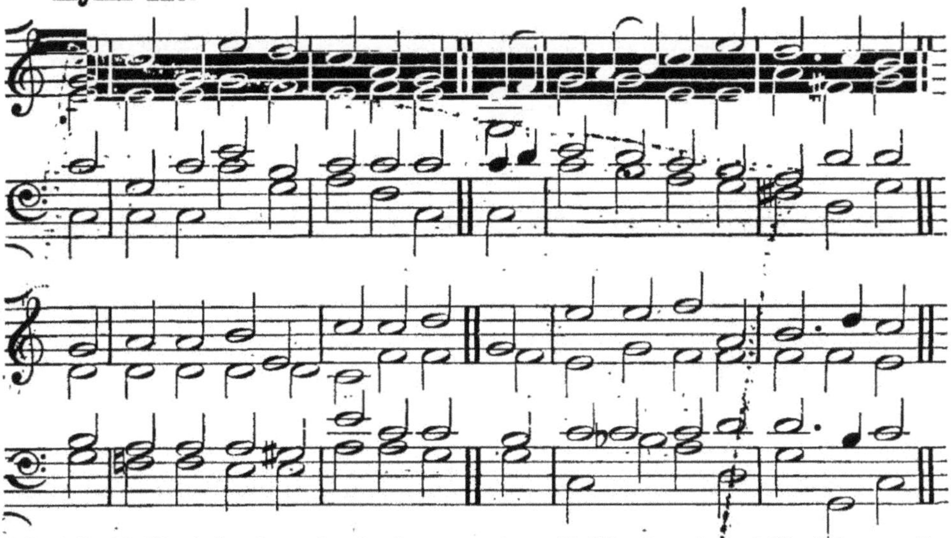

"Buried with Him in baptism, wherein also ye are risen with Him through the faith of the operation of God, Who hath raised Him from the dead."

O CHRIST, the heavens' Eternal King,
  Creator, unto Thee we sing,
With GOD the FATHER ever ONE,
Co-equal, co-eternal SON,

Thy Hand, when first the world began,
Made in Thine own pure Image man,
And linked to fleshly form of earth
A living soul of heavenly birth.

And when the envious crafty foe
Had marred Thy noblest work below,
Thou didst our ruined state repair
By deigning flesh Thyself to wear.

Once of a Virgin born to save,
And now new-born from death's dark grave,
O CHRIST, Thou bidd'st us rise with Thee
From death to immortality.

Eternal Shepherd! Thou art wont
To cleanse Thy sheep within the font,
That mystic bath, that grave of sin,
Where ransomed souls new life begin.

p Divine Redeemer, Thou didst deign
To bear for us the Cross of pain,
And freely pay the precious price
Of all Thy Blood in sacrifice.

mf JESU, do Thou to every heart
Unceasing Paschal joy impart:
From death of sin and guilty strife
Set free the new-born sons of life.

f All praise be Thine, O risen LORD,
From death to endless life restored;
All praise to GOD the FATHER be
And HOLY GHOST eternally.

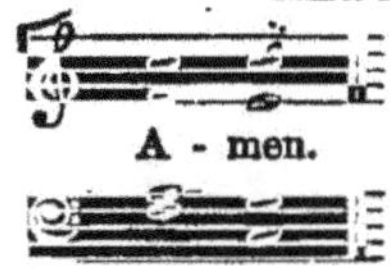

Easter.

Hymn 130.

To be sung in Unison.

Easter.

"This is the day which the Lord hath made; we will rejoice and be glad in it."

f ALLELUIA! ALLELUIA! ALLELUIA!
O sons and daughters, let us sing!
The King of heaven, the glorious King,
O'er death to-day rose triumphing.
Alleluia!

mf That Easter morn, at break of day,
The faithful women went their way
To seek the tomb where JESUS lay.
Alleluia!

An Angel clad in white they see,
Who sat, and spake unto the three,
"Your LORD doth go to Galilee."
Alleluia!

p That night the Apostles met in fear;
cr Amidst them came their LORD most dear,
And said, *(p)* "My peace be on all here."
Alleluia!

mf When Thomas first the tidings heard,
How they had seen the risen LORD,
He doubted the disciples' word.
Alleluia!

p "My piercèd Side, O Thomas, see;
My Hands, My Feet I shew to thee;
Not faithless, but believing be."
Alleluia!

mf No longer Thomas then denied;
He saw the Feet, the Hands, the Side;
f "Thou art my LORD and GOD," he cried.
Alleluia!

How blest are they who have not seen,
And yet whose faith hath constant been,
For they eternal life shall win.
Alleluia!

On this most holy day of days,
To GOD your hearts and voices raise
In laud, and jubilee, and praise.
ff Alleluia!

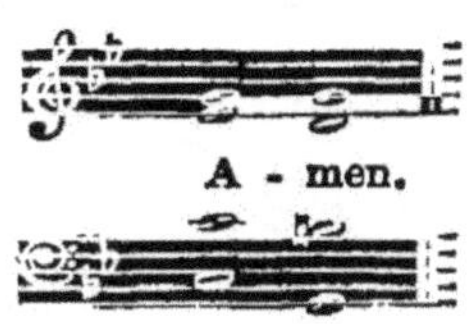

Easter.

Hymn 131.

Easter.

"Worthy is the Lamb that was slain to receive power, and riches, and wisdom, and strength, and honour, and glory, and blessing."

f CHRIST the LORD is risen to-day;
Christians, haste your vows to pay;
Offer ye your praises meet
At the Paschal Victim's feet.
mf For the sheep the LAMB hath bled,
Sinless in the sinner's stead;
ff "CHRIST is risen," to-day we cry;
Now He lives no more to die.

f CHRIST, the Victim undefiled,
Man to GOD hath reconciled;
Whilst in strange and awful strife
Met together Death and Life:
Christians, on this happy day
Haste with joy your vows to pay;
ff "CHRIST is risen," to-day we cry;
Now He lives no more to die.

mf CHRIST, Who once for sinners bled,
f Now the first-born from the dead,
ff Throned in endless might and power,
Lives and reigns for evermore.
Hail, Eternal Hope on high!
Hail, Thou King of victory!
Hail, Thou Prince of life adored!
mf Help and save us, gracious LORD.

Easter.

Hymn 132.

Easter.

"Jesus met them, saying, All hail."

THE Day of Resurrection!
Earth, tell it out abroad;
The Passover of gladness,
The Passover of God!
From death to life eternal,
From earth unto the sky,
Our Christ hath brought us over
With hymns of victory.

mf Our hearts be pure from evil,
That we may see aright
The Lord in rays eternal
Of resurrection-light;
And, listening to His accents,
May hear so calm and plain
His own "All hail," and, hearing,
May raise the victor strain.

f Now let the heavens be joyful,
And earth her song begin,
The round world keep high triumph,
And all that is therein;
Let all things seen and unseen
Their notes of gladness blend,
ff For Christ the Lord is risen,
Our Joy that hath no end.

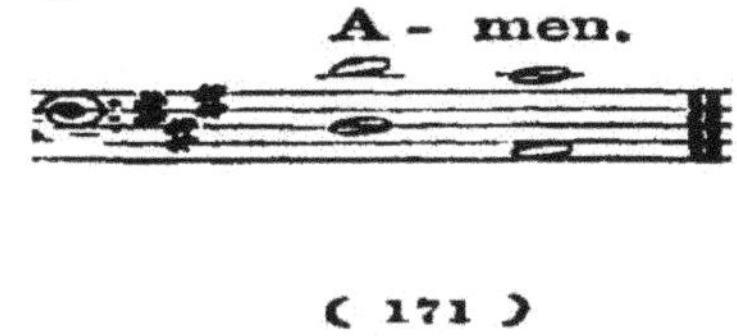

Easter.

Hymn 133.

Easter.

"Lo, the winter is past."

f COME, ye faithful, raise the strain
Of triumphant gladness;
God hath brought His Israel
Into joy from sadness;
mf Loosed from Pharaoh's bitter yoke
Jacob's sons and daughters;
f Led them with unmoistened foot
Through the Red Sea waters.

'Tis the spring of souls to-day;
Christ hath burst His prison,
And from three days' sleep in death
As a sun hath risen;
mf All the winter of our sins,
Long and dark, is flying
f From His Light, to Whom we give
Laud and praise undying.

Now the Queen of seasons, bright
With the Day of splendour,
With the royal Feast of feasts,
Comes its joy to render;
Comes to glad Jerusalem,
Who with true affection
Welcomes in unwearied strains
Jesu's Resurrection.

ff Alleluia now we cry
To our King Immortal,
Who triumphant burst the bars
Of the tomb's dark portal;
Alleluia, with the Son
God the Father praising;
Alleluia yet again
To the Spirit raising.

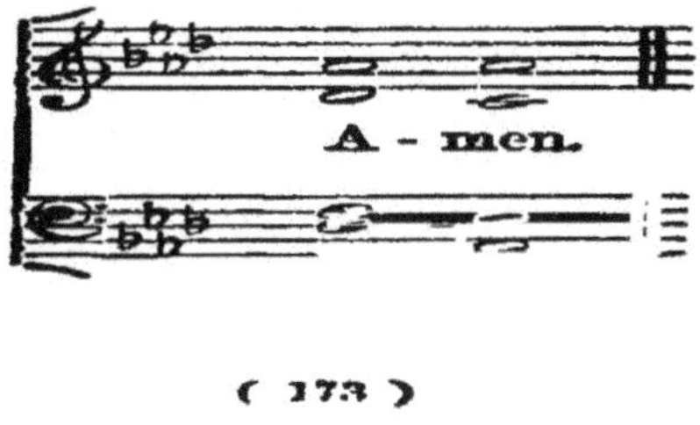

Easter.

Hymn 134. (First Tune.)

Easter.

" The Lord is risen indeed."

f JESUS CHRIST is risen to-day,
Alleluia!
Our triumphant holy day,
Alleluia!
mf Who did once, upon the Cross,
Alleluia!
Suffer to redeem our loss.
Alleluia!

f Hymns of praise then let us sing
Alleluia!
Unto CHRIST, our heavenly King,
Alleluia!
mf Who endured the Cross and grave,
Alleluia!
Sinners to redeem and save.
Alleluia!

But the pain which He endured
Alleluia!
f Our salvation hath procured;
Alleluia!
ff Now above the sky He's King,
Alleluia!
Where the Angels ever sing.
Alleluia!

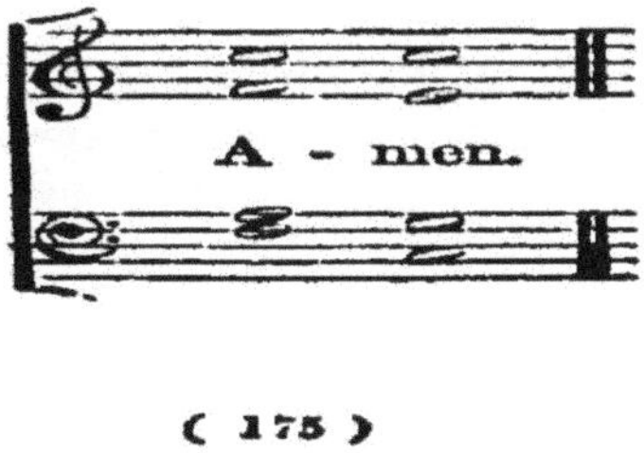

Easter.

Hymn 134. (Second Tune.)

Easter.

"The Lord is risen indeed."

f JESUS CHRIST is risen to-day,
Alleluia!—
Our triumphant holy day,
Alleluia!
mf Who did once, upon the Cross,
Alleluia!
Suffer to redeem our loss.
Alleluia!

f Hymns of praise then let us sing
Alleluia!
Unto CHRIST, our heavenly King,
Alleluia!
mf Who endured the Cross and grave,
Alleluia!
Sinners to redeem and save.
Alleluia!

But the pain which He endured
Alleluia!
f Our salvation hath procured;
Alleluia!
ff Now above the sky He's King,
Alleluia!
Where the Angels ever sing.
Alleluia!

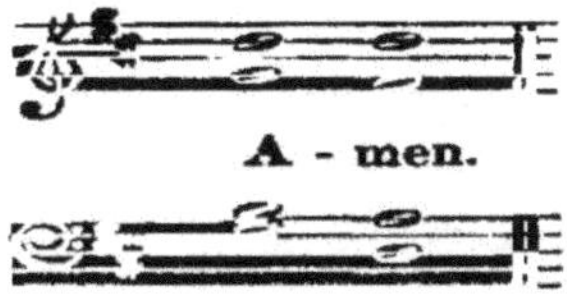

Easter.

Hymn 135.

"O sing unto the Lord a new song; for He hath done marvellous things."

f ALLELUIA! ALLELUIA! ALLELUIA!
The strife is o'er, the battle done;
Now is the Victor's triumph won;
ff O let the song of praise be sung.
Alleluia!

f Death's mightiest powers have done their
And JESUS hath His foes dispersed; [worst,
ff Let shouts of praise and joy outburst.
Alleluia!

f On the third morn He rose again
Glorious in majesty to reign;
O let us swell the joyful strain.
Alleluia!

p LORD, by the stripes which wounded
Thee [free,
From death's dread sting Thy servants
f That we may live, and sing to Thee
ff Alleluia!

Easter.

Hymn 136.

"Alleluia! for the Lord God Omnipotent reigneth."

f CHRIST the LORD is risen again;
CHRIST hath broken every chain;
Hark! Angelic voices cry,
Singing evermore on high,
Alleluia!

mf He, Who gave for us His life,
Who for us endured the strife,
Is our Paschal LAMB to-day;
f We too sing for joy, and say
Alleluia!

mf He, Who bore all pain and loss
Comfortless upon the Cross,
f Lives in glory now on high,
Pleads for us, and hears our cry;
Alleluia!

mf He, Who slumbered in the grave,
f Is exalted now to save;
ff Now through Christendom it rings
That the LAMB is King of kings.
Alleluia!

mf Now He bids us tell abroad
How the lost may be restored,
How the penitent forgiven,
How we too may enter heaven.
Alleluia!

Thou, our Paschal LAMB indeed,
CHRIST, Thy ransomed people feed:
Take our sins and guilt away,
f Let us sing by night and day
ff Alleluia!

Easter.

Hymn 137.

Easter.

"Now is Christ risen from the dead, and become the first-fruits of them that slept."

f ALLELUIA! Alleluia! Hearts to heaven and voices raise;
Sing to God a hymn of gladness, sing to God a hymn of praise;
p He, Who on the Cross a Victim for the world's salvation bled,
f Jesus Christ, the King of glory, now is risen from the dead.

Christ is risen, Christ the first-fruits of the holy harvest field,
Which will all its full abundance at His second coming yield;
Then the golden ears of harvest will their heads before Him wave,
Ripened by His glorious sunshine from the furrows of the grave.

mf Christ is risen, we are risen; shed upon us heavenly grace,
Rain, and dew, and gleams of glory from the brightness of Thy Face;
That we, with our hearts in heaven, here on earth may fruitful be,
And by Angel-hands be gathered, and be ever, Lord, with Thee.

ff Alleluia! Alleluia! Glory be to God on high;
Alleluia to the Saviour, Who has gained the victory;
Alleluia to the Spirit, fount of love and sanctity;
Alleluia! Alleluia! to the Triune Majesty.

Easter.

Hymn 138.

Easter.

"He is risen."

f CHRIST is risen! CHRIST is risen!
He hath burst His bonds in twain,
CHRIST is risen! CHRIST is risen!
Alleluia! swell the strain!
mf For our gain He suffered loss
By Divine decree;
p He hath died upon the Cross,
f But our GOD is He.
ff CHRIST is risen! CHRIST is risen!
He hath burst His bonds in twain;
CHRIST is risen! CHRIST is risen!
Alleluia! swell the strain!

mf See the chains of death are broken;
Earth below and heaven above
Joy in each amazing token
Of His rising, LORD of love;
f He for evermore shall reign
By the FATHER's side,
dim Till He comes to earth again,
Comes to claim His bride.

ff CHRIST is risen! CHRIST is risen!
He hath burst His bonds in twain;
CHRIST is risen! CHRIST is risen!
Alleluia! swell the strain!

mf Glorious Angels downward thronging
Hail the LORD of all the skies;
Heaven, with joy and holy longing
For the WORD Incarnate, cries,
f "CHRIST is risen! Earth, rejoice!
Gleam, ye starry train!
All creation find a voice;
He o'er all shall reign."
ff CHRIST is risen! CHRIST is risen!
He hath burst His bonds in twain;
CHRIST is risen! CHRIST is risen,
O'er the universe to reign.

Easter.

Hymn 139.

"The First-begotten of the dead."

mf COME see the place where JESUS lay,
And hear Angelic watchers say,
f "He lives, Who once was slain:
mf Why seek the living 'midst the dead?
Remember how the Saviour said
f That He would rise again."

O joyful sound! O glorious hour,
When by His own Almighty power
He rose, and left the grave!
ff Now let our songs His triumph tell,
Who burst the bands of death and hell,
And ever lives to save.

f The First-begotten of the dead,
For us He rose, our glorious Head,
Immortal life to bring;
What though the saints like Him shall [die,
They share their Leader's victory,
And triumph with their King.

mf No more they tremble at the grave,
For JESUS will their spirits save,
And raise their slumbering dust:
f O risen LORD, in Thee we live,
dim To Thee our ransomed souls we give,
p To Thee our bodies trust.

Easter.

Hymn 140. (First Tune.)

"I am He that liveth, and was dead; and behold, I am alive for evermore, Amen; and have the keys of hell and of death."

JESUS lives! no longer now
  Can thy terrors, death, appal us;
Jesus lives! by this we know
  Thou, O grave, canst not enthral us.
    Alleluia!

Jesus lives! henceforth is death
  But the gate of life immortal;
This shall calm our trembling breath,
  When we pass its gloomy portal.
    mf Alleluia!

Jesus lives! (*p*) for us He died;
f Then, alone to Jesus living,
Pure in heart may we abide,
  Glory to our Saviour giving.
    Alleluia!

f Jesus lives! our hearts know well
  Nought from us His love shall sever;
Life, nor death, nor powers of hell
  Tear us from His keeping ever.
    Alleluia!

Jesus lives! to Him the Throne
  Over all the world is given;
mf May we go where He is gone,
cr Rest and reign with Him in heaven.
    Alleluia!

Easter.

Hymn 140. (Second Tune.)

"I am He that liveth, and was dead; and behold, I am alive for evermore, Amen; and have the keys of hell and of death."

f Jesus lives! no longer now
Can thy terrors, death, appal us;
Jesus lives! by this we know
Thou, O grave, canst not enthral us.
Alleluia!

Jesus lives! henceforth is death
But the gate of life immortal;
p This shall calm our trembling breath,
When we pass its gloomy portal.
mf Alleluia!

f Jesus lives! *(p)* for us He died;
mf Then, alone to Jesus living,
Pure in heart may we abide,
Glory to our Saviour giving.
Alleluia!

f Jesus lives! our hearts know well
Nought from us His love shall sever;
Life, nor death, nor powers of hell
Tear us from His keeping ever.
Alleluia!

Jesus lives! to Him the Throne
Over all the world is given;
mf May we go where He is gone,
cr Rest and reign with Him in heaven.
Alleluia!

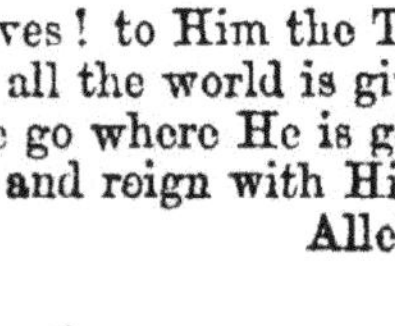

Easter.

Hymn 141.

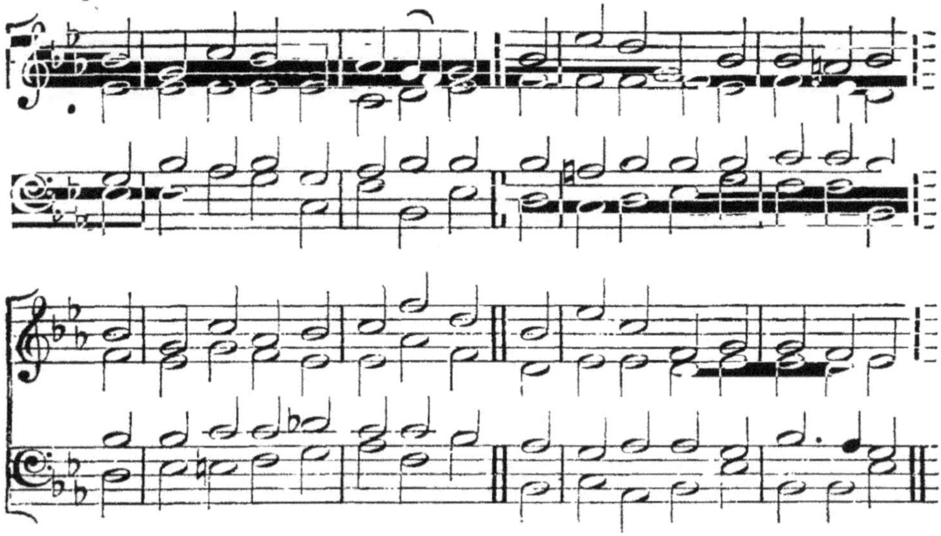

"*When thou liest down, thou shalt not be afraid, yea, thou shalt lie down, and thy sleep shall be sweet.*"

For a Late Evening Service.

f JESU, the world's redeeming Lord,
The Father's co-eternal Word,
Of Light invisible true Light,
Thine Israel's Keeper day and night;

Our great Creator and our Guide,
Who times and seasons dost divide,
Refresh at night with quiet rest
Our limbs by daily toil oppressed;

That while in this frail house of clay
A little longer here we stay,
Our flesh in Thee may sweetly sleep,
Our souls with Thee their vigils keep.

mf We pray Thee, while we dwell below,
Preserve us from our ghostly foe;
Nor let his wiles victorious be
O'er them that are redeemed by Thee.

O Lord of all, with us abide
In this our joyful Easter-tide;
From every weapon death can wield
Thine own redeemed for ever shield.

f All praise be Thine, O risen Lord,
From death to endless life restored;
All praise to God the Father be
And Holy Ghost eternally.

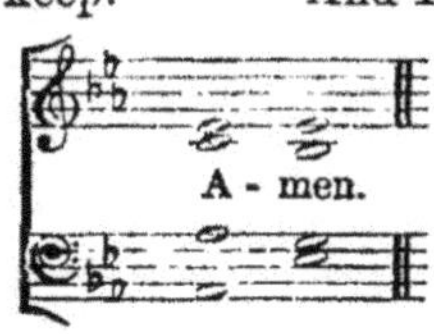

The following Hymns are suitable for this season.

197 The King of love my Shepherd is.
232 Light's abode, celestial Salem.
302 Come, ye faithful, raise the anthem.

Rogation Days.

Hymn 142.

Rogation Days.

"Lord, Thou art become gracious unto Thy land."

TO Thee our God we fly
  For mercy and for grace;
O hear our lowly cry,
  And hide not Thou Thy Face.
O Lord, stretch forth Thy mighty hand,
And guard and bless our Fatherland.

Arise, O Lord of hosts,
  Be jealous for Thy Name,
And drive from out our coasts
  The sins that put to shame.
O Lord, stretch forth Thy mighty hand,
And guard and bless our Fatherland.

Thy best gifts from on high
  In rich abundance pour,
That we may magnify
  And praise Thee more and more.
O Lord, stretch forth Thy mighty hand,
And guard and bless our Fatherland.

The powers ordained by Thee
  With heavenly wisdom bless;
May they Thy servants be,
  And rule in righteousness.
O Lord, stretch forth Thy mighty hand,
And guard and bless our Fatherland.

The Church of Thy dear Son
  Inflame with love's pure fire,
Bind her once more in one,
  And life and truth inspire.
O Lord, stretch forth Thy mighty hand,
And guard and bless our Fatherland.

The Pastors of Thy fold
  With grace and power endue,
That faithful, pure, and bold,
  They may be Pastors true.
f O Lord, stretch forth Thy mighty hand,
mf And guard and bless our Fatherland.

O let us love Thy house,
  And sanctify Thy day,
Bring unto Thee our vows,
  And loyal homage pay.
f O Lord, stretch forth Thy mighty hand,
mf And guard and bless our Fatherland.

p Give peace, Lord, in our time;
  O let no foe draw nigh,
Nor lawless deed of crime
  Insult Thy Majesty.
f O Lord, stretch forth Thy mighty hand,
mf And guard and bless our Fatherland.

p Though vile and worthless, still
  Thy people, Lord, are we;
cr And for our God we will
  None other have but Thee.
f O Lord, stretch forth Thy mighty hand,
And guard and bless our Fatherland.

This Hymn may also be sung at other seasons.

Rogation Days.

Hymn 143.

"The eyes of all wait upon Thee, O Lord; and Thou givest them their meat in due season."

mf LORD, in Thy Name Thy servants plead,
And Thou hast sworn to hear;
Thine is the harvest, Thine the seed,
The fresh and fading year.

Our hope, when autumn winds blew wild,
We trusted, LORD, with Thee:
And still, now spring has on us smiled,
We wait on Thy decree.

The former and the latter rain,
The summer sun and air,
The green ear, and the golden grain,
All Thine, are ours by prayer.

Thine too by right, and ours by grace,
The wondrous growth unseen,
The hopes that soothe, the fears that
The love that shines serene. [brace,

So grant the precious things brought
By sun and moon below, [forth
That Thee in Thy new heaven and earth
We never may forego.

The following Hymn is suitable for this season:
468 Litany for the Rogation Days.

Ascensiontide.

Hymn 144.

"All power is given unto Me in heaven and in earth."

mf O LORD most High, Eternal King,
By Thee redeemed Thy praise we sing;
The bonds of death are burst by Thee,
And grace has won the victory.

Ascending to the FATHER'S Throne
Thou claim'st the kingdom as Thine own;
Thy days of mortal weakness o'er,
All power is Thine for evermore.

To Thee the whole creation now
Shall, in its threefold order, bow,
Of things on earth, and things on high,
And things that underneath us lie.

p In awe and wonder Angels see
How changed is man's estate by Thee,
How Flesh makes pure as flesh did stain,
And Thou, True GOD, in Flesh dost reign.

f Be Thou our Joy, O mighty LORD,
As Thou wilt be our great Reward;
Let all our glory be in Thee
Both now and through eternity.

All praise from every heart and tongue
To Thee, ascended LORD, be sung;
All praise to GOD the FATHER be
And HOLY GHOST eternally.

Ascensiontide.

Hymn 145.

"This same Jesus, which is taken up from you into heaven, shall so come in like manner as ye have seen Him go into heaven."

O CHRIST our Joy, gone up on high
  To fill Thy Throne above the sky,
    How glorious dost Thou shine!
Thy Sovereign rule the worlds obey,
And earthly joys all fade away
    In that pure light of Thine.

To Thee in prayer Thy people bow;
O may our sins Thy pardon know,
    The cleansing of Thy grace;
r Then lift our hearts to Thee above,
On wings of faithfulness and love,
    To seek Thy holy place.

mf So, when the sudden call shall sound,
  And with Thy robe of clouds around
    Thou, CHRIST, shalt come once more,
dim Thyself our Judge may'st turn away
  The penalty our sins should pay,
cr   And our lost crowns restore.

f Ascended up from mortal sight,
  JESU, we praise Thee in the height,
    Our Joy, our great Reward;
  Whom with the FATHER we confess,
  And with the HOLY SPIRIT bless,
    ONE ever-glorious LORD.

Ascensiontide.

Hymn 146.

"By His own Blood He entered in once into the holy place."

mf O SAVIOUR, Who for man hast trod
The winepress of the wrath of GOD,
f Ascend, and claim again on high
Thy glory left for us to die.

A radiant cloud is now Thy seat,
And earth lies stretched beneath Thy feet;
Ten thousand thousands round Thee sing,
And share the triumph of their King.

The Angel-host enraptured waits:
"Lift up your heads, eternal gates!"
O GOD-and-MAN! the FATHER'S Throne
Is now for evermore Thine own.

Our great High Priest and Shepherd Thou
Within the veil art entered now,
f To offer there Thy precious Blood
Once poured on earth a cleansing flood.

mf And thence the Church, Thy chosen Bride,
With countless gifts of grace supplied,
Through all her members draws from Thee
Her hidden life of sanctity.

O CHRIST, our LORD, of Thy dear care
Thy lowly members heaven-ward bear;
Be ours with Thee to suffer pain,
With Thee for evermore to reign.

f All praise from every heart and tongue
To Thee, ascended LORD, be sung;
All praise to GOD the FATHER be
And HOLY GHOST eternally.

Ascensiontide.

Hymn 147.

Ascensiontide.

"Lift up your heads, O ye gates, and be ye lift up, ye everlasting doors; and the King of glory shall come in."

HAIL the day that sees Him rise
Alleluia!
To His Throne above the skies;
Alleluia!
CHRIST, the LAMB for sinners given,
Alleluia!
Enters now the highest heaven.
Alleluia!

There for Him high triumph waits;
Alleluia!
Lift your heads, eternal gates;
Alleluia!
He hath conquered death and sin;
Alleluia!
Take the King of glory in.
Alleluia!

Lo! the heaven its LORD receives,
Alleluia!
Yet He loves the earth He leaves;
Alleluia!
Though returning to His Throne,
Alleluia!
Still He calls mankind His own.
Alleluia!

See! He lifts His Hands above;
Alleluia!
p See! He shews the prints of love;
Alleluia!
f Hark! His gracious lips bestow
Alleluia!
Blessings on His Church below.
Alleluia!

p Still for us He intercedes,
Alleluia!
His prevailing death He pleads,
Alleluia!
cr Near Himself prepares our place,
Alleluia!
f He the first-fruits of our race.
Alleluia!

p LORD, though parted from our sight
Alleluia!
cr Far above the starry height,
Alleluia!
Grant our hearts may thither rise,
Alleluia!
f Seeking Thee above the skies.
Alleluia!

Ascensiontide.

Hymn 148. (First Part.)

Ascensiontide.

" Thou art gone up on high, Thou hast led captivity captive, and received gifts for men."

f SEE the Conqueror mounts in triumph, see the King in royal state
Riding on the clouds His chariot to His heavenly palace gate;
Hark! the choirs of Angel voices joyful Alleluias sing,
And the portals high are lifted to receive their Heavenly King.

mf Who is this that comes in glory, with the trump of jubilee?
f Lord of battles, God of armies, He has gained the victory;
p He Who on the Cross did suffer, *(mf)* He Who from the grave arose,
f He has vanquished sin and Satan, He by death has spoiled His foes.

mf While He lifts His Hands in blessing, He is parted from His friends;
While their eager eyes behold Him, He upon the clouds ascends;
He Who walked with God, and pleased Him, preaching truth and doom to come,
He, our Enoch, is translated to His everlasting home.

p Now our heavenly Aaron enters, with His Blood, within the veil;
mf Joshua now is come to Canaan, and the kings before Him quail;
Now He plants the tribes of Israel in their promised resting-place;
Now our great Elijah offers double portion of His grace.

He has raised our human nature on the clouds to God's right hand;
There we sit in heavenly places, there with Him in glory stand:
f Jesus reigns, adored by Angels; Man with God is on the Throne;
Mighty Lord, in Thine Ascension *(p)* we by faith behold our own.

The following Doxology may be sung at the end of either Part.

ff Glory be to God the Father; glory be to God the Son,
Dying, risen, ascending for us, Who the heavenly realm has won;
Glory to the Holy Spirit; to One God in Persons Three
Glory both in earth and heaven, glory, endless glory be.

M 2

Ascensiontide.

Hymn 148. (Second Part.)

Ascensiontide.

"Thou art gone up on high, Thou hast led captivity captive, and received gifts for men."

Part 2.

mf Holy Ghost, Illuminator, shed Thy beams upon our eyes,
Help us to look up with Stephen, and to see, beyond the skies,
Where the Son of Man in glory standing is at God's right hand,
Beckoning on His Martyr army, succouring His faithful band;

f See Him, Who is gone before us heavenly mansions to prepare,
p See Him, Who is ever pleading for us with prevailing prayer,
f See Him, Who with sound of trumpet and with His Angelic train,
Summoning the world to judgment, on the clouds will come again.

mf Raise us up from earth to heaven, give us wings of faith and love,
Gales of holy aspirations wafting us to realms above;
That, with hearts and minds uplifted, we with Christ our Lord may dwell,
Where He sits enthroned in glory in His heavenly citadel.

So at last, when He appeareth, we from out our graves may spring,
With our youth renewed like eagles, flocking round our Heavenly King,
cr Caught up on the clouds of heaven, and may meet Him in the air,
Rise to realms where He is reigning, and may reign for ever there.

The following Doxology may be sung at the end of either Part.

ff Glory be to God the Father; glory be to God the Son,
Dying, risen, ascending for us, Who the heavenly realm has won;
Glory to the Holy Spirit; to One God in Persons Three
Glory both in earth and heaven, glory, endless glory be.

Ascensiontide.

Hymn 149. (First Tune.)

Ascensiontide.

Hymn 149. (Second Tune.)

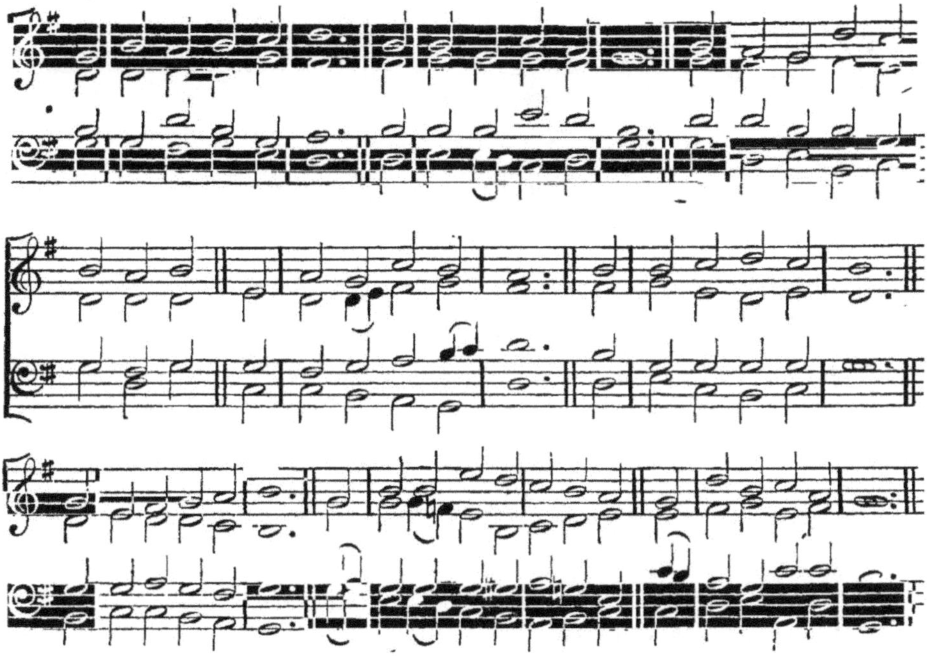

"Who is gone into heaven."

f THOU art gone up on high,
 To mansions in the skies;
And round Thy Throne unceasingly
 The songs of praise arise;
p But we are lingering here,
 With sin and care oppressed;
cr Lord, send Thy promised Comforter,
 And lead us to Thy rest.

f Thou art gone up on high;
p But Thou didst first come down,
Through earth's most bitter misery
cr To pass unto Thy Crown;
p And girt with griefs and fears
 Our onward course must be;
cr But only let this path of tears
 Lead us at last to Thee.

f Thou art gone up on high;
 But Thou shalt come again,
With all the bright ones of the sky
 Attendant in Thy train.
mf Lord, by Thy saving power
 So make us live and die,
cr That we may stand in that dread hour
f At Thy right hand on high.

1. 

2. 

Ascensiontide.

Hymn 150.

"Who being the brightness of His glory, and the express Image of His person, and upholding all things by the word of His power, when He had by Himself purged our sins, sat down on the right hand of the Majesty on high."

mf JESU, our Hope, our heart's Desire,
 Thy work of grace we sing;
Redeemer of the world art Thou,
 Its Maker and its King.

p How vast the mercy and the love,
 Which laid our sins on Thee,
And led Thee to a cruel death,
 To set Thy people free!

f But now the bonds of death are burst;
 The ransom has been paid;
And Thou art on Thy FATHER'S Throne,
 In glorious robes arrayed.

mf O may Thy mighty love prevail
 Our sinful souls to spare!
O may we stand around Thy Throne,
 And see Thy glory there!

JESU, our only Joy be Thou,
 As Thou our Prize wilt be;
In Thee be all our glory now
 And through eternity.

f All praise to Thee Who art gone up
 Triumphantly to heaven;
All praise to GOD the FATHER'S Name
 And HOLY GHOST be given.

The following Hymns are suitable for this season:

201 Where high the heavenly temple stands.
202 Rejoice, the LORD is King.
300 All hail the power of JESU'S Name.
301 The Head that once was crowned with thorns.
304 Crown Him with many crowns.
469 Litany of JESUS Glorified.

Whitsun-Even.

Hymn 151.

"If I go not away, the Comforter will not come unto you; but if I depart, I will send Him unto you."

mf RULER of the hosts of light,
Death hath yielded to Thy might;
And Thy Blood hath marked a road
Which will lead us back to God.

From Thy dwelling-place above,
From Thy Father's Throne of love,
With Thy look of mercy bless
p Those without Thee comfortless.

Bitter were Thy throes on earth,
Giving to the Church her birth
From the spear-wound opening wide
In Thine own life-giving Side.

f Now in glory Thou dost reign
Won by all Thy toil and pain;
mf Thence the promised Spirit send,
While our prayers to Thee ascend.

Jesu, praise to Thee be given
With the Father high in heaven;
Holy Spirit, praise to Thee,
Now and through eternity.

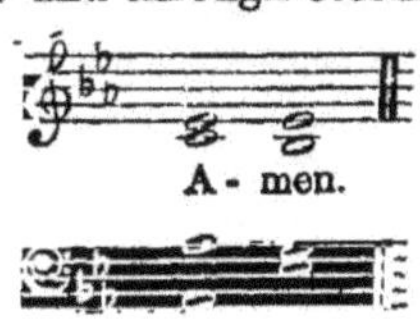

Whitsuntide.

Hymn 152.

"And when the day of Pentecost was fully come, they were all with one accord in one place."

mf ABOVE the starry spheres,
  To where He was before,
CHRIST had gone up, the FATHER's gift
  Upon the Church to pour.

  At length had fully come,
  On mystic circle borne
Of seven times seven revolving days,
  The Pentecostal morn:

  When, as the Apostles knelt
  At the third hour in prayer,
cr A sudden rushing sound proclaimed
p That GOD Himself was there.

mf Forthwith a tongue of fire
  Is seen on every brow,
Each heart receives the FATHER's light,
  The WORD's enkindling glow;

  The HOLY GHOST on all
  Is mightily outpoured,
Who straight in divers tongues declare
  The wonders of the LORD.

  While strangers of all climes
  Flock round from far and near,
And their own tongue, wherever born,
  All with amazement hear.

  But Judah, faithless still,
  Denies the hand Divine;
And, mocking, jeers the saints of CHRIST
  As full of new-made wine.

  Till Peter, in the midst,
  By Joel's ancient word
Rebukes their unbelief, *(cr)* and wins
  Three thousand to the LORD.

f The FATHER and the SON
  And SPIRIT we adore;
O may the SPIRIT's gifts be poured
  On us for evermore.

Whitsuntide.

Hymn 153.

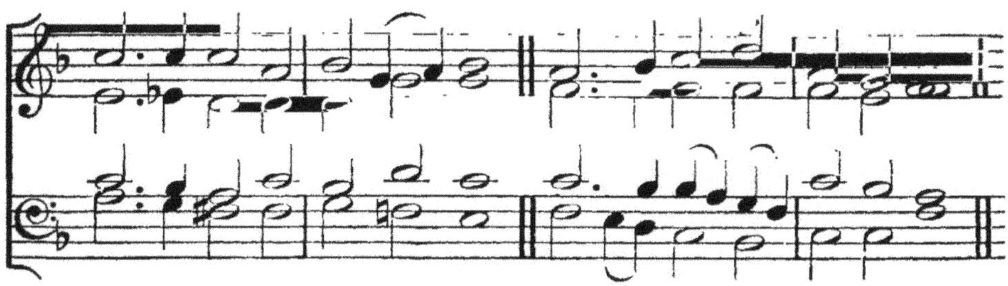

"I will pour out My Spirit upon all flesh."

f JOY! because the circling year
Brings our day of blessings here;
Day when first the light Divine
On the Church began to shine.

mf Like to quivering tongues of flame
Unto each the SPIRIT came,
Tongues, that earth might hear their call,
Fire, that love might burn in all.

f So the wondrous works of GOD
Wondrously were spread abroad;
Every tribe's familiar tone
Made the glorious marvel known.

mf Hardened scoffers vainly jeered;
Listening strangers heard and feared,
Knew the prophet's word fulfilled,
Owned the work which GOD had willed.

Still Thy SPIRIT's fulness, LORD,
On Thy waiting Church be poured;
p Grant our burdened hearts release;
Grant us Thine abiding peace.

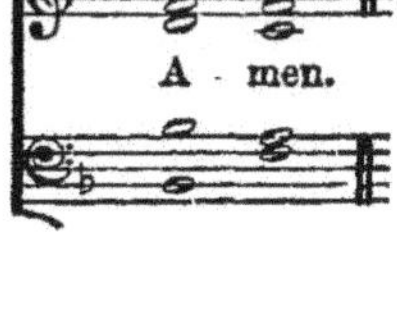

Whitsuntide.

Hymn 154.

"And suddenly there came a sound from heaven, as of a rushing mighty wind."

mf WHEN God of old came down from heaven,
In power and wrath He came;
Before His feet the clouds were riven,
Half darkness and half flame:

p But, when He came the second time,
He came in power and love;
Softer than gale at morning prime
Hovered His holy Dove.

mf The fires, that rushed on Sinai down
In sudden torrents dread,
p Now gently light, *(cr)* a glorious crown,
On every sainted head.

f And as on Israel's awe-struck ear
The voice exceeding loud,
The trump, that Angels quake to hear,
Thrilled from the deep, dark cloud;

So, when the Spirit of our God
Came down His flock to find,
A voice from heaven was heard abroad,
A rushing, mighty wind.

mf It fills the Church of God; It fills
The sinful world around;
Only in stubborn hearts and wills
No place for It is found.

p Come Lord, come Wisdom, Love, and Power,
Open our ears to hear;
Let us not miss the accepted hour;
Save, Lord, by love or fear.

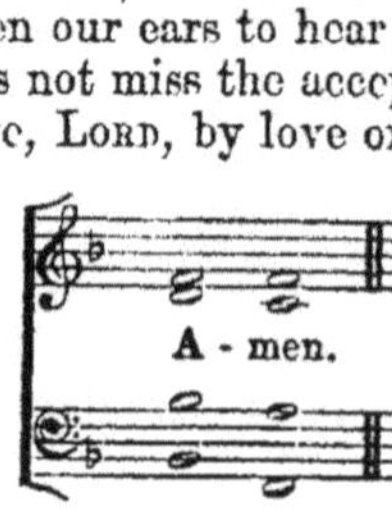

Whitsuntide.

Hymn 155.

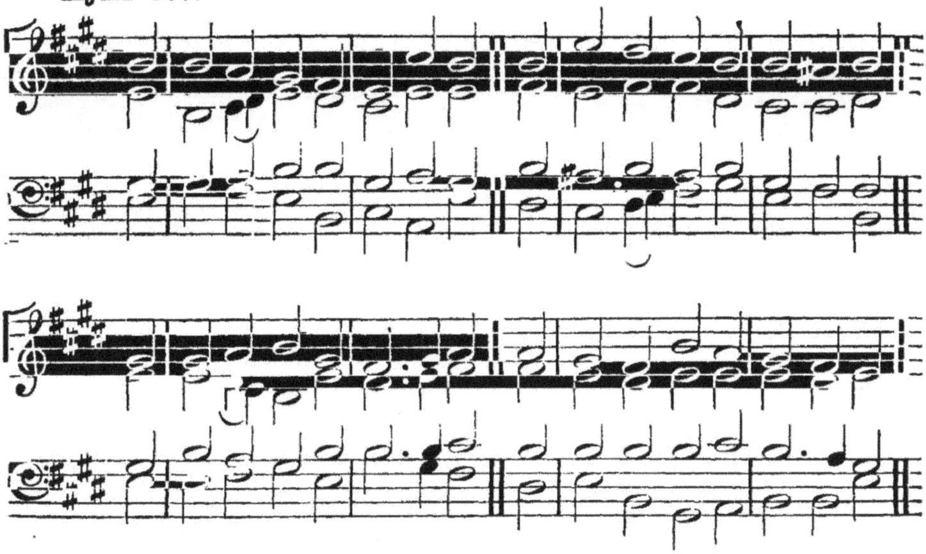

"And the same day there were added unto them about three thousand souls."

mf SPIRIT of mercy, truth, and love,
O shed Thine influence from above;
And still from age to age convey
The wonders of this sacred day.

f In every clime, by every tongue,
Be God's surpassing glory sung;
Let all the listening earth be taught
The acts our great Redeemer wrought.

mf Unfailing Comfort, Heavenly Guide,
Still o'er Thy Holy Church preside;
Still let mankind Thy blessings prove,
Spirit of mercy, truth, and love.

Whitsuntide.

Hymn 156.

Whitsuntide.

"When Thou lettest Thy breath go forth they shall be made, and Thou shalt renew the face of the earth."

mf COME, Thou HOLY SPIRIT, come;
And from Thy celestial home
Shed a ray of light Divine;
Come, Thou Father of the poor,
Come, Thou source of all our store,
Come, within our bosoms shine:

Thou of Comforters the best,
Thou the soul's most welcome guest,
p Sweet refreshment here below;
In our labour rest most sweet,
Grateful coolness in the heat,
Solace in the midst of woe.

mf O most Blessèd Light Divine,
Shine within these hearts of Thine,
And our inmost being fill;
p Where Thou art not, man hath nought,
Nothing good in deed or thought,
Nothing free from taint of ill.

mf Heal our wounds; our strength renew;
On our dryness pour Thy dew;
Wash the stains of guilt away:
Bend the stubborn heart and will;
Melt the frozen, warm the chill;
Guide the steps that go astray.

On the faithful, who adore
And confess Thee, evermore
In Thy sevenfold gifts descend:
Give them virtue's sure reward,
cr Give them Thy salvation, LORD,
f Give them joys that never end.

This Hymn may also be sung at other seasons.

Whitsuntide.

Hymn 157. (First Tune.)

To be sung in Unison.

Whitsuntide.

"The Comforter which is the Holy Ghost."

mf COME, HOLY GHOST, our souls inspire,
And lighten with celestial fire;
Thou the anointing SPIRIT art,
Who dost Thy sevenfold gifts impart:

Thy blessèd unction from above
Is comfort, life, and fire of love;
Enable with perpetual light
The dulness of our blinded sight:

Anoint and cheer our soilèd face
With the abundance of Thy grace:
Keep far our foes, give peace at home;
Where Thou art Guide no ill can come.

Teach us to know the FATHER, SON,
And THEE, of Both, to be but ONE;
That through the ages all along
This may be our endless song,

This Hymn may also be sung at other seasons.

Hymn 157. (Second Tune.)

"The Comforter which is the Holy Ghost."

mf COME, Holy Ghost, our souls inspire,
And lighten with celestial fire;
Thou the anointing Spirit art,
Who dost Thy sevenfold gifts impart:

Thy blessèd unction from above
Is comfort, life, and fire of love;
Enable with perpetual light
The dulness of our blinded sight:

Anoint and cheer our soilèd face
With the abundance of Thy grace:
Keep far our foes, give peace at home;
Where Thou art Guide no ill can come.

Teach us to know the Father, Son,
And Thee, of Both, to be but One;
That through the ages all along
This may be our endless song,

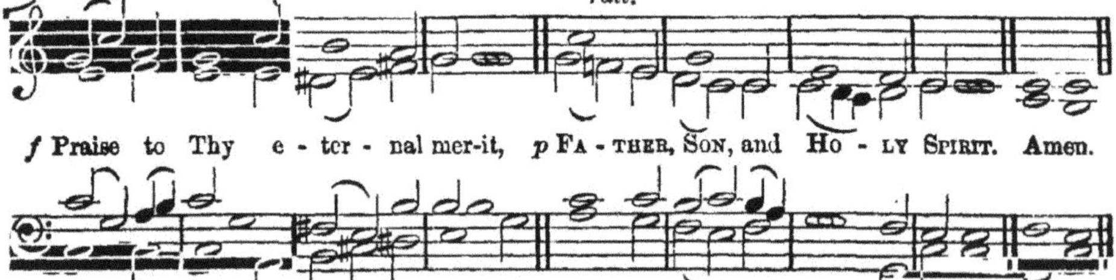

This Hymn may also be sung at other seasons.

The following Hymns are suitable for this season:

207 Our Blest Redeemer, ere He breathed.
208 O Holy Spirit, Lord of grace.
209 Come, gracious Spirit, heavenly Dove.
210 Gracious Spirit, Holy Ghost.
211 O Holy Ghost, Thy people bless.
212 To Thee, O Comforter Divine.
470 Litany of the Holy Ghost.

Trinity Sunday.

Hymn 158. *(To be sung in Unison.)*

"And one cried unto another, and said, Holy, Holy, Holy, is the Lord of hosts."

ALL hail, Adorèd TRINITY;
All hail, Eternal UNITY;
O GOD the FATHER, GOD the SON,
And GOD the SPIRIT, ever ONE.

mf Behold to Thee, this festal day,
We meekly pour our thankful lay;
O let our work accepted be,
That sweetest work of praising Thee.

f THREE Persons praise we evermore,
ONE only GOD our hearts adore;
In Thy sure mercy ever kind
May we our true protection find.

p O TRINITY! O UNITY!
Be present as we worship Thee;
cr And with the songs that Angels sing
Unite the hymns of praise we bring.

Trinity Sunday.

Hymn 159.

Trinity Sunday.

"O praise God in His holiness."

mf WITH hearts renewed, and cleansed from guilt of sin,
Send we our voices pealing to the skies;
Let a pure conscience echo joy within,
And all our powers in emulation rise:
To FATHER, SON, and HOLY SPIRIT's praise,
THREE Whom One Essence joins, one anthem here we raise.

Maker of all, the FATHER uncreate,
Of Him from everlasting born, the SON,
And the Blest SPIRIT of co-equal state
From Both proceeding, are of Substance One:
So in this TRINITY the Persons THREE
One Perfect Being are, ONE GOD, One Majesty.

Yet, none the less, each Person of the Trine
GOD, in His attributes distinct, we own;
Vainly would reason grasp the things Divine,
p Man can but bend adoring at GOD's Throne:
cr O may the FATHER, SON, and SPIRIT be
Our help in time of need, our joy eternally.

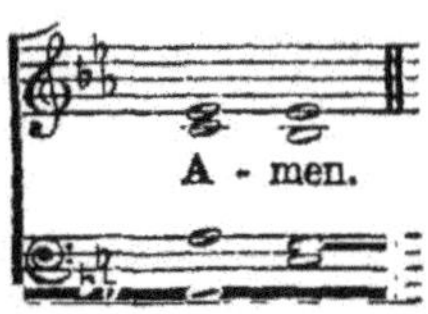

The following Hymns are suitable for this Festival:

160 Holy, Holy, Holy! LORD GOD Almighty!
161 Bright the vision that delighted.
162 Have mercy on us, GOD most High.
163 THREE in ONE, and ONE in THREE.

General Hymns.

Hymn 160.

"They rest not day and night, saying, Holy, Holy, Holy, Lord God Almighty, Which was, and is, and is to come."

p HOLY, Holy, Holy! *(mf)* LORD GOD Almighty!
  Early in the morning our song shall rise to Thee:
p Holy, Holy, Holy! *(mf)* Merciful and Mighty!
f   GOD in THREE Persons, Blessèd TRINITY!

p Holy, Holy, Holy! *(mf)* all the Saints adore Thee,
  Casting down their golden crowns around the glassy sea;
Cherubim and Seraphim falling down before Thee,
  Which wert, and art, and evermore shalt be.

p Holy, Holy, Holy! though the darkness hide Thee,
  Though the eye of sinful man Thy glory may not see,
mf Only Thou art Holy: there is none beside Thee
  Perfect in power, in love, and purity.

p Holy, Holy, Holy! *(mf)* LORD GOD Almighty!
ff   All Thy works shall praise Thy Name, in earth, and sky, and sea:
mf Holy, Holy, Holy! Merciful and Mighty!
f   GOD in THREE Persons, Blessèd TRINITY!

General Hymns.

Hymn 161.

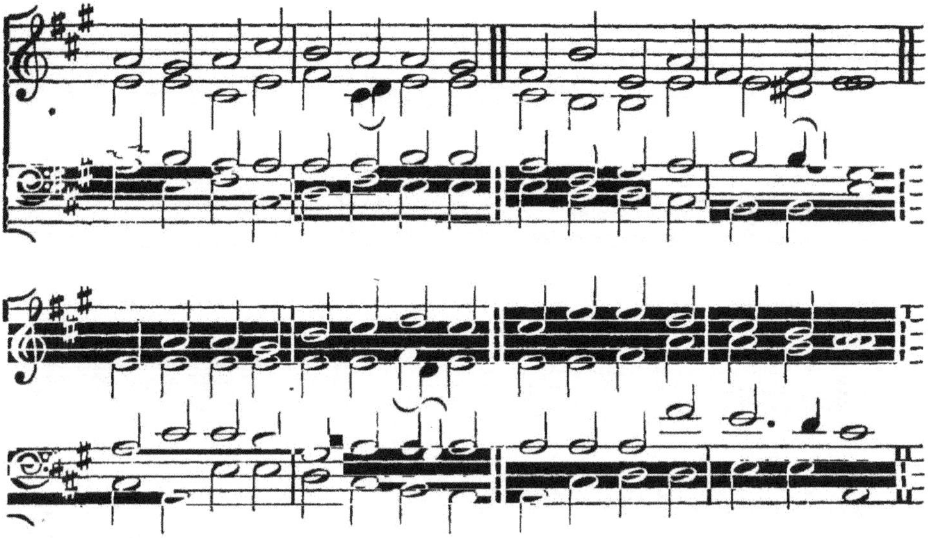

"And one cried unto another, and said, Holy, Holy, Holy, is the Lord of hosts; the whole earth is full of His glory."

mf BRIGHT the vision that delighted
  Once the sight of Judah's seer;
Sweet the countless tongues united
  To entrance the prophet's ear.

Round the LORD in glory seated
  Cherubim and Seraphim
Filled His temple, and repeated
  Each to each the alternate hymn;

f "LORD, Thy glory fills the heaven;
  Earth is with its fulness stored;
Unto Thee be glory given,
p   Holy, Holy, Holy, LORD."

f Heaven is still with glory ringing,
  Earth takes up the Angels' cry,
p "Holy, Holy, Holy," singing,
cr   "LORD of hosts, LORD GOD most High."

mf With His seraph train before Him,
  With His holy Church below,
Thus unite we to adore Him,
  Bid we thus our anthem flow;

f "LORD, Thy glory fills the heaven;
  Earth is with its fulness stored;
Unto Thee be glory given,
p   Holy, Holy, Holy, LORD."

Hymn 162.

"Thou art God from everlasting, and world without end."

p HAVE mercy on us, God most High,
  Who lift our hearts to Thee;
Have mercy on us worms of earth,
  Most Holy Trinity.

Most ancient of all mysteries!
  Before Thy Throne we lie;
Have mercy now, most Merciful,
  Most Holy Trinity.

mf When heaven and earth were yet unmade,
  When time was yet unknown,
Thou, in Thy bliss and majesty,
  Didst live and love alone.

How wonderful creation is,
  The work that Thou didst bless;
And oh, what then must Thou be like,
  Eternal Loveliness!

Most ancient of all mysteries!
p Low at Thy Throne we lie;
Have mercy now, most Merciful,
  Most Holy Trinity.

General Hymns.

Hymn 163.

"Sing unto the Lord, and praise His Name."

mf THREE in ONE, and ONE in THREE,
Ruler of the earth and sea,
Hear us, while we lift to Thee
Holy chant and psalm.

Light of lights! with morning shine;
Lift on us Thy Light Divine;
And let charity benign
p Breathe on us her balm.

Light of lights! when falls the even,
Let it close on sin forgiven;
Fold us in the peace of heaven;
Shed a holy calm.

mf THREE in ONE and ONE in THREE,
Dimly here we worship Thee;
cr With the Saints hereafter we
Hope to bear the palm.

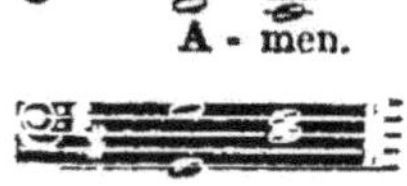

General Hymns.

Hymn 164.

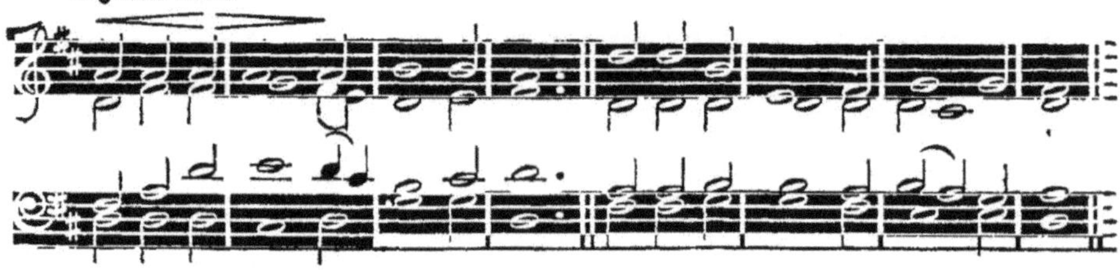

"Let us therefore come boldly unto the throne of grace, that we may obtain mercy, and find grace to help in time of need."

mf FATHER of heaven, Whose love profound
A ransom for our souls hath found,
p Before Thy Throne we sinners bend,
mf To us Thy pardoning love extend.

Almighty SON, Incarnate WORD,
Our Prophet, Priest, Redeemer, LORD,
p Before Thy Throne we sinners bend,
mf To us Thy saving grace extend.

Eternal SPIRIT, by Whose breath
The soul is raised from sin and death,
p Before Thy Throne we sinners bend,
mf To us Thy quickening power extend.

Thrice Holy! FATHER, SPIRIT, SON;
Mysterious GODHEAD, THREE in ONE,
p Before Thy Throne we sinners bend,
mf Grace, pardon, life to us extend.

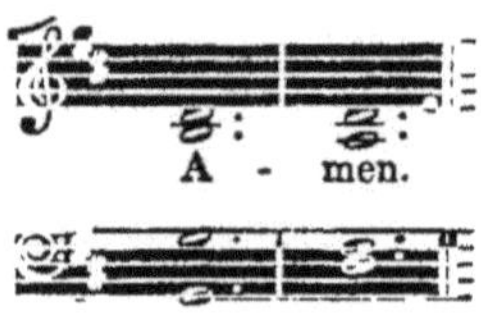

General Hymns.

Hymn 165.

"Lord, Thou hast been our refuge from one generation to another."

f O GOD, our help in ages past,
  Our hope for years to come,
Our shelter from the stormy blast,
  And our eternal home;

mf Beneath the shadow of Thy Throne
  Thy saints have dwelt secure;
Sufficient is Thine Arm alone,
  And our defence is sure.

Before the hills in order stood,
  Or earth received her frame,
cr From everlasting Thou art God,
  To endless years the Same.

p A thousand ages in Thy sight
  Are like an evening gone,
Short as the watch that ends the night
  Before the rising sun.

Time, like an ever-rolling stream,
  Bears all its sons away;
They fly forgotten, as a dream
  Dies at the opening day.

f O God, our help in ages past,
  Our hope for years to come,
Be Thou our guard while troubles last,
  And our eternal home.

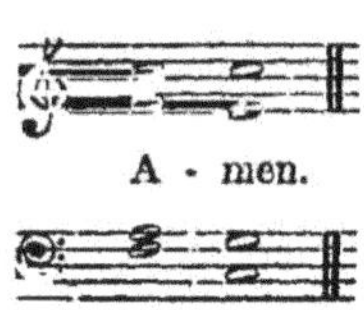

General Hymns.

Hymn 166. (First Version.)

"O be joyful in the Lord, all ye lands."

f ALL people that on earth do dwell,
Sing to the Lord with cheerful voice;
Him serve with fear, His praise forth tell,
Come ye before Him, and rejoice.

mf The Lord, ye know, is God indeed;
Without our aid He did us make;
We are His flock, He doth us feed,
And for His sheep He doth us take.

f O enter then His gates with praise,
Approach with joy His courts unto;
Praise, laud, and bless His Name always,
For it is seemly so to do.

mf For why? the Lord our God is good;
His mercy is for ever sure;
His truth at all times firmly stood,
And shall from age to age endure.

ff To Father, Son, and Holy Ghost,
The God Whom heaven and earth adore,
From men and from the Angel-host
Be praise and glory evermore.

General Hymns.

Hymn 166. (Second Version.)

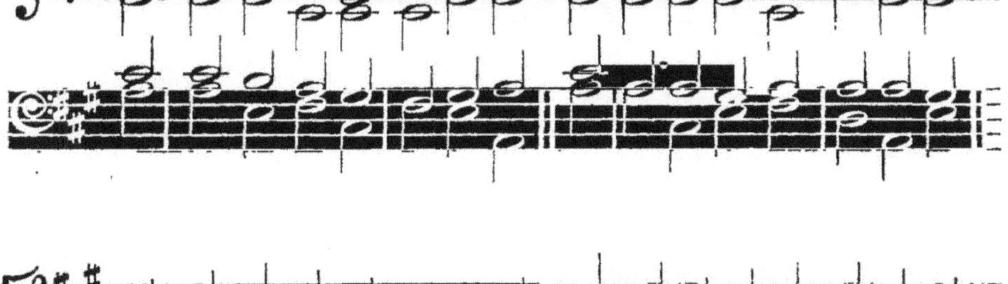

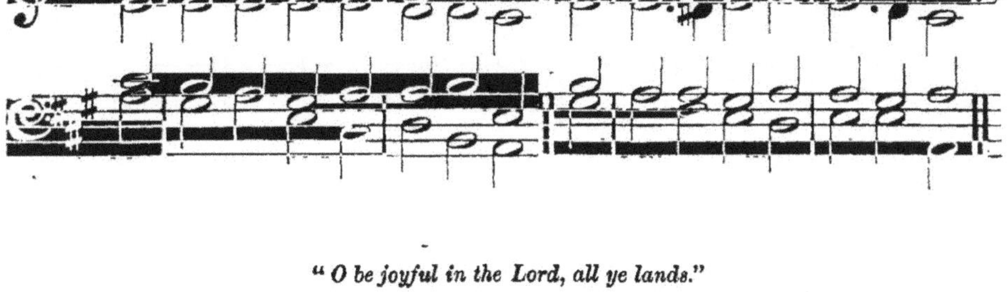

"O be joyful in the Lord, all ye lands."

f ALL people that on earth do dwell,
Sing to the Lord with cheerful voice;
Him serve with fear, His praise forth tell,
Come ye before Him, and rejoice.

mf The Lord, ye know, is God indeed;
Without our aid He did us make;
We are His flock, He doth us feed,
And for His sheep He doth us take.

f O enter then His gates with praise,
Approach with joy His courts unto;
Praise, laud, and bless His Name always,
For it is seemly so to do.

mf For why? the Lord our God is good;
His mercy is for ever sure;
His truth at all times firmly stood,
And shall from age to age endure.

ff To Father, Son, and Holy Ghost,
The God Whom heaven and earth adore,
From men and from the Angel-host
Be praise and glory evermore.

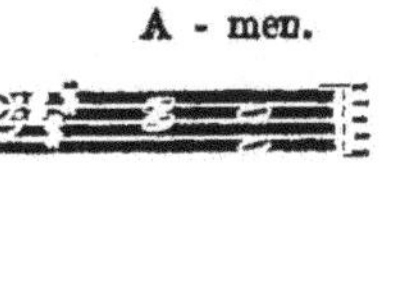

General Hymns.

Hymn 167.

General Hymns.

Praise the ***Lord,*** *O my soul: O* ***Lord*** *my* ***God, Thou*** *art become exceeding glorious;* ***Thou*** *art clothed with majesty and honour."*

f O WORSHIP the King All-glorious above;
O gratefully sing His power and His love;
Our Shield and Defender, the Ancient of days,
Pavilioned in splendour, and girded with praise.

O tell of His might, O sing of His grace,
Whose robe is the light, Whose canopy space;
His chariots of wrath the deep thunder clouds form,
And dark is His path on the wings of the storm.

mf The earth with its store of wonders untold,
Almighty, Thy power hath founded of old;
Hath stablished it fast by a changeless decree,
And round it hath cast, like a mantle, the sea.

Thy bountiful care what tongue can recite?
It breathes in the air, it shines in the light;
It streams from the hills, it descends to the plain,
And sweetly distils in the dew and the rain.

p Frail children of dust, and feeble as frail,
In Thee do we trust, nor find Thee to fail.
cr Thy mercies how tender! how firm to the end!
Our Maker, Defender, Redeemer, and Friend.

f O measureless Might, ineffable Love,
While Angels delight to hymn Thee above,
Thy ransomed creation, *(p)* though feeble their lays,
cr With true adoration shall sing to Thy praise.

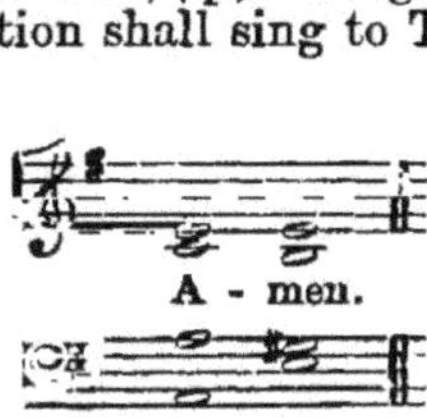

General Hymns.

Hymn 168.

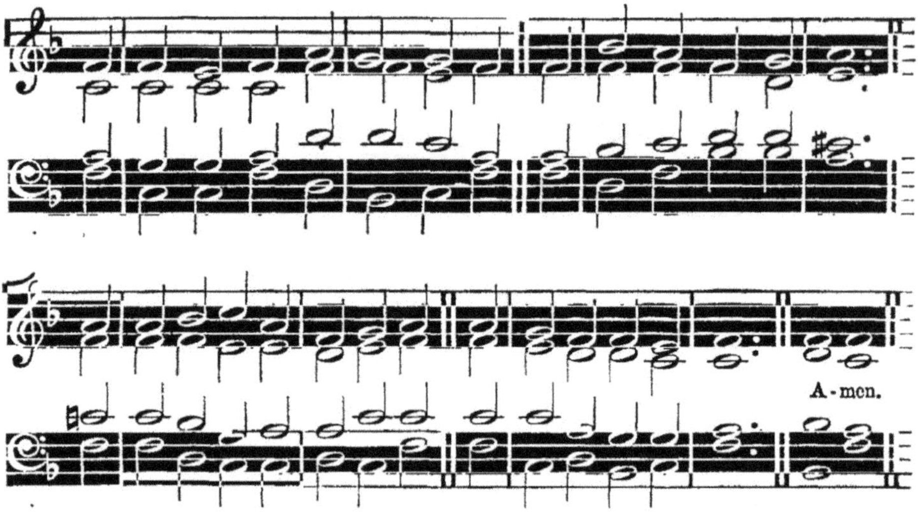

"The invisible things of Him from the creation of the world are clearly seen, being understood by the things that are made."

mf THERE is a book, who runs may read,
Which heavenly truth imparts,
And all the lore its scholars need,
Pure eyes and Christian hearts.

The works of God, above, below,
Within us and around,
Are pages in that book to show
How God Himself is found.

The glorious sky, embracing all,
Is like the Maker's love,
Wherewith encompassed, great and small
In peace and order move.

The moon above, the Church below,
A wondrous race they run;
But all their radiance, all their glow,
Each borrows of its Sun.

The Saviour lends the light and heat
That crown His holy hill;
The Saints, like stars, around His seat
Perform their courses still.

p The dew of heaven is like Thy grace,
It steals in silence down;
cr But, where it lights, the favoured place
By richest fruits is known.

f One Name, above all glorious names,
With its ten thousand tongues
The everlasting sea proclaims,
Echoing Angelic songs.

The raging fire, the roaring wind
Thy boundless power display;
p But in the gentler breeze we find
Thy Spirit's viewless way.

mf Two worlds are ours: 'tis only sin
Forbids us to descry
The mystic heaven and earth within,
Plain as the sea and sky.

Thou, Who hast given me eyes to see
And love this sight so fair,
Give me a heart to find out Thee,
And read Thee everywhere.

General Hymns.

Hymn 169.

"*Thus saith the high and lofty One that inhabiteth eternity, Whose name is Holy: I dwell in the high and holy place, with him also that is of a contrite and humble spirit.*"

mf MY GOD, how wonderful Thou art,
Thy majesty how bright,
How beautiful Thy mercy-seat,
In depths of burning light!

How dread are Thine eternal years,
O everlasting LORD,
By prostrate spirits day and night
Incessantly adored!

mf How wonderful, how beautiful,
The sight of Thee must be,
Thine endless wisdom, boundless power,
And awful purity!

v Oh, how I fear Thee, Living GOD,
With deepest, tenderest fears,
And worship Thee with trembling hope,
And penitential tears!

cr Yet I may love Thee too, O LORD,
Almighty as Thou art,
For Thou hast stooped to ask of me
dim The love of my poor heart.

mf No earthly father loves like Thee,
No mother, e'er so mild,
Bears and forbears as Thou hast done
With me Thy sinful child.

FATHER of JESUS, love's reward,
What rapture will it be,
Prostrate before Thy Throne to lie,
And gaze and gaze on Thee.

General Hymns.

Hymn 170.

General Hymns.

"In the beginning was the Word, and the Word was with God, and the Word was God. All things were made by Him."

f JESUS is GOD: *(mf)* the solid earth,
The ocean broad and bright,
The countless stars, like golden dust,
That strew the skies at night,
f The wheeling storm, the dreadful fire,
mf The pleasant wholesome air,
The summer's sun, the winter's frost,
His own creations were.

f JESUS is GOD: *(mf)* the glorious bands
Of golden Angels sing
Songs of adoring praise to Him,
Their Maker and their King.
He was true GOD in Bethlehem's crib,
On Calvary's Cross true GOD;
He, Who in heaven Eternal reigned,
In time on earth abode.

f JESUS is GOD: *(p)* let sorrow come,
And pain, and every ill,
cr All are worth while, for all are means
His glory to fulfil;
mf Worth while a thousand years of woe
To speak one little word,
If by that "I believe" we own
f The GODHEAD of our LORD.

General Hymns.

Hymn 171.

General Hymns.

"Worthy is the Lamb that was slain to receive power, and riches, and wisdom, and strength, and honour, and glory, and blessing."

f FROM highest heaven the Eternal Son,
With God the Father ever One,
p Came down to suffer and to die;
mf For love of sinful man He bore
Our human griefs and troubles sore,
p Our load of guilt and misery.

f Rejoice, ye saints of God, and praise
The Lamb Who died, His flock to raise
From sin and everlasting woe;
With Angels round the Throne above
O tell the wonders of His love,
The joys that from His mercy flow.

p In darkest shades of night we lay,
Without a beam to guide our way,
Or hope of aught beyond the grave;
mf But He has brought us life and light,
And opened heaven to our sight,
f And lives for ever strong to save.

ff Rejoice, ye saints of God, rejoice;
Sing out, and praise with cheerful voice
The Lamb Whom heaven and earth adore;
To Him Who gave His only Son,
To God the Spirit, with Them One,
Be praise and glory evermore.

General Hymns.

Hymn 172.

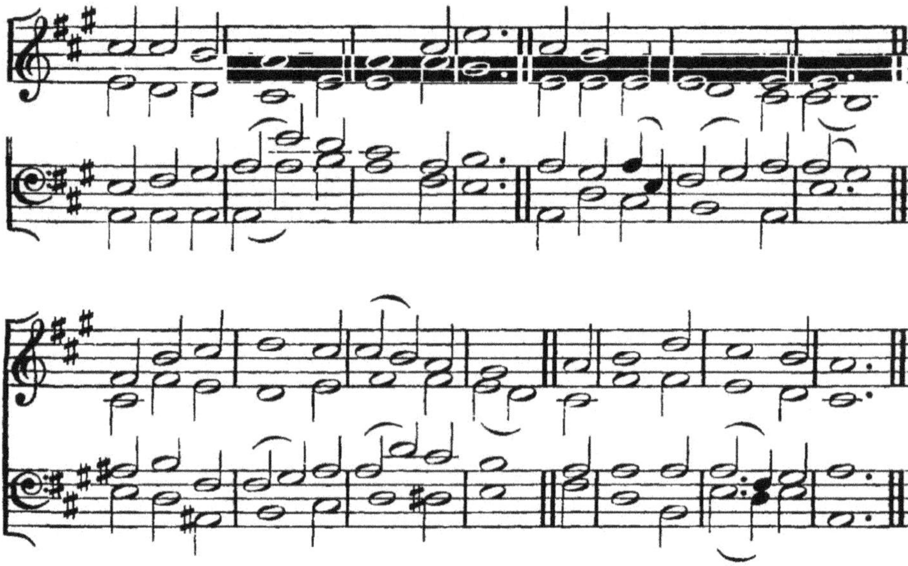

"The second Man is the Lord from heaven."

f PRAISE to the Holiest in the height,
And in the depth be praise;
In all His words most wonderful,
Most sure in all His ways.

mf O loving wisdom of our God!
p When all was sin and shame,
cr A second Adam to the fight
f And to the rescue came.

mf O wisest love! that flesh and blood,
p Which did in Adam fail,
cr Should strive afresh against the foe,
f Should strive and should prevail;

mf And that a higher gift than grace
Should flesh and blood refine,
p God's Presence and His very Self,
And Essence all-divine.

mf O generous love! that He, Who smote
In Man for man the foe,
The double agony in Man
For man should undergo;

p And in the garden secretly,
And on the Cross on high,
cr Should teach His brethren, and inspire
To suffer and to die.

f Praise to the Holiest in the height,
And in the depth be praise:
In all His words most wonderful,
Most sure in all His ways.

General Hymns.

Hymn 173.

"The love of Christ which passeth knowledge."

mf O LOVE, how deep! how broad! how high!
It fills the heart with ecstasy,
That God, the Son of God, should take
Our mortal form for mortals' sake.

He sent no Angel to our race
Of higher or of lower place,
p But wore the robe of human frame
Himself, and to this lost world came.

f For us He was baptized, and bore
His holy fast, and hungered sore;
For us temptations sharp He knew;
mf For us the tempter overthrew.

For us He prayed, for us He taught,
For us His daily works He wrought,
By words, and signs, and actions, thus
Still seeking not Himself but us.

p For us to wicked men betrayed,
Scourged, mocked, in purple robe arrayed,
He bore the shameful Cross and death;
For us at length gave up His breath.

f For us He rose from death again,
For us He went on high to reign,
For us He sent His Spirit here
To guide, to strengthen, and to cheer.

To Him Whose boundless love has won
Salvation for us through His Son,
To God the Father, glory be
Both now and through eternity.

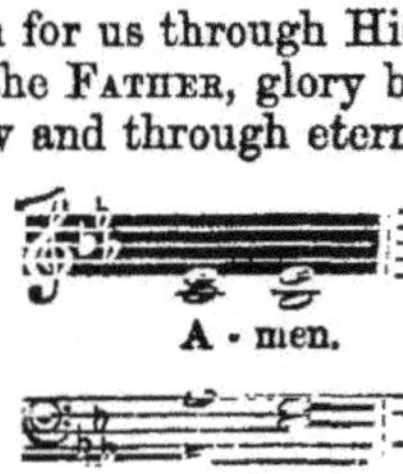

General Hymns.

Hymn 174.

General Hymns.

"Blessed are they that have not seen, and yet have believed."

mf WE saw Thee not when Thou didst come
    To this poor world of sin and death,
Nor e'er beheld Thy cottage-home
    In that despisèd Nazareth;
f But we believe Thy footsteps trod
Its streets and plains, Thou SON of GOD.

mf We did not see Thee lifted high
    Amid that wild and savage crew,
dim Nor heard Thy meek, imploring cry,
    "Forgive, they know not what they do;"
f Yet we believe the deed was done,
dim Which shook the earth and veiled the sun.

mf We stood not by the empty tomb
    Where late Thy sacred Body lay,
cr Nor sat within that upper room,
    Nor met Thee in the open way;
f But we believe that Angels said,
"Why seek the living with the dead?"

mf We did not mark the chosen few,
    When Thou didst through the clouds ascend,
First lift to heaven their wondering view,
p Then to the earth all prostrate bend;
f Yet we believe that mortal eyes
Beheld that journey to the skies.

And now that Thou dost reign on high,
    And thence Thy waiting people bless,
mf No ray of glory from the sky
    Doth shine upon our wilderness;
ff But we believe Thy faithful Word,
And trust in our Redeeming LORD.

General Hymns.

Hymn 175.

"Thou shalt call His name Jesus, for He shall save His people from their sins."

mf CONQUERING kings their titles take
From the foes they captive make :
f Jesus, by a nobler deed,
From the thousands He hath freed.

mf Yes : none other name is given
Unto mortals under heaven,
Which can make the dead arise,
And exalt them to the skies.

That which Christ so hardly wrought,
That which He so dearly bought,
That salvation, brethren, say,
Shall we madly cast away ?

Rather gladly for that Name
Bear the cross, endure the shame ;
Joyfully for Him to die
Is not death but victory.

p Jesu, Who dost condescend
To be called the sinner's Friend,
Hear us, as to Thee we pray,
cr Glorying in Thy Name to-day.

f Glory to the Father be,
Glory, Holy Son, to Thee,
Glory to the Holy Ghost,
From the Saints and Angel-host.

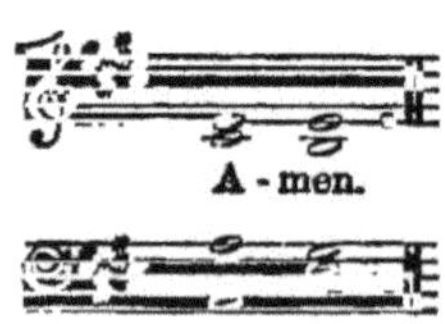

General Hymns.

Hymn 176.

"Unto you therefore which believe He is precious."

mf HOW sweet the Name of Jesus sounds
In a believer's ear!
It soothes his sorrows, heals his wounds,
And drives away his fear.

It makes the wounded spirit whole,
And calms the troubled breast;
'Tis manna to the hungry soul,
p And to the weary rest.

mf Dear Name! the rock on which I build,
My shield and hiding-place,
My never-failing treasury filled
With boundless stores of grace.

Jesus! my Shepherd, Husband, Friend,
My Prophet, Priest, and King,
My Lord, my Life, my Way, my End,
Accept the praise I bring.

p Weak is the effort of my heart,
And cold my warmest thought;
cr But when I see Thee as Thou art,
I'll praise Thee as I ought.

f Till then I would Thy love proclaim
With every fleeting breath;
dim And may the music of Thy Name
p Refresh my soul in death.

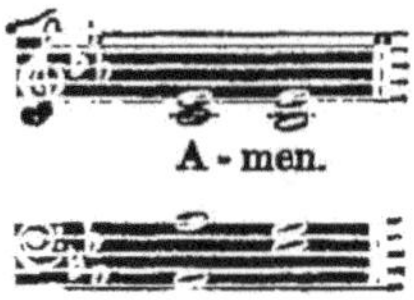

General Hymns.

Hymn 177. (First Tune.)

To be sung in Unison.

General Hymns.

Hymn 177. (Second Tune.)

"Thy Name is as ointment poured forth."

p JESU! the very thought is sweet;
In that dear Name all heart-joys meet:
cr But oh! than honey sweeter far
The glimpses of His Presence are.

mf No word is sung more sweet than this,
No sound is heard more full of bliss,
No thought brings sweeter comfort nigh,
Than Jesus, Son of God most High.

Jesu, the hope of souls forlorn,
How good to them for sin that mourn!
To them that seek Thee, oh how kind!
cr But what art Thou to them that find?

mf No tongue of mortal can express,
No pen can write the blessedness,
He only who hath proved it knows
What bliss from love of Jesus flows.

f O Jesu, King of wondrous might!
O Victor, glorious from the fight!
mf Sweetness that may not be expressed,
And altogether loveliest!

p Abide with us, O Lord, to-day,
Fulfil us with Thy grace, we pray;
cr And with Thine own true sweetness feed
Our souls from sin and darkness freed.

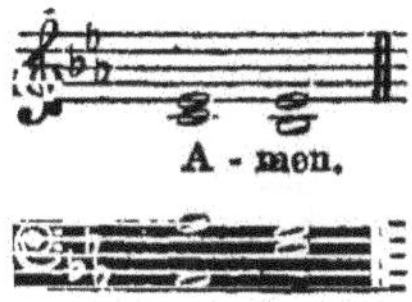

General Hymns.

Hymn 178. (First Tune.)

Hymn 178. (Second Tune.)

General Hymns.

"Thy Name is as ointment poured forth."

mf JESU, the very thought of Thee
  With sweetness fills the breast;
But sweeter far Thy Face to see,
  And in Thy Presence rest.

No voice can sing, no heart can frame,
  Nor can the memory find
A sweeter sound than JESU'S Name,
  The Saviour of mankind.

O Hope of every contrite heart,
  O Joy of all the meek,
To those who ask how kind Thou art,
  How good to those who seek!

But what to those who find? Ah! this
  Nor tongue nor pen can show;
The love of JESUS, what it is
  None but His loved ones know.

f JESU, our only Joy be Thou,
  As Thou our Prize wilt be;
In Thee be all our glory now,
  And through eternity.

PART 2.

f O JESU, King most wonderful,
  Thou Conqueror renowned,
mf Thou Sweetness most ineffable,
  In Whom all joys are found!

When once Thou visitest the heart,
  Then truth begins to shine,
Then earthly vanities depart,
  Then kindles love Divine.

f O JESU, Light of all below,
  Thou Fount of living fire,
Surpassing all the joys we know,
  And all we can desire;

mf JESU, may all confess Thy Name,
  Thy wondrous love adore,
And, seeking Thee, themselves inflame
  To seek Thee more and more.

Thee, JESU, may our voices bless,
  Thee may we love alone,
And ever in our lives express
  The image of Thine Own.

PART 3.

mf O JESU, Thou the Beauty art
  Of Angel-worlds above;
Thy Name is music to the heart,
  Inflaming it with love.

Celestial Sweetness unalloyed,
  Who eat Thee hunger still;
Who drink of Thee still feel a void
  Which only Thou canst fill.

p O most sweet JESU, hear the sighs
  Which unto Thee we send;
To Thee our inmost spirit cries,
  To Thee our prayers ascend.

Abide with us, and let Thy Light
cr Shine, LORD, on every heart;
Dispel the darkness of our night,
  And joy to all impart.

f JESU, our Love and Joy, to Thee,
  The Virgin's Holy Son,
All might, and praise, and glory be,
  While endless ages run.

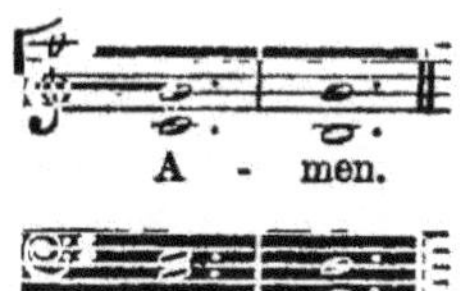

1.

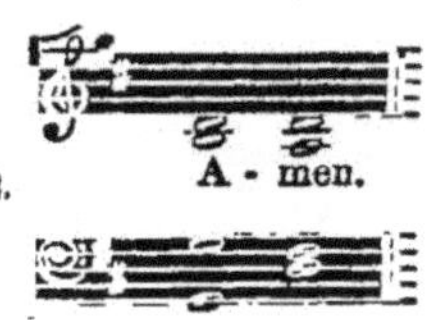

2.

General Hymns.

Hymn 179.

General Hymns.

"There is none other name under heaven given among men whereby we must be saved."

f TO the Name of our Salvation
Laud and honour let us pay,
p Which for many a generation
Hid in God's foreknowledge lay,
f But with holy exultation
We may sing aloud to-day.

mf Jesus is the Name we treasure,
Name beyond what words can tell;
Name of gladness, Name of pleasure,
Ear and heart delighting well;
Name of sweetness passing measure,
Saving us from sin and hell.

'Tis the Name for adoration,
Name for songs of victory,
Name for holy meditation
In this vale of misery,
Name for joyful veneration
By the citizens on high.

'Tis the Name that whoso preacheth
Speaks like music to the ear;
p Who in prayer this Name beseecheth
Sweetest comfort findeth near;
cr Who its perfect wisdom reacheth
mf Heavenly joy possesseth here.

f Jesus is the Name exalted
Over every other name;
In this Name, whene'er assaulted,
We can put our foes to shame;
Strength to them who else had halted,
Eyes to blind, and feet to lame.

p Therefore we in love adoring
This most blessèd Name revere,
cr Holy Jesu, Thee imploring
So to write it in us here,
That hereafter heavenward soaring
ff We may sing with Angels there.

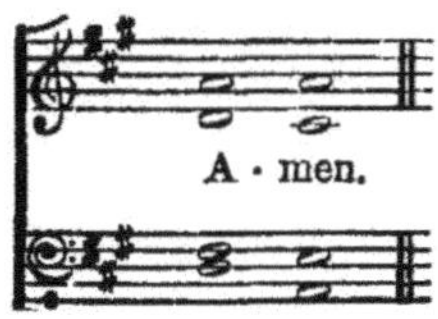

General Hymns.

Hymn 180.

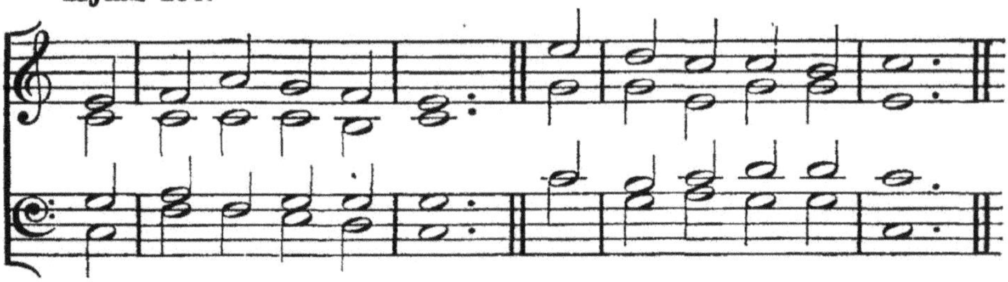

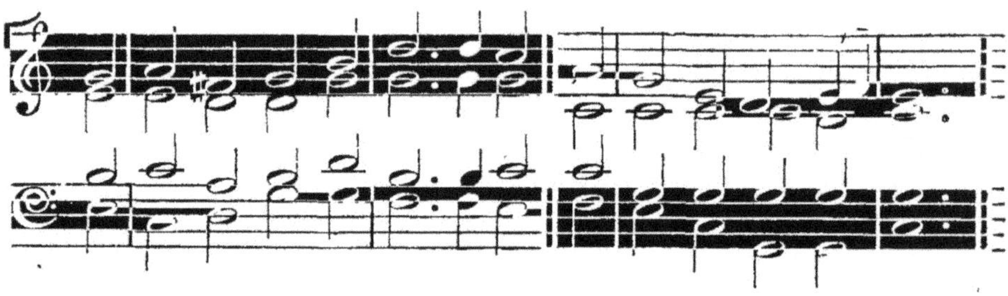

"The everlasting Father, the Prince of peace."

mf TO CHRIST, the Prince of peace,
And SON of GOD most high,
The FATHER of the world to come,
We lift our joyful cry.

p Deep in His Heart for us
The wound of love He bore,
cr That love which He enkindles still
In hearts that Him adore.

mf O JESU, Victim Blest,
What else but love Divine
Could Thee constrain to open thus
That sacred Heart of Thine?

O wondrous Fount of love,
O Well of waters free,
O heavenly Flame, refining Fire,
O burning Charity!

p Hide us in Thy dear Heart,
JESU, our Saviour Blest,
mf So shall we find Thy plenteous grace,
And heaven's eternal rest.

General Hymns.

Hymn 181.

"Thou hast been my succour: leave me not, neither forsake me, O God of my salvation."

mf We know Thee Who Thou art,
Lord Jesus, Mary's Son;
We know the yearnings of Thy Heart
To end Thy work begun.

That sacred Fount of grace,
'Mid all the bliss of heaven,
Has joy whene'er we seek Thy Face,
And kneel to be forgiven.

p Brought home from ways perverse,
At peace Thine Arms within,
We pray Thee shield us from the curse
Of falling back to sin.

mf We dare not ask to live
Henceforth from trials free;
But oh! when next they tempt us, give
More strength to cling to Thee.

We know Thee Who Thou art,
Our own redeeming Lord;
Be Thou by will, and mind, and heart,
Accepted, loved, adored.

General Hymns.

Hymn 182.

"Thou art a place to hide me in."

p JESU, grant me this, I pray,
Ever in Thy Heart to stay;
Let me evermore abide
Hidden in Thy wounded Side.

mf If the evil one prepare,
Or the world, a tempting snare,
cr I am safe when I abide
p In Thy Heart and wounded Side.

mf If the flesh, more dangerous still,
Tempt my soul to deeds of ill,
cr Nought I fear when I abide
In Thy Heart and wounded Side.

Death will come one day to me;
mf JESU, cast me not from Thee:
p Dying let me still abide
In Thy Heart and wounded Side.

General Hymns.

Hymn 183.

"Lord, to whom shall we go?"

p WHEN wounded sore the stricken heart
Lies bleeding and unbound,
cr One only Hand, *(p)* a piercèd Hand,
mf Can salve the sinner's wound.

p When sorrow swells the laden breast,
And tears of anguish flow,
cr One only Heart, *(p)* a broken Heart,
mf Can feel the sinner's woe.

p When penitential grief has wept
Over some foul dark spot,
cr One only Stream, *(p)* a Stream of Blood,
mf Can wash away the blot.

'Tis JESUS' Blood that washes white,
His Hand that brings relief,
cr His Heart is touched with all our joys,
p And feels for all our grief.

mf Lift up Thy bleeding Hand, O LORD,
Unseal that cleansing Tide;
We have no shelter from our sin
p But in Thy wounded Side.

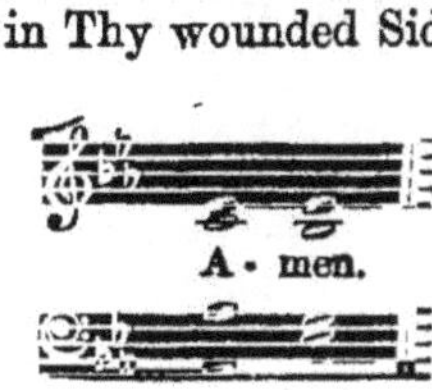

General Hymns.

Hymn 184.

"*That rock was Christ.*"

mf ROCK of ages, cleft for me,
Let me hide myself in Thee;
Let the Water and the Blood,
From Thy riven Side which flowed,
Be of sin the double cure,
Cleanse me from its guilt and power.

Not the labours of my hands
Can fulfil Thy law's demands;
Could my zeal no respite know,
Could my tears for ever flow,
All for sin could not atone;
Thou must save, and Thou alone.

p Nothing in my hand I bring,
Simply to Thy Cross I cling;
Naked, come to Thee for dress;
Helpless, look to Thee for grace;
Foul, I to the Fountain fly;
cr Wash me, Saviour, *(p)* or I die.

mf While I draw this fleeting breath,
p When my eyelids close in death,
cr When I soar through tracts unknown,
See Thee on Thy Judgment Throne:
p Rock of ages, cleft for me,
pp Let me hide myself in Thee.

General Hymns.

Hymn 185.

"O look Thou upon me, and be merciful unto me."

p LORD JESUS, think on me,
And purge away my sin;
cr From earthborn passions set me free,
And make me pure within.

p LORD JESUS, think on me
With many a care opprest,
cr Let me Thy loving servant be,
And taste Thy promised rest.

mf LORD JESUS, think on me,
Nor let me go astray;
Through darkness and perplexity
cr Point Thou the heavenly way.

p LORD JESUS, think on me,
That, when the flood is passed,
cr I may the eternal brightness see,
And share Thy joy at last.

mf LORD JESUS, think on me,
cr That I may sing above
f Praise to the FATHER, and to THEE,
And to the HOLY DOVE.

General Hymns.

Hymn 186.

General Hymns.

"Without Me ye can do nothing."

mf I COULD not do without Thee,
O Saviour of the lost,
cr Whose precious Blood redeemed me
dim At such tremendous cost;
mf Thy righteousness, Thy pardon,
Thy precious Blood must be
My only hope and comfort,
My glory and my plea.

I could not do without Thee,
I cannot stand alone,
I have no strength or goodness,
No wisdom of my own;
cr But Thou, belovèd Saviour,
Art all in all to me,
And weakness will be power
If leaning hard on Thee.

mf I could not do without Thee,
p For, oh, the way is long,
And I am often weary,
And sigh replaces song;
How could I do without Thee?
I do not know the way;
cr Thou knowest, and Thou leadest,
And wilt not let me stray.

mf I could not do without Thee,
O JESUS, Saviour dear;
E'en when my eyes are holden,
I know that Thou art near;
How dreary and how lonely
This changeful life would be
Without the sweet communion,
The secret rest with Thee.

I could not do without Thee;
No other friend can read
The spirit's strange deep longings,
Interpreting its need;
No human heart could enter
Each dim recess of mine,
dim And soothe, and hush, and calm it,
cr O Blessèd LORD, but Thine.

mf I could not do without Thee,
p For years are fleeting fast,
And soon in solemn loneliness
The river must be passed;
cr But Thou wilt never leave me,
And though the waves roll high,
f I know Thou wilt be near me,
p And whisper, "It is I."

General Hymns.

Hymn 187. (First Tune.)

Hymn 187. (Second Tune.)

Slow.

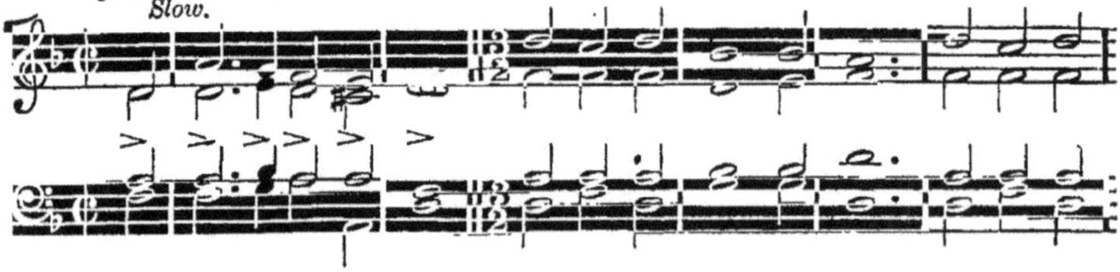

General Hymns.

"Behold the Lamb of God, which taketh away the sin of the world."

mf BEHOLD the LAMB of GOD!
p O Thou for sinners slain,
Let it not be in vain
That Thou hast died:
mf Thee for my Saviour let me take,
My only refuge let me make
p Thy piercèd Side.

mf Behold the LAMB of GOD!
p Into the sacred flood
Of Thy most precious Blood
My soul I cast:
mf Wash me and make me clean within,
And keep me pure from every sin,
p Till life be past.

mf Behold the LAMB of GOD!
All hail, Incarnate WORD,
Thou everlasting LORD,
Saviour most Blest;
Fill us with love that never faints,
Grant us with all Thy blessèd Saints
p Eternal rest.

mf Behold the LAMB of GOD!
f Worthy is He alone
To sit upon the Throne
Of GOD above;
One with the Ancient of all days,
One with the Comforter in praise,
All Light and Love.

1.

2.
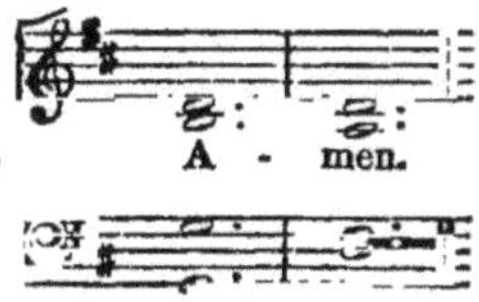

General Hymns.

Hymn 188.

"I, if I be lifted up from the earth, will draw all men unto Me."

mf JESU, meek and lowly,
Saviour, pure and holy,
On Thy love relying
Hear me humbly crying.

Prince of life and power,
My salvation's tower,
p On the Cross I view Thee
Calling sinners to Thee.

mf There behold me gazing
At the sight amazing;
p Bending low before Thee,
Helpless I adore Thee.

By Thy red Wounds streaming,
With Thy Life-blood gleaming,
Blood for sinners flowing,
Pardon free bestowing;

By that Fount of blessing,
Thy dear love expressing,
All my aching sadness
cr Turn Thou into gladness.

mf LORD, in mercy guide me,
Be Thou e'er beside me;
In Thy ways direct me,
'Neath Thy wings protect me.

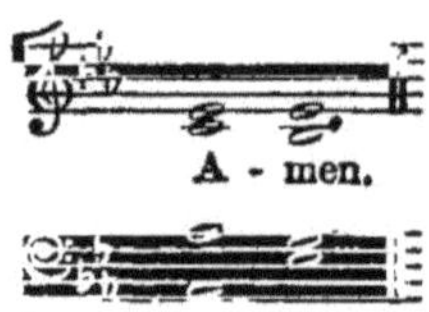

General Hymns.

Hymn 189.

"I have loved thee with an everlasting love; therefore with loving-kindness have I drawn thee."

mf JESU, Thy mercies are untold
  Through each returning day;
Thy love exceeds a thousandfold
  Whatever we can say;

That love which in Thy Passion drained
  For us Thy precious Blood:
mf That love whereby the Saints have gained
  The vision of their GOD.

'Tis Thou hast loved us from the womb,
  Pure Source of all our bliss,
Our only hope of life to come,
  Our happiness in this.

p LORD, grant us, while on earth we stay
cr   Thy love to feel and know;
p And, when from hence we pass away,
mf   To us Thy glory show.

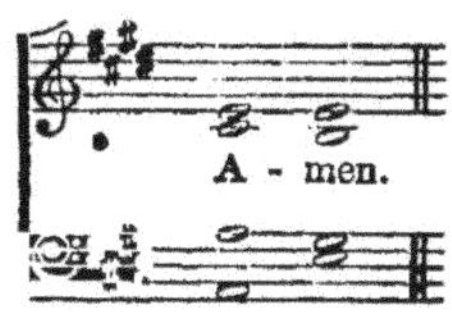

General Hymns.

Hymn 190.

"He is altogether lovely."

mf JESU, Thou Joy of loving hearts!
Thou Fount of life, Thou Light of men!
From the best bliss that earth imparts
We turn unfilled to Thee again.

Thy truth unchanged hath ever stood;
Thou savest those that on Thee call;
To them that seek Thee Thou art good;
To them that find Thee All in all.

We taste Thee, O Thou Living Bread,
And long to feast upon Thee still;
We drink of Thee, the Fountain-head,
And thirst our souls from Thee to fill.

p Our restless spirits yearn for Thee,
Where'er our changeful lot is cast;
cr Glad when Thy gracious smile we see,
Blest when our faith can hold Thee fast.

p O Jesu, ever with us stay;
Make all our moments calm and bright;
cr Chase the dark night of sin away;
Shed o'er the world Thy holy light.

General Hymns.

Hymn 191.

"Whom have I in heaven but Thee? and there is none upon earth that I desire in comparison of Thee."

mf JESU, my LORD, my GOD, my All,
Hear me, Blest Saviour, when I call;
Hear me, and from Thy dwelling-place
Pour down the riches of Thy grace;
JESU, my LORD, I Thee adore,
cr O make me love Thee more and more.

JESU, too late I Thee have sought,
How can I love Thee as I ought?
And how extol Thy matchless fame,
mf The glorious beauty of Thy Name?
JESU, my LORD, I Thee adore,
cr O make me love Thee more and more.

p JESU, what didst Thou find in me,
That Thou hast dealt so lovingly?
f How great the joy that Thou hast brought,
So far exceeding hope or thought!
mf JESU, my LORD, I Thee adore,
cr O make me love Thee more and more.

f JESU, of Thee shall be my song,
To Thee my heart and soul belong;
All that I have or am is Thine,
And Thou, Blest Saviour, Thou art mine.
mf JESU, my LORD, I Thee adore,
cr O make me love Thee more and more.

General Hymns.

Hymn 192.

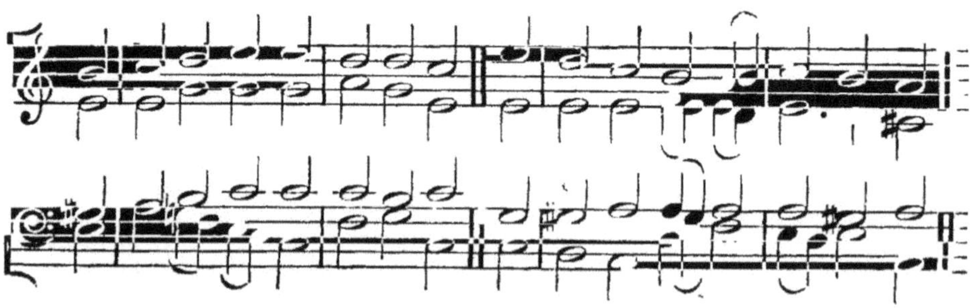

General Hymns.

"God is Love."

mf O LOVE, Who formedst me to wear
The image of Thy GODHEAD here;
p Who soughtest me with tender care
Through all my wanderings wild and drear;
cr O LOVE, I give myself to Thee,
mf Thine ever, only Thine to be.

O LOVE, Who ere life's earliest dawn
On me Thy choice hast gently laid;
p O LOVE, Who here as Man wast born,
And wholly like to us wast made;
cr O LOVE, I give myself to Thee,
mf Thine ever, only Thine to be.

p O LOVE, Who once in time wast slain,
Pierced through and through with bitter woe;
O LOVE, Who wrestling thus didst gain
That we eternal joy might know;
cr O LOVE, I give myself to Thee,
mf Thine ever, only Thine to be.

O LOVE, Who lovest me for aye,
Who for my soul dost ever plead;
p O LOVE, Who didst that ransom pay
Whose power sufficeth in my stead;
cr O LOVE, I give myself to Thee,
mf Thine ever, only Thine to be.

O LOVE, Who once shalt bid me rise
From out this dying life of ours;
O LOVE, Who once o'er yonder skies
Shalt set me in the fadeless bowers;
cr O LOVE, I give myself to Thee,
Thine ever, only Thine to be.

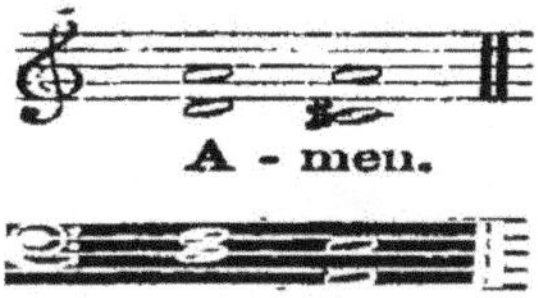

General Hymns.

Hymn 193.

General Hymns.

"A Man shall be as an hiding place from the wind, and a covert from the tempest."

p JESU, Lover of my soul,
Let me to Thy Bosom fly,
cr While the gathering waters roll,
While the tempest still is high:
mf Hide me, O my Saviour, hide,
Till the storm of life be past;
dim Safe into the haven guide,
p O receive my soul at last.

mf Other refuge have I none;
Hangs my helpless soul on Thee;
p Leave, ah! leave me not alone,
Still support and comfort me.
cr All my trust on Thee is stayed,
All my help from Thee I bring;
Cover my defenceless head
p With the shadow of Thy wing.

mf Plenteous grace with Thee is found,
Grace to cleanse from every sin;
cr Let the healing streams abound;
f Make and keep me pure within;
Thou of Life the Fountain art;
Freely let me take of Thee;
Spring Thou up within my heart,
Rise to all eternity.

General Hymns.

Hymn 194.

"Lord, save us."

p JESU, meek and gentle,
Son of God most High,
Pitying, loving Saviour,
Hear Thy children's cry.

Pardon our offences,
Loose our captive chains,
Break down every idol
Which our soul detains.

mf Give us holy freedom,
Fill our hearts with love,
Draw us, Holy Jesus,
To the realms above.

p Lead us on our journey,
cr Be Thyself the Way
Through terrestrial darkness
f To celestial day.

p Jesu, meek and gentle,
Son of God most High,
Pitying, loving Saviour,

General Hymns.

Hymn 195.

"Mary hath chosen that good part, which shall not be taken away from her."

mf O LOVE Divine, how sweet thou art!
When shall I find my willing heart
All taken up by thee?
cr I thirst, I faint, I die to prove
The greatness of redeeming love,
The love of Christ to me.

mf Stronger His love than death or hell;
Its riches are unsearchable;
The first-born sons of light
Desire in vain its depths to see;
They cannot reach the mystery,
The length, and breadth, and height.

God only knows the love of God;
O that it now were shed abroad
In this poor stony heart!
For love I sigh, for love I pine;
This only portion, Lord, be mine,
Be mine this better part.

For ever would I take my seat
With Mary at the Master's feet;
Be this my happy choice;
My only care, delight, and bliss,
cr My joy, my heaven on earth, be this,
To hear the Bridegroom's voice.

General Hymns.

Hymn 196.

"This God is our God for ever and ever; He shall be our guide unto death."

mf GUIDE me, O Thou great Redeemer,
  Pilgrim through this barren land;
I am weak, but *(f)* Thou art mighty,
  Hold me with Thy powerful hand;
    Bread of heaven,
cr Feed me now and evermore.

mf Open now the crystal fountain,
  Whence the healing streams do flow:
Let the fiery cloudy pillar
  Lead me all my journey through;
    Strong Deliverer,
Be Thou still my Strength and Shield.

p When I tread the verge of Jordan,
  Bid my anxious fears subside:
f Death of death, and hell's Destruction,
  Land me safe on Canaan's side;
ff   Songs of praises
I will ever give to Thee.

General Hymns.

Hymn 197.

"The Lord is my Shepherd."

mf THE King of love my Shepherd is,
   Whose goodness faileth never;
I nothing lack if I am His
   And He is mine for ever.

Where streams of living water flow
   My ransomed soul He leadeth,
And, where the verdant pastures grow,
   With food celestial feedeth.

p Perverse and foolish oft I strayed,
cr   But yet in love He sought me,
dim And on His Shoulder gently laid,
f   And home, rejoicing, brought me.

p In death's dark vale I fear no ill
cr   With Thee, dear LORD, beside me;
Thy rod and staff my comfort still,
   Thy Cross before to guide me.

mf Thou spread'st a Table in my sight;
   Thy Unction grace bestoweth;
f And oh, what transport of delight
   From Thy pure Chalice floweth!

mf And so through all the length of days
   Thy goodness faileth never:
cr Good Shepherd, may I sing Thy praise
   Within Thy house for ever.

General Hymns.

Hymn 198.

General Hymns.

"Behold, I stand at the door and knock."

p O JESU, Thou art standing,
Outside the fast-closed door,
In lowly patience waiting
To pass the threshold o'er:
f Shame on us, Christian brethren,
His Name and sign who bear,
Oh shame, thrice shame upon us
p To keep Him standing there!

O Jesu, Thou art knocking:
And lo! that Hand is scarred,
And thorns Thy Brow encircle,
And tears Thy Face have marred
cr O love that passeth knowledge
So patiently to wait!
dim O sin that hath no equal
p So fast to bar the gate!

O Jesu, Thou art pleading
In accents meek and low,
"I died for you, My children,
cr And will ye treat Me so?"
mf O Lord, with shame and sorrow
We open now the door:
Dear Saviour, enter, enter,
And leave us never more.

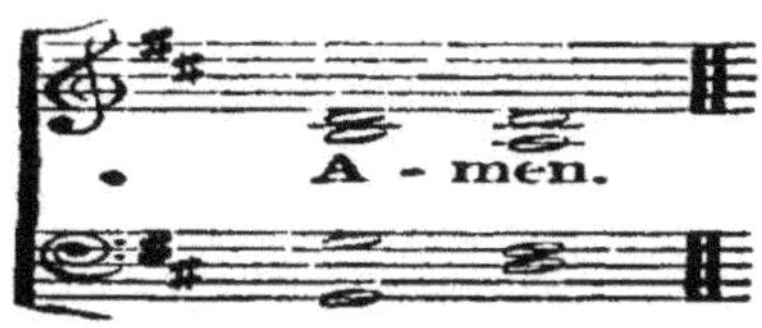

General Hymns.

Hymn 199.

"Jesus saith unto him, I am the way, the truth, and the life."

mf THOU art the Way; by Thee alone
  From sin and death we flee:
And he who would the Father seek
  Must seek Him, Lord, by Thee.

Thou art the Truth; Thy Word alone
  True wisdom can impart;
Thou only canst inform the mind,
  And purify the heart.

Thou art the Life; *(f)* the rending tomb
  Proclaims Thy conquering arm;
mf And those who put their trust in Thee
  Nor death nor hell shall harm.

Thou art the Way, the Truth, the Life,
p Grant us that Way to know,
That Truth to keep, that Life to win,
mf Whose joys eternal flow.

General Hymns.

Hymn 200.

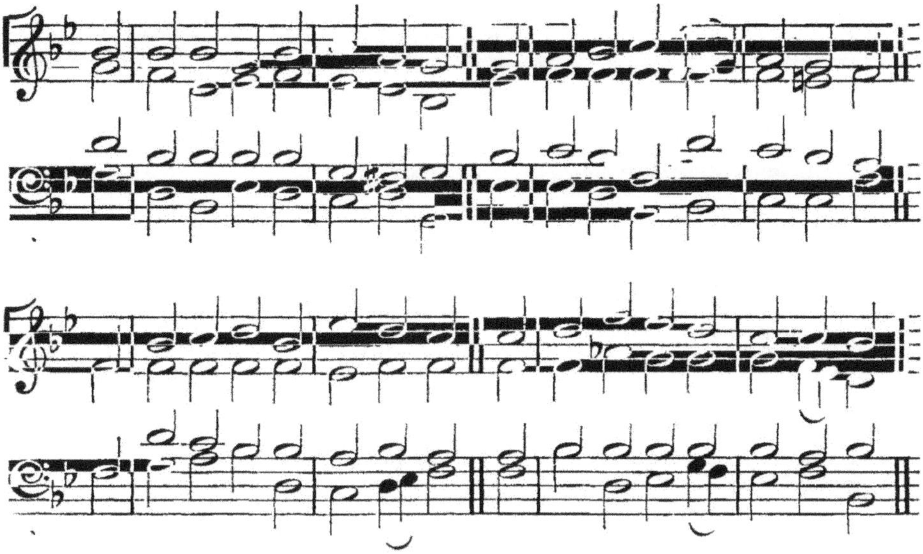

"God forbid that I should glory, save in the cross of our Lord Jesus Christ."

mf WE sing the praise of Him Who died,
p Of Him Who died upon the Cross;
cr The sinner's hope let men deride,
For this we count the world but loss.

mf Inscribed upon the Cross we see
In shining letters, "God is Love;"
p He bears our sins upon the Tree;
cr He brings us mercy from above.

f The Cross! it takes our guilt away;
It holds the fainting spirit up;
It cheers with hope the gloomy day,
And sweetens every bitter cup.

It makes the coward spirit brave,
And nerves the feeble arm for fight;
It takes its terror from the grave,
And gilds the bed of death with light.

The balm of life, the cure of woe,
The measure and the pledge of love,
The sinner's refuge here below,
The Angel's theme in heaven above.

mf To Christ, Who won for sinners grace
p By bitter grief and anguish sore,
f Be praise from all the ransomed race
For ever and for evermore.

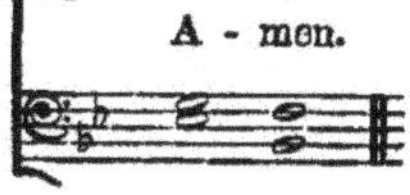

General Hymns.

Hymn 201.

"Who also maketh intercession for us."

mf WHERE high the heavenly temple stands,
The house of God not made with hands,
A great High-Priest our nature wears,
The Guardian of mankind appears.

He Who for men their Surety stood,
p And poured on earth His precious Blood,
cr Pursues in heaven His mighty plan,
The Saviour and the Friend of man.

mf Though now ascended up on high,
He bends on earth a brother's eye;
Partaker of the human name,
He knows the frailty of our frame.

Our fellow-sufferer yet retains
A fellow-feeling of our pains;
And still remembers in the skies
p His tears, His agonies, and cries.

mf In every pang that rends the heart
The Man of Sorrows had a part;
He sympathizes with our grief,
And to the sufferer sends relief.

With boldness therefore at the Throne
Let us make all our sorrows known;
And ask the aid of heavenly power
To help us in the evil hour.

General Hymns.

Hymn 202.

"Rejoice in the Lord alway, and again I say, rejoice."

f REJOICE, the LORD is King,
dim Your LORD and King adore;
cr Mortals, give thanks and sing,
And triumph evermore:
f Lift up your heart, lift up your voice;
Rejoice, again I say, rejoice.

mf JESUS, the Saviour, reigns,
The GOD of truth and love:
p When He had purged our stains,
cr He took His seat above:
f Lift up your heart, lift up your voice;
Rejoice, again I say, rejoice.

mf His Kingdom cannot fail;
He rules o'er earth and heaven;
The keys of death and hell
Are to our JESUS given:
f Lift up your heart, lift up your voice;
Rejoice, again I say, rejoice.

mf He sits at GOD's right hand
Till all His foes submit,
And bow to His command,
And fall beneath His feet:
f Lift up your heart, lift up your voice;
ff Rejoice, again I say, rejoice.

General Hymns.

Hymn 203.

General Hymns.

"He . . . saith, Surely I come quickly; Amen. Even so, come, Lord Jesus."

f THOU art coming, O my Saviour,
Thou art coming, O my King,
mf In Thy beauty all-resplendent,
cr In Thy glory all-transcendent;
f Well may we rejoice and sing;
p Coming! *(cr)* In the opening east
Herald brightness slowly swells;
p Coming! *(cr)* O my glorious Priest,
dim Hear we not Thy golden bells?

mf Thou art coming; we are waiting
With a hope that cannot fail,
Asking not the day or hour,
Resting on Thy word of power,
Anchored safe within the veil.
p Time appointed may be long,
cr But the vision must be sure;
Certainty shall make us strong,
Joyful patience can endure.

mf Thou art coming, Thou art coming;
We shall meet Thee on Thy way,
We shall see Thee, we shall know Thee,
cr We shall bless Thee, we shall show Thee
All our hearts could never say;
mf What an anthem that will be
Ringing out our love to Thee,
Pouring out our rapture sweet
cr At Thine own all-glorious Feet.

f O the joy to see Thee reigning,
Thee, my own belovèd LORD!
Every tongue Thy Name confessing,
Worship, honour, glory, blessing
Brought to Thee with one accord,
p Thee, my Master, and my Friend,
f Vindicated and enthroned,
cr Unto earth's remotest end
Glorified, adored, and owned!

mf Thou art coming; at Thy Table
We are witnesses for this;
p While remembering hearts Thou meetest
In communion clearest, sweetest,
cr Earnest of our coming bliss,
mf Shewing not Thy death alone,
And Thy love exceeding great,
cr But Thy coming, and Thy Throne,
dim All for which we long and wait.

General Hymns.

Hymn 204.

General Hymns.

"He . . . saith, Surely I come quickly: Amen. Even so, come, Lord Jesus."

mf O QUICKLY come, dread Judge of all;
p For, awful though Thine advent be,
cr All shadows from the truth will fall,
dim And falsehood die, in sight of Thee:
cr O quickly come: for doubt and fear
Like clouds dissolve when Thou art near.

mf O quickly come, great King of all;
Reign all around us, and within;
Let sin no more our souls enthral,
Let pain and sorrow die with sin:
cr O quickly come: for Thou alone
Canst make Thy scattered people one.

mf O quickly come, true Life of all;
p For death is mighty all around;
On every home his shadows fall,
On every heart his mark is found:
cr O quickly come: for grief and pain
f Can never cloud Thy glorious reign.

mf O quickly come, sure Light of all,
p For gloomy night broods o'er our way;
And weakly souls begin to fall
With weary watching for the day:
cr O quickly come: for round Thy Throne
f No eye is blind, no night is known.

General Hymns.

Hymn 205.

Rather Slow.

"Take ye heed, watch and pray; for ye know not when the time is."

p THOU Judge of quick and dead,
Before Whose bar severe
mf With holy joy, or (*p*) guilty dread,
We all shall soon appear;

mf Our wakened souls prepare
For that tremendous day,
And fill us now with watchful care,
And stir us up to pray:

To pray, and wait the hour,
p The awful hour unknown,
cr When, robed in majesty and power,
Thou shalt from heaven come down,

mf The immortal SON of Man,
To judge the human race,
With all Thy FATHER's dazzling train,
With all Thy glorious grace.

p To sober earthly joys,
To quicken holy fears,
cr For ever let the Archangel's voice
Be sounding in our ears;

p The solemn midnight cry,
f "Ye dead, the Judge is come!
Arise, and meet Him in the sky,
And meet your instant doom!"

p O may we thus be found
Obedient to His Word,
cr Attentive to the trumpet's sound,
And looking for our LORD.

mf O may we thus insure
Our lot among the blest,
And watch a moment, to secure
An everlasting rest.

General Hymns.

Hymn 206.

Slow.

"The day of the Lord will come as a thief in the night."

mf THAT day of wrath, that dreadful day,
When heaven and earth shall pass away,
What power shall be the sinner's stay?
How shall he meet that dreadful day?

When, shrivelling like a parchèd scroll,
The flaming heavens together roll;
cr When louder yet, and yet more dread,
ff Swells the high trump that wakes the dead;

p Oh, on that day, that wrathful day,
When man to judgment wakes from clay,
cr Be Thou, O CHRIST, the sinner's stay,
dim Though heaven and earth shall pass away.

General Hymns.

Hymn 207.

"If I go not away, the Comforter will not come unto you; but if I depart, I will send Him unto you."

p OUR Blest Redeemer, ere He breathed
His tender last farewell,
A Guide, a Comforter, bequeathed
With us to dwell.

mf He came sweet influence to impart,
A gracious willing Guest,
While He can find one humble heart
Wherein to rest.

p And His that gentle voice we hear,
Soft as the breath of even,
That checks each fault, that calms each fear,
And speaks of heaven.

cr And every virtue we possess,
And every conquest won,
And every thought of holiness,
mf Are His alone.

SPIRIT of purity and grace,
Our weakness, pitying, see:
O make our hearts Thy dwelling-place,
And worthier Thee.

General Hymns.

Hymn 208.

"The communion of the Holy Ghost."

mf O HOLY SPIRIT, LORD of grace,
Eternal Fount of love,
Inflame, we pray, our inmost hearts
With fire from heaven above.

As Thou in bond of love dost join
The FATHER and the SON,
So fill us all with mutual love,
And knit our hearts in one.

f All glory to the FATHER be,
All glory to the SON,
All glory, HOLY GHOST, to Thee,
While endless ages run.

General Hymns.

Hymn 209.

"As many as are led by the Spirit of God, they are the sons of God."

mf COME, gracious Spirit, heavenly Dove,
With light and comfort from above;
Be Thou our Guardian, Thou our Guide,
O'er every thought and step preside.

The light of truth to us display,
And make us know and choose Thy way;
p Plant holy fear in every heart,
cr That we from God may ne'er depart.

mf Lead us to Christ, the living Way,
Nor let us from His pastures stray;
Lead us to holiness, the road
That we must take to dwell with God.

Lead us to heaven, that we may share
Fulness of joy for ever there;
Lead us to God, our final rest,
To be with Him for ever blest.

General Hymns.

Hymn 210.

"And now abideth faith, hope, charity, these three; but the greatest of these is charity."

mf GRACIOUS SPIRIT, HOLY GHOST,
  Taught by Thee, we covet most,
Of Thy gifts at Pentecost,
  Holy, heavenly love.

Love is kind and suffers long,
Love is meek, and thinks no wrong,
Love than death itself more strong;
  Therefore give us love.

Prophecy will fade away,
Melting in the light of day;
Love will ever with us stay;
  Therefore give us love.

Faith will vanish into sight;
Hope be emptied in delight;
cr Love in heaven will shine more bright
  Therefore give us love.

mf Faith and hope and love we see
Joining hand in hand agree;
cr But the greatest of the three,
  And the best, is love.

p From the overshadowing
Of Thy gold and silver wing
Shed on us, who to Thee sing,
  Holy, heavenly love.

General Hymns.

Hymn 211.

"Awake, O north wind; and come, thou south; blow upon my garden, that the spices thereof may flow out."

mf O HOLY GHOST, Thy people bless
Who long to feel Thy might,
And fain would grow in holiness
As children of the light.

To Thee we bring, Who art the LORD,
Our selves to be Thy throne;
Let every thought, and deed, and word
Thy pure dominion own.

Life-giving SPIRIT, o'er us move,
dim As on the formless deep;
cr Give life and order, light and love,
p Where now is death or sleep.

f Great Gift of our ascended King,
His saving truth reveal;
Our tongues inspire His praise to sing,
Our hearts His love to feel.

mf True Wind of heaven, from south or [north,
For joy (*dim*) or chastening, blow;
cr The garden-spices shall spring forth
If Thou wilt bid them flow.

f O HOLY GHOST, of sevenfold might,
All graces come from Thee;
p Grant us to know and serve aright
ONE GOD in Persons THREE.

General Hymns.

Hymn 212.

"He is faithful."

mf TO Thee, O Comforter Divine,
For all Thy grace and power benign,
f Sing we Alleluia!

To Thee, Whose faithful love had place
In GOD's great covenant of grace,
Sing we Alleluia!

mf To Thee, Whose faithful voice doth win
The wandering from the ways of sin,
f Sing we Alleluia!

To Thee, Whose faithful power doth heal,
Enlighten, sanctify, and seal,
Sing we Alleluia!

mf To Thee, Whose faithful truth is shown
By every promise made our own,
f Sing we Alleluia!

To Thee, our Teacher and our Friend,
Our faithful Leader to the end,
Sing we Alleluia!

mf To Thee, by JESUS CHRIST sent down,
f Of all His gifts the sum and crown,
ff Sing we Alleluia!

f To Thee, Who art with GOD the SON
And GOD the FATHER ever ONE,
ff Sing we Alleluia!

General Hymns.

Hymn 213.

"And he shewed me a pure river of water of life, clear as crystal, proceeding out of the throne of God and of the Lamb."

mf A LIVING stream, as crystal clear,
Welling from out the Throne
Of God and of the Lamb on high,
The Lord to man hath shown.

This stream doth water Paradise,
It makes the Angels sing:
cr One precious drop within the heart
Is of all joy the spring:

f Joy past all speech, of glory full,
dim But stored where none may know,
As manna hid in dewy heaven,
As pearls in ocean low.

p Eye hath not seen, nor ear hath heard,
Nor to man's heart hath come
What for those loving Thee in truth
Thou hast in love's own home.

mf But by His Spirit He to us
The secret doth reveal:
cr Faith sees and hears: but O for wings
That we might taste, and feel;

Wings like a dove to waft us on
High o'er the flood of sin!
p Lord of the Ark, put forth Thine hand,
And take Thy wanderers in.

f O praise the Father, praise the Son,
The Lamb for sinners given,
And Holy Ghost, through Whom alone
Our hearts are raised to heaven.

Hymn 214.

"Help us, O God of our salvation, for the glory of Thy Name."

mf LORD of our life, and GOD of our salvation,
Star of our night, and Hope of every nation,
p Hear and *(cr)* receive Thy Church's supplication,
f LORD GOD Almighty.

mf See round Thine ark the hungry billows curling;
See how Thy foes their banners are unfurling;
p LORD, while their *(cr)* darts envenomed they are hurling,
f Thou canst preserve us.

mf LORD, Thou canst help when earthly armour faileth,
LORD, Thou canst save when deadly sin assaileth,
p LORD, o'er Thy *(cr)* Church nor death nor hell prevaileth;
p Grant us Thy peace, LORD.

mf Grant us Thy help till foes are backward driven,
Grant them Thy truth, that they may be forgiven,
p Grant peace on earth, *(cr)* and, after we have striven,
pp Peace in Thy heaven.

General Hymns.

Hymn 215.

General Hymns.

"He is the Head of the body, the Church."

mf THE Church's one foundation
  Is JESUS CHRIST her LORD;
She is His new creation
  By water and the Word:
From heaven He came and sought her
  To be His holy Bride;
p With His own Blood He bought her,
pp   And for her life He died.

mf Elect from every nation,
  Yet one o'er all the earth,
Her charter of salvation
  One LORD, one Faith, one Birth,
One Holy Name she blesses,
  Partakes one Holy Food,
And to one hope she presses
  With every grace endued.

p Though with a scornful wonder
  Men see her sore opprest,
By schisms rent asunder,
  By heresies distrest,
cr Yet Saints their watch are keeping,
  Their cry goes up, "How long?"
mf And soon the night of weeping
cr   Shall be the morn of song.

mf Mid toil, and tribulation,
  And tumult of her war,
She waits the consummation
p   Of peace for evermore;
cr Till with the vision glorious
  Her longing eyes are blest,
f And the great Church victorious
dim   Shall be the Church at rest.

mf Yet she on earth hath union
  With GOD the THREE in ONE,
And mystic sweet communion
  With those whose rest is won:
f O happy ones and holy!
p   LORD, give us grace that we,
Like them the meek and lowly,
cr   On high may dwell with Thee.

General Hymns.

Hymn 216.

General Hymns.

"That they all may be one."

p WHAT time the evening shadows fall
Around the Church on earth,
When darker forms of doubt appal,
And new false lights have birth;
cr Then closer should her faithful band
For Truth together hold,
Hell's last devices to withstand,
And safely guard her fold.

p O FATHER, in that hour of fear
The Church of England keep,
mf Thine Altar to the last to rear,
And feed Thy fainting sheep;
May she the holy truths attest
Apostles taught of yore,
Nor quit the Faith by saints confest,
Though tempted ne'er so sore.

p O CHRIST, Who for Thy flock didst pray
That all might be as one,
mf Unite us all ere fades the day,
Thou Sole-Begotten SON;
The East, the West, together bind
In love's unbroken chain;
cr Give each one hope, one heart, one mind,
One glory, and one gain.

f O SPIRIT, LORD of light and life,
The Church with strength renew,
p Compose the angry voice of strife,
All jealousies subdue:
cr Do Thou in ever-quickening streams
Upon Thy saints descend,
And warm them with reviving beams,
And guide them to the end.

mf Great THREE in ONE, great ONE in THREE,
Our hymns of prayer receive,
And teach us all from sin to flee,
And live as we believe;
cr So, pure in faith, our thoughts and speech
And acts that faith shall own;
f So shall we to Thy Presence reach,
And know as we are known.

General Hymns.

Hymn 217.

"Thy kingdom come."

mf THY kingdom come, O God,
Thy rule, O Christ, begin;
Break with Thine iron rod
The tyrannies of sin.

p Where is Thy reign of peace,
And purity, and love?
When shall all hatred cease,
As in the realms above?

When comes the promised time
That war shall be no more,
And lust, oppression, crime
Shall flee Thy Face before?

mf We pray Thee, Lord, arise,
And come in Thy great might
Revive our longing eyes,
Which languish for Thy sight.

p Men scorn Thy sacred Name,
And wolves devour Thy fold;
By many deeds of shame
We learn that love grows cold.

O'er heathen lands afar
Thick darkness broodeth yet:
cr Arise, O morning Star,
f Arise, and never set.

General Hymns.

Hymn 218.

"God be merciful unto us, and bless us; and shew us the light of His countenance."

mf GOD of mercy, GOD of grace,
Shew the brightness of Thy Face;
Shine upon us, Saviour, shine,
Fill Thy Church with light Divine;
And Thy saving health extend
Unto earth's remotest end.

f Let the people praise Thee, LORD;
Be by all that live adored;
Let the nations shout and sing
Glory to their Saviour King;
p At Thy feet their tribute pay,
And Thy holy Will obey.

f Let the people praise Thee, LORD;
Earth shall then her fruits afford,
GOD to man His blessing give,
Man to GOD devoted live;
All below, and all above,
One in joy, and light, and love.

General Hymns.

Hymn 219.

General Hymns.

"All the earth shall be filled with His Majesty"

f HAIL to the LORD's Anointed,
   Great David's greater Son!
Hail, in the time appointed,
   His reign on earth begun!
He comes to break oppression,
   To set the captive free,
To take away transgression,
   And rule in equity.

mf He shall come down like showers
   Upon the fruitful earth,
And joy and hope, like flowers,
   Spring in His path to birth:
Before Him on the mountains
p   Shall peace, the herald, go;
cr From hill to vale the fountains
   Of righteousness o'erflow.

mf Kings shall bow down before Him,
   And gold and incense bring;
All nations shall adore Him,
   His praise all people sing;
To Him shall prayer unceasing
   And daily vows ascend;
His kingdom still increasing,
   A kingdom without end.

f O'er every foe victorious,
   He on His Throne shall rest;
From age to age more glorious,
   All-blessing and all-blessed:
The tide of time shall never
   His covenant remove;
His Name shall stand for ever,
p   His changeless Name of love.

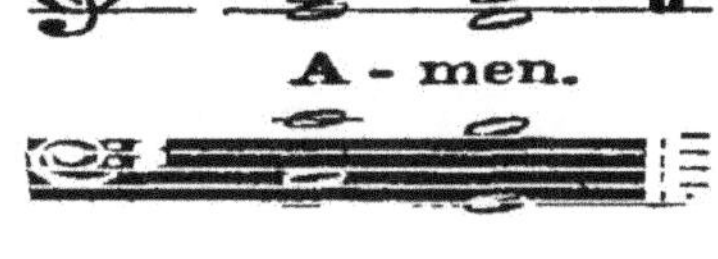

General Hymns.

Hymn 220.

"The kingdoms of this world are become the kingdoms of our Lord and of His Christ; and He shall reign for ever and ever."

f JESUS shall reign where'er the sun
Doth his successive journeys run;
His kingdom stretch from shore to shore,
Till moons shall wax and wane no more.

f Blessings abound where'er He reigns
The prisoner leaps to lose his chains ·
dim The weary find eternal rest,
cr And all the sons of want are blest.

mf People and realms of every tongue
Dwell on His love with sweetest song,
p And infant voices shall proclaim
cr Their early blessings on His Name.

f Let every creature rise and bring
Peculiar honours to our King;
Angels descend with songs again,
And earth repeat the loud Amen.

General Hymns.

Hymn 221.

"Of Whom the whole family in heaven and earth is named."

mf LET saints on earth in concert sing
  With those whose work is done;
For all the servants of our King
  In heaven and earth are one.

One family, we dwell in Him,
  One Church, above, beneath;
dim Though now divided by the stream
p   The narrow stream of death.

mf One army of the living God,
  To His command we bow;
Part of the host have crossed the flood,
p   And part are crossing now.

E'en now to their eternal home
  There pass some spirits blest;
While others to the margin come,
  Waiting their call to rest.

mf Jesu, be Thou our constant Guide;
  Then, when the word is given,
Bid Jordan's narrow stream divide,
cr   And bring us safe to heaven.

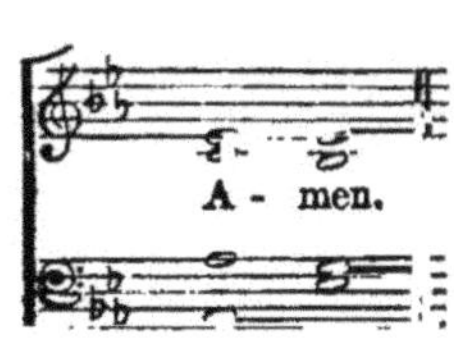

General Hymns.

Hymn 222.

General Hymns.

"*God shall wipe away all tears from their eyes.*"

f TEN thousand times ten thousand,
In sparkling raiment bright,
The armies of the ransomed Saints
Throng up the steeps of light:
mf 'Tis finished! all is finished,
Their fight with death and sin;
f Fling open wide the golden gates,
And let the victors in.

What rush of Alleluias
Fills all the earth and sky!
What ringing of a thousand harps
Bespeaks the triumph nigh!
O day, for which creation
And all its tribes were made!
O joy, for all its former woes
A thousand-fold repaid!

mf Oh, then what raptured greetings
On Canaan's happy shore,
What knitting severed friendships up,
Where partings are no more!
f Then eyes with joy shall sparkle
p That brimmed with tears of late;
cr Orphans no longer fatherless,
Nor widows desolate.

p Bring near Thy great salvation,
Thou LAMB for sinners slain,
cr Fill up the roll of Thine elect,
f Then take Thy power and reign:
mf Appear, Desire of nations,
p Thine exiles long for home;
cr Shew in the heavens Thy promised sign;
f Thou Prince and Saviour, come.

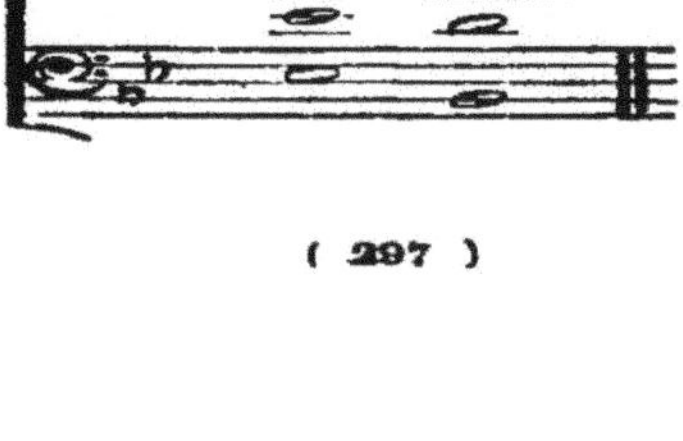

General Hymns.

Hymn 223. (First Tune.)

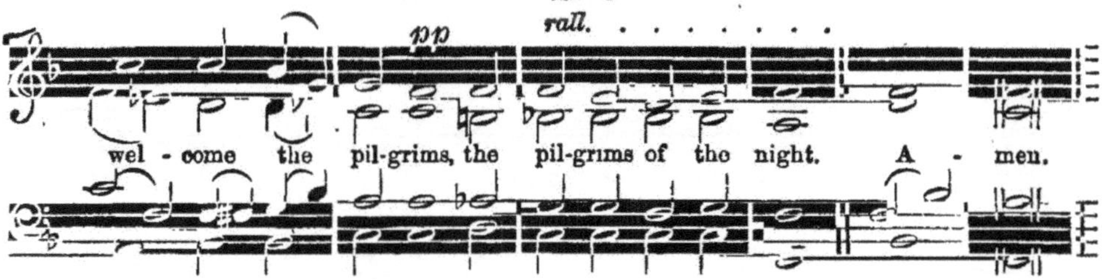

"The night is far spent, the day is at hand."

HARK! hark, my soul! Angelic songs are swelling
  O'er earth's green fields, and ocean's wave-beat shore:
How sweet the truth those blessèd strains are telling
  Of that new life when sin shall be no more.
Angels of JESUS, Angels of light,
Singing to welcome the pilgrims of the night!

Onward we go, for still we hear them singing,
  "Come, weary souls, for JESUS bids you come:"
And through the dark, its echoes sweetly ringing,
  The music of the Gospel leads us home.
Angels of JESUS, Angels of light,
Singing to welcome the pilgrims of the night!

Far, far away, like bells at evening pealing,
  The voice of JESUS sounds o'er land and sea,
And laden souls, by thousands meekly stealing,
  Kind Shepherd, turn their weary steps to Thee.
Angels of JESUS, Angels of light,
Singing to welcome the pilgrims of the night!

Rest comes at length; though life be long and dreary,
  The day must dawn, and darksome night be past;
Faith's journey ends in welcome to the weary,
  And heaven, the heart's true home, will come at last.
Angels of JESUS, Angels of light,
Singing to welcome the pilgrims of the night!

Angels! sing on, your faithful watches keeping,
  Sing us sweet fragments of the songs above;
Till morning's joy shall end the night of weeping,
  And life's long shadows break in cloudless love.
Angels of JESUS, Angels of light,
Singing to welcome the pilgrims of the night!

General Hymns.

Hymn 223. (Second Tune.)

General Hymns.

" The night is far spent, the day is at hand."

mf HARK ! hark, my soul ! Angelic songs are swelling
O'er earth's green fields, and ocean's wave-beat shore
How sweet the truth those blessèd strains are telling
Of that new life when sin shall be no more.
p Angels of Jesus, *(cr)* Angels of light,
f Singing to welcome *(p)* the pilgrims of the night !

mf Onward we go, for still we hear them singing,
p "Come, weary souls, for Jesus bids you come :"
cr And through the dark, its echoes sweetly ringing,
The music of the Gospel leads us home.
p Angels of Jesus, *(cr)* Angels of light,
f Singing to welcome *(p)* the pilgrims of the night !

p Far, far away, like bells at evening pealing,
The voice of Jesus sounds o'er land and sea,
And laden souls, by thousands meekly stealing,
cr Kind Shepherd, turn their weary steps to Thee.
p Angels of Jesus, *(cr)* Angels of light,
f Singing to welcome *(p)* the pilgrims of the night !

mf Rest comes at length ; though life be long and dreary,
The day must dawn, and darksome night be past ;
Faith's journey ends in welcome to the weary,
And heaven, the heart's true home, will come at last.
p Angels of Jesus, *(cr)* Angels of light,
f Singing to welcome *(p)* the pilgrims of the night !

mf Angels ! sing on, your faithful watches keeping,
Sing us sweet fragments of the songs above ;
Till morning's joy shall end the night of weeping,
cr And life's long shadows break in cloudless love.
p Angels of Jesus, *(cr)* Angels of light,
f Singing to welcome the pilgrims of the night !

General Hymns.

Hymn 224.

"The fellowship of His sufferings."

mf O HAPPY band of pilgrims,
If onward ye will tread
With JESUS as your Fellow
To JESUS as your Head!

O happy if ye labour
As JESUS did for men:
O happy if ye hunger
As JESUS hungered then!

p The Cross that JESUS carried
He carried as your due:
f The Crown that JESUS weareth
He weareth it for you.

mf The faith by which ye see Him,
The hope in which ye yearn,
The love that through all troubles
To Him alone will turn,

p The trials that beset you,
The sorrows ye endure,
The manifold temptations
That death alone can cure,

cr What are they but His jewels
Of right celestial worth?
What are they but the ladder
Set up to heaven on earth?

f O happy band of pilgrims,
Look upward to the skies,
dim Where such a light affliction
f Shall win so great a prize.

General Hymns.

Hymn 225.

"Here have we no continuing city, but we seek one to come."

p BRIEF life is here our portion;
Brief sorrow, short-lived care;
cr The life that knows no ending,
The tearless life, is there.

mf O happy retribution!
Short toil, eternal rest;
For mortals and for sinners
A mansion with the blest!

And now we fight the battle,
f But then shall wear the crown
Of full and everlasting
And passionless renown;

p And now we watch and struggle,
And now we live in hope,
And Sion in her anguish
With Babylon must cope;

mf But He, Whom now we trust in,
Shall then be seen and known;
And they that know and see Him
Shall have Him for their own.

cr The morning shall awaken,
The shadows shall decay,
And each true-hearted servant
Shall shine as doth the day.

f There God, our King and Portion
In fulness of His grace,
Shall we behold for ever,
p And worship face to face.

mf O sweet and blessèd country,
The home of God's elect!
O sweet and blessèd country
That eager hearts expect!

p Jesu, in mercy bring us
To that dear land of rest;
mf Who art, with God the Father
And Spirit, ever Blest.

General Hymns.

Hymn 226.

General Hymns.

"The nations of them which are saved shall walk in the light of it."

mf THE world is very evil,
  The times are waxing late,
p Be sober and keep vigil,
  The Judge is at the gate;
The Judge Who comes in mercy,
cr The Judge Who comes with might,
Who comes to end the evil,
f Who comes to crown the right.

mf Arise, arise, good Christian,
  Let right to wrong succeed;
p Let penitential sorrow
cr To heavenly gladness lead,
To light that has no evening,
  That knows nor moon nor sun,
The light so new and golden,
  The light that is but one.

mf O home of fadeless splendour,
  Of flowers that fear no thorn,
Where they shall dwell as children
p Who here as exiles mourn;
mf 'Midst power that knows no limit,
  Where wisdom has no bound,
p The Beatific Vision
cr Shall glad the Saints around.

mf O happy, holy portion,
  Refection for the blest,
True vision of true beauty,
  True cure of the distrest!
f Strive, man, to win that glory;
  Toil, man, to gain that light;
Send hope before to grasp it,
  Till hope be lost in sight.

mf O sweet and blessèd country,
  The home of GOD's elect!
O sweet and blessèd country
  That eager hearts expect!
p JESU, in mercy bring us
  To that dear land of rest;
mf Who art, with GOD the FATHER
  And SPIRIT, ever Blest.

General Hymns.

Hymn 227.

General Hymns.

"A better country, that is, an heavenly."

mf FOR thee, O dear, dear country,
Mine eyes their vigils keep;
For very love, beholding
Thy happy name, they weep.
The mention of thy glory
Is unction to the breast,
And medicine in sickness,
And love, and life, and rest.

O one, O only mansion!
O Paradise of joy!
Where tears are ever banished,
And smiles have no alloy;
f The LAMB is all thy splendour;
The Crucified thy praise;
His laud and benediction
Thy ransomed people raise.

With jasper glow thy bulwarks,
Thy streets with emeralds blaze;
The sardius and the topaz
Unite in thee their rays;
Thine ageless walls are bonded
With amethyst unpriced;
The Saints build up thy fabric,
And the corner-stone is CHRIST.

mf Thou hast no shore, fair ocean!
Thou hast no time, bright day!
Dear fountain of refreshment
To pilgrims far away!
f Upon the Rock of ages
They raise thy holy tower;
Thine is the victor's laurel,
And thine the golden dower.

mf O sweet and blessèd country,
The home of GOD's elect!
O sweet and blessèd country
That eager hearts expect!
p JESU, in mercy bring us
To that dear land of rest;
mf Who art, with GOD the FATHER
And SPIRIT, ever Blest.

General Hymns.

Hymn 228.

General Hymns.

"And the city was pure gold."

mf JERUSALEM the golden,
With milk and honey blest,
Beneath thy contemplation
dim Sink heart and voice opprest.
cr I know not, oh, I know not
What joys await us there,
What radiancy of glory,
p What bliss beyond compare.

f They stand, those halls of Sion,
All jubilant with song,
And bright with many an Angel,
And all the Martyr throng;
The Prince is ever in them,
The daylight is serene:
The pastures of the blessèd
p Are decked in glorious sheen.

mf There is the throne of David;
And there, from care released,
The shout of them that triumph,
The song of them that feast;
f And they, who with their Leader
Have conquered in the fight,
For ever and for ever
p Are clad in robes of white.

mf O sweet and blessèd country,
The home of God's elect!
O sweet and blessèd country
That eager hearts expect!
p Jesu, in mercy bring us
To that dear land of rest;
mf Who art, with God the Father
p And Spirit, ever Blest.

General Hymns.

Hymn 229.

General Hymns.

The things which are seen are temporal ; but the things which are not seen are eternal."

mf THE roseate hues of early dawn,
   The brightness of the day,
The crimson of the sunset sky;
dim How fast they fade away!
cr Oh, for the pearly gates of heaven,
   Oh, for the golden floor,
Oh, for the Sun of righteousness
   That setteth nevermore!

p The highest hopes we cherish here,
   How fast they tire and faint;
How many a spot defiles the robe
   That wraps an earthly saint!
cr Oh, for a heart that never sins,
   Oh, for a soul washed white,
Oh, for a voice to praise our King,
   Nor weary day nor night!

mf Here faith is ours, and heavenly hope,
   And grace to lead us higher;
cr But there are perfectness, and peace,
   Beyond our best desire.
p Oh, by Thy love and anguish, LORD,
   And by Thy life laid down,
cr Grant that we fall not from Thy grace,
   Nor cast away our crown.

General Hymns.

Hymn 230. (First Tune.)

To be sung in Unison.

General Hymns.

"There remaineth therefore a rest to the people of God."

mf THERE is a blessèd home
Beyond this land of woe,
Where trials never come,
Nor tears of sorrow flow;
cr Where faith is lost in sight,
And patient hope is crowned.
f And everlasting light
Its glory throws around.

p There is a land of peace,
Good Angels know it well;
cr Glad songs that never cease
Within its portals swell;
mf Around its glorious Throne
Ten thousand Saints adore
CHRIST, with the FATHER ONE
And SPIRIT, evermore.

f O joy all joys beyond,
To see the LAMB Who died,
p And count each sacred Wound
In Hands, and Feet, and Side;
mf To give to Him the praise
Of every triumph won,
cr And sing through endless days
The great things He hath done.

mf Look up, ye saints of GOD,
Nor fear to tread below
The path your Saviour trod
p Of daily toil and woe;
cr Wait but a little while
In uncomplaining love,
mf His own most gracious smile
Shall welcome you above.

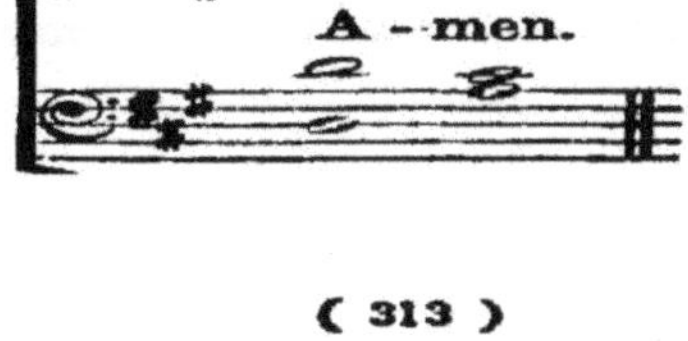

General Hymns.

Hymn 230. (Second Tune.)

General Hymns.

"There remaineth therefore a rest to the people of God."

mf THERE is a blessèd home
  Beyond this land of woe,
Where trials never come,
  Nor tears of sorrow flow;
cr Where faith is lost in sight,
  And patient hope is crowned,
f And everlasting light
  Its glory throws around.

p There is a land of peace,
  Good Angels know it well;
cr Glad songs that never cease
  Within its portals swell;
mf Around its glorious Throne
  Ten thousand Saints adore
CHRIST, with the FATHER ONE
  And SPIRIT, evermore.

f O joy all joys beyond,
  To see the LAMB Who died,
p And count each sacred Wound
  In Hands, and Feet, and Side;
mf To give to Him the praise
  Of every triumph won,
cr And sing through endless days
  The great things He hath done.

mf Look up, ye saints of GOD,
  Nor fear to tread below
The path your Saviour trod
p Of daily toil and woe;
cr Wait but a little while
  In uncomplaining love,
mf His own most gracious smile
  Shall welcome you above.

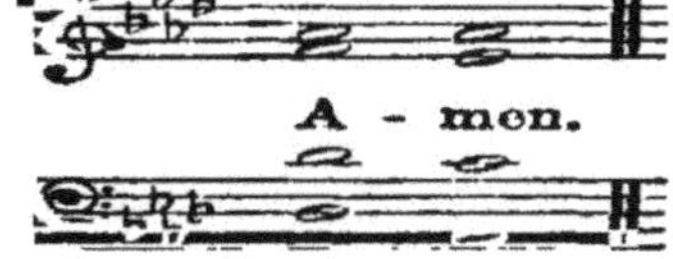

General Hymns.

Hymn 231.

General Hymns.

"And so shall we ever be with the Lord."

mf "FOR ever with the LORD!"
p Amen; so let it be;
cr Life from the dead is in that word,
'Tis immortality.
p Here in the body pent,
Absent from Him I roam,
cr Yet nightly pitch my moving tent
A day's march nearer home.

mf My FATHER'S house on high,
Home of my soul, how near
At times to faith's foreseeing eye
Thy golden gates appear!
p *Ah! then my spirit faints
To reach the land I love,
cr The bright inheritance of Saints,
Jerusalem above.

f "For ever with the LORD!"
mf FATHER, if 'tis Thy Will,
The promise of that faithful word
Even here to me fulfil.
Be Thou at my right hand,
Then can I never fail;
cr Uphold Thou me, and I shall stand,
Fight, and I must prevail.

p So when my latest breath
Shall rend the veil in twain,
cr By death I shall escape from death,
f And life eternal gain.
mf Knowing as I am known,
How shall I love that word,
cr And oft repeat before the Throne,
"For ever with the LORD!"

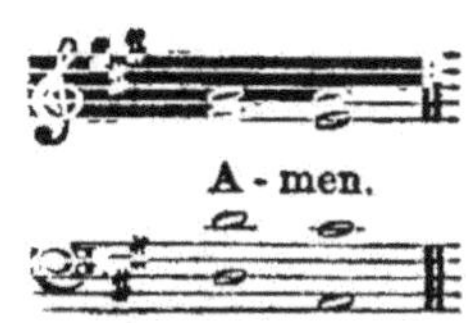

Verse 2, lines 5 and 6.

General Hymns.

Hymn 232. (First Tune.) *To be sung in Unison.*

Hymn 232. (Second Tune.)

General Hymns.

"Eye hath not seen, nor ear heard, neither have entered into the heart of man, the things which God hath prepared for them that love Him. But God hath revealed them unto us by His Spirit."

mf LIGHT'S abode, celestial Salem,
Vision whence true peace doth spring,
Brighter than the heart can fancy,
Mansion of the Highest King;
f Oh, how glorious are the praises
Which of thee the prophets sing!

mf There for ever and for ever
Alleluia is out-poured;
For unending, for unbroken
Is the feast-day of the LORD;
p All is pure and all is holy
That within thy walls is stored.

There no cloud nor passing vapour
Dims the brightness of the air;
mf Endless noon-day, glorious noon-day,
From the Sun of suns is there;
There no night brings rest from labour,
For unknown are toil and care.

f Oh, how glorious and resplendent,
Fragile body, shalt thou be,
When endued with so much beauty,
Full of health, and strong, and free,
Full of vigour, full of pleasure
That shall last eternally!

mf Now with gladness, now with courage,
Bear the burden on thee laid,
p That hereafter these thy labours
May with endless gifts be paid,
cr And in everlasting glory
Thou with brightness be arrayed.

f Laud and honour to the FATHER,
Laud and honour to the SON,
Laud and honour to the SPIRIT,
Ever THREE and ever ONE,
Consubstantial, Co-eternal,
While unending ages run.

General Hymns.

Hymn 233.

General Hymns.

"Our conversation is in heaven."

mf JERUSALEM on high
My song and city is,
My home whene'er I die,
The centre of my bliss:
f O happy place!
When shall I be,
My God, with Thee,
p To see Thy Face?

mf There dwells my Lord, my King,
p Judged here unfit to live;
mf There Angels to Him sing,
And lowly homage give:
f O happy place!
When shall I be,
My God, with Thee,
p To see Thy Face?

mf The Patriarchs of old
There from their travels cease;
The Prophets there behold
Their longed-for Prince of peace:
f O happy place!
When shall I be,
My God, with Thee,
p To see Thy Face?

mf The Lamb's Apostles there
I might with joy behold,
The harpers I might hear
Harping on harps of gold:
f O happy place!
When shall I be,
My God, with Thee,
p To see Thy Face?

p The bleeding Martyrs, they
Within these courts are found,
cr Clothèd in pure array,
Their scars with glory crowned:
f O happy place!
When shall I be,
My God, with Thee,
p To see Thy Face?

Ah me! ah me! that I
In Kedar's tents here stay;
No place like that on high;
cr Lord, thither guide my way:
f O happy place
When shall I be,
My God, with Thee,
p To see Thy Face?

General Hymns.

Hymn 234. (First Tune.)

Hymn 234. (Second Tune.)

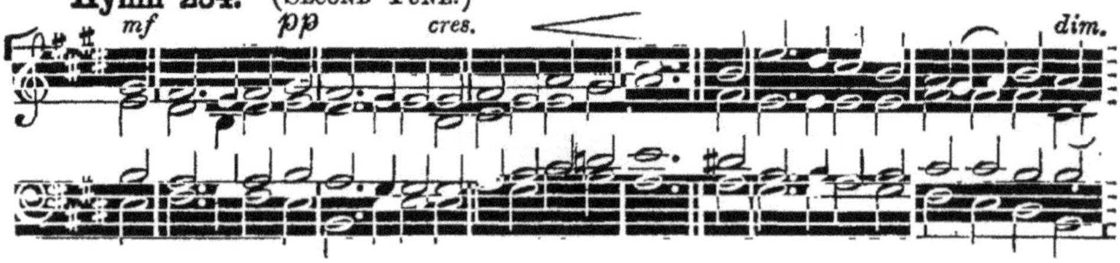

General Hymns.

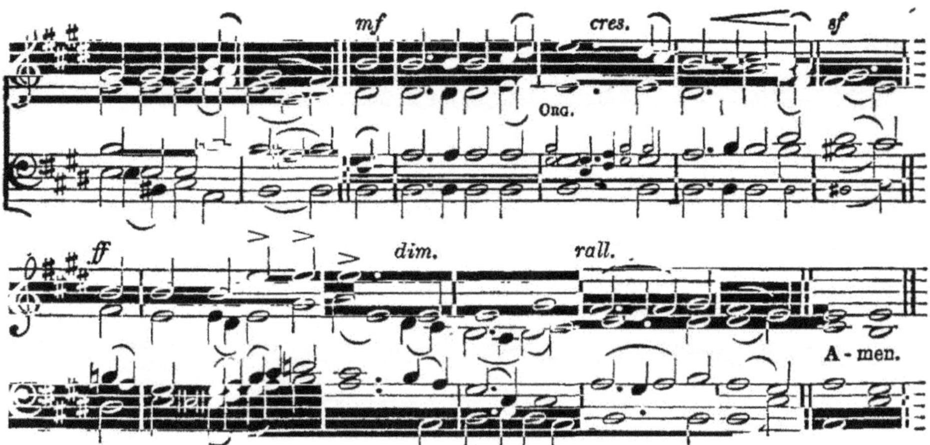

"The Paradise of God."

mf O PARADISE! O Paradise!
Who doth not crave for rest?
Who would not seek the happy land
Where they that loved are blest;
f Where loyal hearts and true
Stand ever in the light,
All rapture through and through,
dim In God's most holy sight?

mf O Paradise! O Paradise!
p The world is growing old;
cr Who would not be at rest and free
Where love is never cold;
f Where loyal hearts and true
Stand ever in the light,
All rapture through and through,
dim In God's most holy sight?

mf O Paradise! O Paradise!
p 'Tis weary waiting here;
cr I long to be where Jesus is,
To feel, to see Him near;
f Where loyal hearts and true
Stand ever in the light,
All rapture through and through,
dim In God's most holy sight.

mf O Paradise! O Paradise!
I want to sin no more,
I want to be as pure on earth
As on thy spotless shore;
f Where loyal hearts and true
Stand ever in the light,
All rapture through and through,
dim In God's most holy sight.

mf O Paradise! O Paradise!
I greatly long to see
The special place my dearest Lord
In love prepares for me;
f Where loyal hearts and true
Stand ever in the light,
All rapture through and through,
dim In God's most holy sight.

p Lord Jesu, King of Paradise,
O keep me in Thy love,
cr And guide me to that happy land
Of perfect rest above;
f Where loyal hearts and true
Stand ever in the light,
All rapture through and through,
dim In God's most holy sight.

General Hymns.

Hymn 235.

* *For the 1st verse, the slur is better over the 3rd and 4th notes of this bar.*

General Hymns.

"There remaineth therefore a rest to the people of God."

mf OH, what the joy and the glory must be,
Those endless Sabbaths the blessèd ones see;
Crown for the valiant, *(p)* to weary ones rest;
cr God shall be All and in all ever Blest.

mf What are the Monarch, His Court, and His Throne?
What are the peace and the joy that they own?
O that the blest ones, who in it have share,
All that they feel could as fully declare!

Truly Jerusalem name we that shore,
p Vision of peace, *(cr)* that brings joy evermore;
mf Wish and fulfilment can severed be ne'er,
Nor the thing prayed for come short of the prayer.

p There, where no troubles distraction can bring,
cr We the sweet anthems of Sion shall sing,
While for Thy grace, Lord, their voices of praise
Thy blessèd people eternally raise.

mf There dawns no Sabbath, no Sabbath is o'er,
Those Sabbath-keepers have one evermore;
f One and unending is that triumph-song
Which to the Angels and us shall belong.

p Now in the meanwhile, with hearts raised on high,
We for that country must yearn and must sigh;
Seeking Jerusalem, dear native land,
Through our long exile on Babylon's strand.

mf Low before Him with our praises we fall,
Of Whom, and in Whom, and through Whom are all;
f Of Whom, the Father; and in Whom, the Son;
Through Whom, the Spirit, with Them ever One.

General Hymns.

Hymn 236.

"When shall I come to appear before the presence of God?"

mf JERUSALEM, my happy home,
  Name ever dear to me,
When shall my labours have an end?
  Thy joys when shall I see?

When shall these eyes thy heaven-built [walls
  And pearly gates behold?
Thy bulwarks with salvation strong,
  And streets of shining gold?

f Apostles, Martyrs, Prophets, there
  Around my Saviour stand;
And all I love in CHRIST below
  Will join the glorious band.

mf Jerusalem, my happy home,
  When shall I come to thee?
When shall my labours have an end?
  Thy joys when shall I see?

p O CHRIST, do Thou my soul prepare
  For that bright home of love;
cr That I may see Thee and adore,
  With all Thy Saints above.

General Hymns.

Hymn 237.

"O how amiable are Thy dwellings, Thou Lord of hosts."

mf O GOD of hosts, the mighty LORD,
How lovely is the place,
Where Thou, enthroned in glory, shew'st
The brightness of Thy Face!

p My longing soul faints with desire
To view Thy blest abode;
My panting heart and flesh cry out
For Thee the living GOD.

mf For in Thy courts one single day
'Tis better to attend,
Than, LORD, in any place besides
A thousand days to spend.

O LORD of hosts, my King and GOD,
How highly blest are they
Who in Thy temple always dwell,
And there Thy praise display!

f To FATHER, SON, and HOLY GHOST,
The GOD Whom we adore,
Be glory, as it was, is now,
And shall be evermore.

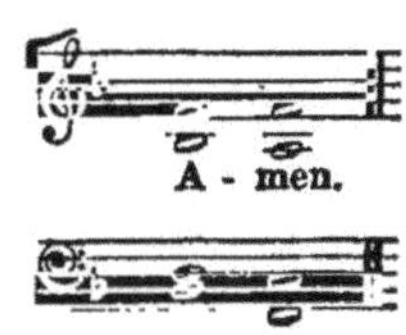

Hymn 238.

"Like as the hart desireth the water-brooks, so longeth my soul after Thee, O God."

p AS pants the hart for cooling streams
When heated in the chase,
So longs my soul, O GOD, for Thee,
And Thy refreshing grace.

For Thee my GOD, the living GOD,
My thirsty soul doth pine:
cr O when shall I behold Thy Face,
Thou Majesty Divine?

p Why restless, why cast down, my soul?
cr Hope still, and thou shalt sing
f The praise of Him Who is thy GOD,
Thy health's eternal Spring.

To FATHER, SON, and HOLY GHOST,
The GOD Whom we adore,
Be glory, as it was, is now,
And shall be evermore.

General Hymns.

Hymn 239.

"The Lord said unto him, . . . I have hallowed this house . . . to put My Name there for ever, and Mine eyes and Mine heart shall be there perpetually."

mf CHRIST is our corner-stone,
  On Him alone we build;
With His true Saints alone
  The courts of heaven are filled:
cr   On His great love
    Our hopes we place
    Of present grace
   And joys above.

f Oh, then with hymns of praise
  These hallowed courts shall ring;
Our voices we will raise
  The Three in One to sing;
   And thus proclaim
    In joyful song,
    Both loud and long,
   That glorious Name.

mf Here, gracious God, do Thou
  For evermore draw nigh;
Accept each faithful vow,
p And mark each suppliant sigh;
mf   In copious shower
    On all who pray
    Each holy day
   Thy blessings pour.

Here may we gain from heaven
  The grace which we implore;
And may that grace, once given,
  Be with us evermore,
p   Until that day
    When all the blest
cr   To endless rest
dim   Are called away.

General Hymns.

Hymn 240.

General Hymns.

"O how amiable are Thy dwellings, Thou Lord of hosts."

mf PLEASANT are Thy courts above
In the land of light and love;
p Pleasant are Thy courts below
In this land of sin and woe:
cr Oh, my spirit longs and faints
For the converse of Thy Saints,
For the brightness of Thy Face,
For Thy fulness, God of grace.

mf Happy birds that sing and fly
Round Thy Altars, O most High;
p Happier souls that find a rest
In a heavenly Father's breast;
Like the wandering dove that found
No repose on earth around,
cr They can to their ark repair,
And enjoy it ever there.

mf Happy souls, their praises flow
p Even in this vale of woe;
cr Waters in the deserts rise,
Manna feeds them from the skies;
f On they go from strength to strength,
Till they reach Thy Throne at length,
p At Thy feet adoring fall,
mf Who hast led them safe through all.

p Lord, be mine this prize to win,
Guide me through a world of sin,
Keep me by Thy saving grace,
Give me at Thy side a place;
mf Sun and Shield alike Thou art,
Guide and guard my erring heart;
f Grace and glory flow from Thee;
dim Shower, O shower them, Lord, on me.

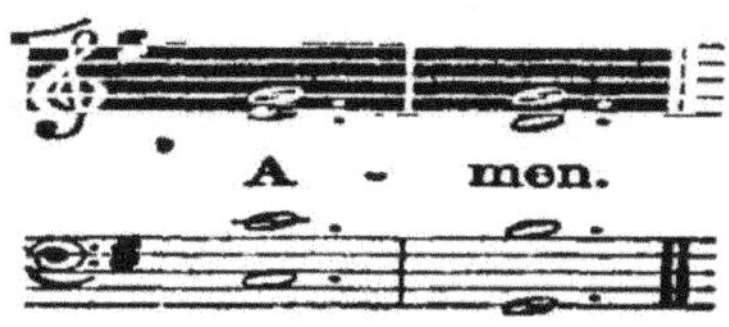

Hymn 241.

"Hosanna in the highest."

mf HOSANNA to the living LORD!
Hosanna to the Incarnate WORD,
To CHRIST, Creator, Saviour, King,
Let earth, let heaven Hosanna sing,
f Hosanna in the highest!

p O Saviour, with protecting care
Abide in this Thy house of prayer,
Where we Thy parting promise claim,
Assembled in Thy sacred Name.
f Hosanna in the highest!

mf But, chiefest, in our cleansèd breast,
ETERNAL, bid Thy SPIRIT rest;
And make our secret soul to be
A temple pure and worthy Thee.
Hosanna in the highest!

f To GOD the FATHER, GOD the SON,
And GOD the SPIRIT, THREE in ONE,
cr Be honour, praise, and glory given
By all on earth and all in heaven.
ff Hosanna in the highest!

Hymn 242.

"Lord, I have loved the habitation of Thy house; and the place where Thine honour dwelleth."

mf WE love the place, O God,
  Wherein Thine honour dwells;
The joy of Thine abode
  All earthly joy excels.

It is the house of prayer,
  Wherein Thy servants meet;
And Thou, O Lord, art there
  Thy chosen flock to greet.

We love the sacred Font;
  For there the Holy Dove
To pour is ever wont
  His blessings from above.

We love Thine Altar, Lord;
  Oh, what on earth so dear?
p For there, in faith adored,
cr   We find Thy Presence near.

mf We love the Word of life,
  The Word that tells of peace,
p Of comfort in the strife,
cr   And joys that never cease.

f We love to sing below
  For mercies freely given·
cr But, oh, we long to know
  The triumph-song of heaven.

p Lord Jesus, give us grace
  On earth to love Thee more,
f In heaven to see Thy Face,
dim   And with Thy Saints adore.

General Hymns.

Hymn 243.

"Thy Word is a lantern unto my feet, and a light unto my paths."

mf LORD, Thy Word abideth,
And our footsteps guideth;
Who its truth believeth
Light and joy receiveth.

p When our foes are near us,
cr Then Thy Word doth cheer us,
Word of consolation,
Message of salvation.

p When the storms are o'er us,
And dark clouds before us,
cr Then its light directeth,
And our way protecteth.

mf Who can tell the pleasure,
Who recount the treasure
By Thy Word imparted
To the simple-hearted?

Word of mercy, giving
Succour to the living;
Word of life, supplying
p Comfort to the dying!

mf O that we discerning
Its most holy learning,
LORD, may love and fear Thee,
Evermore be near Thee.

General Hymns.

Hymn 244.

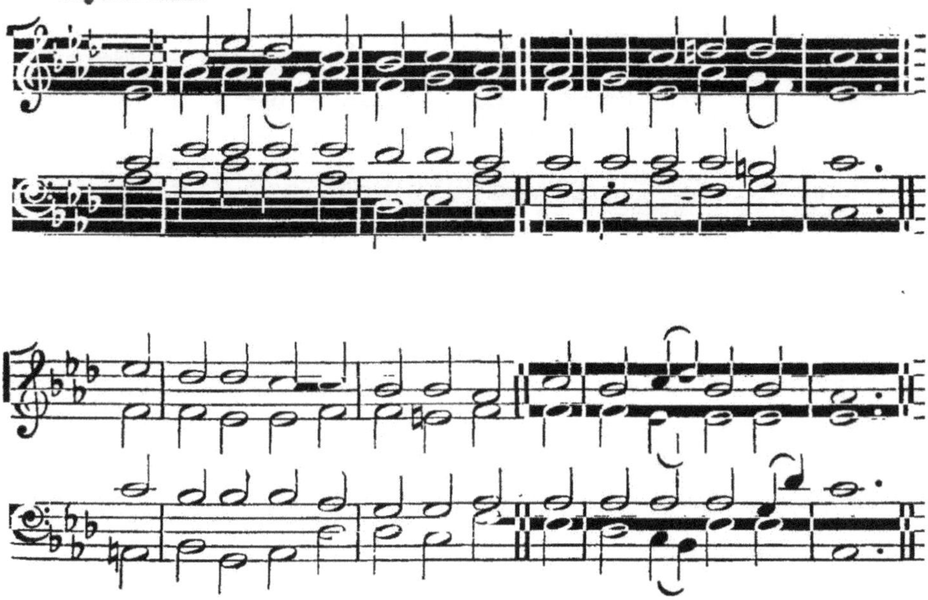

" A broken and contrite heart, O God, shalt Thou not despise."

p LORD, when we bend before Thy Throne,
  And our confessions pour,
Teach us to feel the sins we own,
  And hate what we deplore.

Our broken spirits pitying see;
  True penitence impart;
cr Then let a kindling glance from Thee
  Beam hope upon the heart.

mf When we disclose our wants in prayer,
  May we our wills resign,
And not a thought our bosoms share
  Which is not wholly Thine.

May faith each weak petition fill,
  And waft it to the skies,
And teach our hearts 'tis goodness still
  That grants it or denies.

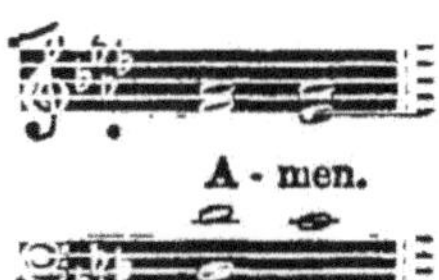

Hymn 245.

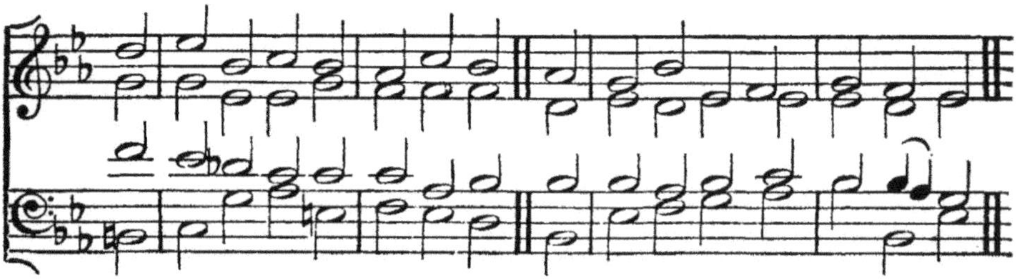

"If any man sin, we have an Advocate with the Father, Jesus Christ the Righteous."

p WHEN at Thy footstool, LORD, I bend,
And plead with Thee for mercy there,
cr Think of the sinner's dying Friend,
And for His sake receive my prayer.

p O think not of my shame and guilt,
My thousand stains of deepest dye;
cr Think of the Blood which JESUS spilt,
And let that Blood my pardon buy.

mf Think, LORD, how I am still Thine own,
p The trembling creature of Thy hand;
Think how my heart to sin is prone,
And what temptations round me stand.

mf O think upon Thy holy Word,
And every plighted promise there;
How prayer should evermore be heard
And how Thy glory is to spare.

p O think not of my doubts and fears,
My strivings with Thy grace Divine;
Think upon JESUS' woes and tears,
cr And let His merits stand for mine.

mf Thine eye, Thine ear, they are not dull
Thine arm can never shortened be:
Behold me here; my heart is full;
p Behold, and spare, and succour me.

General Hymns.

Hymn 246.

"Men ought always to pray, and not to faint."

mf WHAT various hindrances we meet
In coming to the Mercy-seat;
Yet who, that knows the worth of prayer,
But wishes to be often there?

Prayer makes the darkened cloud withdraw,
Prayer climbs the ladder Jacob saw,
Gives exercise to faith and love,
Brings every blessing from above.

p Restraining prayer we cease to fight;
cr Prayer makes the Christian's armour bright;
And Satan trembles when he sees
The weakest saint upon his knees.

mf When Moses stood with arms spread wide,
Success was found on Israel's side;
p But when through weariness they failed,
That moment Amalek prevailed.

mf Have we no words? ah, think again;
Words flow apace when we complain,
And fill our fellow-creature's ear
With the sad tale of all our care.

Were half the breath thus vainly sper
To heaven in supplication sent,
Our cheerful song would oftener be,
f "Hear what the LORD hath done for me.

mf O LORD, increase our faith and love,
That we may all Thy goodness prove,
And gain from Thy exhaustless store
The fruits of prayer for evermore.

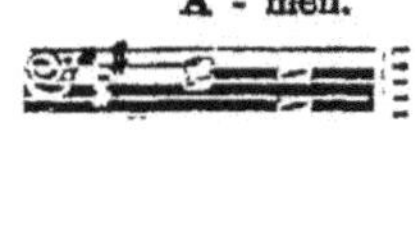

General Hymns.

Hymn 247.

"Thou preparest their heart, and Thine ear hearkeneth thereto."

mf LORD, teach us how to pray aright
With reverence and with fear;
p Though dust and ashes in Thy sight,
cr We may, we must draw near.

mf We perish if we cease from prayer;
O grant us power to pray;
And, when to meet Thee we prepare,
Lord, meet us by the way.

God of all grace, we bring to Thee
p A broken contrite heart;
mf Give, what Thine eye delights to see,
Truth in the inward part;

Faith in the only Sacrifice
That can for sin atone;
To cast our hopes, to fix our eyes,
cr On Christ, on Christ alone;

p Patience to watch, and wait, and weep,
Though mercy long delay;
cr Courage our fainting souls to keep,
And trust Thee though Thou slay;

mf Give these, and then Thy Will be done;
Thus, strengthened with all might,
We, through Thy Spirit and Thy Son,
Shall pray, and pray aright.

General Hymns.

Hymn 248.

"And he said, I will not let thee go, except thou bless me."

mf SHEPHERD Divine, our wants relieve
In this our evil day;
To all Thy tempted followers give
The power to watch and pray.

p Long as our fiery trials last,
Long as the cross we bear,
cr O let our souls on Thee be cast
In never-ceasing prayer.

mf The Spirit of interceding grace
Give us in faith to claim;
To wrestle till we see Thy Face,
And know Thy hidden Name.

Till Thou Thy perfect love impart,
Till Thou Thyself bestow,
Be this the cry of every heart,
"I will not let Thee go."

I will not let Thee go, unless
Thou tell Thy Name to me;
With all Thy great salvation bless,
And make me all like Thee.

Then let me on the mountain-top
Behold Thy open Face;
f Where faith in sight is swallowed up,
And prayer in endless praise.

General Hymns.

Hymn 249.

"Have mercy upon me, O God, after Thy great goodness: according to the multitude of Thy mercies do away mine offences."

p HAVE mercy, LORD, on me,
As Thou wert ever kind;
Let me, opprest with loads of guilt,
Thy wonted mercy find.

Wash off my foul offence,
And cleanse me from my sin;
For I confess my crime, and see
How great my guilt has been.

mf The joy Thy favour gives
Let me again obtain,
And Thy free SPIRIT'S firm support
My fainting soul sustain.

f To GOD the FATHER, SON,
And SPIRIT glory be;
As 'twas, and is, and shall be so
To all eternity.

General Hymns.

Hymn 250.

"Out of the deep have I called unto Thee, O Lord."

p OUT of the deep I call
To Thee, O LORD, to Thee;
Before Thy Throne of grace I fall;
Be merciful to me.

Out of the deep I cry,
The woful deep of sin,
Of evil done in days gone by,
Of evil now within.

Out of the deep of fear,
And dread of coming shame,
From morning watch till night is near
cr I plead the Precious Name.

mf LORD, there is mercy now
As ever was, with Thee;
Before Thy Throne of grace I bow;
p Be merciful to me.

General Hymns.

Hymn 251.

General Hymns.

"Jesus, Master, have mercy on us."

p SAVIOUR, when in dust to Thee
 Low we bow the adoring knee,
When, repentant, to the skies
Scarce we lift our weeping eyes,
O, by all Thy pains and woe
Suffered once for man below,
Bending from Thy Throne on high,
Hear our solemn litany.

mf By Thy helpless infant years;
By Thy life of want and tears;
By Thy days of sore distress
In the savage wilderness;
By the dread mysterious hour
Of the insulting tempter's power;
Turn, O turn a favouring eye;
p Hear our solemn litany.

mf By the sacred grief that wept
O'er the grave where Lazarus slept;
By the boding tears that flowed
Over Salem's loved abode;
By the mournful word that told
Treachery lurked within Thy fold;
From Thy seat above the sky
p Hear our solemn litany.

By Thine hour of whelming fear;
By Thine agony of prayer;
By the cross, the nail, the thorn,
Piercing spear, and torturing scorn;
By the gloom that veiled the skies
O'er the dreadful Sacrifice;
Listen to our humble cry;
Hear our solemn litany.

pp By Thy deep expiring groan;
By the sad sepulchral stone;
By the vault whose dark abode
cr Held in vain the rising GOD,
f O, from earth to heaven restored,
Mighty, re-ascended LORD,
mf Listen, listen to the cry
p Of our solemn litany.

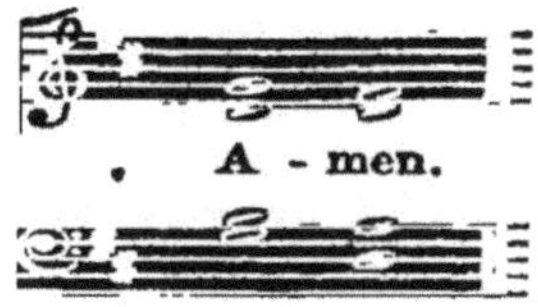

General Hymns.

Hymn 252. (First Tune.)

Hymn 252. (Second Tune.)

General Hymns.

"In Whom we have redemption through His Blood, the forgiveness of sins."

p WEARY of earth and láden with my sin,
I look at heaven and long to enter in;
But there no evil thíng may find a home,
cr And yet I hear a voice that bids me, "Come."

p So vile I am, how dáre I hope to stand
In the pure glory of that holy land?
Before the whiteness óf that Throne appear?
cr Yet there are Hands stretched out to draw me near.

p The while I fain would tréad the heavenly way,
Evil is ever with me day by day;
cr Yet on mine ears the grácious tidings fall,
"Repent, confess, thou shalt be loosed from all."

mf It is the voice of JÉSUS that I hear,
His are the Hands stretched out to draw me near,
And His the Blood that cán for all atone,
And set me faultless there before the Throne.

'Twas He Who found me ón the deathly wild,
And made me heir of heaven, the FATHER's child,
And day by day, wherebý my soul may live,
Gives me His grace of pardon, and will give.

p O great Absolver, gránt my soul may wear
The lowliest garb of penitence and prayer,
cr That in the FATHER's coúrts my glorious dress
May be the garment of Thy righteousness.

mf Yea, Thou wilt answer fór me, Righteous LORD;
Thine all the merits, mine the great reward;
p Thine the sharp thorns, and *(mf)* míne the golden crown;
Mine the life won, and *(p)* Thine the life laid down.

mf Nought can I bring, dear LÓRD, for all I owe,
Yet let my full heart what it can bestow;
cr Like Mary's gift let mý devotion prove,
Forgiven greatly, how I greatly love.

1.

2.

General Hymns.

Hymn 253.

"When he thought thereon, he wept."

p O JESU CHRIST, if aught there be
  That, more than all beside,
In ever-painful memory
  Must in my heart abide,

It is that deep ingratitude
  Which I to Thee have shown,
Who didst for me in tears and Blood
  Upon the Cross atone.

Alas, how with my actions all
  Has this defect entwined;
How has it poisoned with its gall
  My spirit, heart, and mind!

mf Alas, through this, how many a gem
  I've rudely cast away,
That might have formed my diadem
  In everlasting day!

p Yet though the time be past and gone,
  Though little more remains,
Though nought is all that can be done,
  E'en with my utmost pains;

mf Still will I strive, O Saviour mine,
  To do what in me lies;
For never did Thy glance Divine
  A contrite heart despise.

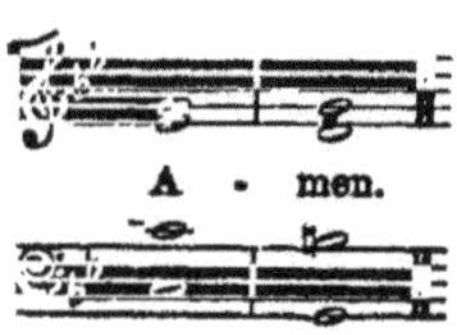

General Hymns.

Hymn 254. (First Tune.)

Slowly, and with expression.

"Come unto Me, all ye that labour and are heavy laden, and I will give you rest."

p ART thou weary, art thou languid,
Art thou sore distrest?
mf "Come to Me," saith One, "and coming
p Be at rest!"

mf Hath He marks to lead me to Him,
If He be my guide?
p "In His Feet and Hands are Wound-prints,
And His Side."

mf Hath He diadem as Monarch
That His Brow adorns?
"Yea, a Crown, in very surety,
p But of thorns."

mf If I find Him, if I follow,
What His guerdon here?
p "Many a sorrow, many a labour,
Many a tear."

mf If I still hold closely to Him,
What hath He at last?
f "Sorrow vanquished, labour ended,
Jordan past."

mf If I ask Him to receive me,
Will He say me nay?
f "Not till earth, and not till heaven
Pass away."

mf Finding, following, keeping, struggling
Is He sure to bless?
ff "Angels, Martyrs, Prophets, Virgins,
Answer, Yes!"

General Hymns.

Hymn 254. (Second Tune.)

"Come unto Me, all ye that labour and are heavy laden, and I will give you rest."

p ART thou weary, art thou languid,
Art thou sore distrest?
mf "Come to Me," saith One, "and coming
p Be at rest!"

mf Hath He marks to lead me to Him,
If He be my guide?
p "In His Feet and Hands are Wound-prints,
And His Side."

mf Hath He diadem as Monarch
That His Brow adorns?
"Yea, a Crown, in very surety,
p But of thorns."

mf If I find Him, if I follow,
What His guerdon here?
p "Many a sorrow, many a labour,
Many a tear."

mf If I still hold closely to Him,
What hath He at last?
f "Sorrow vanquished, labour ended,
Jordan past."

mf If I ask Him to receive me,
Will He say me nay?
f "Not till earth, and not till heaven
Pass away."

mf Finding, following, keeping, struggling
Is He sure to bless?
ff "Angels, Martyrs, Prophets, Virgins,
Answer, Yes!"

Hymn 255.

"Him that cometh to Me I will in no wise cast out."

JUST as I am, without one plea
But that Thy Blood was shed for me,
And that Thou bidd'st me come to Thee,
O LAMB of GOD, I come.

Just as I am, though tossed about
With many a conflict, many a doubt,
Fightings and fears within, without,
O LAMB of GOD, I come.

Just as I am, poor, wretched, blind;
cr Sight, riches, healing of the mind,
Yea all I need, in Thee to find,
p O LAMB of GOD, I come.

Just as I am, *(mf)* Thou wilt receive,
Wilt welcome, pardon, cleanse, relieve;
cr Because Thy promise I believe,
O LAMB of GOD, I come.

p Just as I am, *(mf)* (Thy love unknown
Has broken every barrier down),
cr Now to be Thine, yea, Thine alone,
O LAMB of GOD, I come.

p Just as I am, *(mf)* of that free love
The breadth, length, depth, and height to prove,
cr Here for a season, then above,
p O LAMB of GOD, I come.

General Hymns.

Hymn 256.

Note.—*It is suggested that the first two lines of each verse should be sung by Tenors and Basses only, but if necessary they may be sung in Octaves by all the voices.*

General Hymns.

" Him that cometh to Me I will in no wise cast out."

mf " COME unto Me, ye weary,
And I will give you rest."
p O blessèd voice of JESUS,
cr Which comes to hearts opprest;
mf It tells of benediction,
Of pardon, grace, and peace,
f Of joy that hath no ending,
Of love which cannot cease.

mf " Come unto Me, ye wanderers,
And I will give you light."
p O loving voice of JESUS,
cr Which comes to cheer the night;
p Our hearts were filled with sadness,
And we had lost our way;
f But He has brought us gladness
And songs at break of day.

mf " Come unto Me, ye fainting,
And I will give you life."
O cheering voice of JESUS,
cr Which comes to aid our strife;
mf The foe is stern and eager,
The fight is fierce and long;
f But He has made us mighty,
And stronger than the strong.

mf " And whosoever cometh,
I will not cast him out."
O welcome voice of JESUS,
cr Which drives away our doubt;
mf Which calls us very sinners,
p Unworthy though we be,
cr Of love so free and boundless,
p To come, dear LORD, to Thee.

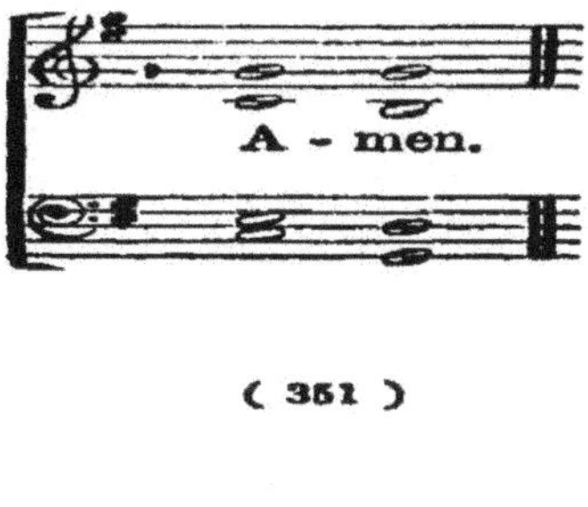

General Hymns.

Hymn 257.

General Hymns.

"He that cometh to Me shall never hunger; and he that believeth on Me shall never thirst."

p I HEARD the voice of Jesus say,
mf "Come unto Me and rest;
cr Lay down, thou weary one, lay down
Thy head upon My Breast:"
p I came to Jesus as I was,
Weary, and worn, and sad;
cr I found in Him a resting-place,
ff And He has made me glad.

p I heard the voice of Jesus say,
mf "Behold, I freely give
cr The living water, thirsty one,
Stoop down, and drink, and live:"
p *I came to Jesus, and I drank
cr Of that life-giving stream;
My thirst was quenched, my soul revived,
ff And now I live in Him.

p I heard the voice of Jesus say,
mf "I am this dark world's Light;
cr Look unto Me, thy morn shall rise,
And all thy day be bright:"
p *I looked to Jesus, and I found
cr In Him my Star, my Sun;
And in that Light of life I'll walk
dim Till travelling days are done.

* *In verses 2 and 3, for music of lines 5 and 6, substitute the following:—*

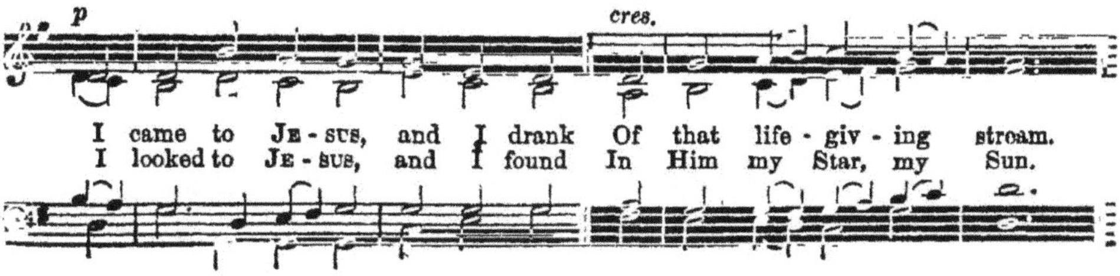

General Hymns.

Hymn 258.

General Hymns.

When he hath found it, he layeth it on his shoulders rejoicing."

p I WAS a wandering sheep,
I did not love the fold,
I did not love my Shepherd's voice,
I would not be controlled.
I was a wayward child,
I did not love my home,
I did not love my FATHER'S voice,
I loved afar to roam.

mf The Shepherd sought His sheep,
The FATHER sought His child,
They followed me o'er vale and hill,
O'er deserts waste and wild;
They found me *(p)* nigh to death,
Famished, and faint, and lone;
cr They bound me with the bands of love,
They saved the wandering one.

mf They spoke in tender love,
They raised my drooping head,
They gently closed my bleeding wounds,
My fainting soul they fed;
They washed my filth away,
They made me clean and fair;
cr They brought me to my home in peace,
dim The long-sought wanderer.

f JESUS my Shepherd is,
'Twas He that loved my soul,
'Twas He that washed me in His Blood,
'Twas He that made me whole;
'Twas He that sought the lost,
dim That found the wandering sheep;
cr 'Twas He that brought me to the fold,
'Tis He that still doth keep.

p I was a wandering sheep,
I would not be controlled;
f But now I love my Shepherd's voice,
I love, I love the fold.
p I was a wayward child,
I once preferred to roam;
f But now I love my FATHER'S voice,
I love, I love His home.

 U

General Hymns.

Hymn 259.

Slow and soft.

General Hymns.

What reward shall I give unto the Lord for all the benefits that He hath done unto me?"

p THY life was given for me,
Thy Blood, O LORD, was shed,
cr That I might ransomed be,
And quickened from the dead;
p Thy life was given for me;
What have I given for Thee?

Long years were spent for me
In weariness and woe,
cr That through eternity
Thy glory I might know;
p Long years were spent for me;
Have I spent one for Thee?

mf Thy FATHER's home of light,
Thy rainbow-circled Throne,
dim Were left for earthly night,
For wanderings sad and lone;
p Yea, all was left for me;
Have I left aught for Thee?

Thou, LORD, hast borne for me
More than my tongue can tell
Of bitterest agony,
To rescue me from hell;
Thou suff'redst all for me;
What have I borne for Thee?

mf And Thou hast brought to me
Down from Thy home above
cr Salvation full and free,
Thy pardon and Thy love;
mf Great gifts Thou broughtest me;
p What have I brought to Thee?

mf O let my life be given,
My years for Thee be spent;
World-fetters all be riven,
And joy with suffering blent;
cr Thou gav'st Thyself for me,
I give myself to Thee.

General Hymns.

Hymn 260.

"Lovest thou Me?"

mf HARK, my soul! it is the Lord;
'Tis thy Saviour, hear His Word;
Jesus speaks, and speaks to thee,
p "Say, poor sinner, lov'st thou Me?

mf "I delivered thee when bound,
And, when bleeding, healed thy wound;
Sought thee wandering, set thee right,
Turned thy darkness into light.

"Can a woman's tender care
Cease towards the child she bare?
p Yes, she may forgetful be,
cr Yet will I remember thee.

mf "Mine is an unchanging love,
Higher than the heights above,
Deeper than the depths beneath,
cr Free and faithful, strong as death.

f "Thou shalt see My glory soon,
mf When the work of grace is done;
cr Partner of My Throne shalt be;
p Say, poor sinner, *(cr)* lov'st thou Me?"

mf Lord, it is my chief complaint
That my love is weak and faint;
cr Yet I love Thee, *(dim)* and adore;
cr O for grace to love Thee more

General Hymns.

Hymn 261.

"Blessed are the pure in heart, for they shall see God."

mf BLEST are the pure in heart,
For they shall see our God;
The secret of the Lord is theirs;
Their soul is Christ's abode.

p The Lord, Who left the heavens
Our life and peace to bring,
To dwell in lowliness with men,
Their Pattern and their King;

He to the lowly soul
Doth still Himself impart,
cr And for His dwelling and His throne
Chooseth the pure in heart.

p Lord, we Thy presence seek;
May ours this blessing be;
cr Give us a pure and lowly heart,
A temple meet for Thee.

General Hymns.

Hymn 262.

"Now abideth faith, hope, charity, these three; but the greatest of these is charity."

mf GREAT Mover of all hearts, Whose Hand
Doth all the secret springs command
Of human thought and will,
Thou, since the world was made, dost bless
Thy saints with fruits of holiness,
Their order to fulfil.

Faith, hope, and love here weave one chain;
But love alone shall then remain
When this short day is gone:
O Love, O Truth, O endless Light,
When shall we see Thy Sabbath bright
With all our labours done?

p We sow 'mid perils here and tears:
cr There the glad hand the harvest bears,
dim Which here in grief hath sown:
mf Great Three in One, the increase give;
Thy gifts of grace, by which we live,
cr With heavenly glory crown.

General Hymns.

Hymn 263.

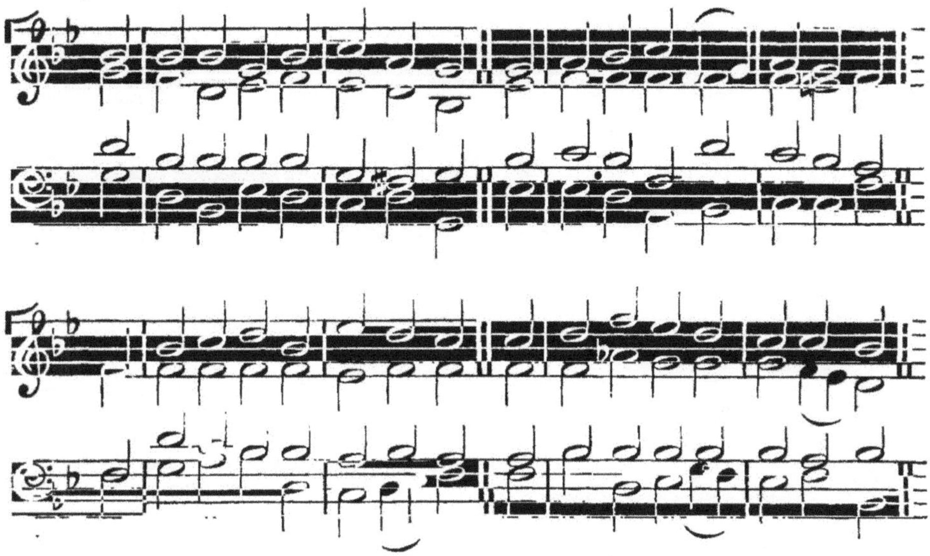

"If any man will come after Me, let him deny himself, and take up his cross, and follow Me."

mf TAKE up thy cross, the Saviour said,
If thou wouldst My disciple be;
Deny thyself, the world forsake,
And humbly follow after Me.

Take up thy cross; let not its weight
Fill thy weak spirit with alarm;
His strength shall bear thy spirit up,
And brace thy heart, and nerve thine arm.

Take up thy cross, nor heed the shame;
Nor let thy foolish pride rebel;
p Thy LORD for thee the Cross endured,
cr To save thy soul from death and hell.

mf Take up thy cross then in His strength,
And calmly every danger brave;
'Twill guide thee to a better home,
cr And lead to victory o'er the grave.

mf Take up thy cross, and follow CHRIST,
Nor think till death to lay it down;
For only he who bears the cross
cr May hope to wear the glorious crown.

f To Thee, Great LORD, the ONE in THREE
All praise for evermore ascend;
dim O grant us in our home to see
f The heavenly life that knows no end.

General Hymns.

Hymn 264.

"Thy will be done."

mf. MY God, my Father, whíle I stray,
Far from my home, on lífe's rough way,
O teach me from my heárt to say,
p "Thy Will be done."

Though dark my path, and sád my lot,
Let me be still and múrmur not,
Or breathe the prayer divínely taught,
"Thy Will be done."

What though in lonely gríef I sigh
For friends beloved no lónger nigh,
Submissive would I still reply,
"Thy Will be done."

If Thou shouldst call me tó resign
What most I prize, it ne'ér was mine;
I only yield Thee whát is Thine;
"Thy Will be done."

mf Let but my fainting heárt be blest
With Thy sweet Spirit fór its guest,
My God, to Thee I leáve the rest;
p "Thy Will be done."

mf Renew my will from dáy to day,
Blend it with Thine, and táke away
All that now makes it hárd to say,
p "Thy Will be done."

General Hymns.

Hymn 265.

"Not as I will, but as Thou wilt."

mf THY way, not mine, O Lord,
However dark it be;
Lead me by Thine own Hand,
Choose out the path for me.

Smooth let it be, or rough,
It will be still the best;
Winding, or straight, it leads
Right onward to Thy rest.

p I dare not choose my lot;
I would not if I might;
mf Choose Thou for me, my God,
So shall I walk aright.

The kingdom that I seek
Is Thine, so let the way
That leads to it be Thine,
p Else I must surely stray.

mf Take Thou my cup, and it
With joy or sorrow fill,
As best to Thee may seem;
Choose Thou my good or ill.

Choose Thou for me my friends,
My sickness or my health;
p Choose Thou my cares for me,
My poverty or wealth.

mf Not mine, not mine the choice
In things or great or small;
cr Be Thou my Guide, my Strength,
f My Wisdom, and my All.

General Hymns.

Hymn 266.

General Hymns.

"In the day time also He led them with a cloud, and all the night through with a light of fire."

mf LEAD, kindly Light, amid the encircling gloom,
Lead Thou me on;
p The night is dark, and I am far from home,
Lead Thou me on.
cr Keep Thou my feet; I do not ask to see
The distant scene; *(p)* one step enough for me.

mf I was not ever thus, nor prayed that Thou
Shouldst lead me on;
I loved to choose and see my path; *(p)* but now
Lead Thou me on.
cr I loved the garish day, and, spite of fears,
Pride ruled my will: *(p)* remember not past years.

mf So long Thy power hath blest me, sure it still
Will lead me on
O'er moor and fen, o'er crag and torrent, *(p)* till
The night is gone,
cr And with the morn those angel faces smile,
Which I have loved long since, *(p)* and lost awhile.

General Hymns.

Hymn 267.

"Let this mind be in you, which was also in Christ Jesus."

p LORD, as to Thy dear Cross we flee,
And plead to be forgiven,
cr So let Thy life our pattern be,
And form our souls for heaven.

mf Help us, through good report and ill,
Our daily cross to bear;
Like Thee, to do our FATHER'S Will,
p Our brethren's griefs to share.

mf Let grace our selfishness expel,
Our earthliness refine;
And kindness in our bosoms dwell,
As free and true as Thine.

If joy shall at Thy bidding fly,
p And grief's dark day come on,
We in our turn would meekly cry,
pp "FATHER, Thy Will be done."

mf Kept peaceful in the midst of strife,
Forgiving and forgiven,
cr O may we lead the pilgrim's life,
And follow Thee to heaven.

General Hymns.

Hymn 268.

"Blessed are those servants whom the Lord when He cometh shall find watching'

mf YE servants of the LORD,
Each in his office, wait,
Observant of His heavenly Word,
And watchful at His gate.

Let all your lamps be bright,
And trim the golden flame;
Gird up your loins as in His sight,
For awful is His Name.

Watch! 'tis your LORD's command,
And while we speak He's near;
Mark the first signal of His hand,
And ready all appear.

Oh, happy servant he,
In such a posture found!
He shall his LORD with rapture see,
And be with honour crowned.

CHRIST shall the banquet spread
With His own royal hand,
And raise that faithful servant's head
Amid the Angelic band.

f All glory, LORD, to Thee,
Whom heaven and earth adore,
To FATHER, SON, and HOLY GHOST,
ONE GOD for evermore.

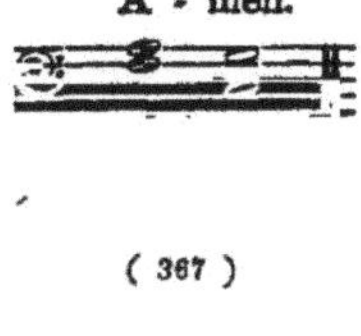

Hymn 269.

"Watch and pray."

mf "CHRISTIAN! seek not yet repose,"
p Hear thy guardian Angel say;
mf Thou art in the midst of foes;
p "Watch and pray."

mf Principalities and powers,
Mustering their unseen array,
Wait for thy unguarded hours:
p "Watch and pray."

mf Gird thy heavenly armour on,
Wear it ever night and day;
cr Ambushed lies the evil one;
p "Watch and pray."

f Hear the victors who o'ercame;
dim Still they mark each warrior's way;
cr All with one sweet voice exclaim,
"Watch and pray."

mf Hear, above all, hear thy LORD,
Him thou lovest to obey;
p Hide within thy heart His Word,
"Watch and pray."

mf Watch, as if on that alone
Hung the issue of the day;
Pray, that help may be sent down;
"Watch and pray."

Hymn 270.

"Put on the whole armour of God."

f SOLDIERS of CHRIST, arise,
And put your armour on,
Strong in the strength which GOD supplies
Through His Eternal SON;

Strong in the LORD of hosts,
And in His mighty power;
p Who in the strength of JESUS trusts
cr Is more than conqueror.

f Stand then in His great might,
With all His strength endued;
mf And take, to arm you for the fight,
The panoply of GOD.

From strength to strength go on,
Wrestle, and fight, and pray;
cr Tread all the powers of darkness down,
ff And win the well-fought day.

mf That having all things done,
And all your conflicts past,
Ye may obtain, through CHRIST alone,
cr A crown of joy at last.

p JESU, Eternal SON,
cr We praise Thee and adore,
f Who art with GOD the FATHER ONE
And SPIRIT evermore.

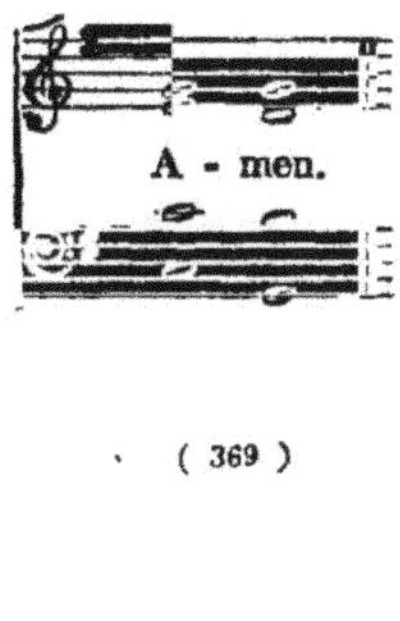

General Hymns.

Hymn 271.

General Hymns.

"If any man serve Me, let him follow Me; and where I am, there shall also My servant be."

mf O JESUS, I have promised
  To serve Thee to the end;
Be Thou for ever near me,
  My Master and my Friend;
I shall not fear the battle
  If Thou art by my side,
Nor wander from the pathway,
  If Thou wilt be my Guide.

O let me feel Thee near me:
  The world is ever near;
I see the sights that dazzle,
  The tempting sounds I hear;
p My foes are ever near me,
  Around me and within;
cr But, Jesus, draw Thou nearer,
  And shield my soul from sin.

mf O let me hear Thee speaking
  In accents clear and still,
Above the storms of passion,
  The murmurs of self-will;
O speak to re-assure me,
  To hasten, or control;
O speak, and make me listen,
  Thou Guardian of my soul.

O Jesus, Thou hast promised
  To all who follow Thee,
That where Thou art in glory
  There shall Thy servant be;
And, Jesus, I have promised
  To serve Thee to the end;
O give me grace to follow,
  My Master and my Friend.

p O let me see Thy foot-marks,
  And in them plant mine own;
My hope to follow duly
  Is in Thy strength alone.
cr O guide me, call me, draw me,
  Uphold me to the end;
And then in heaven receive me,
  My Saviour and my Friend.

General Hymns.

Hymn 272.

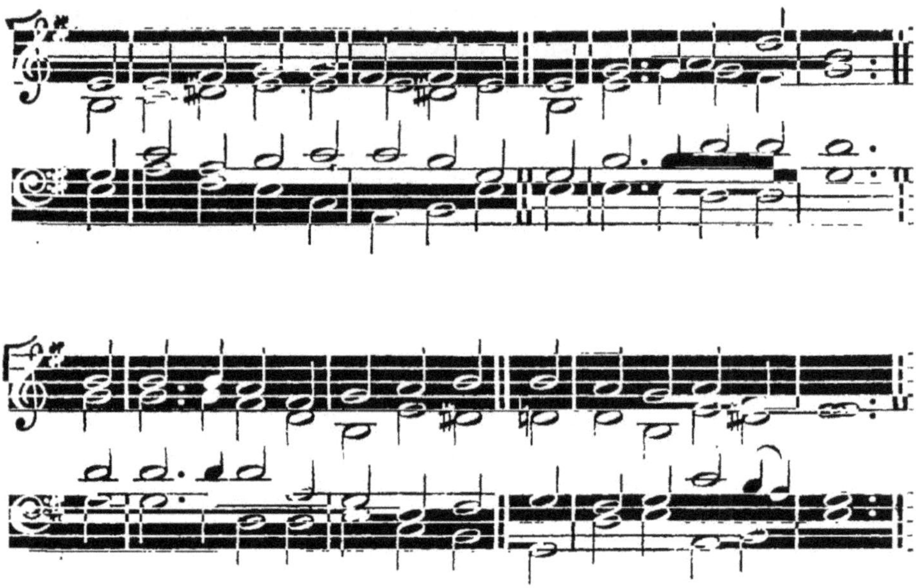

"Christ in you, the hope of glory."

mf O SAVIOUR, may we never rest
Till Thou art formed within,
Till Thou hast calmed our troubled breast,
And crushed the power of sin.

mf Until, released from carnal ties,
Our spirit upward springs,
And sees true peace above the skies
True joy in heavenly things.

p O may we gaze upon Thy Cross,
cr Until the wondrous sight
Makes earthly treasures seem but dross,
p And earthly sorrows light:

p There as we gaze, may we become
United, LORD, to Thee,
cr And, in a fairer, happier home,
Thy perfect beauty see.

General Hymns.

Hymn 273.

"Behold, how good and joyful a thing it is, brethren, to dwell together in unity!"

mf O LORD, how joyful 'tis to see
The brethren join in love to Thee!
On Thee alone their heart relies,
Their only strength Thy grace supplies.

How sweet within Thy holy place
With one accord to sing Thy grace,
Besieging Thine attentive ear
With all the force of fervent prayer!

O may we love the House of God,
p Of peace and joy the blest abode;
cr O may no angry strife destroy
That sacred peace, that holy joy.

mf The world without may rage, but we
Will only cling more close to Thee,
With hearts to Thee more wholly given,
More weaned from earth, more fixed on heaven.

p Lord, shower upon us from above
The sacred gift of mutual love;
Each other's wants may we supply,
cr And reign together in the sky.

f Praise God, from Whom all blessings flow,
Praise Him, all creatures here below,
Praise Him above, Angelic host,
Praise Father, Son, and Holy Ghost.

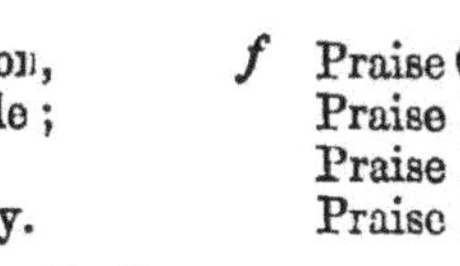

General Hymns.

Hymn 274.

"One hope of your calling."

mf THROUGH the night of doubt and sorrow
Onward goes the pilgrim band,
Singing songs of expectation,
Marching to the Promised Land.

Clear before us through the darkness
Gleams and burns the guiding Light;
Brother clasps the hand of brother,
Stepping fearless through the night.

One the Light of GOD's own Presence
O'er His ransomed people shed,
Chasing far the gloom and terror,
Brightening all the path we tread:

One the object of our journey,
One the faith which never tires,
One the earnest looking forward,
One the hope our GOD inspires:

One the strain that lips of thousands
Lift as from the heart of one;
One the conflict, one the peril,
One the march in GOD begun:

f One the gladness of rejoicing
On the far eternal shore,
Where the One Almighty FATHER
Reigns in love for evermore.

mf Onward therefore, pilgrim brothers,
Onward with the Cross our aid!
Bear its shame, and fight its battle,
p Till we rest beneath its shade.

cr Soon shall come the great awaking,
Soon the rending of the tomb;
f Then the scattering of all shadows,
And the end of toil and gloom.

General Hymns.

Hymn 275.

"That they all may be one."

mf FATHER of all, from land and sea
The nations sing, "Thine, LORD, are we,
Countless in number, but in Thee
May we be one."

O SON of GOD, Whose love so free
For men did make Thee Man to be,
p *cr* United to our GOD in Thee
May we be one.

p Thou, LORD, didst once for all atone;
mf Thee may both Jew and Gentile own
Of their two walls the Corner Stone,
Making them one.

In Thee we are GOD's Israel,
Thou art the world's Emmanuel,
In Thee the saints for ever dwell,
Millions, but one.

Thou art the Fountain of all good,
p Cleansing with Thy most precious Blood,
cr And feeding us with Angels' Food,
Making us one.

mf Join high and low, join young and old
In love that never waxes cold;
cr Under one Shepherd, in one Fold,
Make us all one.

p O SPIRIT Blest, Who from above
Cam'st gently gliding like a dove,
Calm all our strife, give faith and love;
O make us one.

mf O TRINITY in UNITY,
ONE only GOD, in Persons THREE,
Dwell ever in our hearts; like Thee
May we be one.

f So, when the world shall pass away,
May we awake with joy and say,
"Now in the bliss of endless day
We all are one."

General Hymns.

Hymn 276. (First Tune.)

General Hymns.

Hymn 276. (Second Tune.)

"Casting all your care upon Him; for He careth for you."

mf O LORD, how happy should we be
If we could cast our care on Thee,
If we from self could rest;
And feel at heart that One above
In perfect wisdom, perfect love,
Is working for the best.

p How far from this our daily life,
How oft disturbed by anxious strife,
By sudden wild alarms;
cr Oh, could we but relinquish all
Our earthly props, and simply fall
On Thine Almighty arms!

p Could we but kneel and cast our load,
E'en while we pray, upon our God,
cr Then rise with lightened cheer;
mf Sure that the Father, Who is nigh
To still the famished raven's cry,
Will hear in that we fear.

p We cannot trust Him as we should;
So chafes weak nature's restless mood
To cast its peace away;
cr But birds and flowerets round us preach,
All, all the present evil teach
Sufficient for the day.

mf Lord, make these faithless hearts of ours
Such lessons learn from birds and flowers;
Make them from self to cease,
Leave all things to a Father's Will,
And taste, before Him lying still,
p E'en in affliction peace.

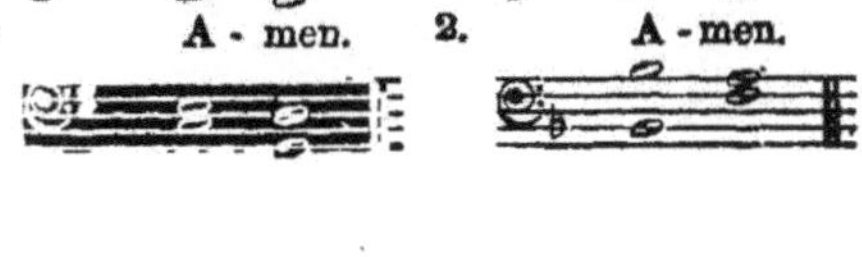

 X 2

General Hymns.

Hymn 277.

General Hymns.

"Whom have I in heaven but Thee? and there is none upon earth that I desire in comparison of Thee."

mf NEARER, my God, to Thee,
Nearer to Thee;
p E'en though it be a cross
That raiseth me,
cr Still all my song shall be,
dim Nearer, my God, to Thee,
Nearer to Thee.

p Though, like the wanderer,
The sun gone down,
Darkness comes over me,
My rest a stone,
cr Yet in my dreams I'd be
dim Nearer, my God, to Thee,
Nearer to Thee.

mf There let my way appear
Steps unto heaven,
All that Thou sendest me
In mercy given,
cr Angels to beckon me
dim Nearer, my God, to Thee,
Nearer to Thee.

mf Then, with my waking thoughts
Bright with Thy praise,
Out of my stony griefs
Beth-el I'll raise;
cr So by my woes to be
dim Nearer, my God, to Thee,
Nearer to Thee.

General Hymns.

Hymn 278.

"And the Apostles said unto the Lord, Increase our faith."

mf O FOR a faith that will not shrink,
  Though pressed by many a foe;
That will not tremble on the brink
  Of poverty or woe;

p That will not murmur nor complain
  Beneath the chastening rod,
cr But in the hour of grief or pain
  Can lean upon its God;

mf A faith that shines more bright and clear
  When tempests rage without;
That when in danger knows no fear,
  In darkness feels no doubt;

A faith that keeps the narrow way
  Till life's last spark is fled,
And with a pure and heavenly ray
  Lights up the dying bed.

p Lord, give me such a faith as this,
  And then, whate'er may come,
cr I taste e'en now the hallowed bliss
  Of an eternal home.

General Hymns.

Hymn 279.

"Lord, help me."

p O HELP us, Lord; each hour of need
 Thy heavenly succour give;
mf Help us in thought, and word, and deed,
 Each hour on earth we live.

p O help us when our spirits bleed
 With contrite anguish sore;
And when our hearts are cold and dead,
cr O help us, Lord, the more.

mf O help us through the prayer of faith
 More firmly to believe;
For still the more the servant hath,
 The more shall he receive.

O help us, Jesu, from on high;
 We know no help but Thee;
O help us so to live and die
cr As Thine in heaven to be.

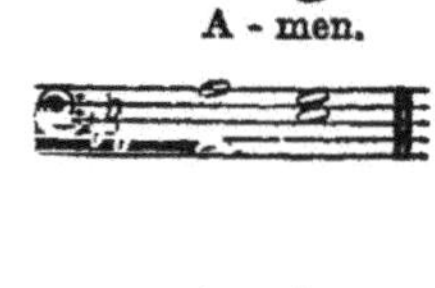

General Hymns.

Hymn 280. (First Tune.)

"And they shall be Mine, saith the Lord of hosts, in that day when I make up My jewels."

mf THINE for ever! God of love,
Hear us from Thy Throne above;
Thine for ever may we be
Here and in eternity.

Thine for ever! Lord of life,
Shield us through our earthly strife;
Thou the Life, the Truth, the Way,
Guide us to the realms of day.

Thine for ever! oh, how blest
They who find in Thee their rest!
Saviour, Guardian, Heavenly Friend,
O defend us to the end.

Thine for ever! Saviour, keep
p Us Thy frail and trembling sheep;
Safe alone beneath Thy care,
cr Let us all Thy goodness share.

mf Thine for ever; Thou our Guide,
All our wants by Thee supplied,
All our sins by Thee forgiven,
cr Lead us, Lord, from earth to heaven.

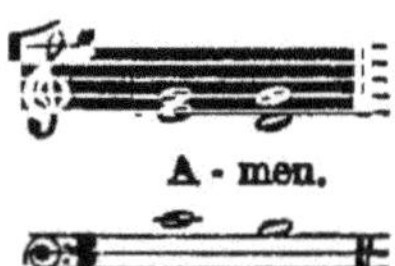

General Hymns.

Hymn 280. (Second Tune.)

"And they shall be Mine, saith the Lord of hosts, in that day when I make up My jewels."

mf THINE for ever! God of love,
Hear us from Thy Throne above;
Thine for ever may we be
Here and in eternity.

Thine for ever! Lord of life,
Shield us through our earthly strife;
Thou the Life, the Truth, the Way,
Guide us to the realms of day.

Thine for ever! oh, how blest
They who find in Thee their rest!
Saviour, Guardian, Heavenly Friend,
O defend us to the end.

Thine for ever! Saviour, keep
p Us Thy frail and trembling sheep;
Safe alone beneath Thy care,
cr Let us all Thy goodness share.

mf Thine for ever; Thou our Guide,
All our wants by Thee supplied,
All our sins by Thee forgiven,
cr Lead us, Lord, from earth to heaven.

General Hymns.

Hymn 281.

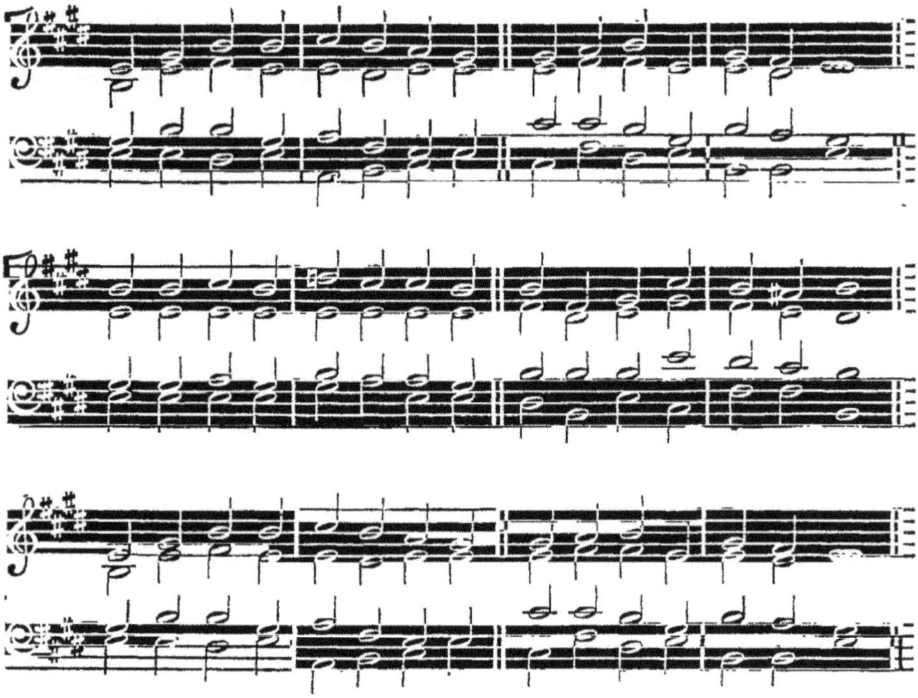

"I am the Lord thy God . . . . which leadeth thee by the way that thou shouldest go."

mf LEAD us, Heavenly FATHER, lead us
  O'er the world's tempestuous sea;
Guide us, guard us, keep us, feed us,
  For we have no help but Thee,
Yet possessing every blessing,
  If our GOD our FATHER be.

p SAVIOUR, breathe forgiveness o'er us,
  All our weakness Thou dost know;
Thou didst tread this earth before us,
  Thou didst feel its keenest woe;
Lone and dreary, faint and weary,
  Through the desert Thou didst go.

mf SPIRIT of our GOD, descending,
  Fill our hearts with heavenly joy,
Love with every passion blending,
  Pleasure that can never cloy;
Thus provided, pardoned, guided,
  Nothing can our peace destroy.

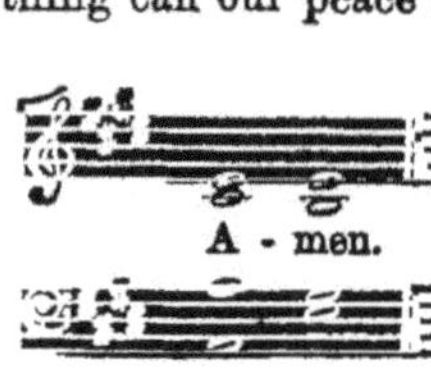

General Hymns.

Hymn 282.

"O hold Thou up my goings in Thy paths; that my footsteps slip not."

mf BE Thou my Guardian and my Guide,
And hear me when I call;
Let not my slippery footsteps slide,
And hold me lest I fall.

p And if I tempted am to sin,
And outward things are strong,
cr Do Thou, O LORD, keep watch within,
And save my soul from wrong.

p The world, the flesh, and Satan dwell
Around the path I tread;
cr O save me from the snares of hell,
f Thou Quickener of the dead.

mf Still let me ever watch and pray,
p And feel that I am frail;
That if the tempter cross my way,
cr Yet he may not prevail.

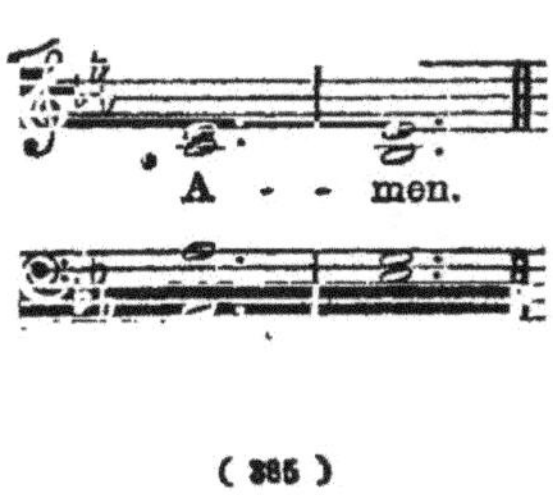

General Hymns.

Hymn 283.

"Lord, remember me."

mf O THOU, from Whom all goodness flows,
  I lift my soul to Thee;
p In all my sorrows, conflicts, woes,
  Good LORD, remember me.

When on my aching burdened heart
  My sins lie heavily,
cr Thy pardon grant, Thy peace impart;
p Good LORD, remember me.

When trials sore obstruct my way,
  And ills I cannot flee,
mf Then let my strength be as my day;
p Good LORD, remember me.

If worn with pain, disease, and grief
  This feeble frame should be,
cr Grant patience, rest, and kind relief;
p Good LORD, remember me.

And, oh, when in the hour of death
  I bow to Thy decree,
JESU, receive my parting breath;
pp Good LORD, remember me.

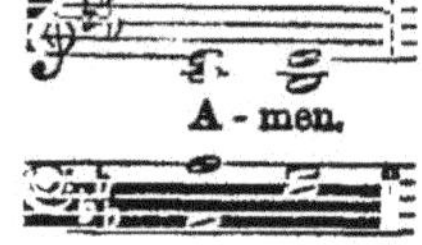

General Hymns.

Hymn 284.

"My soul thirsteth for Thee, my flesh also longeth after Thee; in a barren and dry land where no water is."

p FAR from my heavenly home,
Far from my FATHER's breast,
Fainting I cry, "Blest SPIRIT, come,
cr And speed me to my rest."

mf My spirit homeward turns,
And fain would thither flee;
dim My heart, O Sion, droops and yearns,
When I remember thee.

mf To thee, to thee, I press,
p A dark and toilsome road;
When shall I pass the wilderness,
cr And reach the Saints' abode?

mf GOD of my life, be near;
On Thee my hopes I cast;
p O guide me through the desert here,
cr And bring me home at last.

Hymn 285.

"And He arose and rebuked the wind, and said unto the sea, Peace, be still."

f FIERCE raged the tempest o'er the deep,
Watch did Thine anxious servants keep,
dim But Thou wast wrapped in guileless sleep,
pp Calm and still.

mf "Save, LORD, we perish," was their cry,
"O save us in our agony!"
cr Thy Word above the storm rose high,
p "Peace, be still."

pp The wild winds hushed; *(f)* the angry deep
dim Sank, like a little child, to sleep;
The sullen billows ceased to leap,
cr At Thy Will.

mf So, when our life is clouded o'er,
And storm-winds drift us from the shore,
Say, lest we sink to rise no more,
pp "Peace, be still."

General Hymns.

Hymn 286.

"Our light affliction, which is but for a moment, worketh for us a far more exceeding and eternal weight of glory."

mf O LET him, whose sorrow
No relief can find,
Trust in God, and borrow
Ease for heart and mind.

p Where the mourner weeping
Sheds the secret tear,
cr God His watch is keeping,
dim Though none else be near.

mf God will never leave thee,
All thy wants He knows,
Feels the pain that grieves thee,
Sees thy cares and woes.

Raise thine eyes to heaven
When thy spirits quail,
When, by tempests driven,
Heart and courage fail.

p When in grief we languish,
cr He will dry the tear,
Who His children's anguish
Soothes with succour near.

p All our woe and sadness,
In this world below,
cr Balance not the gladness
We in heaven shall know.

p Jesu, Holy Saviour,
cr In the realms above
mf Crown us with Thy favour,
Fill us with Thy love.

General Hymns.

Hymn 287.

General Hymns.

"Let my supplication come before Thee; deliver me, according to Thy Word."

mf JESUS, Lord of life and glory,
  Bend from heaven Thy gracious ear;
While our waiting souls adore Thee,
  Friend of helpless sinners, hear:
p   By Thy mercy,
  O deliver us, good Lord.

mf From the depths of nature's blindness,
  From the hardening power of sin,
From all malice and unkindness,
  From the pride that lurks within,
p   By Thy mercy,
  O deliver us, good Lord.

When temptation sorely presses,
  In the day of Satan's power,
In our times of deep distresses,
  In each dark and trying hour,
    By Thy mercy,
  O deliver us, good Lord.

mf When the world around is smiling,
  In the time of wealth and ease,
Earthly joys our hearts beguiling,
  In the day of health and peace,
p   By Thy mercy,
  O deliver us, good Lord.

In the weary hours of sickness,
  In the times of grief and pain,
When we feel our mortal weakness,
  When the creature's help is vain,
    By Thy mercy,
  O deliver us, good Lord.

In the solemn hour of dying,
  In the awful judgment day,
cr May our souls, on Thee relying,
  Find Thee still our Hope and Stay:
p   By Thy mercy,
  O deliver us, good Lord.

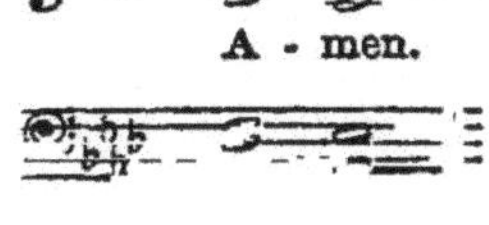

General Hymns.

Hymn 288.

General Hymns.

"The time is short."

mf A FEW more years shall roll,
A few more seasons come,
dim And we shall be with those that rest
p Asleep within the tomb:
Then, O my LORD, prepare *(cr)*
My soul for that great day;
cr e dim O wash me in Thy precious Blood,
p And take my sins away.

mf A few more suns shall set
O'er these dark hills of time,
And we shall be where suns are not,
A far serener clime:
p Then, O my LORD, prepare *(cr)*
My soul for that bright day;
cr e dim O wash me in Thy precious Blood,
p And take my sins away.

mf A few more storms shall beat
On this wild rocky shore,
cr And we shall be where tempests cease,
And surges swell no more:
p Then, O my LORD, prepare *(cr)*
My soul for that calm day;
cr e dim O wash me in Thy precious Blood,
p And take my sins away.

A few more struggles here,
A few more partings o'er,
A few more toils, a few more tears,
cr And we shall weep no more:
p Then, O my LORD, prepare *(cr)*
My soul for that blest day;
cr e dim O wash me in Thy precious Blood,
p And take my sins away.

mf 'Tis but a little while
And He shall come again,
p Who died that we might live, *(f)* Who lives
That we with Him may reign:
p Then, O my LORD, prepare *(cr)*
My soul for that glad day;
cr e dim O wash me in Thy precious Blood,
p And take my sins away.

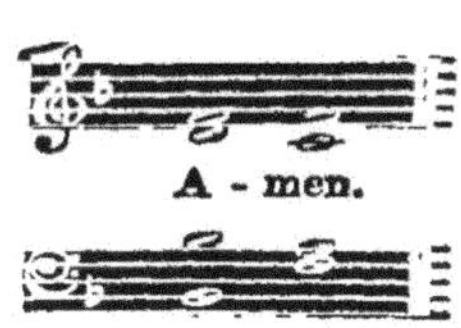

General Hymns.

Hymn 289.

In slow time.

"So soon passeth it away, and we are gone."

mf DAYS and moments quickly flying
Blend the living with the dead;
p Soon will you and I be lying
Each within his narrow bed.

Soon our souls to GOD Who gave them
Will have sped their rapid flight:
cr Able now by grace to save them,
Oh, that while we can we might!

mf JESU, Infinite Redeemer,
Maker of this mighty frame,
dim Teach, O teach us to remember
What we are and whence we came;

Whence we came, and whither wending;
p Soon we must through darkness go,
f To inherit bliss unending,
p Or eternity of woe.

After the 4th verse.
mf
O by Thy power grant, Lord, that we
dim.
At our last hour fall not from Thee;
p
cres.
Saved by Thy grace, Thine may we be
All through the days of e - ter - - - - - - - - ni - ty.
dim.
A - - men.

Y

General Hymns.

Hymn 290.

"I will alway give thanks unto the Lord: His praise shall ever be in my mouth."

mf THROUGH all the changing scenes of life,
  In trouble and in joy,
The praises of my GOD shall still
  My heart and tongue employ.

O magnify the LORD with me,
  With me exalt His Name;
p When in distress to Him I called,
f   He to my rescue came.

mf The hosts of GOD encamp around
  The dwellings of the just;
Deliverance He affords to all
  Who on His succour trust.

O make but trial of His love,
  Experience will decide
How blessed are they, and only they,
  Who in His truth confide.

Fear Him, ye saints, and you will the
  Have nothing else to fear;
Make you His service your delight,
  Your wants shall be His care.

f To FATHER, SON, and HOLY GHOST,
  The GOD Whom we adore,
Be glory, as it was, is now,
  And shall be evermore.

General Hymns.

Hymn 291.

"Fight the good fight of faith, lay hold on eternal life."

mf OFT in danger, oft in woe,
Onward, Christians, onward go;
Bear the toil, maintain the strife,
Strengthened with the Bread of Life!

Let not sorrow dim your eye,
cr Soon shall every tear be dry;
mf Let not fear your course impede,
f Great your strength, if *(dim)* great your need.

mf Let your drooping hearts be glad;
March in heavenly armour clad;
Fight, nor think the battle long,
f Soon shall victory wake your song.

Onward then to glory move;
More than conquerors ye shall prove;
dim Though opposed by many a foe,
f Christian soldiers, onward go!

Hymns of glory and of praise,
mf Father, unto Thee we raise:
Holy Jesus, praise to Thee
With the Spirit ever be.

General Hymns.

Hymn 292. (First Tune.)

General Hymns.

Hymn 292. (Second Tune.)

"O praise the Lord of heaven, praise Him in the height."

ff PRAISE the Lord! ye heavens, adore Him,
Praise Him, Angels, in the height;
Sun and moon, rejoice before Him,
Praise Him, all ye stars and light:
f Praise the Lord! for He hath spoken,
Worlds His mighty voice obeyed;
ff Laws, which never shall be broken,
For their guidance He hath made.

f Praise the Lord! for He is glorious;
Never shall His promise fail;
ff God hath made His saints victorious,
Sin and death shall not prevail.
Praise the God of our salvation;
Hosts on high, His power proclaim;
Heaven and earth, and all creation,
Laud and magnify His Name!

1.

2.

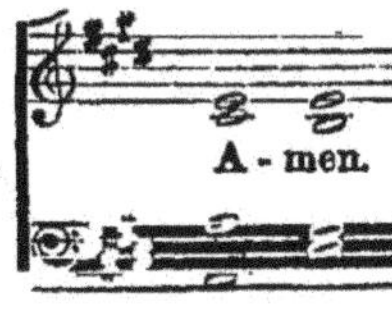

General Hymns.

Hymn 293.

General Hymns.

O that men would therefore praise the Lord for His goodness."

f SING praise to God Who reigns above,
The God of all creation,
The God of power, *(p)* the God of love,
f The God of our salvation;
mf With healing balm my soul He fills,
And every faithless murmur stills;
f To God all praise and glory.*

mf The Angel-host, O King of kings,
Thy praise for ever telling,
In earth and sky all living things
Beneath Thy shadow dwelling,
Adore the wisdom which could span,
And power which formed creation's plan:
f To God all praise and glory.

mf What God's Almighty power hath made
His gracious mercy keepeth;
cr By morning glow *(p)* or evening shade
His watchful eye ne'er sleepeth;
mf Within the kingdom of His might
Lo! all is just and all is right;
f To God all praise and glory.

mf The Lord is never far away,
p But, through all grief distressing,
cr An ever-present help and stay,
Our peace and joy and blessing;
dim As with a mother's tender hand,
cr He leads His own, His chosen band;
f To God all praise and glory.

mf Thus all my toilsome way along
cr I sing aloud Thy praises,
That men may hear the grateful song
My voice unwearied raises:
f Be joyful in the Lord, my heart;
Both soul and body bear your part;
ff To God all praise and glory.

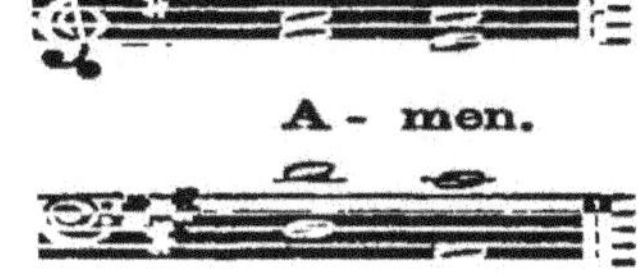

Hymn 294.

Who led His people through the wilderness; for His mercy endureth for ever."

f O PRAISE our Great and Gracious LORD,
  And call upon His Name;
To strains of joy tune every chord,
  His mighty acts proclaim;
mf Tell how He led His chosen race
  To Canaan's promised land;
Tell how His covenant of grace
f   Unchanged shall ever stand.

mf He gave the shadowing cloud by day,
  The moving fire by night;
To guide His Israel on their way,
  He made their darkness light;
And have not we a sure retreat,
  A Saviour ever nigh,
cr The same clear light to guide our feet,
  The Day-spring from on high?

mf We too have Manna from above,
  The Bread that came from heaven;
To us the same kind hand of love
  Has living waters given;
A Rock have we, from whence the spring
  In rich abundance flows;
f That Rock is CHRIST, our Priest, our King,
  Who life and health bestows.

mf O may we prize this blessèd Food,
  And trust our heavenly Guide;
p So shall we find death's fearful flood
  Serene as Jordan's tide,
cr And safely reach that happy shore,
p   The land of peace and rest,
cr Where Angels worship and adore
  In GOD's own Presence blest.

General Hymns.

Hymn 295.

"All Thy works praise Thee, O Lord."

f The strain upraise of joy and praise, Alle-	-lu - - - ia!	To the glory of their King Let the ransomed	peo - ple sing
And the choirs that . . .	dwell on high	Swell the chorus	in the sky,
mf Ye, through the fields of .	Paradise that roam,	Ye blessèd ones, repeat through	that bright home
(*Unison.*) Ye planets glittering on your	heaven - ly way,	Ye shining constellations,	join and say
(*Harmony.*) *p* Ye clouds that onward sweep, Ye winds on	pin - ions light,	*f* Ye thunders, echoing loud and deep, Ye lightnings,	wild - ly bright,
mf Ye floods and ocean billows, Ye storms and	win - ter snow,	Ye days of cloudless beauty, Hoar frost and	sum - mer glow,
(*Trebles only.*) *p* First let the birds, with painted	plum - age gay,	Exalt their great Creater's	praise, and say
(*Men only.*) Then let the beasts of earth, with	vary - ing strain,	Join in creation's hymn, and	cry a - gain
(*Men only.*) *f* Here let the mountains thunder forth so-	-nor - - ous	Alle - - - - - - -	-lu - - ia!
(*Men only.*) *mf* Thou jubilant abyss of . .	o - cean, cry	Alle - - - - - - -	-lu - - ia!
(*Harmony.*) To God, Who all cre - -	-a - tion made,	The frequent hymn be	du - ly paid,
This is the strain, the eternal strain, the Lord of	all things loves,	Alle - - - - - - -	-lu - - ia!
Wherefore we sing, both heart and voice a-	-wak - - ing,	Alle - - - - - - -	-lu - - ia!
(*Unison.*) Now from all men . . .	be out-poured	Alleluia	to the Lord;
(*Harmony.*) *ff* Praise be done to the . .	Three in One.	Alle - - - - - - -	-lu - - ia!

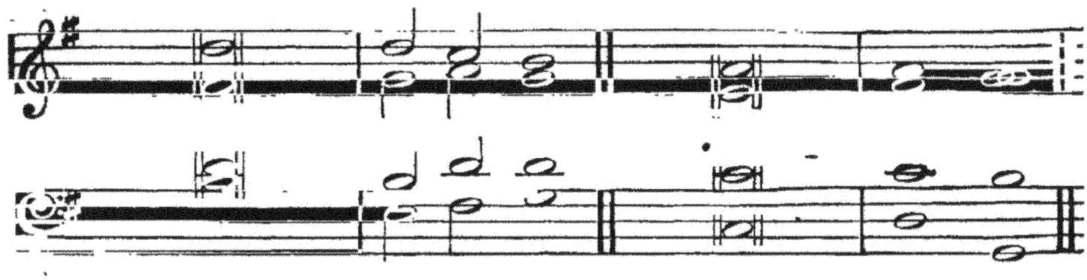

	Alle - - - - - -	-lu - - ia !	Alle - - -	- lu - - ia !
	Alle - - - - - -	-lu - - ia !	Alle - - -	- lu - - ia !
	Alle - - - - - -	-lu - - ia !	Alle - - -	- lu - - ia !
f	Alle - - - - - -	-lu - - ia !	Alle - - -	- lu - - ia !
p	In sweet con- - - - -	-sent u - nite	your Alle - -	- lu - - ia !
	Ye groves that wave in spring, And glorious	fo - rests, sing	*f* Alle - - -	- lu - - ia !
f	Alle - - - - - -	-lu - - ia !	Alle - - -	- lu - - ia !
	Alle - - - - - -	-lu - - ia !	Alle - - -	- lu - - ia !
p	(*Trebles only.*) There let the valleys sing in gentler	cho - - rus	Alle - - -	- lu - - ia !
	(*Trebles only.*) Ye tracts of earth and conti-	-nents, re - ply	Alle - - -	- lu - - ia !
f	Alle - - - - - -	-lu - - ia !	Alle - - -	- lu - - ia !
	This is the song, the heavenly song, that CHRIST Him-	-self ap - proves,	Alle - - -	- lu - - ia !
p	(*Trebles only.*) And children's voices echo, answer	mak - - ing,	Alle - - -	- lu - - ia !
	With Alleluia . . .	e - ver - more	The SON and SPIRIT	we - - adore.
	Alle - - - -	-lu - ia !	Alle - - -	- lu - - ia !
				A - - men.

General Hymns.

"And all her streets shall say, Alleluia."

Hymn 296. (First Tune.)

General Hymns.

General Hymns.

Hymn 296. (Second Tune.)

"And all her streets shall say, Alleluia."

f SING Alleluia forth in duteous praise,
Ye citizens of heaven; O sweetly raise
ff An endless Alleluia.

mf Ye Powers, who stand before the Eternal Light,
cr In hymning choirs re-echo to the height
f An endless Alleluia.

mf The Holy City shall take up your strain,
cr And with glad songs resounding wake again
f An endless Alleluia.

mf In blissful antiphons ye thus rejoice
To render to the Lord with thankful voice
f An endless Alleluia.

mf Ye who have gained at length your palms in bliss,
cr Victorious ones, your chant shall still be this,
f An endless Alleluia.

There, in one grand acclaim, for ever ring
The strains which tell the honour of your King,
ff An endless Alleluia.

p This is sweet rest for weary ones brought back,
This is glad food and drink which ne'er shall lack,
mf An endless Alleluia.

While Thee, by Whom were all things made, we praise
For ever, and tell out in sweetest lays
f An endless Alleluia.

Almighty Christ, to Thee our voices sing
Glory for evermore; to Thee we bring
ff An endless Alleluia.

General Hymns.

Hymn 297.

" When I laid the foundations of the earth . . . . when the morning stars sang together, and all the sons of God shouted for joy."

mf SONGS of praise the Angels sang,
Heaven with Alleluias rang,
When creation was begun,
When God spake and it was done.

Songs of praise awoke the morn
p When the Prince of peace was born;
cr Songs of praise arose when He
f Captive led captivity.

p Heaven and earth must pass away,
mf Songs of praise shall crown that day;
God will make new heavens and earth,
f Songs of praise shall hail their birth.

p And will man alone be dumb
Till that glorious kingdom come?
cr No, the Church delights to raise
f Psalms and hymns and songs of praise.

mf Saints below, with heart and voice,
Still in songs of praise rejoice;
Learning here, by faith and love,
Songs of praise to sing above.

f Hymns of glory, songs of praise,
Father, unto Thee we raise,
Jesu, glory unto Thee,
With the Spirit, ever be.

General Hymns.

Hymn 298.

"Praise the Lord, O my soul; and all that is within me praise His Holy Name."

mf PRAISE, my soul, the King of heaven,
To His feet thy tribute bring;
Ransomed, healed, restored, forgiven,
Evermore His praises sing;
f Alleluia! Alleluia!
Praise the everlasting King.

mf Praise Him for His grace and favour
To our fathers in distress;
Praise Him still the same as ever,
Slow to chide, and swift to bless;
f Alleluia! Alleluia!
Glorious in His faithfulness.

p Father-like, He tends and spares us,
Well our feeble frame He knows;
In His hands He gently bears us,
Rescues us from all our foes;
f Alleluia! Alleluia!
Widely yet His mercy flows.

Angels in the height, adore Him;
Ye behold Him face to face;
Saints triumphant, bow before Him,
Gathered in from every race;
ff Alleluia! Alleluia!
Praise with us the God of grace.

General Hymns.

Hymn 299.

"I heard the voice of many angels . . . saying, . . . Worthy is the Lamb that was slain to receive power, and riches, and wisdom, and strength, and honour, and glory, and blessing."

f COME let us join our cheerful songs
With Angels round the Throne;
Ten thousand thousand are their tongues,
But all their joys are one.

"Worthy the LAMB that died," they cry,
"To be exalted thus;"
"Worthy the LAMB," our lips reply,
p "For He was slain for us."

mf JESUS is worthy to receive
Honour and power Divine;
cr And blessings, more than we can give,
Be, LORD, for ever Thine.

f Let all creation join in one
To bless the sacred Name
Of Him that sits upon the Throne,
p And to adore the LAMB.

General Hymns.

Hymn 300. (First Tune.)

301 Orig. Ed.

General Hymns.

Hymn 300. (Second Tune.)

"King of kings, and Lord of lords."

f ALL hail the power of Jesu's Name;
dim Let Angels prostrate fall;
cr Bring forth the royal diadem
To crown Him Lord of all.

mf Crown Him, ye morning stars of light,
Who fixed this floating ball;
f Now hail the Strength of Israel's might,
And crown Him Lord of all.

mf Crown Him, ye Martyrs of your God,
Who from His Altar call;
Extol the Stem-of-Jesse's Rod,
And crown Him Lord of all.

Ye seed of Israel's chosen race,
Ye ransomed of the fall,
cr Hail Him Who saves you by His grace,
And crown Him Lord of all.

mf Hail Him, ye heirs of David's line,
Whom David Lord did call,
p The God Incarnate, Man Divine,
And crown Him Lord of all.

Sinners, whose love can ne'er forget
The wormwood and the gall,
cr Go spread your trophies at His feet,
And crown Him Lord of all.

f Let every tribe and every tongue
Before Him prostrate fall,
And shout in universal song
The crownèd Lord of all.

The last line of every verse is to be sung as marked in the music.

General Hymns.

Hymn 301.

"To him that overcometh will I grant to sit with Me in My throne, even as I also overcame, and am set down with My Father in His throne."

p THE Head that once was crowned with thorns
f Is crowned with glory now:
A royal diadem adorns
The mighty Victor's Brow.

The highest place that heaven affords
Is His, is His by right,
The King of kings, and LORD of lords,
And heaven's eternal Light.

mf The Joy of all who dwell above,
The Joy of all below,
To whom He manifests His love,
And grants His Name to know.

p To them the Cross, with all its shame,
cr With all its grace, is given:
f Their name an everlasting name,
Their joy the joy of heaven.

p They suffer with their LORD below,
f They reign with Him above;
mf Their profit and their joy to know
The mystery of His love.

The Cross He bore is life and health,
Though shame and death to Him;
His people's hope, His people's wealth,
f Their everlasting theme.

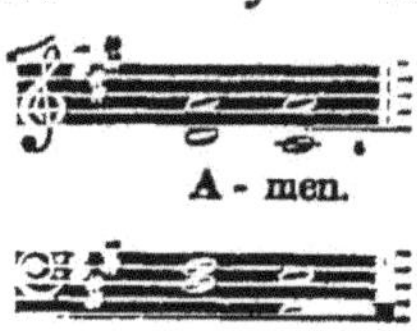

General Hymns.

Hymn 302.

"The four beasts and four and twenty elders fell down before the Lamb, having every one of them harps, and golden vials full of odours, which are the prayers of saints."

f COME, ye faithful, raise the anthem,
Cleave the skies with shouts of praise;
Sing to Him Who found the ransom,
Ancient of eternal days,
God of God, the Word Incarnate,
Whom the heaven of heaven obeys.

mf Ere He raised the lofty mountains,
Formed the seas, or built the sky,
Love eternal, free, and boundless,
p Moved the Lord of Life to die,
cr Fore-ordained the Prince of princes
p For the throne of Calvary.

There, for us and our redemption,
See Him all His Life-blood pour!
cr There He wins our full salvation,
Dies that we may die no more;
f Then, arising, lives for ever,
ff Reigning where He was before.

f High on yon celestial mountains
Stands His gem-built Throne, all bright,
Midst unending Alleluias
Bursting from the sons of light;
Sion's people tell His praises,
ff Victor after hard-won fight.

mf Bring your harps, and bring your odours,
Sweep the string and pour the lay;
f Let the earth proclaim His wonders,
King of that celestial day;
p He the Lamb once slain is worthy,
Who was dead, *(f)* and lives for aye.

ff Laud and honour to the Father,
Laud and honour to the Son,
Laud and honour to the Spirit,
Ever Three and ever One,
Consubstantial, Co-eternal,
While unending ages run.

General Hymns.

Hymn 303.

General Hymns.

"In everything give thanks."

mf WHEN morning gilds the skies,
My heart awaking cries,
f May JESUS CHRIST be praised:
p Alike at work and prayer
cr To JESUS I repair;
May JESUS CHRIST be praised.

mf Whene'er the sweet church bell
Peals over hill and dell,
f May JESUS CHRIST be praised:
p O hark to what it sings,
cr As joyously it rings,
May JESUS CHRIST be praised.

mf My tongue shall never tire
Of chanting with the choir,
f May JESUS CHRIST be praised:
p This song of sacred joy,
cr It never seems to cloy,
May JESUS CHRIST be praised.

p When sleep her balm denies,
My silent spirit sighs,
mf May JESUS CHRIST be praised:
p When evil thoughts molest,
cr With this I shield my breast,
May JESUS CHRIST be praised.

p Does sadness fill my mind?
cr A solace here I find,
mf May JESUS CHRIST be praised:
p Or fades my earthly bliss?
cr My comfort still is this,
May JESUS CHRIST be praised.

mf The night becomes as day,
When from the heart we say,
f May JESUS CHRIST be praised:
p The powers of darkness fear,
cr When this sweet chant they hear,
May JESUS CHRIST be praised.

f In heaven's eternal bliss
The loveliest strain is this,
ff May JESUS CHRIST be praised:
f Let earth, and sea, and sky
cr From depth to height reply,
May JESUS CHRIST be praised.

mf Be this, while life is mine,
My canticle Divine,
f May JESUS CHRIST be praised:
Be this the eternal song
Through ages all along,
cr May JESUS CHRIST be praised.

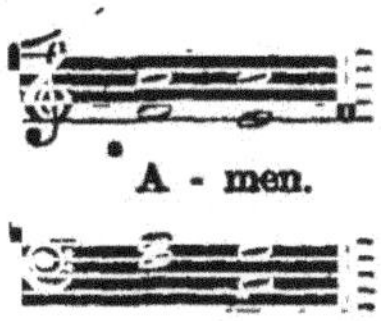

General Hymns.

Hymn 304.

General Hymns.

"And on His Head were many crowns."

f CROWN Him with many crowns,
The LAMB upon His Throne;
Hark! how the heavenly anthem drowns
All music but its own:
Awake, my soul, and sing
p Of Him Who died for thee,
cr And hail Him as thy matchless King
Through all eternity.

f Crown Him the Virgin's Son,
p The GOD Incarnate born,
cr Whose Arm those crimson trophies won
Which now His Brow adorn:
p Fruit of the mystic Rose,
cr As of that Rose the Stem;
mf The Root whence mercy ever flows,
p The Babe of Bethlehem.

mf Crown Him the LORD of love:
p Behold His Hands and Side,
cr Rich Wounds yet visible above
In beauty glorified:
p No Angel in the sky
Can fully bear that sight,
pp rit. But downward bends his burning eye
At mysteries so bright.

mf Crown Him the LORD of peace,
cr Whose power a sceptre sways
From pole to pole, that wars may cease,
And all be prayer and praise:
f His reign shall know no end,
p And round His piercèd Feet
Fair flowers of Paradise extend
cr Their fragrance ever sweet.

f Crown Him the LORD of years,
The Potentate of time,
Creator of the rolling spheres,
Ineffably Sublime:
All hail, Redeemer, hail!
p For Thou hast died for me;
ff Thy praise shall never, never fail
Throughout eternity.

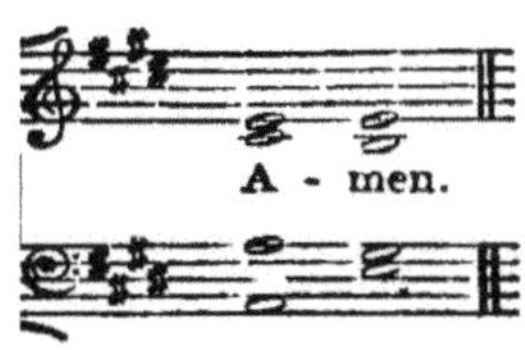

General Hymns.

Hymn 305.

General Hymns.

"Every day will I give thanks unto Thee, and praise Thy Name for ever and ever."

mf SAVIOUR, Blessèd Saviour,
Listen whilst we sing,
Hearts and voices raising
Praises to our King;
p All we have we offer;
All we hope to be,
f Body, soul, and spirit,
All we yield to Thee.

Nearer, ever nearer,
CHRIST, we draw to Thee,
Deep in adoration
Bending low the knee;
Thou for our redemption
Cam'st on earth to die;
Thou, that we might follow,
Hast gone up on high.

mf Great and ever greater
Are Thy mercies here,
f True and everlasting
Are the glories there,
p Where no pain, or sorrow,
Toil, or care, is known,
f Where the Angel-legions
Circle round Thy Throne.

p Dark and ever darker
Was the wintry past,
cr Now a ray of gladness
O'er our path is cast;
p Every day that passeth,
Every hour that flies,
f Tells of love unfeignèd,
Love that never dies.

mf Clearer still and clearer
Dawns the light from heaven,
In our sadness bringing
News of sin forgiven;
Life has lost its shadows,
Pure the light within;
f Thou hast shed Thy radiance
On a world of sin.

Brighter still and brighter
Glows the western sun,
Shedding all its gladness
O'er our work that's done;
p Time will soon be over,
Toil and sorrow past,
mf May we, Blessèd Saviour,
Find a rest at last.

Onward, ever onward,
Journeying o'er the road
cr Worn by saints before us,
Journeying on to GOD;
p Leaving all behind us,
cr May we hasten on,
Backward never looking
Till the prize is won.

f Bliss, all bliss excelling,
When the ransomed soul,
Earthly toils forgetting,
Finds its promised goal;
p Where in joys unheard of
cr Saints with Angels sing,
f Never weary raising
Praises to their King.

General Hymns.

Hymn 306.

* *In verse 5 sing this chord to the first word of line 2, and divide the ○ of the melody to the same.*

General Hymns.

"Wherefore God also hath highly exalted Him, and given Him a name which is above every name: that at the name of Jesus every knee should bow."

mf AT the Name of JESUS
  Every knee shall bow,
cr Every tongue confess Him
f   King of glory now;
mf 'Tis the FATHER's pleasure
  We should call Him LORD,
cr Who from the beginning
  Was the Mighty WORD.

f At His voice creation
  Sprang at once to sight,
All the Angel faces,
  All the hosts of light,
Thrones and Dominations,
  Stars upon their way,
All the heavenly Orders,
  In their great array.

p Humbled for a season,
  To receive a Name
From the lips of sinners
  Unto whom He came,
cr Faithfully He bore it
  Spotless to the last,
Brought it back victorious,
  When from death He passed:

f Bore it up triumphant,
p   With its human light,
cr Through all ranks of creatures,
  To the central height;
f To the Throne of GODHEAD,
  To the FATHER's breast,
Filled it with the glory
dim Of that perfect rest.

f Name Him, brothers, name Him,*
  With love as strong as death,
p But with awe and wonder,
pp   And with 'bated breath;
p He is GOD the Saviour,
  He is CHRIST the LORD,
cr Ever to be worshipped,
  Trusted, and adored.

mf In your hearts enthrone Him;
  There let Him subdue
All that is not holy,
  All that is not true:
cr Crown Him as your Captain
  In temptation's hour;
Let His Will enfold you
  In its light and power.

f Brothers, this LORD JESUS
  Shall return again,
With His FATHER's glory,
  With His Angel train;
ff For all wreaths of empire
  Meet upon His Brow,
And our hearts confess Him
rall. King of glory now.

* *See note on opposite page.*

General Hymns.

Hymn 307.

General Hymns.

"So shall the King have pleasure in thy beauty: for He is thy Lord God, and worship thou Him."

mf O SAVIOUR, precious Saviour,
  Whom yet unseen we love,
cr O Name of might and favour,
  All other names above!
 p We worship Thee, *(cr)* we bless Thee,
   To Thee alone we sing;
 f We praise Thee, and confess Thee
   Our holy LORD and King.

mf O Bringer of salvation,
  Who wondrously hast wrought,
Thyself the revelation
  Of love beyond our thought;
 p We worship Thee, *(cr)* we bless Thee,
   To Thee alone we sing;
 f We praise Thee, and confess Thee
 dim Our gracious LORD and King.

f In Thee all fulness dwelleth,
  All grace and power Divine;
The glory that excelleth,
  O SON of GOD, is Thine;
 p We worship Thee, *(cr)* we bless Thee,
   To Thee alone we sing;
 f We praise Thee, and confess Thee
   Our glorious LORD and King.

mf O grant the consummation
  Of this our song above
In endless adoration,
  And everlasting love;
 f Then shall we praise and bless Thee
   Where perfect praises ring,
 And evermore confess Thee
   Our Saviour and our King.

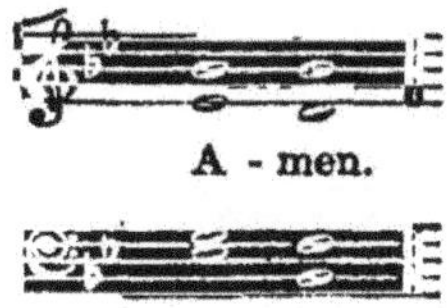

General Hymns.

Hymn 308.

General Hymns.

"O praise the Lord."

f O PRAISE ye the Lord!
  Praise Him in the height;
Rejoice in His Word,
  Ye Angels of light;
Ye heavens, adore Him
  By Whom ye were made,
p And worship before Him,
cr   In brightness arrayed.

f O praise ye the Lord!
  Praise Him upon earth,
mf In tuneful accord,
  Ye sons of new birth;
f Praise Him Who hath brought you
  His grace from above,
Praise Him Who hath taught you
  To sing of His love.

O praise ye the Lord,
  All things that give sound;
Each jubilant chord,
  Re-echo around;
Loud organs, His glory
  Forth tell in deep tone,
p And sweet harp, the story
  Of what He hath done.

f O praise ye the Lord!
  Thanksgiving and song
To Him be outpoured
  All ages along:
mf For love in creation,
cr   For heaven restored,
f For grace of salvation
  O praise ye the Lord!

Holy Communion.

Hymn 309. (First Tune.)

To be sung in Unison.

Holy Communion.

"The cup of blessing which we bless, is it not the communion of the Blood of Christ? The bread which we break, is it not the communion of the Body of Christ?"

mf NOW, my tongue, the mystery telling
Of the glorious Body sing,
And the Blood, all price excelling,
Which the Gentiles' LORD and King,
p In a Virgin's womb once dwelling,
Shed for this world's ransoming.

mf Given for us, and condescending
p To be born for us below,
cr He, with men in converse blending,
Dwelt the seed of truth to sow,
Till He closed with wondrous ending
p His most patient life of woe.

mf That last night, at supper lying,
'Mid the Twelve, His chosen band,
JESUS, with the law complying,
Keeps the feast its rites demand;
Then, more precious Food supplying,
Gives Himself with His own Hand.

p WORD-made-Flesh true bread He maketh
cr By His Word His Flesh to be;
p Wine His Blood; *(mf)* which whoso taketh
Must from carnal thoughts be free;
f Faith alone, though *(dim)* sight forsaketh,
mf Shews true hearts the mystery.

PART 2.

p Therefore we, before Him bending,
This great Sacrament revere;
cr Types and shadows have their ending,
For the newer rite is here;
mf Faith, our outward sense befriending,
Makes our inward vision clear.

f Glory let us give, and blessing
To the FATHER, and the SON,
Honour, might, and praise addressing,
While eternal ages run;
Ever too His love confessing,
Who from Both with Both is ONE.

Holy Communion.

Hymn 309. (Second Tune.)

Hymn 309. (Third Tune.)

Holy Communion.

"The cup of blessing which we bless, is it not the communion of the Blood of Christ? The bread which we break, is it not the communion of the Body of Christ?"

mf NOW, my tongue, the mystery telling
Of the glorious Body sing,
And the Blood, all price excelling,
Which the Gentiles' LORD and King,
p In a Virgin's womb once dwelling,
Shed for this world's ransoming.

mf Given for us, and condescending
p To be born for us below,
cr He, with men in converse blending,
Dwelt the seed of truth to sow,
Till He closed with wondrous ending
p His most patient life of woe.

mf That last night, at supper lying,
'Mid the Twelve, His chosen band,
JESUS, with the law complying,
Keeps the feast its rites demand;
Then, more precious Food supplying,
Gives Himself with His own Hand.

p WORD-made-Flesh true bread He maketh
cr By His Word His Flesh to be;
p Wine His Blood; *(mf)* which whoso taketh
Must from carnal thoughts be free;
f Faith alone, tho' *(dim)* sight forsaketh,
mf Shews true hearts the mystery.

PART 2.

p Therefore we, before Him bending,
This great Sacrament revere;
cr Types and shadows have their ending,
For the newer rite is here;
mf Faith, our outward sense befriending,
Makes our inward vision clear.

f Glory let us give, and blessing
To the FATHER, and the SON,
Honour, might, and praise addressing,
While eternal ages run;
Ever too His love confessing,
Who from Both with Both is ONE.

Holy Communion.

Hymn 310.

" So man did eat angels' food."

cres.
f
Cal.
Thine e-ter-nal goodness send us In the land of life to see: Ons. pp
pp
Thou Who all things canst and know - est, Who on earth such Food be - stow - est,
p
cres.
Grant us with Thy Saints, though low - est, Where the heav'n-ly Feast Thou show-est,
cres.
dim.
rall.
Fel-low heirs and guests . . to be. A - men.
dim.
rall.

Holy Communion.

Hymn 311.* (First Tune.)

To be sung in Unison.

* *The Tune "Melcombe" (Hymn 4) may also be sung to this Hymn, for which it was composed.*

Holy Communion.

Hymn 311. (Second Tune.)

"As the living Father hath sent Me, and I live by the Father, so he that eateth Me, even he shall live by Me."

mf THE Heavenly Word proceeding forth,
Yet leaving not the Father's side,
Accomplishing His work on earth
Had reached at length life's eventide.

mf By false disciple to be given
To foemen for His life athirst,
Himself, the very Bread of Heaven,
He gave to His disciples first.

He gave Himself in either kind,
His precious Flesh, His precious Blood;
cr In love's own fulness thus designed
Of the whole man to be the Food.

p By Birth their Fellow-man was He;
cr Their Meat, when sitting at the Board;
p He died, their Ransomer to be;
f He ever reigns, their great Reward.

Part 2.

p O Saving Victim, *(cr)* opening wide
mf The gate of heaven to *(dim)* man below,
cr Our foes press on from every side,
mf Thine aid supply, Thy strength *(dim)* bestow.

mf All praise and thanks to Thee ascend
For evermore, Blest One in Three;
p O grant us life that shall not end
cr In our true native land with Thee.

Holy Communion.

Hymn 312. (First Tune.)

Hymn 312. (Second Tune.)

Holy Communion.

Hymn 312. (Third Tune.)

"Jesus said unto them, I am the Bread of Life."

p THEE we adore, O hidden Sáviour, Thee,
Who in Thy Sacrament dost deígn to be;
Both flesh and spirit át Thy Presence fail,
Yet here Thy Presence wé devoutly hail.

mf O blest Memorial of our dýing Lord,
Who living Bread to men doth hére afford!
O may our souls for éver feed on Thee,
And Thou, O Christ, for éver precious be.

Fountain of goodness, Jesu, Lórd and God,
p Cleanse us, unclean, with Thy most cléansing Blood;
cr Increase our faith and lóve, that we may know
The hope and peace which fróm Thy Presence flow.

p O Christ, Whom now beneath a véil we see,
May what we thirst for soon our pórtion be,
cr To gaze on Thee unvéiled, and see Thy Face,
f The vision of Thy glóry and Thy grace.

2 and 3.

Holy Communion.

Hymn 313. (First Tune.)

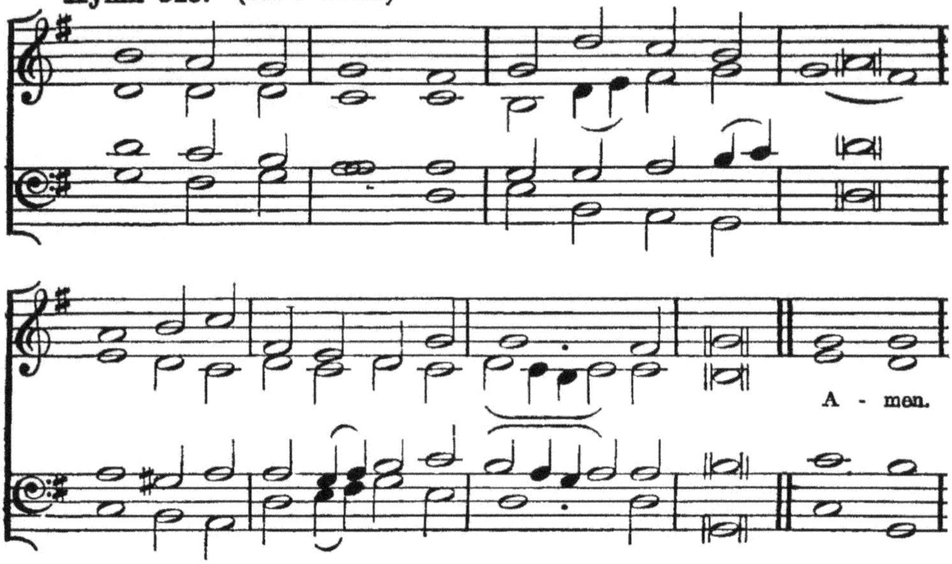

Hymn 313. (Second Tune.)

Holy Communion.

Hymn 313. (Third Tune.)

"Wisdom saith, Come eat of my bread, and drink of the wine which I have mingled."

p DRAW nigh and take the Body óf the Lord,
And drink the holy Blóod for you out-poured.

Saved by that Body and that hóly Blood,
cr With souls refreshed, we rénder thanks to God.

Salvation's Giver, Christ, the Ónly Son,
By His dear Cross and Blóod the victory won.

p Offered was He for greatest ánd for least,
Himself the Victim, ánd Himself the Priest.

Victims were offered by the láw of old,
Which in a type this heávenly mystery told.

mf He, Ransomer from death, and Líght from shade,
Now gives His holy gráce His saints to aid.

p Approach ye then with faithful héarts sincere,
cr And take the safeguard óf salvation here.

mf He, that His saínts in this world rules and shields,
To all believers lífe eternal yields;

With heavenly bread makes them that húnger whole,
Gives living waters tó the thirsting soul.

p Alpha and Omega, to Whóm shall bow
All nations at the Dóom, is with us now.

Holy Communion.

Hymn 314.

"He that eateth My Flesh and drinketh My Blood dwelleth in Me and I in him."

mf O FOOD that weary pilgrims love,
O Bread of Angel-hosts above,
O Manna of the Saints,
The hungry soul would feed on Thee;
cr Ne'er may the heart unsolaced be
Which for Thy *(dim)* sweetness faints.

mf O Fount of love, O cleansing Tide,
p Which from the Saviour's piercèd Side
And Sacred Heart dost flow,
cr Be ours to drink of Thy pure rill,
Which only can our spirits fill,
And all we need bestow.

p Lord Jesu, Whom, by power Divine
Now hidden 'neath the outward sign,
We worship and adore,
mf Grant, when the veil away is rolled,
cr With open face we may behold
Thyself for evermore.

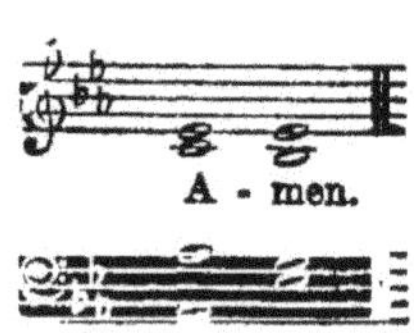

Hymn 315.

"We have an Altar."

mf ONCE, only once, and once for all,
His precious life He gave;
Before the Cross our spirits fall,
And own it strong to save.

"One offering, single and complete,"
With lips and heart we say;
But what He never can repeat
He shews forth day by day.

For, as the Priest of Aaron's line
Within the Holiest stood,
And sprinkled all the mercy-shrine
With sacrificial blood;

So He, Who once atonement wrought,
Our Priest of endless power,
Presents Himself for those He bought
p In that dark noontide hour.

mf His Manhood pleads where now It lives
On heaven's eternal Throne,
And where in mystic rite He gives
Its Presence to His own.

And so we shew Thy death, O Lord,
Till Thou again appear;
And feel, when we approach Thy Board,
We have an Altar here.

f All glory to the Father be,
All glory to the Son,
All glory, Holy Ghost, to Thee,
While endless ages run.

Holy Communion.

Hymn 316.

Holy Communion.

"Thou art a Priest for ever."

f ALLELUIA! sing to JESUS!
His the sceptre, His the Throne;
Alleluia! His the triumph,
His the victory alone;
p Hark! the songs of peaceful Sion
cr Thunder like a mighty flood;
f JESUS out of every nation
Hath redeemed us *(p)* by His Blood.

mf Alleluia! not as orphans
Are we left in sorrow now;
Alleluia! He is near us,
Faith believes, nor questions how:
Though the cloud from sight received Him,
When the forty days were o'er,
or Shall our hearts forget His promise,
"I am with you evermore?"

mf Alleluia! Bread of Angels,
Thou on earth our Food, our Stay;
Alleluia! *(p)* here the sinful
Flee to Thee from day to day;
Intercessor, Friend of sinners,
or Earth's Redeemer, plead for me,
Where the songs of all the sinless
Sweep across the crystal sea.

mf Alleluia! King Eternal,
Thee the LORD of lords we own;
Alleluia! *(p)* born of Mary,
or Earth Thy footstool, heaven Thy Throne:
mf Thou within the veil hast entered,
Robed in flesh, our great High Priest;
Thou on earth both Priest and Victim
In the Eucharistic Feast.

f Alleluia! sing to JESUS!
His the sceptre, His the Throne;
Alleluia! His the triumph,
His the victory alone;
p Hark! the songs of peaceful Sion
or Thunder like a mighty flood;
f JESUS out of every nation
Hath redeemed us *(p)* by His Blood.

Holy Communion.

Hymn 317.

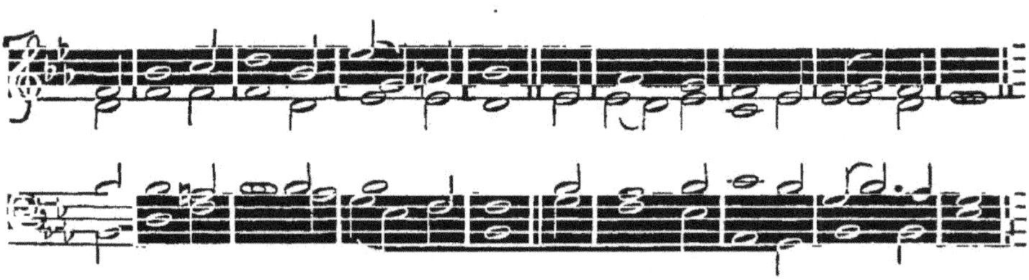

"Come, for all things are now ready."

p MY GOD, and is Thy Table spread,
And doth Thy Cup with love o'erflow?
cr Thither be all Thy children led,
And let them all Thy sweetness know.

mf Hail, sacred Feast, which JESUS makes,
Rich banquet of His Flesh and Blood!
cr Thrice happy he who here partakes
That sacred Stream, that heavenly Food.

mf Why are its dainties all in vain
Before unwilling hearts displayed?
Was not for them the Victim slain?
Are they forbid the children's Bread?

O let Thy Table honoured be,
And furnished well with joyful guests;
And may each soul salvation see,
That here its sacred pledges tastes.

f To FATHER, SON, and HOLY GHOST,
The GOD Whom heaven and earth adore,
From men and from the Angel-host
Be praise and glory evermore.

Holy Communion.

Hymn 318.

"This do in remembrance of Me."

nf BREAD of heaven, on Thee we feed,
For Thy Flesh is meat indeed;
Ever may our souls be fed
With this true and living Bread;
r Day by day with strength supplied
im Through the life of Him Who died.

mf Vine of heaven, Thy Blood supplies
This blest Cup of Sacrifice;
p LORD, Thy Wounds our healing give,
To Thy Cross we look and live:
cr JESUS, may we ever be
Grafted, rooted, built in Thee.

Holy Communion.

Hymn 319.

"The Lord's Table."

mf AUTHOR of life Divine,
Who hast a Table spread,
Furnished with mystic Wine
And everlasting Bread,
cr Preserve the life Thyself hast given,
And feed and train us up to heaven.

mf Our needy souls sustain
With fresh supplies of love,
Till all Thy life we gain,
And all Thy fulness prove,
cr And, strengthened by Thy perfect grace,
dim Behold without a veil Thy Face.

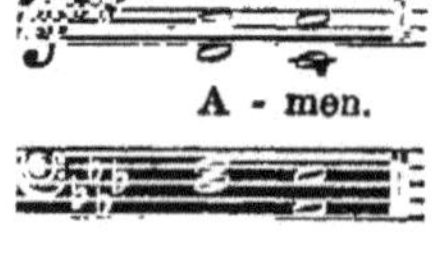

Holy Communion.

Hymn 320.

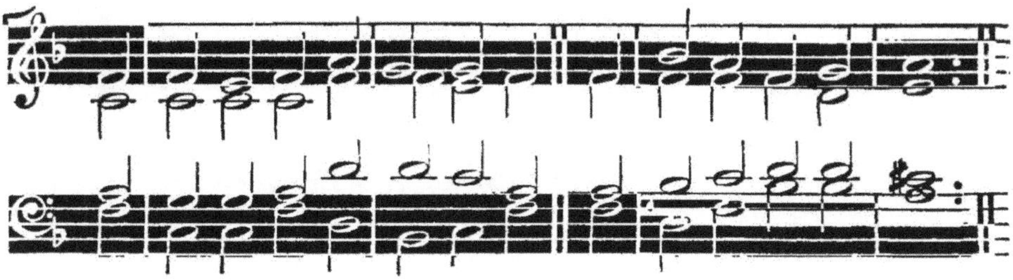

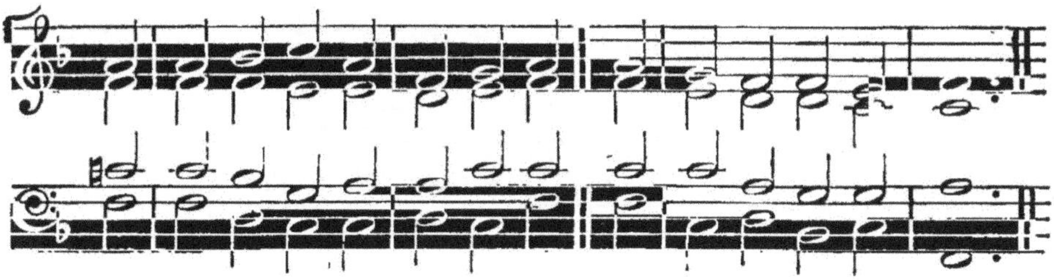

"My Flesh is meat indeed, and My Blood is drink indeed."

p O GOD, unseen yet ever near,
Thy Presence may we feel;
And, thus inspired with holy fear,
Before Thine Altar kneel.

We come, obedient to Thy Word,
To feast on heavenly Food;
Our meat the Body of the LORD,
Our drink His precious Blood.

mf Here may Thy faithful people know
The blessings of Thy love,
The streams that through the desert flow,
The manna from above.

p Thus may we all Thy Word obey,
cr For we, O GOD, are Thine;
f And go rejoicing on our way,
Renewed with strength Divine.

Holy Communion.

Hymn 321.

Holy Communion.

"I love them that love Me: and those that seek Me early shall find Me."

mf WE pray Thee, heavenly Father,
To hear us in Thy love,
And pour upon Thy children
The unction from above;
That so in love abiding,
From all defilement free,
cr We may in pureness offer
Our Eucharist to Thee.

mf Be Thou our Guide and Helper,
O Jesu Christ, we pray;
So may we well approach Thee,
If Thou wilt be the Way:
cr Thou, very Truth, hast promised
To help us in our strife,
dim Food of the weary pilgrim,
cr Eternal Source of Life.

mf And Thou, Creator Spirit,
Look on us, we are Thine;
Renew in us Thy graces,
Upon our darkness shine;
cr That, with Thy benediction
Upon our souls outpoured,
We may receive in gladness
p The Body of the Lord.

mf O Trinity of Persons!
O Unity most High!
On Thee alone relying
Thy servants would draw nigh:
p Unworthy in our weakness,
cr On Thee our hope is stayed,
mf And blest by Thy forgiveness
We will not be afraid.

Holy Communion.

Hymn 322.

Holy Communion.

"In every place incense shall be offered unto My Name, and a pure offering."

p AND now, O FATHER, mindful of the love
That bought us, once for all, on Calvary's Tree,
And having with us Him that pleads above,
cr We here present, we here spread forth to Thee
mf That only Offering perfect in Thine eyes,
The one true, pure, immortal Sacrifice.

p Look, FATHER, look on His Anointed Face,
And only look on us as found in Him;
Look not on our misusings of Thy grace,
Our prayer so languid, and our faith so dim;
cr For lo! between our sins and their reward
We set the Passion of Thy SON our LORD.

p And then for those, our dearest and our best,
By this prevailing Presence we appeal;
cr O fold them closer to Thy mercy's breast,
O do Thine utmost for their souls' true weal;
From tainting mischief keep them white and clear,
And crown Thy gifts with strength to persevere.

p And so we come; O draw us to Thy feet,
Most patient Saviour, Who canst love us still;
cr And by this Food, so awful and so sweet,
Deliver us from every touch of ill:
f In Thine own service make us glad and free,
And grant us never more to part with Thee.

Holy Communion.

Hymn 323.

"The centurion answered and said, Lord, I am not worthy that Thou shouldest come under my roof; but speak the word only, and my servant shall be healed."

p I AM not worthy, Holy LORD,
That Thou shouldst come to me;
cr Speak but the Word; one gracious Word
Can set the sinner free.

p I am not worthy; cold and bare
The lodging of my soul;
How canst Thou deign to enter there?
cr LORD, speak, and make me whole.

p I am not worthy; *(cr)* yet, my GOD,
How can I say Thee nay;
Thee, Who didst give Thy Flesh and Blood
My ransom-price to pay?

mf O come! in this sweet morning hour
Feed me with Food Divine;
And fill with all Thy love and power
p This worthless heart of mine.

Holy Communion.

Hymn 324.

"He that eateth Me, even he shall live by Me."

p JESU, gentlest Saviour,
Thou art in us now,
cr Fill us with Thy Goodness,
Till our hearts o'erflow.

p Multiply our graces,
Chiefly love and fear,
cr And, dear LORD, the chiefest,
Grace to persevere.

mf Oh, how can we thank Thee
For a Gift like this,
Gift that truly maketh
Heaven's eternal bliss!

p Ah! when wilt Thou always
Make our hearts Thy home?
cr We must wait for heaven;
Then the day will come.

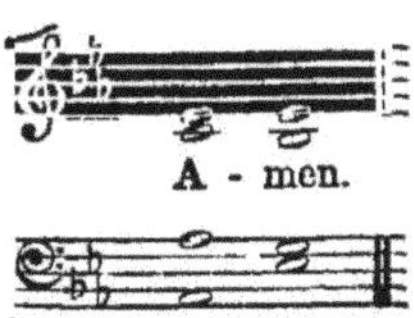

The following Hymns are suitable:

107 Glory be to JESUS.
177 JESU! the very thought is sweet.
178 JESU, the very thought of Thee.
182 JESU, grant me this, I pray.
187 Behold the LAMB of GOD!
190 JESU, Thou Joy of loving hearts
191 JESU, my LORD, my GOD, my All.
192 O Love, Who formedst me to wear.
193 JESU, Lover of my soul.
197 The King of love my Shepherd is.
260 Hark, my soul! it is the LORD.
307 O Saviour, precious Saviour.

Baptism.

Hymn 325.

Baptism.

Ask, and it shall be given you ; seek, and ye shall find ; knock, and it shall be opened unto you.'

mf O FATHER, Thou Who hast creáted all
  In wisest love, we pray,
Look on this babe, who at Thy grácious call
  Is entering on life's way ;
p Bend o'er *him* in Thy tenderness,
Thine image on *his* soul impress ;
  cr O FATHER, hear !

p O SON of GOD, Who diedst for ús, behold,
  We bring our child to Thee ;
Thou tender Shepherd, take *him* tó Thy fold,
  Thine own for aye to be ;
cr Defend *him* through this earthly strife,
And lead *him* on the path of life,
  f O SON of GOD !

mf O HOLY GHOST, Who broodedst ó'er the wave,
  Descend upon this child ;
Give *him* undying life, *his* spírit lave
  With waters undefiled ;
p Grant *him*, while yet a babe, to be
cr A child of GOD, a home for Thee,
  O HOLY GHOST !

mf O TRIUNE GOD, what Thou commánd'st is done ;
  We speak, but Thine the might ;
This child hath scarce yet seen our éarthly sun,
  Yet pour on *him* Thy light,
cr In faith and hope, in joy and love,
f Thou Sun of all below, above,
  O TRIUNE GOD !

 2 B

Baptism.

Hymn 326.

Baptism.

'Baptizing them in the Name of the Father, and of the Son, and of the Holy Ghost.'

mf WITHIN the Church's sacred fold,
By holy Sacrament enrolled,
Another lamb we lay :
p An heir before of sin and shame,
cr Now in the Holy TRIUNE Name
His guilt is washed away.

mf O loving FATHER, Thee we pray
Look on this babe new-born to-day,
Thine own adopted child;
An Angel guard do Thou bestow
To lead *him* in Thy paths below,
And guide *him* through the wild.

O GOD the SON, Thou heavenly Vine,
Protect this tender branch of Thine
Through all that may betide;
For ever nourished may *he* be
With sap Divine that flows from Thee,
In Thee for aye abide.

Blest SPIRIT, Whose indwelling grace
Has given this little one a place
Among the heirs of life,
O breathe Thy sevenfold gifts within,
And keep Thy temple pure from sin
In midst of worldly strife.

So, Holy TRINITY, by Thee
Divinely trained this babe may be
In faith and hope and love;
cr So may *he* gain, earth's waves o'erpast,
His bright inheritance at last
With all Thy Saints above.

 2 B 2

Baptism.

Hymn 327.

"The washing of regeneration."

mf 'TIS done! that new and heavenly birth,
Which re-creates the sons of earth,
Has cleansed from guilt of Adam's sin
A soul which JESUS *(p)* died to win.

mf 'Tis done! the Cross upon the brow
Is marked for weal or sorrow now,
cr To shine with heavenly lustre bright,
pp Or burn in everlasting night.

mf O ye who came that babe to lay
Within a Saviour's Arms to-day,
Watch well and guard with careful eye
The heir of immortality.

Teach *him* to know a FATHER's love,
And seek for happiness above,
To CHRIST *his* heart and treasure give,
And in the SPIRIT ever live;

cr That so before the judgment-seat
In joy and triumph ye may meet;
f The battle fought, the struggle o'er,
The kingdom yours for evermore.

Praise GOD, from Whom all blessings flow,
Praise Him, all creatures here below,
Praise Him above, Angelic host,
Praise FATHER, SON, and HOLY GHOST.

Hymn 328.

"Be not thou therefore ashamed of the testimony of our Lord."

mf IN token that thou shalt not fear
  CHRIST Crucified to own,
We print the Cross upon thee here,
  And stamp thee His alone.

In token that thou shalt not blush
  To glory in His Name,
We blazon here upon thy front
  His glory *(dim)* and His shame.

mf In token that thou shalt not flinch
  CHRIST's quarrel to maintain,
But 'neath His banner manfully
  Firm at thy post remain;

In token that thou too shalt tread
  The path He travelled by,
Endure the cross, despise the shame,
cr And sit thee down on high;

mf Thus outwardly and visibly
  We seal thee for His own;
And may the brow that wears His Cross
cr Hereafter share His Crown.

This Hymn may also be sung when a child who has been privately baptized is received into the congregation; and at the baptism of an adult.

For the Young.

Hymn 329.

For the Young.

"The Child Jesus."

mf ONCE in royal David's city
  Stood a lowly cattle shed,
p Where a Mother laid her Baby
  In a manger for His bed;
mf Mary was that Mother mild,
p Jesus Christ her little Child.

He came down to earth from heaven
f Who is God and Lord of all,
p And His shelter was a stable,
  And His cradle was a stall;
With the poor, and mean, and lowly,
Lived on earth our Saviour Holy.

mf And, through all His wondrous Childhood,
  He would honour and obey,
Love, and watch the lowly Maiden,
  In whose gentle arms He lay;
Christian children all must be
Mild, obedient, good as He.

For He is our childhood's pattern,
  Day by day like us He grew,
p He was little, weak, and helpless,
  Tears and smiles like us He knew;
And He feeleth for our sadness,
cr And He shareth in our gladness.

f And our eyes at last shall see Him,
  Through His own redeeming love,
p For that Child so dear and gentle
f Is our Lord in heaven above;
And He leads His children on
To the place where He is gone.

mf Not in that poor lowly stable,
  With the oxen standing by,
We shall see Him; *(f)* but in heaven,
  Set at God's right hand on high;
When like stars His children crowned
All in white shall wait around.

For the Young.

Hymn 330.

For the Young.

" The love of Christ."

mf I LOVE to hear the story
  Which Angel voices tell,
p How once the King of glory
  Came down on earth to dwell.
I am both weak and sinful,
cr But this I surely know,
The Lord came down to save me,
  Because He loved me so.
mf   I love to hear the story
    Which Angel voices tell,
   How once the King of glory
    Came down on earth to dwell.

I'm glad my Blessèd Saviour
  Was once a Child like me
To shew how pure and holy
  His little ones might be·
And if I try to follow
  His footsteps here below,
He never will forget me,
  Because He loves me so.
   I love to hear the story
    Which Angel voices tell,
   How once the King of glory
    Came down on earth to dwell.

f To sing His love and mercy
  My sweetest songs I'll raise;
mf And though I cannot see Him
  I know He hears my praise;
For He has kindly promised
  That even I may go
cr To sing among His Angels,
  Because He loves me so.
f   I love to hear the story
    Which Angel voices tell,
p   How once the King of glory
    Came down on earth to dwell.

For the Young.

Hymn 331.

"Even a child is known by his doings."

mf WE are but little children weak,
Nor born in any high estate;
What can we do for JESUS' sake,
cr Who is so high and good and great?

mf We know the Holy Innocents
Laid down for Him their infant life,
And Martyrs brave and patient Saints
Have stood for Him in fire and strife.

We wear the cross they wore of old,
Our lips have learned like vows to make;
We need not die; we cannot fight;
What may we do for JESUS' sake?

Oh, day by day, each Christian child
Has much to do, without, within;
A death to die, for JESUS' sake,
A weary war to wage with sin.

p When deep within our swelling hearts
The thoughts of pride and anger rise,
When bitter words are on our tongues,
And tears of passion in our eyes;

cr Then we may stay the angry blow,
Then we may check the hasty word,
p Give gentle answers back again,
f And fight a battle for our LORD.

mf With smiles of peace, and looks of love
Light in our dwellings we may make,
Bid kind good humour brighten there,
p And still do all for JESUS' sake.

mf There's not a child so small and weak
But has his little cross to take,
His little work of love and praise
p That he may do for JESUS' sake.

For the Young.

Hymn 332.

"While we were yet sinners, Christ died for us."

mf THERE is a green hill far away,
Without a city wall,
p Where the dear LORD was crucified,
Who died to save us all.

We may not know, we cannot tell
What pains He had to bear,
But we believe it was for us
He hung and suffered there.

mf He died that we might be forgiven,
He died to make us good,
cr That we might go at last to heaven,
p Saved by His precious Blood.

mf There was no other good enough
To pay the price of sin,
He only could unlock the gate
Of heaven, and let us in.

Oh, dearly, dearly has He loved,
And we must love Him too,
And trust in His redeeming Blood,
And try His works to do.

For the Young.

Hymn 333.

For the Young.

"He took them up in His arms."

f CHRIST, Who once amongst us
As a Child did dwell.
Is the children's Saviour,
And He loves us well;
mf If we keep our promise
Made Him at the Font,
f He will be our Shepherd,
And we shall not want.

mf There it was they laid us
In those tender Arms,
Where the lambs are carried
Safe from all alarms;
If we trust His promise,
He will let us rest
In His Arms for ever,
Leaning on His Breast.

Though we may not see Him
For a little while,
We shall know He holds us,
Often feel His smile;
p Death will be to slumber
In that sweet embrace,
f And we shall awaken
To behold His Face.

mf He will be our Shepherd
After as before,
By still heavenly waters
Lead us evermore,
Make us lie in pastures
Beautiful and green,
Where none thirst or hunger,
And no tears are seen.

p Jesus, our good Shepherd,
Laying down Thy life,
Lest Thy sheep should perish
In the cruel strife,
cr Help us to remember
All Thy love and care,
f Trust in Thee, and love Thee
Always, everywhere.

For the Young.

Hymn 334.

"My sheep hear My voice, and I know them, and they follow Me."

mf LOVING Shepherd of Thy sheep,
Keep Thy lamb, in safety keep;
Nothing can Thy power withstand,
None can pluck me from Thy Hand.

Loving Saviour, Thou didst give
Thine own life that we might live,
And the Hands outstretched to bless
p Bear the cruel nails' impress.

f I would praise Thee every day,
Gladly all Thy Will obey,
Like Thy blessèd ones above
Happy in Thy precious love.

mf Loving Shepherd, ever near,
Teach Thy lamb Thy voice to hear,
Suffer not my steps to stray
From the straight and narrow way.

Where Thou leadest I would go,
Walking in Thy steps below,
cr Till before my FATHER's Throne
I shall know as I am known.

For the Young.

Hymn 335. *

"He shall give His angels charge over thee, to keep thee in all thy ways."

mf AROUND the Throne of God a band
Of glorious Angels ever stand;
cr Bright things they see, sweet harps they hold,
f And on their heads are crowns of gold.

mf Some wait around Him, ready still
To sing His praise and do His Will;
And some, when He commands them, go
To guard His servants here below.

Lord, give Thy Angels every day
Command to guide us on our way,
And bid them every evening keep
p Their watch around us while we sleep.

mf So shall no wicked thing draw near,
To do us harm or cause us fear;
cr And we shall dwell, when life is past,
f With Angels round Thy Throne at last.

* *This Tune may be sung in Two Parts (Treble and Alto), if preferred; or in the absence of the other voices.*

For the Young.

Hymn 336.

For the Young.

"Praise our God, all ye His servants, and ye that fear Him, both small and great."

mf ABOVE the clear blue sky,
In heaven's bright abode,
The Angel host on high
Sing praises to their God:
f Alleluia!
mf They love to sing
To God their King
f Alleluia!

mf But God from infant tongues
On earth receiveth praise;
cr We then our cheerful songs
In sweet accord will raise:
f Alleluia!
mf We too will sing
To God our King
f Alleluia!

p O Blessèd Lord, Thy Truth
To us Thy babes impart,
cr And teach us in our youth
To know Thee as Thou art.
f Alleluia!
mf Then shall we sing
To God our King
f Alleluia!

mf O may Thy holy Word
Spread all the world around;
And all with one accord
Uplift the joyful sound,
f Alleluia!
mf All then shall sing
To God their King
f Alleluia!

For the Young.

Hymn 338.

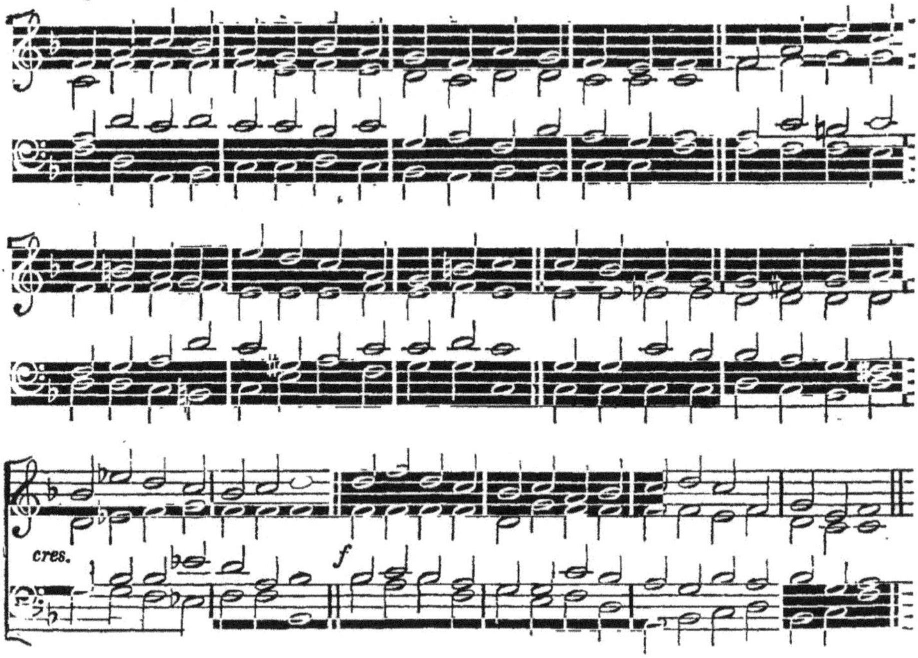

"Be ye therefore followers of God, as dear children."

mf HEAVENLY FATHER, send Thy blessing
On Thy children gathered here,
May they all, Thy Name confessing,
Be to Thee for ever dear:
May they be, like Joseph, loving,
Dutiful, and chaste, and pure;
f And their faith, like David, proving,
Steadfast unto death endure.

p Holy SAVIOUR, Who in meekness
Didst vouchsafe a Child to be,
cr Guide their steps, and help their weakness,
Bless and make them like to Thee;
Bear Thy lambs, when they are weary,
In Thine Arms and at Thy Breast;
Through life's desert, dry and dreary,
Bring them to Thy heavenly rest.

mf Spread Thy golden pinions o'er them,
HOLY SPIRIT, from above,
Guide them, lead them, go before them,
Give them peace, and joy, and love:
Thy true temples, HOLY SPIRIT,
cr May they with Thy glory shine,
f And immortal bliss inherit,
And for evermore be Thine.

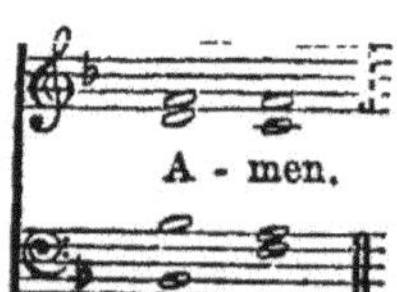

For the Young.

Hymn 339.

"Thou shalt not delay to offer the first of thy ripe fruits."

mf FAIR waved the golden corn
In Canaan's pleasant land,
cr When full of joy, some shining morn,
Went forth the reaper-band.

f To God so good and great
Their cheerful thanks they pour;
Then carry to His temple-gate
The choicest of their store.

mf Like Israel, Lord, we give
Our earliest fruits to Thee,
And pray that, long as we shall live,
We may Thy children be.

Thine is our youthful prime,
And life and all its powers;
Be with us in our morning time,
p And bless our evening hours.

cr In wisdom let us grow,
As years and strength are given,
That we may serve Thy Church below,
f And join Thy Saints in heaven.

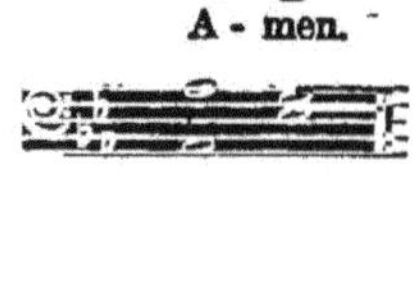

For the Young.

Hymn 340.

"The children crying in the temple, and saying Hosanna."

This may be sung as an accompanied Melody, or in Harmony.

For the Young.

For the Young.

Hymn 341.

For the Young.

"My song shall be alway of the loving-kindness of the Lord.

f COME, sing with holy gladness,
High Alleluias sing,
Uplift your loud Hosannas
To JESUS, LORD and King;
Sing, boys, in joyful chorus
Your hymn of praise to-day,
p And sing, ye gentle maidens,
cr Your sweet responsive lay.

mf 'Tis good for boys and maidens
Sweet hymns to CHRIST to sing,
'Tis meet that children's voices
Should praise the children's King;
For JESUS is salvation,
And glory, grace, and rest;
To babe, and boy, and maiden
The one Redeemer Blest.

O boys, be strong in JESUS,
To toil for Him is gain,
And JESUS wrought with Joseph
With chisel, saw, and plane;
O maidens, live for JESUS,
Who was a maiden's Son;
Be patient, pure, and gentle,
And perfect grace begun.

f Soon in the golden city
The boys and girls shall play,
And through the dazzling mansions
Rejoice in endless day;
p O CHRIST, prepare Thy children
cr With that triumphant throng
f To pass the burnished portals,
And sing the eternal song.

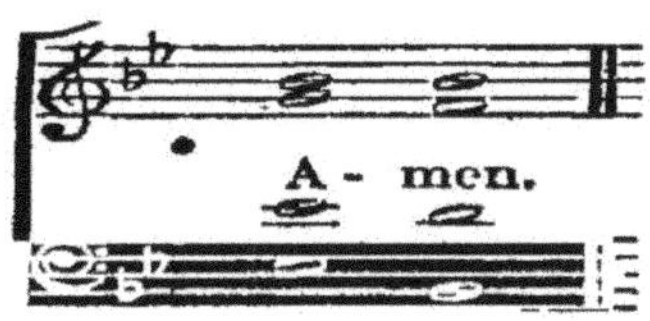

For the Young.

Hymn 342.

For the Young.

"He shall feed His flock like a shepherd; He shall gather the lambs with His arm, and carry them in His bosom."

mf GRACIOUS Saviour, gentle Shepherd,
Little ones are dear to Thee;
Gathered with Thine Arms, and carried
In Thy Bosom may we be;
p Sweetly, fondly, safely tended,
cr From all want and danger free.

mf Tender Shepherd, never leave us
From Thy fold to go astray;
By Thy look of love directed
May we walk the narrow way;
Thus direct us, and protect us,
Lest we fall an easy prey.

Cleanse our hearts from sinful folly
In the stream Thy love supplied,
p Mingled stream of Blood and Water,
Flowing from Thy wounded Side;
cr And to heavenly pastures lead us,
dim Where Thine own still waters glide.

mf Let Thy holy Word instruct us;
Guide us daily by its light;
Let Thy love and grace constrain us
To approve whate'er is right,
Take Thine easy yoke, and wear it,
cr Strengthened with Thy heavenly might

mf Taught to lisp the holy praises
Which on earth Thy children sing,
Both with lips and hearts unfeignèd
May we our thank-offerings bring;
f Then with all the Saints in glory
Join to praise our LORD and King.

For the Young.

Hymn 343.

"Out of the mouth of babes and sucklings Thou hast perfected praise."

f GOD Eternal, Mighty King,
Unto Thee our praise we bring;
All the earth doth worship Thee,
We amid the throng would be.

pp Holy, Holy, Holy! cry
p Angels round Thy Throne on high:
cr LORD of all the heavenly powers,
Be the same loud anthem ours.

f Glorified Apostles raise
Night and day continual praise;
mf Hast Thou not a mission too
For Thy children here to do?

With the Prophets' goodly line
We in mystic bond combine;
For Thou hast to babes revealed
Things that to the wise were sealed.

Martyrs, in a noble host,
Of the cross are heard to boast;
p O that we our cross may bear,
f And a crown of glory wear.

ff GOD Eternal, Mighty King,
Unto Thee our praise we bring;
To the FATHER, and the SON,
And the SPIRIT, THREE in ONE.

For the Young.

Hymn 344.

"Thy Holy Child Jesus."

FOR A SCHOOL FEAST.

mf LORD JESUS, GOD and Man,
For love of man a Child,
The Very GOD, yet born on earth
Of Mary undefiled;

LORD JESUS, GOD and Man,
cr In this our festal day
To Thee for precious gifts of grace
dim Thy ransomed people pray.

mf We pray for childlike hearts,
For gentle holy love,
For strength to do Thy Will below
As Angels do above.

We pray for simple faith,
For hope that never faints,
cr For true communion evermore
With all Thy blessèd Saints.

mf On friends around us here
O let Thy blessing fall;
cr We pray for grace to love them well,
But Thee beyond them all.

f O joy to live for Thee!
O joy in Thee to die!
ff O very joy of joys to see
Thy Face eternally!

p LORD JESUS, GOD and Man,
cr We praise Thee and adore,
Who art with GOD the FATHER ONE
And SPIRIT evermore.

For the Young.

Hymn 345.

For the Young.

"In Him was Life, and the Life was the Light of men."

mf O LIGHT, Whose beams illumine all
From twilight dawn to perfect day,
Shine Thou before the shadows fall
dim That lead our wandering feet astray:
mf At morn and eve Thy radiance pour,
cr That youth may love, and age adore.

mf O Way, through Whom our souls draw near
To yon eternal home of peace,
f Where perfect love shall cast out fear,
And earth's vain toil and wandering cease;
mf In strength or weakness may we see
cr Our heavenward path, O LORD, through Thee.

mf O Truth, before Whose shrine we bow,
Thou priceless pearl for all who seek,
To Thee our earliest strength we vow,
Thy love will bless the pure and meek;
p When dreams or mists beguile our sight,
cr Turn Thou our darkness into light.

mf O Life, the well that ever flows
To slake the thirst of those that faint,
f Thy power to bless what Seraph knows?
Thy joy supreme what words can paint?
p In earth's last hour of fleeting breath
cr Be Thou our Conqueror over death.

f O Light, O Way, O Truth, O Life,
O JESU, born mankind to save,
p Give Thou Thy peace in deadliest strife,
Shed Thou Thy calm on stormiest wave;
f Be Thou our Hope, our Joy, our Dread,
LORD of the living *(dim)* and the dead.

For the Young.

Hymn 346.

"*When thou liest down thou shalt not be afraid; yea, thou shalt lie down and thy sleep shall be sweet.*"

EVENING.

p NOW the day is over,
Night is drawing nigh,
Shadows of the evening
Steal across the sky.

Now the darkness gathers,
Stars begin to peep,
Birds, and beasts, and flowers
Soon will be asleep.

mf JESU, give the weary
Calm and sweet repose;
p With Thy tenderest blessing
May mine eyelids close.

cr Grant to little children
Visions bright of Thee;
Guard the sailors tossing
On the deep blue sea.

p Comfort every sufferer
Watching late in pain;
Those who plan some evil
cr From their sin restrain.

p Through the long night watches
May Thine Angels spread
Their white wings above me,
cr Watching round my bed.

mf When the morning wakens,
Then may I arise
Pure, and fresh, and sinless
In Thy Holy Eyes.

f Glory to the FATHER,
Glory to the SON,
And to Thee, Blest SPIRIT,
Whilst all ages run.

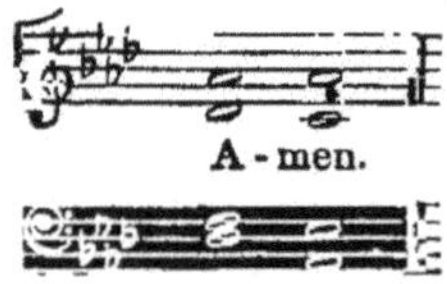

Confirmation.

Hymn 347.

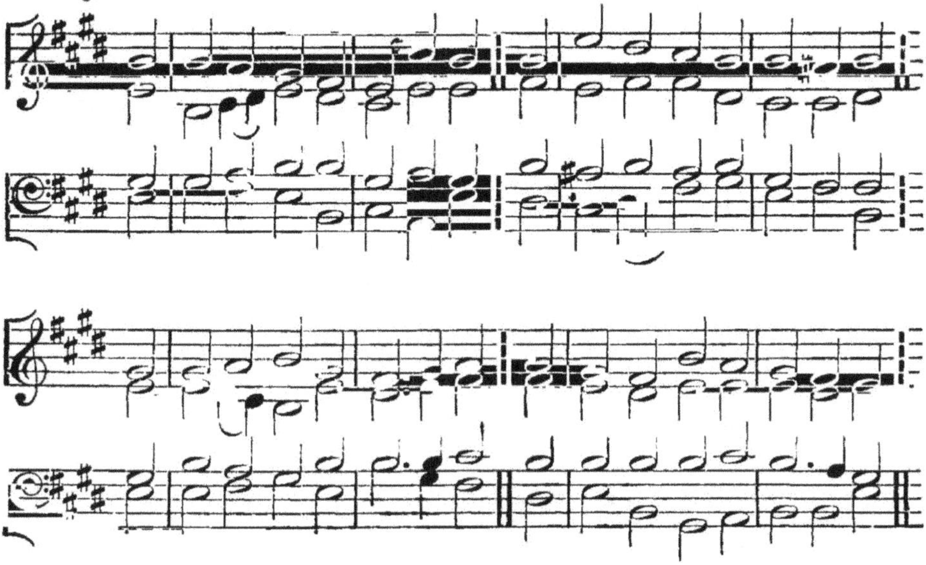

"The Comforter which is the Holy Ghost."

mf COME, Holy Ghost, Creator Blest,
Vouchsafe within our souls to rest;
Come with Thy grace and heavenly aid,
And fill the hearts which Thou hast made.

p To Thee, the Comforter, we cry,
To Thee, the Gift of God most High,
The Fount of life, the Fire of love,
The soul's Anointing from above.

mf O Finger of the Hand Divine,
The sevenfold gifts of grace are Thine;
True promise of the Father Thou,
Who dost the tongue with power endow.

cr Thy light to every sense impart,
And shed Thy love in every heart;
f Thine own unfailing might supply
dim To strengthen our infirmity.

mf Drive far away our ghostly foe,
And Thine abiding peace bestow;
If Thou be our preventing Guide,
No evil can our steps betide.

Grant us through Thee, O Holy One,
To know the Father and the Son;
And this be our unchanging creed,
That Thou dost from Them Both proceed.

f Praise we the Father, and the Son,
And Holy Spirit with Them One:
p And may the Son on us bestow
cr The gifts that from the Spirit flow.

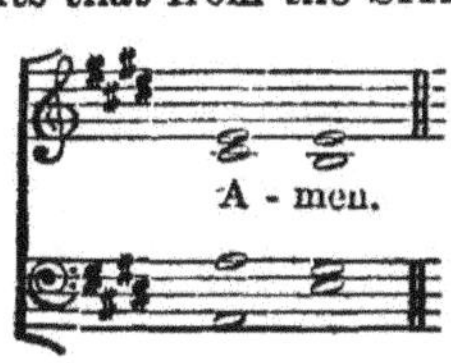

Confirmation.

Hymn 348.

Confirmation.

Then laid they their hands on them, and they received the Holy Ghost."

mf BEHOLD us, LORD, before Thee met
Whom each bright Angel serves and fears,
Who on Thy Throne rememberest yet
p Thy spotless Boyhood's quiet years,
Whose Feet the hills of Nazareth trod,
cr Who art true Man and perfect GOD.

mf To Thee we look, in Thee confide,
Our help is in Thine own dear Name;
cr For who on JESUS e'er relied
And found not JESUS still the same?
mf Thus far Thy love our souls hath brought,
cr O stablish well what Thou hast wrought.

mf From Thee was our baptismal grace,
The holy seed by Thee was sown;
And now before our FATHER'S Face
We make the three great vows our own,
And ask, in Thine appointed way,
Confirm us in Thy grace to-day.

We need Thee more than tongue can speak,
'Mid foes that well might cast us down;
cr But thousands, *(dim)* once as young and weak,
cr Have fought the fight, and won the crown;
p We ask the help that *(cr)* bore them through;
We trust the Faithful and the True.

mf So bless us with the gift complete
By hands of Thy chief Pastors given,
p That awful Presence kind and sweet
Which comes in sevenfold might from heaven;
pp Eternal CHRIST, to Thee we bow:
cr Give us Thy SPIRIT here and now.

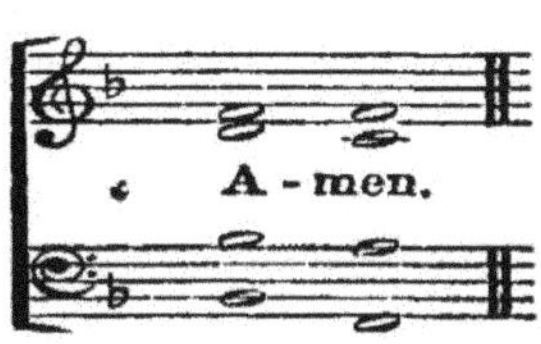

Confirmation.

Hymn 349.

"With my whole heart have I sought Thee; O let me not go wrong out of Thy commandments."

mf MY God, accept my heart this day,
And make it always Thine,
That I from Thee no more may stray,
No more from Thee decline.

p Before the Cross of Him Who died,
Behold, I prostrate fall;
Let every sin be crucified,
cr And Christ be All in all.

Anoint me with Thy heavenly grace,
And seal me for Thine own;
f That I may see Thy glorious Face,
p And worship near Thy Throne.

mf Let every thought, and work, and word
To Thee be ever given;
Then life shall be Thy service, Lord,
cr And death the gate of heaven.

f All glory to the Father be,
All glory to the Son,
All glory, Holy Ghost, to Thee,
While endless ages run.

The following Hymns are suitable:

156 Come, Thou Holy Spirit, come.
157 Come, Holy Ghost, our souls inspire.
207 Our Blest Redeemer, ere He breathed.
270 Soldiers of Christ, arise.
271 O Jesus, I have promised.
280 Thine for ever! God of love.

Holy Matrimony.

Hymn 350.

"A threefold cord is not quickly broken."

mf THE voice that breathed o'er Eden,
  That earliest wedding day,
The primal marriage blessing,
  It hath not passed away:

Still in the pure espousal
  Of Christian man and maid
The Holy Three are with us,
  The threefold grace is said,

For dower of blessèd children,
  For love and faith's sweet sake,
For high mysterious union
  Which nought on earth may break

p Be present, awful Father,
cr   To give away this bride,
As Eve Thou gav'st to Adam
  Out of his own pierced side;

p Be present, Son of Mary,
cr   To join their loving hands,
As Thou didst bind two natures
  In Thine Eternal bands;

p Be present, Holiest Spirit,
cr   To bless them as they kneel,
As Thou for Christ, the Bridegroom,
  The heavenly spouse dost seal.

mf O spread Thy pure wing o'er them,
  Let no ill power find place,
When onward to Thine Altar
  The hallowed path they trace,

f To cast their crowns before Thee
  In perfect sacrifice,
Till to the home of gladness
  With Christ's own Bride they rise.

Holy Matrimony.

Hymn 351.

"Both Jesus was called, and His disciples, to the marriage."

mf HOW welcome was the call,
And sweet the festal lay,
cr When Jesus deigned in Cana's hall
To bless the marriage day!

mf And happy was the Bride,
And glad the Bridegroom's heart,
For He Who tarried at their side
Bade grief and ill depart.

His gracious power Divine
The water vessels knew;
cr And plenteous was the mystic wine
The wondering servants drew.

p O Lord of life and love,
Come Thou again to-day;
cr And bring a blessing from above
That ne'er shall pass away.

mf O bless, as erst of old,
The Bridegroom and the Bride;
Bless with the holier stream that flowed
p Forth from Thy piercèd Side.

Before Thine Altar-throne
This mercy we implore;
cr As Thou dost knit them, Lord, in one,
f So bless them evermore.

Ember Days.

Hymn 352.

"As My Father hath sent Me, even so send I you."

mf CHRIST is gone up; yet ere He passed
  From earth, in heaven to reign,
He formed one holy Church to last
  Till He should come again.

His twelve Apostles first He made
  His ministers of grace;
And they their hands on others laid,
  To fill in turn their place.

So age by age, and year by year,
  His grace was handed on;
And still the holy Church is here,
  Although her LORD is gone.

p Let those find pardon, LORD, from Thee,
  Whose love to her is cold:
cr Bring wanderers in, and let there be
  One Shepherd and one fold.

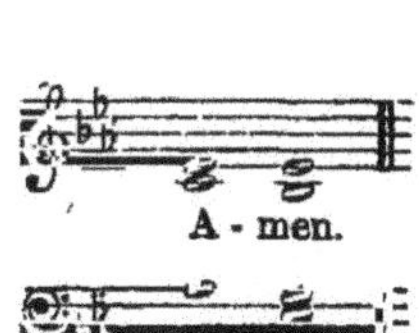

Hymn 353.

"He gave some Apostles, . . . and some pastors and teachers, for the perfecting of the saints, for the work of the ministry, for the edifying of the body of Christ."

mf O THOU Who makest souls to shine
With light from lighter worlds above,
And droppest glistening dew Divine
On all who seek a Saviour's love;

Do Thou Thy benediction give
On all who teach, on all who learn,
That so Thy Church may holier live,
And every lamp more brightly burn.

Give those, who teach, pure hearts and wise,
Faith, hope, and love, all warmed by prayer;
Themselves first training for the skies,
They best will raise their people there.

Give those, who learn, the willing ear,
The spirit meek, the guileless mind;
Such gifts will make the lowliest here
Far better than a kingdom find.

cr O bless the shepherd; bless the sheep;
That guide and guided both be one,
One in the faithful watch they keep,
Until this hurrying life be done.

mf If thus, Good LORD, Thy grace be given,
In Thee to live, *(p)* in Thee to die,
cr Before we upward pass to heaven,
f We taste our immortality.

Ember Days.

Hymn 354.

"The harvest truly is plenteous, but the labourers are few."

mf THE earth, O LORD, is one wide field
Of all Thy chosen seed;
The crop prepared its fruit to yield;
p The labourers few indeed.

We therefore come before Thee now
With fasting, and with prayer,
cr Beseeching of Thy love that Thou
Wouldst send more labourers there.

mf Not for our land alone we pray,
Though that above the rest;
The realms and islands far away,
O let them all be blest.

Endue the Bishops of Thy flock
With wisdom and with grace,
cr Against false doctrine, like a rock,
To set the heart and face.

mf To all Thy Priests Thy truth reveal,
And make Thy judgments clear;
Make Thou Thy Deacons full of zeal,
And humble, and sincere:

And give their flocks a lowly mind
To hear and to obey;
That each and all may mercy find
At Thine appearing-day.

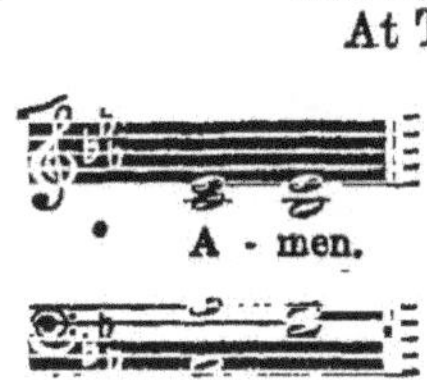

Ember Days.

Hymn 355.

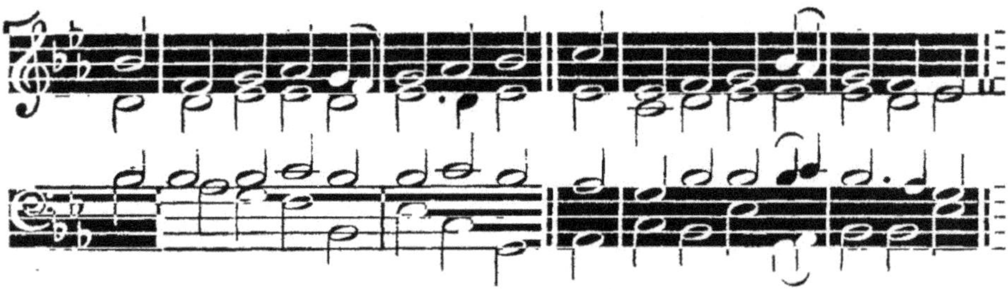

"Let Thy priests be clothed with righteousness."

mf LORD, pour Thy SPIRIT from on high,
And Thine ordainèd servants bless;
Graces and gifts to each supply,
And clothe Thy Priests with righteousness.

Within Thy temple when they stand,
To teach the truth as taught by Thee,
cr Saviour, like stars in Thy right hand,
Let all Thy Church's Pastors be.

mf Wisdom, and zeal, and faith impart,
Firmness with meekness, from above,
To bear Thy people in their heart,
And love the souls whom Thou dost love:

p To watch, and pray, and never faint,
By day and night their guard to keep,
To warn the sinner, cheer the saint,
To feed Thy lambs, and tend Thy sheep

mf So, when their work is finished here,
May they in hope their charge resign;
cr So, when their Master shall appear,
May they with crowns of glory shine.

These Hymns for Ember Days are also suitable for meetings of Clergy.

Lay Helpers.

Hymn 356.

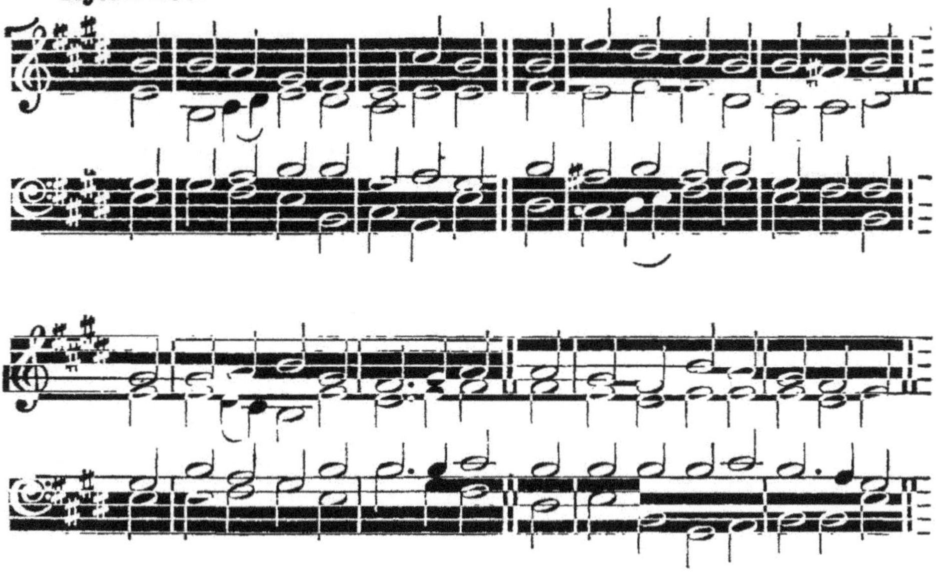

"My helpers in Christ Jesus."

mf LORD, speak to me, that I may speak
In living echoes of Thy tone;
As Thou hast sought, so let me seek
Thy erring children lost and lone.

O lead me, LORD, that I may lead
The wandering and the wavering feet;
O feed me, LORD, that I may feed
Thy hungering ones with manna sweet.

O strengthen me, that while I stand
Firm on the Rock, and strong in Thee,
I may stretch out a loving hand
To wrestlers with the troubled sea.

O teach me, LORD, that I may teach
The precious things Thou dost impart;
And wing my words, that they may reach
The hidden depths of many a heart.

p O give Thine own sweet rest to me,
That I may speak with soothing power
A word in season, as from Thee,
To weary ones in needful hour.

f O fill me with Thy fulness, LORD,
Until my very heart o'erflow
In kindling thought and glowing word,
Thy love to tell, Thy praise to show.

mf O use me, LORD, use even me,
Just as Thou wilt, and when, and where;
cr Until Thy Blessèd Face I see,
Thy rest, Thy joy, Thy glory share.

Lay Helpers.

Hymn 357.

The original form of this Tune is given with Hymn 369.

Lay Helpers.

"If any man serve Me, let him follow Me; and where I am, there shall also My servant be."

mf HOW blessèd, from the bonds of sin
And earthly fetters free,
In singleness of heart and aim
Thy servant, LORD, to be;
The hardest toil to undertake
With joy at Thy command,
p The meanest office to receive
With meekness at Thy hand.

mf With willing heart and longing eyes
To watch before Thy gate,
Ready to run the weary race,
To bear the heavy weight;
No voice of thunder to expect,
p But follow calm and still;
cr For love can easily divine
The One Belovèd's Will.

mf Thus may I serve Thee, gracious LORD;
Thus ever Thine alone,
My soul and body given to Thee,
The purchase Thou hast won,
Through evil or through good report
Still keeping by Thy side,
By life or death, in this poor flesh,
Let CHRIST be magnified.

f How happily the working days
In this dear service fly,
p How rapidly the closing hour,
The time of rest, draws nigh,
cr When all the faithful gather home,
f A joyful company,
And ever where the Master is
Shall His blest servants be.

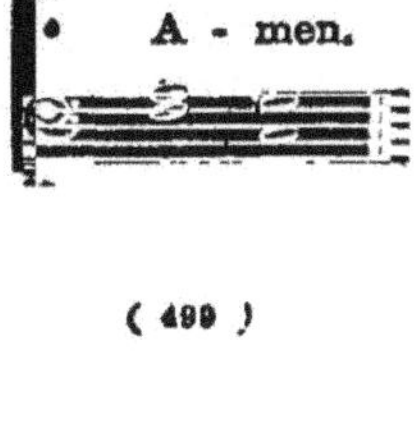

Missions.

Hymn 358.

Missions.

"Come over . . . and help us."

mf FROM Greenland's icy mountains,
From India's coral strand,
Where Afric's sunny fountains
Roll down their golden sand,
From many an ancient river,
From many a palmy plain,
They call us to deliver
Their land from error's chain.

What though the spicy breezes
Blow soft o'er Ceylon's isle,
Though every prospect pleases
dim And only man is vile,
mf In vain with lavish kindness
The gifts of God are strown,
p The heathen in his blindness
Bows down to wood and stone.

mf Can we, whose souls are lighted
With wisdom from on high,
Can we to men benighted
The lamp of life deny?
f Salvation! oh, salvation!
The joyful sound proclaim,
Till each remotest nation
Has learnt Messiah's name.

ff Waft, waft, ye winds, His story,
And you, ye waters, roll,
Till, like a sea of glory,
It spreads from pole to pole;
p Till o'er our ransomed nature
The Lamb for sinners slain,
cr Redeemer, King, Creator,
f In bliss returns to reign.

Missions.

Hymn 359.

Missions.

"So shall He sprinkle many nations."

mf SAVIOUR, sprinkle many nations,
Fruitful let Thy sorrows be;
By Thy pains and consolations
Draw the Gentiles unto Thee:
Of Thy Cross the wondrous story,
Be it to the nations told;
f Let them see Thee in Thy glory,
And Thy mercy manifold.

mf Far and wide, though all unknowing,
Pants for Thee each mortal breast;
p Human tears for Thee are flowing,
Human hearts in Thee would rest;
Thirsting, as for dews of even,
As the new-mown grass for rain,
cr Thee they seek, as GOD of heaven,
dim Thee, as Man, for sinners slain.

mf Saviour, lo! the isles are waiting,
Stretched the hand, and strained the sight,
For Thy SPIRIT new creating,
Love's pure flame and wisdom's light;
cr Give the word, and of the preacher
Speed the foot, and touch the tongue,
f Till on earth by every creature
Glory to the LAMB be sung.

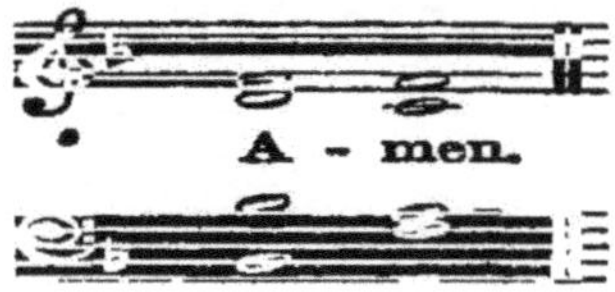

Missions.

Hymn 360. (First Tune.)

Hymn 360. (Second Tune.)

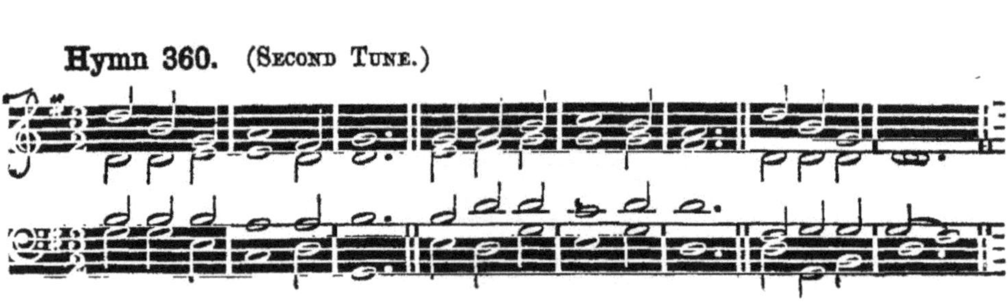

Missions.

"And God said, Let there be light; and there was light."

mf THOU, Whose Almighty Word
Chaos and darkness heard,
And took their flight,
p Hear us, we humbly pray,
cr And where the Gospel-day
Sheds not its glorious ray,
Let there be light.

mf Thou, Who didst come to bring
On Thy redeeming wing
Healing and sight,
Health to the sick in mind,
Sight to the inly blind,
cr O now to all mankind
f Let there be light.

mf SPIRIT of truth and love,
Life-giving, HOLY DOVE,
Speed forth Thy flight;
p Move on the waters' face,
cr Bearing the lamp of grace,
And in earth's darkest place
f Let there be light.

mf Holy and Blessèd THREE,
Glorious TRINITY,
Wisdom, Love, Might;
f Boundless as ocean's tide
Rolling in fullest pride,
cr Through the earth, far and wide,
ff Let there be light.

Missions.

Hymn 361.

Missions.

" Come over into Macedonia, and help us."

p THROUGH midnight gloom from Macedon
The cry of myriads as of one,
The voiceful silence of despair,
Is eloquent in awful prayer,
cr The soul's exceeding bitter cry,
" Come o'er and help us, *(dim)* or we die."

p How mournfully it echoes on!
For half the earth is Macedon;
mf These brethren to their brethren call,
And by the Love which loved them all,
And by the whole world's Life they cry,
cr " O ye that live, *(dim)* behold we die!"

mf By other sounds the world is won
Than that which wails from Macedon;
The roar of gain is round it rolled,
Or men unto themselves are sold,
And cannot list the alien cry,
p " O hear and help us, lest we die!"

mf Yet with that cry from Macedon
The very car of CHRIST rolls on;
" I come; who would abide My day
In yonder wilds prepare My way;
My voice is crying in their cry;
Help ye the dying, lest ye die."

JESU, for men of Man the Son,
Yea, Thine the cry from Macedon;
cr O by the kingdom and the power
And glory of Thine advent hour,
Wake heart and will to hear their cry;
Help us to help them, lest we die!

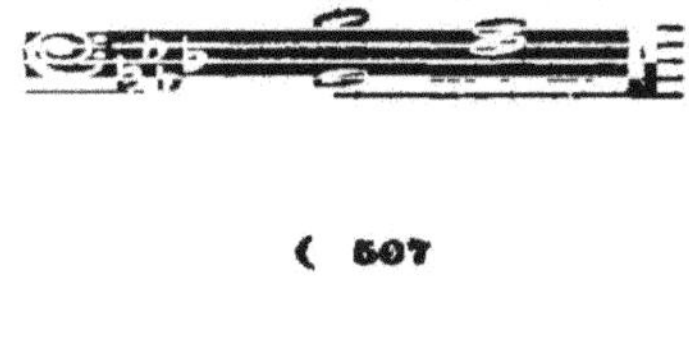

Missions.

Hymn 362.

"Waiting for the coming of our Lord Jesus Christ."

LORD, her watch Thy Church is keeping;
cr When shall earth Thy rule obey?
When shall end the night of weeping?
When shall break the promised day?
p See the whitening harvest languish,
Waiting still the labourer's toil;
cr Was it vain, Thy SON's deep anguish?
Shall the strong retain the spoil?

p Tidings, sent to every creature,
Millions yet have never heard;
cr Can they hear without a preacher?
LORD Almighty, give the Word:
mf Give the Word; in every nation
Let the Gospel-trumpet sound,
Witnessing a world's salvation
cr To the earth's remotest bound.

f Then the end: Thy Church completed,
All Thy chosen gathered in,
With their King in glory seated,
Satan bound, and banished sin;
p Gone for ever parting, weeping,
Hunger, sorrow, death, and pain;
cr Lo! her watch Thy Church is keeping;
Come, LORD JESUS, come to reign.

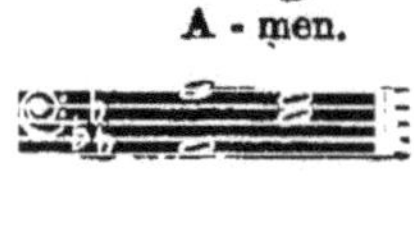

Missions.

Hymn 363. (First Tune.)

"Turn us then, O God our Saviour."

mf ALMIGHTY God, Whose only Son
O'er sin and death the triumph won,
And ever lives to intercede
For souls who Thy sweet mercy need;

In His dear Name to Thee we pray
For all who err and go astray,
For sinners, wheresoe'er they be,
Who do not serve and honour Thee.

p There are who never yet have heard
The tidings of Thy blessèd Word,
But still in heathen darkness dwell,
Without one thought of heaven or hell;

And some within Thy sacred fold
To holy things are dead and cold,
And waste the precious hours of life
In selfish ease, or toil, or strife;

And many a quickened soul within
There lurks the secret love of sin,
A wayward will, or anxious fears,
Or lingering taint of bygone years:

mf O give repentance true and deep
To all Thy lost and wandering sheep,
cr And kindle in their hearts the fire
Of holy love and pure desire.

f That so from Angel-hosts above
May rise a sweeter song of love,
And we, with all the Blest, adore
Thy Name, O God, for evermore.

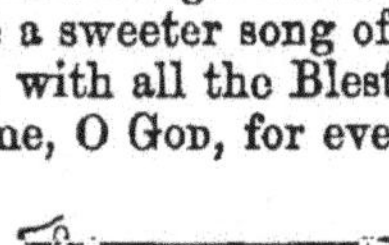

Missions.

Hymn 363. (Second Tune.)

"Turn us then, O God our Saviour."

mf ALMIGHTY God, Whose only Son
O'er sin and death the triumph won,
And ever lives to intercede
For souls who Thy sweet mercy need;

In His dear Name to Thee we pray
For all who err and go astray,
For sinners, wheresoe'er they be,
Who do not serve and honour Thee.

p There are who never yet have heard
The tidings of Thy blessèd Word,
But still in heathen darkness dwell,
Without one thought of heaven or hell,

And some within Thy sacred fold
To holy things are dead and cold,
And waste the precious hours of life
In selfish ease, or toil, or strife;

And many a quickened soul within
There lurks the secret love of sin,
A wayward will, or anxious fears,
Or lingering taint of bygone years:

mf O give repentance true and deep
To all Thy lost and wandering sheep,
cr And kindle in their hearts the fire
Of holy love and pure desire.

f That so from Angel-hosts above
May rise a sweeter song of love,
And we, with all the Blest, adore
Thy Name, O God, for evermore.

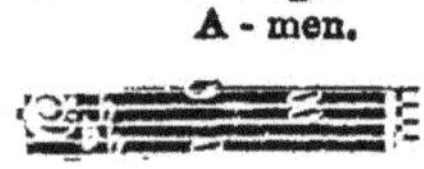

Missions.

Hymn 364.

"That Thy way may be known upon earth, Thy saving health among all nations."

p GOD of grace, O let Thy light
Bless our dim and blinded sight;
cr Like the day-spring on the night,
Bid Thy grace to shine.

mf To the nations led astray
Thine eternal love display;
Let Thy truth direct their way
cr Till the world be Thine.

f Praise to Thee, the faithful LORD;
Let all tongues in glad accord
Learn the good thanksgiving word,
Ever praising Thee.

mf Let them moved to gladness sing,
Owning Thee their Judge and King;
Righteous truth shall bloom and spring
Where Thy rule shall be.

ff Praise to Thee, all faithful LORD;
Let all tongues in glad accord
Speak the good thanksgiving word,
Heart-rejoicing praise.

mf So the fruitful earth's increase,
Bounty of the GOD of peace,
Never in its course shall cease
Through the length of days;

While His grace our life shall cheer,
Furthest lands shall own His fear,
Brought to Him in worship near,
Taught His mercy's ways.

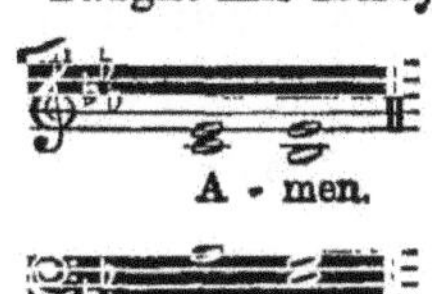

The following Hymns are suitable:

217 Thy kingdom come, O GOD.
218 GOD of mercy, GOD of grace.
220 JESUS shall reign where'er the sun.

Almsgiving.

Hymn 365.

"Freely ye have received, freely give."

f O LORD of heaven, and earth, and sea,
To Thee all praise and glory be;
How shall we shew our love to Thee,
Who givest all?

mf The golden sunshine, vernal air,
Sweet flowers and fruit, Thy love declare;
When harvests ripen, Thou art there,
Who givest all.

For peaceful homes, and healthful days,
For all the blessings earth displays,
cr We owe Thee thankfulness and praise,
Who givest all.

p Thou didst not spare Thine Only Son,
But gav'st Him for a world undone,
cr And freely with that Blessèd One
Thou givest all.

mf Thou giv'st the HOLY SPIRIT's dower,
SPIRIT of life, and love, and power,
And dost His sevenfold graces shower
Upon us all.

For souls redeemed, for sins forgiven,
For means of grace and hopes of heaven,
cr FATHER, what can to Thee be given,
Who givest all?

p We lose what on ourselves we spend,
f We have as treasure without end
Whatever, LORD, to Thee we lend,
Who givest all.

mf Whatever, LORD, we lend to Thee
cr Repaid a thousandfold will be;
f Then gladly will we give to Thee,
Who givest all;

To Thee, from Whom we all derive
Our life, our gifts, our power to give:
p O may we ever with Thee live,
Who givest all.

Almsgiving.

Hymn 366.

"Whoso hath this world's good, and seeth his brother have need, and shutteth up his bowels of compassion from him, how dwelleth the love of God in him?"

mf WE give Thee but Thine own,
Whate'er the gift may be:
All that we have is Thine alone,
A trust, O LORD, from Thee.

May we Thy bounties thus
As stewards true receive,
And gladly, as Thou blessest us,
To Thee our first-fruits give.

p Oh, hearts are bruised and dead,
And homes are bare and cold,
And lambs, for whom the Shepherd bled,
Are straying from the fold.

cr To comfort and to bless,
To find a balm for woe,
To tend the lone and fatherless,
Is Angels' work below.

The captive to release,
To GOD the lost to bring,
To teach the way of life and peace,
It is a Christ-like thing.

And we believe Thy Word,
dim Though dim our faith may be;
cr Whate'er for Thine we do, O LORD,
We do it unto Thee.

f All might, all praise be Thine,
FATHER, Co-equal SON,
And SPIRIT, Bond of love Divine,
While endless ages run.

Almsgiving.

Hymn 367.

Almsgiving.

"Ye ought . . . to remember the words of the Lord Jesus, how He said, It is more blessed to give than to receive."

mf LORD of glory, Who hast bought us
  With Thy Life-blood as the price,
Never grudging for the lost ones
  That tremendous Sacrifice,
And with that hast freely given
  Blessings, countless as the sand,
To the unthankful and the evil
  With Thine own unsparing hand;

Grant us hearts, dear LORD, to yield Thee
  Gladly, freely of Thine own;
With the sunshine of Thy goodness
  Melt our thankless hearts of stone;
p Till our cold and selfish natures,
cr   Warmed by Thee, at length believe
That more happy and more blessèd
  'Tis to give than to receive.

mf Wondrous honour hast Thou given
  To our humblest charity
In Thine own mysterious sentence,
  "Ye have done it unto Me."
p Can it be, O gracious Master,
  Thou dost deign for alms to sue,
cr Saying by Thy poor and needy,
  "Give as I have given to you?"

p Yes: the sorrow and the suffering,
  Which on every hand we see,
Channels are for tithes and offerings
  Due by solemn right to Thee;
cr Right of which we may not rob Thee,
  Debt we may not choose but pay,
dim Lest that Face of love and pity
  Turn from us another day.

mf LORD of glory, Who hast bought us
  With Thy Life-blood as the price,
Never grudging for the lost ones
  That tremendous Sacrifice,
cr Give us faith, to trust Thee boldly,
  Hope, to stay our souls on Thee;
f But O, best of all Thy graces,
dim   Give us Thine own charity.

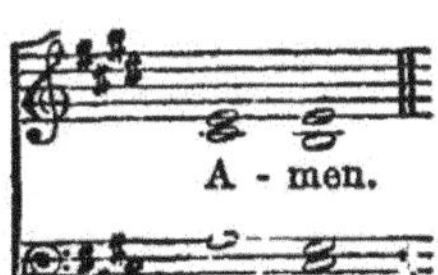

The following Hymn is suitable:

259 Thy life was given for me.

Hospitals.

Hymn 368. (First Tune.)

"They brought unto Him all sick people that were taken with divers diseases . . . and He healed them.'

mf THOU to Whom the sick and dying
Ever came, nor came in vain,
Still with healing word replying
To the wearied cry of pain,
p Hear us, Jesu, as we meet
Suppliants at Thy mercy-seat.

Still the weary, sick, and dying
Need a brother's, sister's care,
cr On Thy higher help relying
May we now their burden share,
mf Bringing all our offerings meet
Suppliants at Thy mercy-seat.

May each child of Thine be willing,
Willing both in hand and heart,
All the law of love fulfilling,
Ever comfort to impart;
Ever bringing offerings meet,
Suppliant to Thy mercy-seat.

So may sickness, sin, and sadness
To Thy healing virtue yield,
cr Till the sick and sad, in gladness,
Rescued, ransomed, cleansèd, heale
f One in Thee together meet,
p Pardoned at Thy judgment-seat.

Hospitals

Hymn 368. (Second Tune.)

"They brought unto Him all sick people that were taken with divers diseases . . . and He healed them."

mf THOU to Whom the sick and dying
Ever came, nor came in vain,
Still with healing word replying
To the wearied cry of pain,
p Hear us, Jesu, as we meet
Suppliants at Thy mercy-seat.

Still the weary, sick, and dying
Need a brother's, sister's care,
cr On Thy higher help relying
May we now their burden share,
mf Bringing all our offerings meet
Suppliants at Thy mercy-seat.

May each child of Thine be willing,
Willing both in hand and heart,
All the law of love fulfilling,
Ever comfort to impart,
Ever bringing offerings meet
Suppliant to Thy mercy-seat.

So may sickness, sin, and sadness
To Thy healing virtue yield,
cr Till the sick and sad, in gladness,
Rescued, ransomed, cleansèd, healed,
f One in Thee together meet,
p Pardoned at Thy judgment-seat.

Hospitals.

Hymn 369. (Original Form.)

Hymn 369. (Modern Form.)

Hospitals.

"They brought unto Him all that were diseased, and besought Him that they might only touch the hem of His garment; and as many as touched were made perfectly whole."

f THINE arm, O LORD, in days of old,
Was strong to heal and save;
It triumphed o'er disease and death,
O'er darkness and the grave;
p To Thee they went, the blind, the dumb,
The palsied and the lame,
The leper with his tainted life,
The sick with fevered frame.

mf And lo! Thy touch brought life and health,
Gave speech, and strength, and sight;
cr And youth renewed and frenzy calmed
Owned Thee, the LORD of light;
f And now, O LORD, be near to bless,
Almighty as of yore,
In crowded street, by restless couch,
As by Gennesareth's shore.

mf Be Thou our great Deliverer still,
Thou LORD of life and death;
Restore and quicken, soothe and bless
With Thine Almighty breath;
To hands that work, and eyes that see,
Give wisdom's heavenly lore,
f That whole and sick, and weak and strong
May praise Thee evermore.

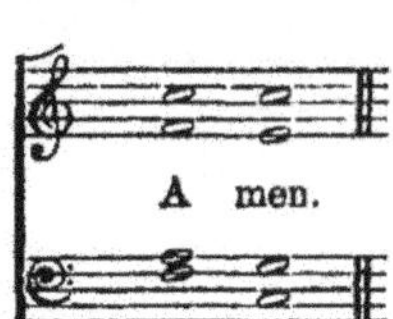

For those at Sea.

Hymn 370.

For those at Sea.

"These men see the works of the Lord, and His wonders in the deep."

mf ETERNAL FATHER, strong to save,
Whose arm hath bound the restless wave,
Who bidd'st the mighty ocean deep
Its own appointed limits keep;
p O hear us *(cr)* when we cry to Thee
dim For those in peril on the sea.

mf O CHRIST, Whose voice the waters heard
p And hushed their raging at Thy word,
cr Who walkedst on the foaming deep,
dim And calm amid the storm didst sleep;
p O hear us *(cr)* when we cry to Thee
dim For those in peril on the sea.

mf O HOLY SPIRIT, Who didst brood
Upon the waters dark and rude,
And bid their angry tumult cease,
And give, for wild confusion, *(p)* peace;
O hear us *(cr)* when we cry to Thee
dim For those in peril on the sea.

mf O TRINITY of love and power,
Our brethren shield in danger's hour;
From rock and tempest, fire and foe,
Protect them wheresoe'er they go;
cr Thus evermore shall rise to Thee
f Glad hymns of praise from land and sea.

For those at Sea.

Hymn 371.

"Thou shalt shew us wonderful things in Thy righteousness, O God of our salvation: Thou that art the hope of all the ends of the earth, and of them that remain in the broad sea."

mf ALMIGHTY FATHER, hear our cry,
As o'er the trackless deep we roam;
Be Thou our haven always nigh,
On homeless waters Thou our home.

p O JESU, Saviour, at Whose voice
The tempest sank to perfect rest,
cr Bid Thou the fearful heart rejoice,
And cleanse and calm the troubled breast.

mf O HOLY GHOST, beneath Whose power
The ocean woke to life and light,
Command Thy blessing in this hour,
Thy fostering warmth, Thy quickening might.

f Great GOD of our salvation, Thee
We love, we worship, we adore;
Our Refuge on time's changeful sea,
Our Joy on heaven's eternal shore.

For those at Sea.

Hymn 372.

"They willingly received Him into the ship."

p ON the waters dark and drear,
  JESUS, Saviour, Thou art near,
cr With our ship where'er it roam,
  As with loving friends at home.

mf Thou hast walked the heaving wave;
f Thou art mighty still to save;
p With one gentle word of peace
  Thou canst bid the tempest cease.

mf Safely from the boisterous main
  Bring us back to port again:
  In our haven we shall be,
  JESU, if we have but Thee.

Only by Thy power and love
Fit us for the port above;
dim Still the deadly storm within,
  Gusts of passion, waves of sin.

f So, when breaks the glorious dawn
  Of the Resurrection morn,
p When the night of toil is o'er,
cr We shall see Thee on the shore.

f Holy FATHER, Holy SON,
  Holy SPIRIT, THREE in ONE,
  Praise unending unto Thee,
  Now and evermore shall be.

The following Hymn is suitable:

285 Fierce raged the tempest o'er the deep.

In Times of Trouble.

Hymn 373.

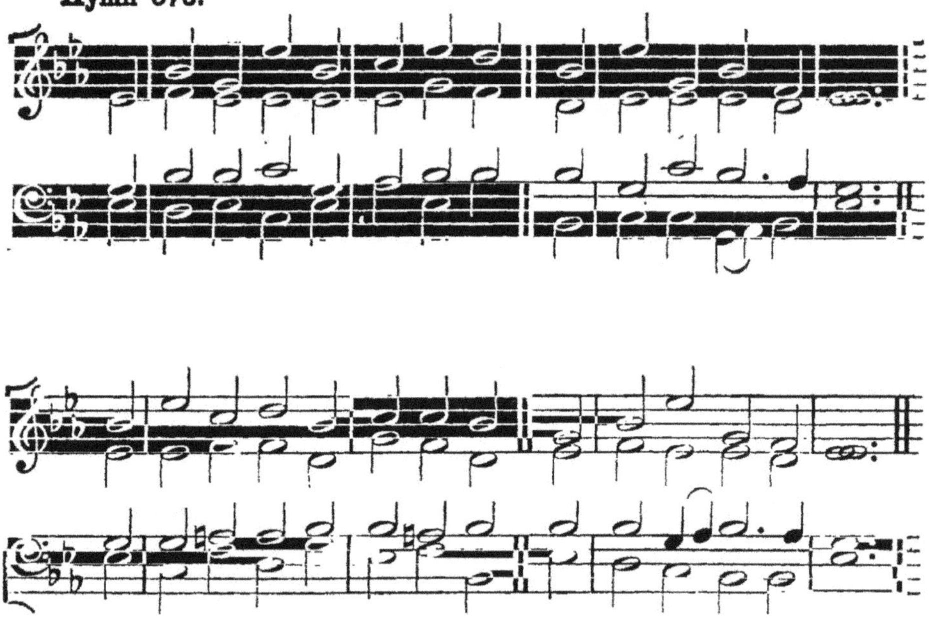

"What I do thou knowest not now; but thou shalt know hereafter."

mf GOD moves in a mysterious way
His wonders to perform;
He plants His footsteps in the sea,
And rides upon the storm.

Deep in unfathomable mines
Of never-failing skill
He treasures up His bright designs
And works His sovereign Will.

Ye fearful saints, fresh courage take;
The clouds ye so much dread
Are big with mercy, and shall break
In blessings on your head.

Judge not the LORD by feeble sense,
But trust Him for His grace;
p Behind a frowning providence
cr He hides a smiling face.

mf Blind unbelief is sure to err,
And scan His work in vain;
cr GOD is His own interpreter,
And He will make it plain.

In Times of Trouble.

Hymn 374.

" God is our hope and strength, a very present help in trouble."

p GOD of our life, to Thee we call,
Afflicted at Thy feet we fall;
When the great water-floods prevail,
Leave not our trembling hearts to fail.

p Did ever mourner plead with Thee,
cr And Thou refuse that mourner's plea?
mf Does not the Word still fixed remain,
That none shall seek Thy Face in vain?

Friend of the friendless and the faint,
Where should we lodge our deep complaint?
cr Where but with Thee, Whose open door
Invites the helpless and the poor?

p Then hear, O LORD, our humble cry,
And bend on us Thy pitying eye:
To Thee their prayer Thy people make,
Hear us for our Redeemer's sake.

In Times of Trouble.

Hymn 375.

In Times of Trouble.

"Thou that hearest the prayer; unto Thee shall all flesh come."

p GREAT King of nations, hear our prayer,
While at Thy feet we fall,
And humbly with united cry
To Thee for mercy call;
The guilt is ours, but grace is Thine,
O turn us not away;
cr But hear us from Thy lofty Throne,
And help us when we pray.

p Our fathers' sins were manifold,
And ours no less we own,
mf Yet wondrously from age to age
Thy goodness hath been shown;
dim When dangers, like a stormy sea,
Beset our country round,
cr To Thee we looked, to Thee we cried,
And help in Thee was found.

p With one consent we meekly bow
Beneath Thy chastening hand,
And, pouring forth confession meet,
Mourn with our mourning land;
cr With pitying eye behold our need,
As thus we lift our prayer;
p Correct us with Thy judgments, LORD,
cr Then let Thy mercy spare.

In Times of Trouble.

Hymn 376.

"The Lord shall give His people the blessing of peace"

War.

mf O GOD of love, O King of peace,
Make wars throughout the world to cease;
The wrath of sinful man restrain,
p Give peace, O God, give peace again.

mf Whom shall we trust but Thee, O Lord?
Where rest but on Thy faithful Word?
cr None ever called on Thee in vain,
p Give peace, O God, give peace again.

mf Remember, Lord, Thy works of old,
The wonders that our fathers told,
Remember not our sin's dark stain,
p Give peace, O God, give peace again.

f Where Saints and Angels dwell above,
All hearts are knit in holy love;
O bind us in that heavenly chain,
p Give peace, O God, give peace again.

In Times of Trouble.

Hymn 377.

"Thou shalt not be afraid . . . for the pestilence that walketh in darkness; nor for the sickness that destroyeth in the noon-day."

PESTILENCE.

p IN grief and fear to Thee, O LORD,
We now for succour fly;
Thine awful judgments are abroad,
cr e dim O shield us lest we die.

p The fell disease on every side
Walks forth with tainted breath;
And pestilence, with rapid stride,
Bestrews the land with death.

mf O look with pity on the scene
Of sadness and of dread;
And let Thine Angel stand between
dim The living and the dead.

p With contrite hearts to Thee, our King
We turn who oft have strayed;
cr Accept the sacrifice we bring,
And let the plague be stayed.

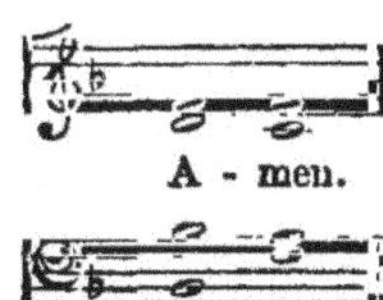

In time of Famine or Scarcity the following Hymn is suitable:
389 What our FATHER does is well.

Thanksgiving.

Hymn 378. (First Version.)

Hymn 378. (Second Version.)

Thanksgiving.

"O praise the Lord, laud ye the Name of the Lord; praise it, O ye servants of the Lord."

f REJOICE to-day with one accord,
  Sing out with exultation;
Rejoice and praise our mighty LORD,
  Whose arm hath brought salvation;
    His works of love proclaim
    The greatness of His Name;
    For He is GOD alone
    Who hath His mercy shown;
dim Let all His saints adore Him!

p When in distress to Him we cried,
  He heard our sad complaining;
cr O trust in Him, whate'er betide,
  His love is all-sustaining;
    f Triumphant songs of praise
    To Him our hearts shall raise;
    Now every voice shall say,
    "O praise our GOD alway;"
dim Let all His saints adore Him!

ff Rejoice to-day with one accord,
  Sing out with exultation;
Rejoice and praise our mighty LORD,
  Whose arm hath brought salvation;
    His works of love proclaim
    The greatness of His Name;
    For He is GOD alone
    Who hath His mercy shown;
  Let all His saints adore Him!

1 and 2.

Thanksgiving.

Hymn 379.

Thanksgiving.

O clap your hands together, all ye people ; O sing unto God with the voice of melody."

f NOW thank we all our God,
With heart, and hands, and voices,
Who wondrous things hath done,
In Whom His world rejoices;
Who from our mother's arms
Hath blessed us on our way
With countless gifts of love,
And still is ours to-day.

mf O may this bounteous God
Through all our life be near us,
With ever joyful hearts
And blessèd peace to cheer us;
And keep us in His grace,
And guide us when perplexed,
And free us from all ills
In this world and the next.

f All praise and thanks to God
The Father now be given,
The Son, and Him Who reigns
With Them in highest heaven,
The One Eternal God,
Whom earth and heaven adore,
For thus it was, is now,
And shall be evermore.

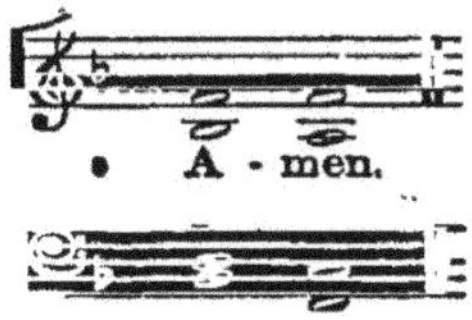

Friendly Societies.

Hymn 380.

"Bear ye one another's burdens, and so fulfil the law of Christ."

f O PRAISE our GOD to-day,
His constant mercy bless,
Whose love hath helped us on our way,
And granted us success.

mf His arm the strength imparts
Our daily toil to bear;
His grace alone inspires our hearts
Each other's load to share.

O happiest work below,
Earnest of joy above,
To sweeten many a cup of woe
By deeds of holy love!

LORD, may it be our choice
This blessèd rule to keep,
cr "Rejoice with them that do rejoice,
dim And weep with them that weep."

f O praise our GOD to-day,
His constant mercy bless,
Whose love hath helped us on our way,
And granted us success.

The following Hymns are suitable:

273 O LORD, how joyful 'tis to see.

274 Through the night of doubt and sorrow.

Harvest.

Hymn 381.

"Who giveth food to all flesh; for His mercy endureth for ever."

PRAISE, O praise our God and King;
Hymns of adoration sing;
For His mercies still endure
Ever faithful, ever sure.

mf Praise Him that He made the sun
Day by day his course to run;
For His mercies still endure
Ever faithful, ever sure;

And the silver moon by night,
Shining with her gentle light;
f For His mercies still endure
Ever faithful, ever sure.

mf Praise Him that He gave the rain
To mature the swelling grain;
f For His mercies still endure
Ever faithful, ever sure;

mf And hath bid the fruitful field
Crops of precious increase yield;
f For His mercies still endure
Ever faithful, ever sure.

ff Praise Him for our harvest-store,
He hath filled the garner-floor;
For His mercies still endure
Ever faithful, ever sure;

p And for richer Food than this,
cr Pledge of everlasting bliss;
f For His mercies still endure
Ever faithful, ever sure.

ff Glory to our Bounteous King;
Glory let creation sing;
Glory to the FATHER, SON,
And Blest SPIRIT, THREE in ONE.

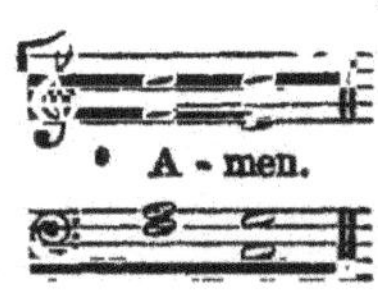

Harvest.

Hymn 382.

Harvest.

"They joy before Thee according to the joy in harvest."

f **COME, ye thankful people, come,**
Raise the song of Harvest-home:
All is safely gathered in,
Ere the winter storms begin;
mf **God, our Maker, doth provide**
For our wants to be supplied;
f **Come to God's own Temple, come;**
Raise the song of Harvest-home.

mf **All this world is God's own field,**
Fruit unto His praise to yield;
Wheat and tares therein are sown,
Unto joy or sorrow grown;
cr **Ripening with a wondrous power**
Till the final Harvest-hour:
p **Grant, O Lord of life, that we**
Holy grain and pure may be.

mf **For we know that Thou wilt come,**
And wilt take Thy people home;
From Thy field wilt purge away
All that doth offend, that day;
p **And Thine Angels charge at last**
In the fire the tares to cast,
f **But the fruitful ears to store**
In Thy garner evermore.

mf **Come then, Lord of mercy, come,**
Bid us sing Thy Harvest-home:
cr **Let Thy saints be gathered in,**
Free from sorrow, free from sin;
f **All upon the golden floor**
Praising Thee for evermore:
Come, with all Thine Angels come;
Bid us sing Thy *(rall)* Harvest-home.

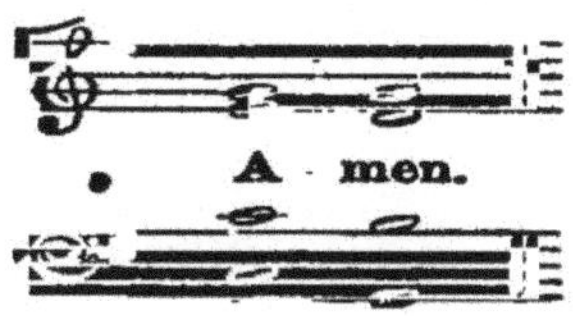

Harvest.

Hymn 383.

Harvest.

"The eyes of all wait upon Thee, O Lord, and Thou givest them their meat in due season."

mf WE plough the fields, and scatter
The good seed on the land,
But it is fed and watered
By God's Almighty Hand;
He sends the snow in winter,
The warmth to swell the grain,
The breezes, and the sunshine,
And soft refreshing rain.
f All good gifts around us
Are sent from heaven above,
ff Then thank the Lord, O thank the Lord,
For all His love.

He only is the Maker
Of all things near and far;
He paints the wayside flower,
He lights the evening star;
The winds and waves obey Him,
By Him the birds are fed;
Much more to us, His children,
He gives our daily bread.
f All good gifts, &c.

mf We thank Thee then, O Father,
For all things bright and good,
The seed-time and the harvest,
Our life, our health, our food;
Accept the gifts we offer
For all Thy love imparts,
And, what Thou most desirest,
p Our humble, thankful hearts.
f All good gifts around us
Are sent from heaven above,
ff Then thank the Lord, O thank the Lord,
For all His love.

Harvest.

Hymn 384.

Harvest.

"Thou crownest the year with Thy goodness."

f TO Thee, O LORD, our hearts we raise
In hymns of adoration,
To Thee bring sacrifice of praise
With shouts of exultation;
mf Bright robes of gold the fields adorn,
The hills with joy are ringing,
The valleys stand so thick with corn
f That even they are singing.

mf And now, on this our festal day,
Thy bounteous Hand confessing,
Upon Thine Altar, LORD, we lay
The first-fruits of Thy blessing;
p By Thee the souls of men are fed
With gifts of grace supernal,
Thou, Who dost give us earthly bread,
Give us the Bread Eternal.

mf We bear the burden of the day,
And often toil seems dreary;
But labour ends with sunset ray,
And rest comes for the weary;
May we, the Angel-reaping o'er,
Stand at the last accepted,
CHRIST'S golden sheaves for evermore
To garners bright elected.

f Oh, blessèd is that land of GOD,
Where Saints abide for ever;
Where golden fields spread far and broad,
Where flows the crystal river:
p The strains of all its holy throng
With ours to-day are blending;
f Thrice blessèd is that harvest-song
Which never hath an ending.

Harvest.

Hymn 385. (First Tune.)

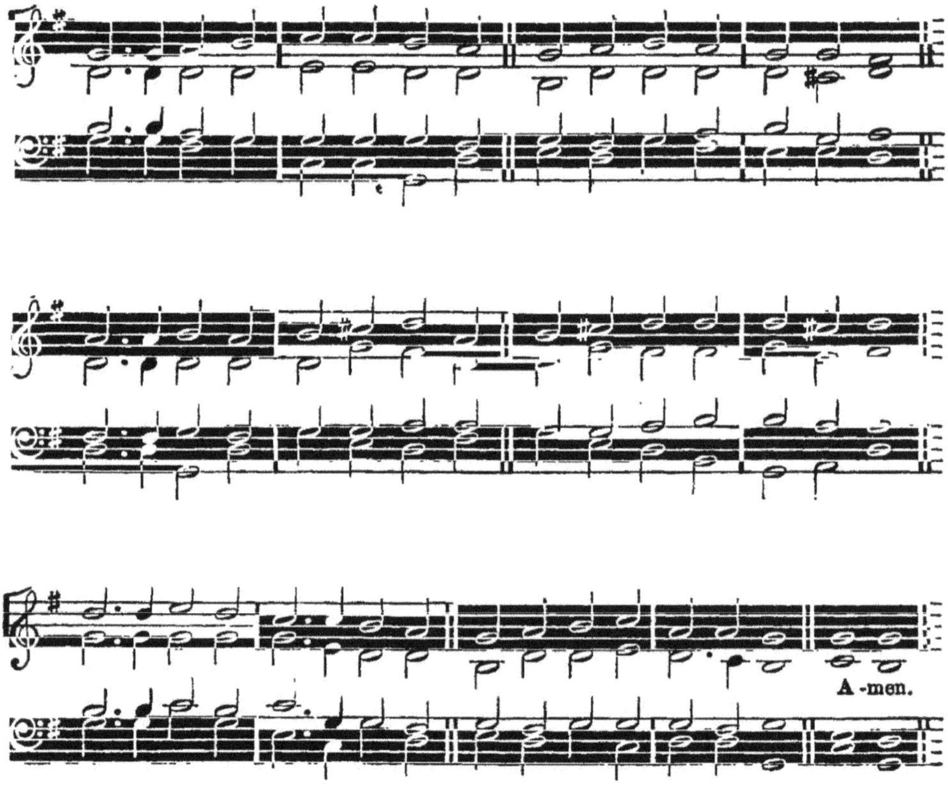

Hymn 385. (Second Tune.)

Harvest.

" While the earth remaineth, seed-time and harvest . . . shall not cease."

mf GOD the FATHER, Whose creation
  Gives to flowers and fruits their birth,
Thou, Whose yearly operation
  Brings the hour of harvest mirth,
Here to Thee we make oblation
  Of the August-gold of earth.

GOD the WORD, the sun maturing
  With his blessèd ray the corn
cr Spake of Thee, O Sun enduring,
  Thee, O everlasting Morn,
p Thee in Whom our woes find curing,
cr Thee that liftest up our horn.

mf GOD the HOLY GHOST, the showers
  That have fattened out the grain,
Types of Thy celestial powers,
  Symbols of baptismal rain,
Shadowed out the grace that dowers
  All the faithful of Thy train.

When the harvest of each nation
  Severs righteousness from sin,
And Archangel-proclamation
  Bids to put the sickle in,
And each age and generation
  Sink to woe, or glory win;

p Grant that we, or young, or hoary,
  Lengthened be our span or brief,
Whatsoe'er the life-long story
  Of our joy or of our grief,
cr May be garnered up in glory
  As Thine own elected sheaf.

f Laud to Him to Whom supernal
  Thrones and Virtues bend the knee;
Laud to Him from Whom infernal
  Powers and Dominations flee;
Laud to Him the Co-eternal
  Paraclete for ever be.

Harvest.

Hymn 386.

Harvest.

"Behold a sower went forth to sow."

THE sower went forth sowing,
 The seed in secret slept
Through weeks of faith and patience,
 Till out the green blade crept;
And warmed by golden sunshine,
 And fed by silver rain,
At last the fields were whitened
 To harvest once again.
O praise the heavenly Sower,
 Who gave the fruitful seed,
And watched and watered duly,
 And ripened for our need.

Behold! the heavenly Sower
 Goes forth with better seed,
The Word of sure salvation,
 With Feet and Hands that bleed;
Here in His Church 'tis scattered,
 Our spirits are the soil;
Then let an ample fruitage
 Repay His pain and toil.
Oh, beauteous is the harvest
 Wherein all goodness thrives,
And this the true thanksgiving,
 The first-fruits of our lives.

p Within a hallowed acre
 He sows yet other grain,
When peaceful earth receiveth
 The dead He died to gain;
For though the growth be hidden,
cr We know that they shall rise;
Yea even now they ripen
 In sunny Paradise.
f O summer land of harvest,
 O fields for ever white
With souls that wear CHRIST'S raiment,
 With crowns of golden light!

mf One day the heavenly Sower
 Shall reap where He hath sown,
cr And come again rejoicing,
 And with Him bring His own;
p And then the fan of judgment
 Shall winnow from His floor
The chaff into the furnace
 That flameth evermore.
mf O holy, awful Reaper,
p Have mercy in the day
Thou puttest in Thy sickle,
rall e pp And cast us not away.

Harvest.

Hymn 387.

Harvest.

The harvest is the end of the world, and the reapers are the angels."

mf LORD of the harvest, once again
We thank Thee for the ripened grain;
For crops safe carried, sent to cheer
Thy servants through another year;
For all sweet holy thoughts supplied
By seed-time, and by harvest-tide.

p The bare dead grain, in autumn sown,
cr Its robe of vernal green puts on;
mf Glad from its wintry grave it springs,
Fresh garnished by the King of kings:
p So, LORD, to those who sleep in Thee
cr Shall new and glorious bodies be.

mf Nor vainly of Thy Word we ask
A lesson from the reaper's task:
So shall Thine Angels issue forth;
The tares be burnt; *(cr)* the just of earth,
To wind and storm exposed no more,
Be gathered to their FATHER's store.

mf Daily, O LORD, our prayers be said,
As Thou hast taught, for daily bread;
But not alone our bodies feed,
Supply our fainting spirits' need:
cr O Bread of life, from day to day,
Be Thou their Comfort, Food, and Stay.

Harvest.

Hymn 388.

"Thou visitest the earth, and blessest it; Thou makest it very plenteous."

mf FATHER of mercies, GOD of love,
Whose gifts all creatures share,
The rolling seasons as they move
Proclaim Thy constant care.

p When in the bosom of the earth
The sower hid the grain,
cr Thy goodness marked its secret birth,
And sent the early rain.

mf The spring's sweet influence, LORD, was Thine,
The seasons knew Thy call;
Thou mad'st the summer sun to shine,
The summer dews to fall.

Thy gifts of mercy from above
Matured the swelling grain;
f And now the harvest crowns Thy love,
And plenty fills the plain.

mf O ne'er may our forgetful hearts
O'erlook Thy bounteous care,
But what our FATHER's Hand imparts
Still own in praise and prayer.

f To FATHER, SON, and HOLY GHOST,
The GOD Whom we adore,
Be glory, as it was, is now,
And shall be evermore.

Harvest.

Hymn 389.

"Although . . . the fields shall yield no meat . . . yet I will rejoice in the Lord, I will joy in the God of my salvation."

mf WHAT our FATHER does is well;
Blessèd truth His children tell!
dim Though He send, for plenty, want,
Though the harvest-store be scant,
cr Yet we rest upon His love,
Seeking better things above.

mf What our FATHER does is well:
Shall the wilful heart rebel?
dim If a blessing He withhold
In the field, or in the fold,
cr Is it not Himself to be
All our store eternally?

mf What our FATHER does is well;
p Though He sadden hill and dell,
cr Upward yet our praises rise
For the strength His Word supplies;
He has called us sons of GOD,
p Can we murmur at His rod?

mf What our FATHER does is well:
May the thought within us dwell;
dim Though nor milk nor honey flow
In our barren Canaan now,
cr GOD can save us in our need,
GOD can bless us, GOD can feed.

f Therefore unto Him we raise
Hymns of glory, songs of praise;
To the FATHER, and the SON,
And the SPIRIT, THREE in ONE,
Honour, might, and glory be
Now, and through eternity.

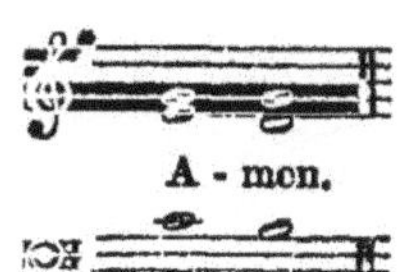

This Hymn may be sung when there is a deficiency in the crops.

Processional.

Hymn 390.

Processional.

"Behold, I have given Him for . . . a leader and commander to the people."

f BRIGHTLY gleams our banner
Pointing to the sky,
Waving wanderers onward
To their home on high.
p Journeying o'er the desert,
Gladly thus we pray,
cr And with hearts united
Take our heavenward way.
f Brightly gleams, &c

mf Jesu, Lord and Master,
At Thy sacred Feet,
Here with hearts rejoicing
See Thy children meet;
p Often have we left Thee,
Often gone astray;
Keep us, mighty Saviour,
In the narrow way.
f Brightly gleams, &c.

mf All our days direct us
In the way we go,
f Lead us on victorious
Over every foe:
p Bid Thine Angels shield us
When the storm-clouds lour,
cr Pardon, Lord, and save us
p In the last dread hour.
f Brightly gleams, &c.

mf Then with Saints and Angels
May we join above,
Offering prayers and praises
At Thy Throne of love;
p When the toil is over,
Then comes rest and peace,
cr Jesus in His beauty,
f Songs that never cease.
ff Brightly gleams, &c.

Processional.

Hymn 391.

Processional.

"Be strong and of a good courage . . And the Lord, He it is that doth go before thee."

f ONWARD, Christian soldiers,
Marching as to war,
With the Cross of JESUS
Going on before.
CHRIST the Royal Master
Leads against the foe;
Forward into battle,
See, His banners go!
ff Onward, Christian soldiers,
Marching as to war,
With the Cross of JESUS
Going on before.

f At the sign of triumph
Satan's host doth flee;
On then, Christian soldiers,
On to victory.
Hell's foundations quiver
At the shout of praise;
Brothers, lift your voices,
Loud your anthems raise.
ff Onward, &c.

f Like a mighty army
Moves the Church of GOD;
mf Brothers, we are treading
Where the Saints have trod;
We are not divided,
All one body we,
cr One in hope and doctrine,
One in charity.
ff Onward, &c.

p Crowns and thrones may perish,
Kingdoms rise and wane,
cr But the Church of JESUS
Constant will remain;
f Gates of hell can never
'Gainst that Church prevail;
We have CHRIST's own promise,
And that cannot fail.
ff Onward, &c.

f Onward, then, ye people,
Join our happy throng,
Blend with ours your voices
In the triumph song;
Glory, laud, and honour
Unto CHRIST the King,
This through countless ages
Men and Angels sing.
ff Onward, Christian soldiers,
Marching as to war,
With the Cross of JESUS
Going on before.

Processional.

Hymn 392.

Processional.

"Speak unto the children of Israel that they go forward."

mf FORWARD! be our watchword,
  Steps and voices joined;
Seek the things before us,
  Not a look behind;
Burns the fiery pillar
  At our army's head;
Who shall dream of shrinking,
  By our Captain led?
    f Forward through the desert,
      Through the toil and fight;
    Jordan flows before us,
      Sion beams with light.

mf Forward, when in childhood
  Buds the infant mind;
All through youth and manhood,
  Not a thought behind;
Speed through realms of nature,
  Climb the steps of grace;
Faint not, till in glory
  Gleams our FATHER'S Face.
    f Forward, all the life-time,
      Climb from height to height;
    Till the head be hoary,
      Till the eve be light.

mf Forward, flock of JESUS,
  Salt of all the earth,
Till each yearning purpose
  Spring to glorious birth;
p Sick, they ask for healing,
  Blind, they grope for day;
cr Pour upon the nations
  Wisdom's loving ray.
    f Forward, out of error,
      Leave behind the night;
    Forward through the darkness,
      Forward into light.

Glories upon glories
  Hath our GOD prepared,
By the souls that love Him
  One day to be shared;
mf Eye hath not beheld them,
  Ear hath never heard;
Nor of these hath uttered
  Thought or speech a word;
    f Forward, marching eastward,
      Where the heaven is bright,
    Till the veil be lifted,
      Till our faith be sight.

mf Far o'er yon horizon
  Rise the city towers,
Where our GOD abideth;
  That fair home is ours:
Flash the streets with jasper,
  Shine the gates with gold;
Flows the gladdening river
  Shedding joys untold.
    f Thither, onward thither,
      In the SPIRIT'S might;
    Pilgrims to your country,
      Forward into light.

mf Into GOD'S high temple
  Onward as we press,
Beauty spreads around us,
  Born of holiness;
Arch, and vault, and carving,
  Lights of varied tone,
p Softened words and holy,
  Prayer and praise alone:
    f Every thought upraising
      To our city bright,
    Where the tribes assemble
      Round the Throne of light.

mf Nought that city needeth
  Of these aisles of stone;
Where the GODHEAD dwelleth,
  Temple there is none;
All the saints, that ever
  In these courts have stood,
p Are but babes, and feeding
  On the children's food.
    f On through sign and token,
      Stars amidst the night,
    Forward through the darkness,
      Forward into light.

ff To the Eternal FATHER
  Loudest anthems raise;
To the SON and SPIRIT
  Echo songs of praise;
To the LORD of glory,
  Blessèd THREE in ONE,
Be by men and Angels
  Endless honours done:
    p Weak are earthly praises;
      Dull the songs of night;
    cr Forward into triumph,
    f Forward into light!

Processional.

Hymn 393.

"*Young men and maidens, old men and children, praise the Name of the Lord.*"

f REJOICE, ye pure in heart,
Rejoice, give thanks and sing;
Your festal banner wave on high,
The Cross of CHRIST your King.

mf Bright youth and snow-crowned age,
Strong men and maidens meek,
Raise high your free exulting song,
GOD's wondrous praises speak.

Yes onward, onward still,
With hymn, and chant, and song,
Thro' gate, and porch, and columned aisle,
The hallowed pathways throng.

With all the Angel choirs,
With all the saints on earth,
Pour out the strains of joy and bliss,
True rapture, noblest, mirth.

f Your clear Hosannas raise,
And Alleluias loud;
Whilst answering echoes upward float,
Like wreaths of incense cloud.

With voice as full and strong
As ocean's surging praise,
Send forth the hymns our fathers loved,
The psalms of ancient days.

mf Yes on, through life's long path,
Still chanting as ye go,
From youth to age, by night and day,
In gladness and in woe.

Still lift your standard high,
Still march in firm array,
As warriors through the darkness toil
Till dawns the golden day.

p At last the march shall end,
The wearied ones shall rest,
cr The pilgrims find their FATHER's house,
Jerusalem the blest.

f Then on, ye pure in heart,
Rejoice, give thanks, and sing;
Your festal banner wave on high,
The Cross of CHRIST your King.

ff Praise Him Who reigns on high,
The LORD Whom we adore,
The FATHER, SON, and HOLY GHOST,
ONE GOD for evermore.

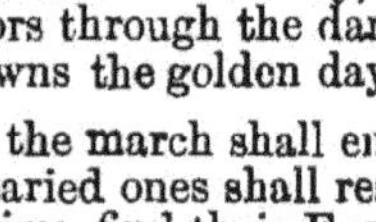

The following Hymns are suitable:

96 The Royal Banners forward go.
179 To the Name of our Salvation.
215 The Church's one foundation.
224 O happy band of pilgrims.
274 Through the night of doubt and sorrow.
302 Come, ye faithful, raise the anthem.
305 Saviour, Blessèd Saviour.
306 At the Name of JESUS.

Laying the Foundation Stone of a Church.

Hymn 394.

"The glory of Lebanon shall come unto thee; the fir tree, the pine tree, and the box together, to beautify the place of My sanctuary."

mf O LORD of hosts, Whose glory fills
The bounds of the eternal hills,
And yet vouchsafes, in Christian lands,
To dwell in temples made with hands;

Grant that all we, who here to-day
Rejoicing this foundation lay,
May be in very deed Thine own,
Built on the precious Corner-stone.

Endue the creatures with Thy grace,
That shall adorn Thy dwelling-place;
The beauty of the oak and pine,
The gold and silver, make them Thine.

To Thee they all belong; to Thee
The treasures of the earth and sea;
And when we bring them to Thy Throne,
We but present Thee with Thine own.

p The heads that guide endue with skill,
The hands that work preserve from ill,
cr That we, who these foundations lay,
May raise the topstone in its day.

mf Both now and ever, LORD, protect
The temple of Thine own elect;
f Be Thou in them, and they in Thee,
O Ever-blessèd TRINITY!

Feast of the Dedication of a Church.

Hymn 395. (First Tune.)

"This is none other but the house of God, and this is the gate of heaven."

f O WORD of God above,
Who fillest all in all,
Hallow this house with Thy sure love,
And bless our Festival.

mf Here from the Font is poured
Grace on each sinful child;
The blest Anointing of the Lord
Brightens the once defiled.

Here Christ to faithful hearts
p His Body gives for food;
cr The Lamb of God Himself imparts
p The Chalice of His Blood.

Here guilty souls that pine
May health and pardon win;
cr The Judge acquits, and grace Divine
Restores the dead in sin.

mf Yea, God enthroned on high
Here also dwells to bless;
Here trains adoring souls that sigh
His mansions to possess.

f Against this holy home
Rude tempests harmless beat,
And Satan's angels fiercely come
But to endure defeat.

ff All might, all praise be Thine,
Father, Co-equal Son,
And Spirit, Bond of love Divine,
While endless ages run.

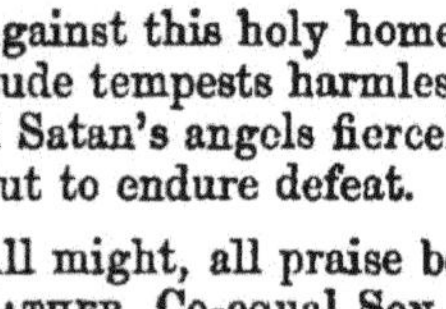

Feast of the Dedication of a Church.

Hymn 395. (Second Tune.)

"This is none other but the house of God, and this is the gate of heaven."

f O WORD of God above,
Who fillest all in all,
Hallow this house with Thy sure love,
And bless our Festival.

mf Here from the Font is poured
Grace on each sinful child;
The blest Anointing of the Lord
Brightens the once defiled.

Here Christ to faithful hearts
p His Body gives for food;
cr The Lamb of God Himself imparts
p The Chalice of His Blood.

Here guilty souls that pine
May health and pardon win;
cr The Judge acquits, and grace Divine
Restores the dead in sin.

mf Yea, God enthroned on high
Here also dwells to bless;
Here trains adoring souls that sigh
His mansions to possess.

f Against this holy home
Rude tempests harmless beat,
And Satan's angels fiercely come
But to endure defeat.

ff All might, all praise be Thine,
Father, Co-equal Son,
And Spirit, Bond of love Divine,
While endless ages run.

Feast of the Dedication of a Church.

Hymn 396. (First Tune.)

To be sung in Unison.

Feast of the Dedication of a Church.

"I, John, saw the holy city, new Jerusalem, coming down from God out of heaven, prepared as a bride adorned for her husband."

mf BLESSED city, heavenly Salem,
Vision dear of peace and love,
f Who of living stones art builded
In the height of heaven above,
mf And, with Angel hosts encircled,
As a bride dost earthward move;

cr From celestial realms descending,
Bridal glory round thee shed,
p Meet for Him Whose love espoused thee,
cr To thy LORD shalt thou be led;
All thy streets, and all thy bulwarks
Of pure gold are fashionèd.

mf Bright thy gates of pearl are shining,
They are open evermore;
cr And by virtue of His merits
Thither faithful souls do soar,
p Who for CHRIST'S dear Name in this world
Pain and tribulation bore.

Many a blow and biting sculpture
Polished well those stones elect,
cr In their places now compacted
By the heavenly Architect,
Who therewith hath willed for ever
That His Palace should be decked.

PART 2.

f CHRIST is made the sure Foundation,
CHRIST the Head and Corner-stone,
mf Chosen of the LORD, and precious,
Binding all the Church in one,
f Holy Sion's help for ever,
And her confidence alone.

mf All that dedicated city,
Dearly loved of GOD on high,
f In exultant jubilation
Pours perpetual melody,
p GOD the ONE in THREE adoring
cr In glad hymns eternally.

mf To this temple, where we call Thee,
Come, O LORD of hosts, to-day;
With Thy wonted loving-kindness
Hear Thy servants, as they pray;
cr And Thy fullest benediction
Shed within its walls alway.

p Here vouchsafe to all Thy servants
What they ask of Thee to gain,
cr What they gain from Thee for ever
With the Blessèd to retain,
f And hereafter in Thy glory
Evermore with Thee to reign.

The following may be sung at the end of each Part:

f Laud and honour to the FATHER,
Laud and honour to the SON,
Laud and honour to the SPIRIT,
Ever THREE, and ever ONE,
Consubstantial, Co-eternal,
While unending ages run.

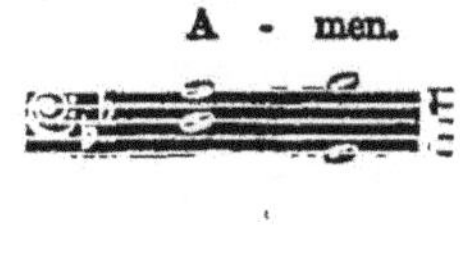

Feast of the Dedication of a Church.

Hymn 396. (Second Tune.)

Feast of the Dedication of a Church.

"I, John, saw the holy city, new Jerusalem, coming down from God out of heaven, prepared as a bride adorned for her husband."

mf BLESSÈD city, heavenly Salem,
Vision dear of peace and love,
f Who of living stones art builded
In the height of heaven above,
mf And, with Angel hosts encircled,
As a bride dost earthward move;

cr From celestial realms descending,
Bridal glory round thee shed,
p Meet for Him Whose love espoused thee,
cr To thy LORD shalt thou be led;
All thy streets, and all thy bulwarks
Of pure gold are fashionèd.

mf Bright thy gates of pearl are shining,
They are open evermore;
cr And by virtue of His merits
Thither faithful souls do soar,
p Who for CHRIST's dear Name in this world
Pain and tribulation bore.

Many a blow and biting sculpture
Polished well those stones elect,
cr In their places now compacted
By the heavenly Architect,
Who therewith hath willed for ever
That His Palace should be decked.

PART 2.

f CHRIST is made the sure Foundation,
CHRIST the Head and Corner-stone,
mf Chosen of the LORD, and precious,
Binding all the Church in one,
f Holy Sion's help for ever,
And her confidence alone.

mf All that dedicated city,
Dearly loved of GOD on high,
f In exultant jubilation
Pours perpetual melody,
p GOD the ONE in THREE adoring
cr In glad hymns eternally.

mf To this temple, where we call Thee,
Come, O LORD of hosts, to-day;
With Thy wonted loving-kindness
Hear Thy servants, as they pray;
cr And Thy fullest benediction
Shed within its walls alway.

p Here vouchsafe to all Thy servants
What they ask of Thee to gain,
cr What they gain from Thee for ever
With the Blessèd to retain,
f And hereafter in Thy glory
Evermore with Thee to reign.

The following may be sung at the end of each Part:

f Laud and honour to the FATHER,
Laud and honour to the SON,
Laud and honour to the SPIRIT,
Ever THREE, and ever ONE,
Consubstantial, Co-eternal,
While unending ages run.

The following Hymns are suitable:

215 The Church's one foundation.
228 Jerusalem the golden.
237 O GOD of hosts, the mighty LORD.
239 CHRIST is our corner-stone.
240 Pleasant are Thy courts above.
241 Hosanna to the living LORD!
242 We love the place, O GOD.

The Restoration of a Church.

Hymn 397.

The Restoration of a Church.

"We are the servants of the God of heaven and earth, and build the house that was builded these many years ago."

f LIFT the strain of high thanksgiving!
Tread with songs the hallowed way!
Praise our fathers' GOD for mercies
New to us their sons to-day:
mf Here they built for Him a dwelling,
cr Served Him here in ages past,
f Fixed it for His sure possession,
Holy ground, while time shall last.

mf When the years had wrought their changes,
He, our own unchanging GOD,
Thought on this His habitation,
Looked on His decayed abode;
Heard our prayers, and helped our counsels,
Blessed the silver and the gold,
cr Till once more His house is standing
f Firm and stately as of old.

mf Entering then Thy gates with praises,
LORD, be ours Thine Israel's prayer;
cr "Rise into Thy place of resting,
Shew Thy promised Presence there!"
p Let the gracious Word be spoken
cr Here, as once on Sion's height,
"This shall be My rest for ever,
This My dwelling of delight."

f Fill this latter house with glory
Greater than the former knew;
mf Clothe with righteousness its Priesthood,
Guide its Choir to reverence true;
Let Thy Holy One's anointing
Here its sevenfold blessing shed;
Spread for us the heavenly Banquet,
Satisfy Thy poor with Bread.

f Praise to Thee, Almighty FATHER,
Praise to Thee, Eternal SON,
Praise to Thee, all-quickening SPIRIT,
Ever-blessèd THREE in ONE;
p Threefold Power and Grace and Wisdom,
cr Moulding out of sinful clay
f Living stones for that true Temple
Which shall never know decay.

Burial of the Dead.

Hymn 398.

"He cometh to judge the earth."

Burial of the Dead.

ff Wondrous sound the trumpet flingeth,
Through earth's sepulchres it ringeth,
All before the Throne it bringeth.
Death is struck, and nature quaking,
All creation is awaking,
To its Judge an answer making.

mf Lo! the Book exactly worded,
Wherein all hath been recorded;
Thence shall judgment be awarded.
When the Judge His seat attaineth,
And each hidden deed arraigneth,
Nothing unavenged remaineth.

p What shall I, frail man, be pleading,
Who for me be interceding,
When the just are mercy needing?
ff King of Majesty tremendous,
mf Who dost free salvation send us,
Fount of pity, *(p)* then befriend us!

Think, good Jesu, my salvation
Caused Thy wondrous Incarnation;
Leave me not to reprobation.
Faint and weary Thou hast sought me,
On the Cross of suffering bought me,
Shall such grace be vainly brought me?

mf Righteous Judge! for sin's pollution
Grant Thy gift of absolution,
Ere that day of retribution.
Guilty, now I pour my moaning,
All my shame with anguish owning;
Spare, O God, Thy suppliant groaning.

Thou the sinful woman savedst;
Thou the dying thief forgavest;
cr And to me a hope vouchsafest.
p Worthless are my prayers and sighing:
Yet, good Lord, in grace complying,
Rescue me from fires undying.

Burial of the Dead.

Burial of the Dead.

Burial of the Dead.

Hymn 399.

"Surely He hath borne our griefs and carried our sorrows."

p WHEN our heads are bowed with woe,
When our bitter tears o'erflow,
When we mourn the lost, the dear,
Jesu, Son of Mary, hear.

mf Thou our throbbing flesh hast worn,
Thou our mortal griefs hast borne,
Thou hast shed the human tear;
Jesu, Son of Mary, hear.

p When the solemn death-bell tolls
For our own departed souls,
When our final doom is near,
Jesu, Son of Mary, hear.

mf Thou hast bowed the dying head,
Thou the blood of life hast shed,
Thou hast filled a mortal bier;
Jesu, Son of Mary, hear.

p When the heart is sad within
With the thought of all its sin,
When the spirit shrinks with fear,
Jesu, Son of Mary, hear.

mf Thou the shame, the grief, hast known,
Though the sins were not Thine own;
cr Thou hast deigned their load to bear:
Jesu, Son of Mary, hear.

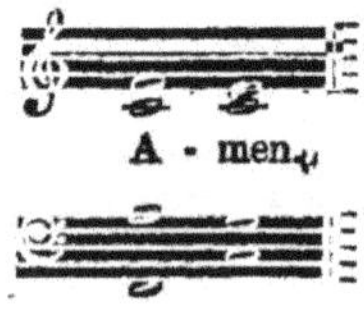

Burial of the Dead.

Hymn 400.

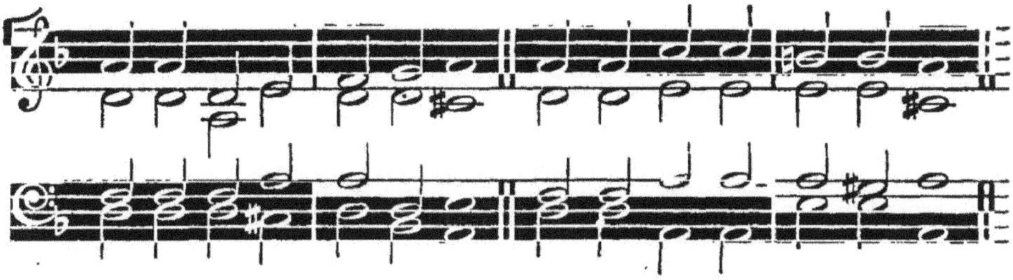

"Where I am there shall also My servant be."

p CHRIST will gather in His own
To the place where He is gone,
mf Where their heart and treasure lie,
Where our life is hid on high.

p Day by day the voice saith, "Come,
Enter thine eternal home;"
Asking not if we can spare
This dear soul it summons there.

Had He asked us, well we know
We should cry, "O spare this blow!"
Yes, with streaming tears should pray,
"LORD, we love *him*, let *him* stay."

mf But the LORD doth nought amiss,
And, since He hath ordered this,
We have nought to do but still
pp Rest in silence on His Will.

mf Many a heart no longer here,
Ah! was all too inly dear;
cr Yet, O Love, 'tis Thou dost call,
f Thou wilt be our All in all.

Burial of the Dead.

Hymn 401.

* *If there is no accompaniment, the small notes may be sung.*

Burial of the Dead.

"The souls of the righteous are in the hand of God, and there shall no torment touch them.

p NOW the labourer's task is o'er;
Now the battle day is past;
cr Now upon the farther shore
Lands the voyager at last.
p FATHER, in Thy gracious keeping
Leave we now Thy servant sleeping.

There the tears of earth are dried;
There its hidden things are clear;
cr There the work of life is tried
By a juster Judge than here.
p FATHER, in Thy gracious keeping
Leave we now Thy servant sleeping.

There the sinful souls, that turn
To the Cross their dying eyes,
cr All the love of CHRIST shall learn
At His Feet in Paradise.
p FATHER, in Thy gracious keeping
Leave we now Thy servant sleeping.

mf There no more the powers of hell
Can prevail to mar their peace;
cr CHRIST the LORD shall guard them wel
He Who died for their release.
p FATHER, in Thy gracious keeping
Leave we now Thy servant sleeping.

"Earth to earth, and dust to dust,"
Calmly now the words we say,
Leaving *him* to sleep in trust
cr Till the Resurrection-day.
p FATHER, in Thy gracious keeping
Leave we now Thy servant sleeping

Burial of the Dead.

Hymn 402.

Slow.

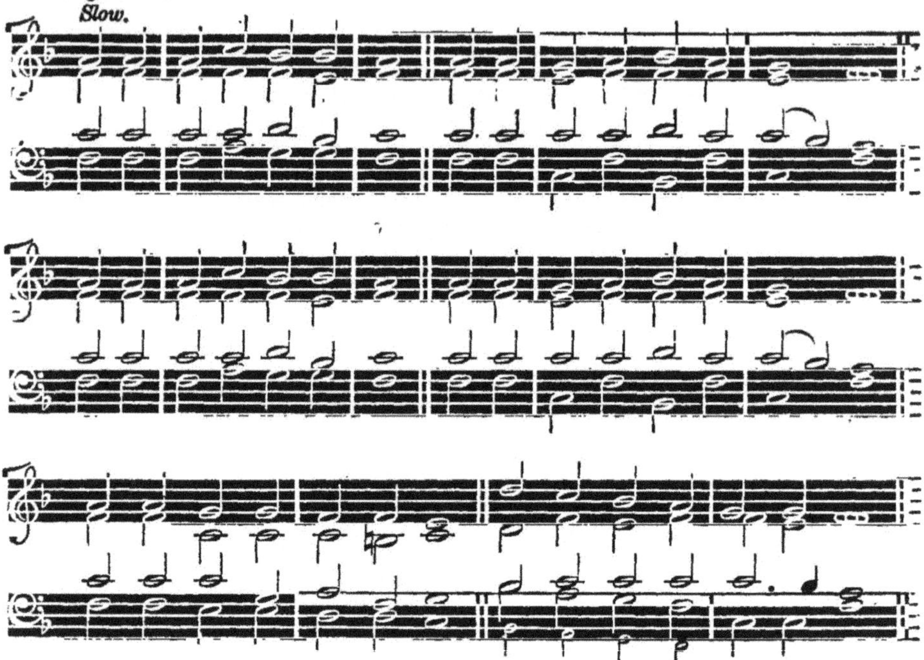

For a Child. *"They are in peace."*

p TENDER Shepherd, Thou hast stilled
Now Thy little lamb's brief weeping;
Oh, how peaceful, pale, and mild,
In its narrow bed 'tis sleeping,
cr And no sigh of anguish sore
p Heaves that little bosom more.

mf In a world of pain and care,
Lord, Thou wouldst no longer leave it;
To Thy meadows bright and fair
Lovingly Thou dost receive it;
cr Clothed in robes of spotless white
Now it dwells with Thee in light.

p Ah, Lord Jesu, grant that we
There may live where it is living,
cr And the blissful pastures see
That its heavenly food are giving;
p Lost awhile our treasured love,
cr Gained for ever, safe above.

The following Hymns are suitable:

140 Jesus lives! no longer now.
225 Brief life is here our portion.
235 Oh, what the joy and the glory must be.
264 My God, my Father, while I stray.
286 O let him, whose sorrow.
288 A few more years shall roll.
289 Days and moments quickly flying.

St. Andrew the Apostle.

Hymn 403.

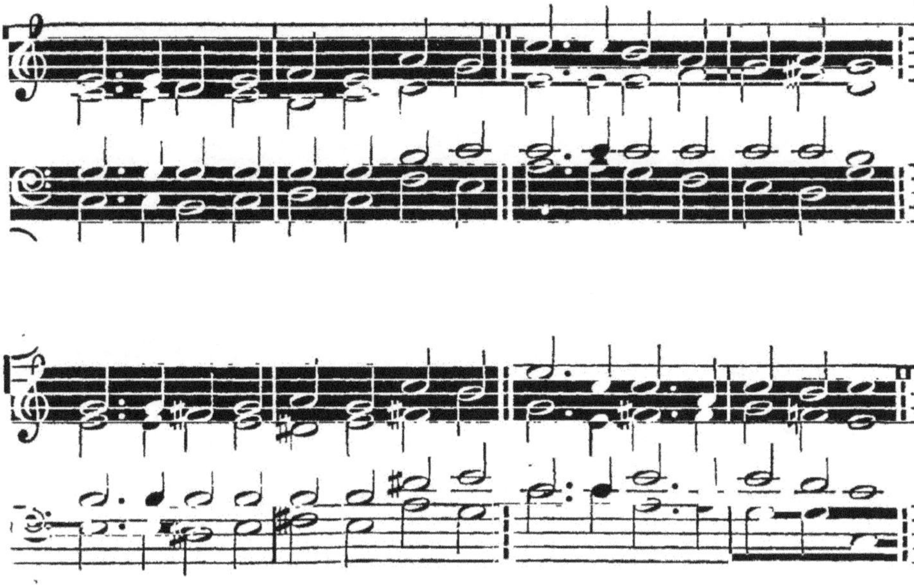

"One of the two which . . . followed Him was Andrew."

mf JESUS calls us; *(cr)* o'er the tumult
Of our life's wild restless sea
Day by day His sweet voice soundeth,
Saying, *(p)* "Christian, follow Me:"

mf As of old Saint Andrew heard it
By the Galilean lake,
Turned from home, and toil, and kindred,
Leaving all for His dear sake.

p Jesus calls us *(cr)* from the worship
Of the vain world's golden store,
From each idol that would keep us,
Saying, *(p)* "Christian, love Me more."

mf In our joys and in our sorrows,
Days of toil and hours of ease,
Still He calls, in cares and pleasures,
That we love Him more than these.

p Jesus calls us: *(cr)* by Thy mercies,
Saviour, make us hear Thy call,
Give our hearts to Thine obedience,
Serve and love Thee best of all.

St. Thomas the Apostle.

Hymn 404.

"Be not faithless, but believing."

mf HOW oft, O LORD, Thy Face hath shone
On doubting souls whose wills were true!
Thou CHRIST of Cephas and of John,
Thou art the CHRIST of Thomas too.

He loved Thee well, and calmly said,
dim "Come, let us go, and die with Him:"
cr Yet when Thine Easter-news was spread,
'Mid all its light *(p)* his eyes were dim.

mf His brethren's word he would not take,
But craved to touch those Hands of Thine:
p The bruisèd reed Thou didst not break;
cr He saw, and hailed his LORD Divine.

f He saw Thee risen; at once he rose
To full belief's unclouded height;
And still through his confession flows
To Christian souls Thy life and light.

mf O Saviour, make Thy presence known
To all who doubt Thy Word and Thee;
And teach them in that Word alone
To find the truth that sets them free.

And we who know how true Thou art,
And Thee as GOD and LORD adore,
Give us, we pray, a loyal heart,
cr To trust and love Thee more and more.

The Conversion of St. Paul.

Hymn 405.

"The voice of the Lord breaketh the cedar trees; yea, the Lord breaketh the cedars of Libanus."

mf THE Shepherd now was smitten;
The wolf was ravening near;
The scattered flock he threatened,
But knew not Whose they were.

cr In zealous fury seeking
To bind and crucify,
A sudden voice withheld him,
A loud and startling cry:

mf "Saul! Saul! why blindly daring
To persecute thy Lord?
p 'Tis Jesus Whom thou hatest,
cr Rebel not at My Word."

mf Then forth in prayer he stretcheth
Those hands prepared to slay;
"What wouldst Thou with Thy servant?
My Lord and Master, say."

Christ's foe becomes His soldier,
The wolf destroys no more,
p A gentle lamb he enters
The sheepfold by the door.

f O voice of God Almighty,
What wonders hath it wrought!
It rends the lofty cedars,
It bends the haughty thought.

p Jesu, our Shepherd, cease not
Thy flock from harm to free,
And, when Thy sheep are wandering,
O lead them back to Thee.

f To Father, Son, and Spirit
All glory, praise, and might,
mf Who called us out of darkness
f To His own glorious light.

The Conversion of St. Paul.

Hymn 406.

The Conversion of St. Paul.

"He which persecuted us in times past now preacheth the faith which once he destroyed."

f WE sing the glorious conquest
Before Damascus' gate,
mf When Saul, the Church's spoiler,
Came breathing threats and hate;
The ravening wolf rushed forward
Full early to the prey;
f But lo! the Shepherd met him,
And bound him fast to-day.

Oh, glory most excelling
That smote across his path!
Oh, light that pierced and blinded
The zealot in his wrath!
p Oh, voice that spake within him
The calm reproving word!
cr Oh, love that sought and held him
The bondman of his LORD!

mf O Wisdom, ordering all things
In order strong and sweet,
cr What nobler spoil was ever
Cast at the Victor's feet?
mf What wiser master-builder
E'er wrought at Thine employ
Than he, till now so furious
Thy building to destroy?

p LORD, teach Thy Church the lesson,
Still in her darkest hour
Of weakness and of danger
To trust Thy hidden power:
cr Thy Grace by ways mysterious
The wrath of man can bind,
And in Thy boldest foeman
Thy chosen Saint can find.

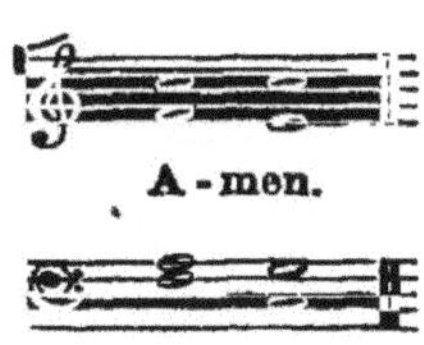

Presentation of Christ in the Temple,

COMMONLY CALLED

The Purification of St. Mary the Virgin.

Hymn 407.

"The Lord, whom ye seek, shall suddenly come to His temple."

mf O SION, open wide thy gates,
Let figures disappear;
A Priest and Victim, both in one,
The Truth Himself, is here.

No more the simple flock shall bleed;
cr Behold, the FATHER'S SON
Himself to His own Altar comes,
dim For sinners to atone.

p Conscious of hidden Deity,
The lowly Virgin brings
Her new-born Babe, with two young doves,
Her tender offerings.

mf The aged Simeon sees at last
His LORD so long desired,
cr And Anna welcomes Israel's Hope
With holy rapture fired.

p But silent knelt the Mother blest
Of the yet silent WORD,
And, pondering all things in her heart,
With speechless praise adored.

f All glory to the FATHER be,
All glory to the SON,
All glory, HOLY GHOST, to Thee,
While endless ages run.

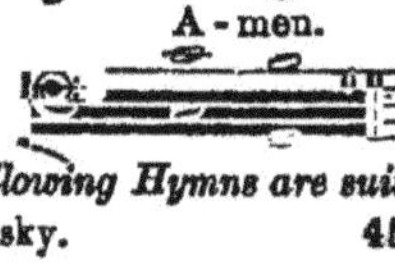

The following Hymns are suitable:

449 The GOD, Whom earth, and sea, and sky.

450 Shall we not love thee, Mother dear

St. Matthias the Apostle.

Hymn 408.

"And they gave forth their lots; and the lot fell upon Matthias; and he was numbered with the eleven Apostles."

mf BISHOP of the souls of men,
p When the foeman's step is nigh,
When the wolf lays wait by night
For the lambs continually,
cr Watch, O LORD, about us keep,
Guard us, Shepherd of the sheep.

p When the hireling flees away,
Caring only for his gold,
And the gate unguarded stands
At the entrance to the fold,
f Stand, O LORD, Thy flock before,
Thou the Guardian, Thou the Door.

mf LORD, Whose guiding finger ruled
In the casting of the lot,
That Thy Church might fill the throne
Of the lost Iscariot,
p In our trouble ever thus
f Stand, good Master, nigh to us.

mf When the Saints their order take
In the New Jerusalem,
f And Matthias stands elect,
p Give us part and lot with him,
cr Where in Thine own dwelling-place
We may witness face to face.

The Annunciation of the Blessed Virgin Mary.

Hymn 409.

"Behold, a Virgin shall be with child, and shall bring forth a Son, and they shall call His Name Emmanuel, which being interpreted is, God with us."

f PRAISE we the Lord this day,
This day so long foretold,
Whose promise shone with cheering ray
On waiting saints of old.

mf The Prophet gave the sign
For faithful men to read;
A Virgin, born of David's line,
Shall bear the promised Seed.

Ask not how this should be,
p But worship and adore;
Like her, whom heaven's majesty
Came down to shadow o'er.

Meekly she bowed her head
To hear the gracious word,
mf Mary, the pure and lowly maid,
The favoured of the Lord.

Blessèd shall be her name
In all the Church on earth,
Thro' whom that wondrous mercy came,
The Incarnate Saviour's birth.

f Jesu, the Virgin's Son,
We praise Thee and adore,
Who art with God the Father One
And Spirit evermore.

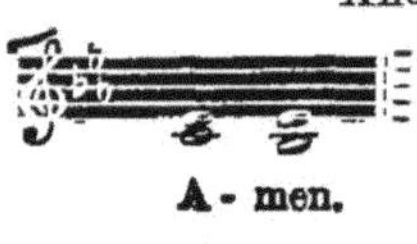

The following Hymns are suitable:

449 The God, Whom earth, and sea, and sky.
450 Shall we not love thee, Mother dear.

St. Mark the Evangelist.

Hymn 410.

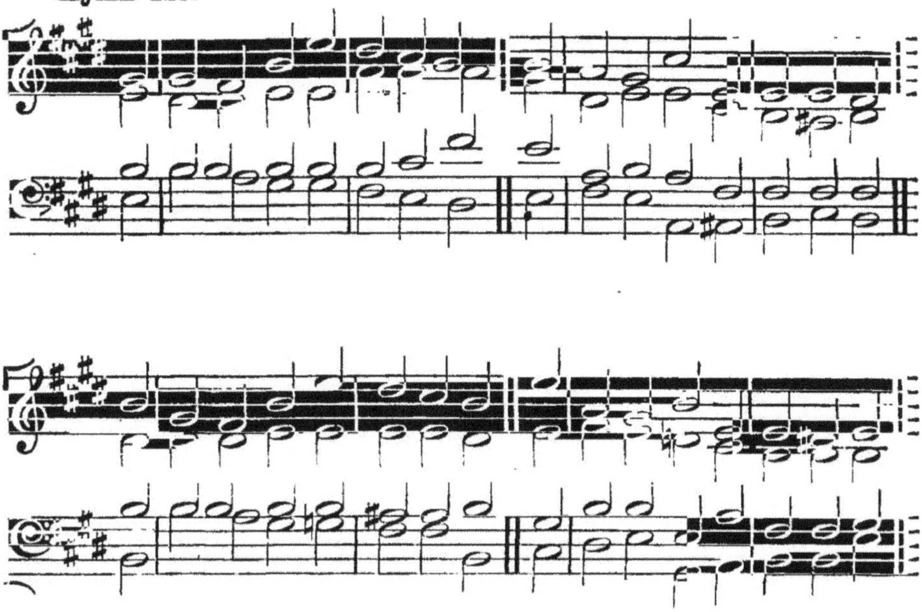

" The face of a lion on the right side."

mf FROM out the cloud of amber light,
Borne on the whirlwind from the north,
Four living creatures winged and bright
Before the Prophet's eye came forth.

f The voice of God was in the Four
p Beneath that awful crystal mist,
cr And every wondrous form they wore
Foreshadowed an Evangelist.

f The lion-faced, he told abroad
The strength of love, the strength of faith;
He shewed the Almighty Son of God,
The Man Divine Who won by death.

O Lion of the Royal Tribe,
Strong Son of God, and strong to save,
All power and honour we ascribe
To Thee Who only makest brave.

mf For strength to love, for will to speak,
f For fiery crowns by Martyrs won,
p For suffering patience, strong and meek,
f We praise Thee, Lord, and Thee alone.

St. Philip and St. James the Apostles.

Hymn 411.

"Philip saith unto Him, Lord, shew us the Father and it sufficeth us."
"James, a servant of God."

mf THERE is one Way, and only one,
Out of our gloom, and sin, and care,
To that far land where shines no sun
Because the Face of God is there.

There is one Truth, the Truth of God,
That Christ came down from heaven to show,
One Life that His redeeming Blood
Has won for all His saints below.

The lore from Philip once concealed,
We know its fulness now in Christ;
In Him the Father is revealed,
And all our longing is sufficed.

And still unwavering faith holds sure
The words that James wrote sternly down;
Except we labour and endure,
We cannot win the heavenly crown.

f O Way Divine, through gloom and strife,
Bring us Thy Father's Face to see;
O heavenly Truth, O precious Life,
p At last, at last, we rest in Thee.

St. Barnabas the Apostle.

Hymn 412.

"He was a good man, and full of the Holy Ghost, and of faith; and much people was added unto the Lord."

mf BRIGHTLY did the light Divine
  From his words and actions shine,
Whom the Twelve, with love unblamed,
"Son of consolation" named.

Full of peace and lively joy
Sped he on his high employ,
By his mild exhorting word
Adding many to the LORD.

p Blessèd SPIRIT, Who didst call
Barnabas and holy Paul,
cr And didst them with gifts endue,
Mighty words and wisdom true,

mf Grant us, LORD of life, to be
By their pattern full of Thee;
cr That beside them we may stand
In that day on CHRIST's right hand.

St. Barnabas the Apostle.

Hymn 413.

St. Barnabas the Apostle.

"Joses, who by the Apostles was surnamed Barnabas, which is, being interpreted, The son of consolation."

mf O SON of God, our Captain of Salvation,
Thyself by suffering schooled to human grief,
cr We bless Thee for Thy sons of consolation,
Who follow in the steps of Thee their Chief;

mf Those whom Thy Spirit's dread vocation severs
To lead the vanguard of Thy conquering host;
Whose toilsome years are spent in brave endeavours
To bear Thy saving Name from coast to coast;

f Those whose bright faith makes feeble hearts grow stronger,
And sends fresh warriors to the great campaign,
p Bids the lone convert feel estranged no longer,
cr And wins the sundered to be one again;

mf And all true helpers, patient, kind, and skilful,
Who shed Thy light across our darkened earth,
Counsel the doubting, and restrain the wilful,
dim e cr Soothe the sick bed, and share the children's mirth.

f Such was Thy Levite, strong in self-oblation
To cast his all at Thine Apostles' feet;
He whose new name, through every Christian nation,
From age to age our thankful strains repeat.

mf Thus, Lord, Thy Barnabas in memory keeping,
Still be Thy Church's watchword, "Comfort ye;"
Till in our Father's house shall end our weeping,
cr And all our wants be satisfied in Thee.

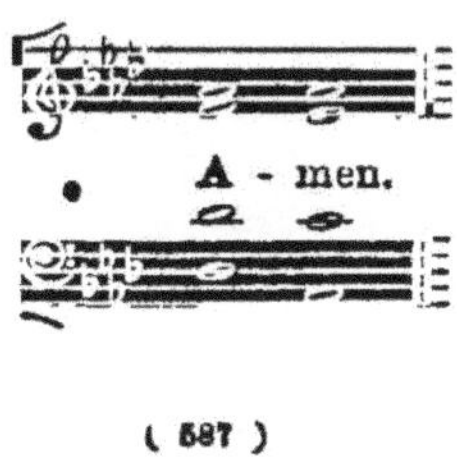

The Nativity of St. John Baptist.

Hymn 414.

The Nativity of St. John Baptist.

"Repent ye, for the kingdom of heaven is at hand."

mf LO! from the desert homes,
Where he hath hid so long,
The new Elias comes,
In sternest wisdom strong;
cr The voice that cries
Of CHRIST from high,
dim And judgment nigh
From opening skies.

mf Your GOD e'en now doth stand
At heaven's opening door;
His fan is in His hand,
And He will purge His floor;
f The wheat He claims
And with Him stows,
p The chaff He throws
To quenchless flames.

f Ye haughty mountains, bow
Your sky-aspiring heads;
p Ye valleys, hiding low,
cr Lift up your gentle meads;
Make His way plain
Your King before,
f For evermore
He comes to reign.

mf May thy dread voice around,
Thou harbinger of Light,
On our dull ears still sound,
dim Lest here we sleep in night,
Till judgment come,
And on our path
Shall burst the wrath,
And deathless doom.

mf O GOD, with love's sweet might,
Who dost anoint and arm
CHRIST's soldier for the fight
With grace that shields from harm,
f Thrice Blessèd THREE,
Heaven's endless days
Shall sing Thy praise
Eternally.

𝔗𝔥𝔢 𝔑𝔞𝔱𝔦𝔳𝔦𝔱𝔶 𝔬𝔣 𝔖𝔱. 𝔍𝔬𝔥𝔫 𝔅𝔞𝔭𝔱𝔦𝔰𝔱.

Hymn 415.

"Behold I will send My messenger, and he shall prepare the way before Me."

mf THE great forerunner of the morn,
The herald of the Word, is born:
And faithful hearts shall never fail
With thanks and praise his light to hail.

With heavenly message Gabriel came,
That John should be that herald's name,
And with prophetic utterance told
His actions great and manifold.

John, still unborn, yet gave aright
His witness to the coming Light;
cr And Christ, the Sun of all the earth,
Fulfilled that witness at His Birth.

f Of woman-born shall never be
A greater Prophet than was he,
Whose mighty deeds exalt his fame
To greater than a Prophet's name.

mf But why should mortal accents raise
The hymn of John the Baptist's praise?
Of whom, or e'er his course was run,
Thus spake the Father to the Son:

p "Behold My herald, who shall go
Before Thy Face Thy way to show,
And shine, as with the day-star's gleam,
Before Thine own eternal beam."

f All praise to God the Father be,
All praise, Eternal Son, to Thee,
Whom with the Spirit we adore
For ever and for evermore.

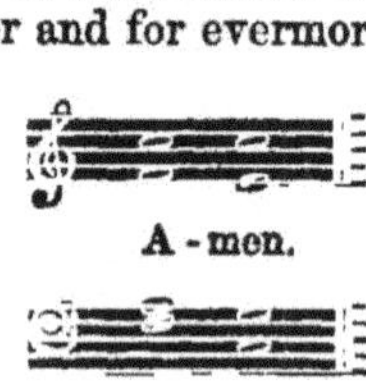

St. Peter the Apostle.

Hymn 416.

"Lovest thou Me?"

FORSAKEN once, and thrice denied,
The risen LORD gave pardon free,
Stood once again at Peter's side,
And asked him, *(p)* "Lov'st thou Me?"

How many times with faithless word
Have we denied His holy Name,
How oft forsaken our dear LORD,
And shrunk when trial came!

Saint Peter, when the cock crew clear,
Went out, and wept his broken faith;
Strong as a rock through strife and fear,
He served his LORD till death.

p How oft his cowardice of heart
We have without his love sincere,
The sin without the sorrow's smart,
The shame without the tear!

mf O oft forsaken, oft denied,
Forgive our shame, wash out our sin;
Look on us from Thy FATHER'S side
p And let that sweet look win.

mf Hear when we call Thee from the deep,
Still walk beside us on the shore,
Give hands to work, *(p)* and eyes to weep,
cr And hearts to love Thee more.

St. Peter the Apostle.

Hymn 417.

"Simon Peter answered and said, Thou art the Christ, the Son of the living God."

f "THOU art the Christ, O Lord,
The Son of God most high!"
For ever be adored
That Name in earth and sky,
dim In which, though mortal strength may fail,
cr The Saints of God at last prevail!

mf Oh, surely he was blest
With blessedness unpriced,
Who, taught of God, confessed
The Godhead in the Christ!
For of Thy Church, Lord, Thou didst own
Thy Saint a true foundation-stone.

p Thrice was he put to shame,
Thrice did the dauntless fall;
But, oh, that look that came
cr From out the judgment-hall!
It pierced and broke the spell-bound heart,
f And foiled the tempter's sifting art.

p Thrice fallen, thrice restored!
The bitter lesson learnt,
cr That heart for Thee, O Lord,
With triple ardour burnt.
The cross he took he laid not down
Until he grasped the Martyr's crown.

f Oh, bright triumphant faith!
Oh, courage void of fears!
Oh, love most strong in death!
p Oh, penitential tears!
mf By these, Lord, keep us lest we fall,
And make us go where Thou shalt call

St. James the Apostle.

Hymn 418.

"He killed James, the brother of John, with the sword."

mf FOR all Thy Saints, a noble throng,
Who fell by fire and sword,
Who soon were called, or waited long,
We praise Thy Name, O Lord;

For him who left his father's side,
Nor lingered by the shore,
p When, softer than the weltering tide,
Thy summons glided o'er;

Who stood beside the maiden dead,
cr Who climbed the mount with Thee,
And saw the glory round Thy Head,
One of Thy chosen three;

p Who knelt beneath the olive shade,
Who drank Thy cup of pain,
And passed from Herod's flashing blade
cr To see Thy Face again.

mf Lord, give us grace, and give us love,
Like him to leave behind
Earth's cares and joys, and look above
With true and earnest mind.

So shall we learn to drink Thy cup,
So meek and firm be found,
cr When Thou shalt come to take us up
Where Thine elect are crowned.

St. Bartholomew the Apostle.

Hymn 419.

St. Bartholomew the Apostle.

“The Lord knoweth them that are His.”

mf KING of Saints, to Whom the number
Of Thy starry host is known,
Many a name, by man forgotten,
Lives for ever round Thy Throne;
Lights, which earth-born mists have darkened,
cr There are shining full and clear,
Princes in the court of heaven,
dim Nameless, unremembered here.

mf In the roll of Thine Apostles
One there stands, Bartholomew,
He for whom to-day we offer,
Year by year, our praises due;
p How he toiled for Thee and suffered
None on earth can now record;
cr All his saintly life is hidden
In the knowledge of his LORD.

mf Was it he, beneath the fig-tree
Seen of Thee, and guileless found;
He who saw the good he longed for
Rise from Nazareth's barren ground;
He who met his risen Master
On the shore of Galilee;
He to whom the Word was spoken,
“Greater things thou yet shalt see?”

p None can tell us; *(cr)* all is written
In the LAMB's great book of life,
All the faith, and prayer, and patience,
All the toiling, and the strife;
f There are told Thy hidden treasures;
p Number us, O LORD, with them,
cr When Thou makest up the jewels
f Of Thy living diadem.

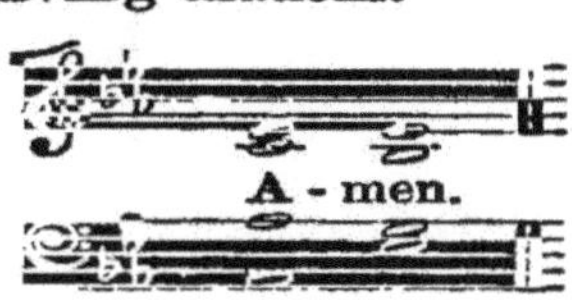

2 I

St. Matthew the Apostle.

Hymn 420.

"Lay up for yourselves treasures in heaven."

mf DEAR LORD, on this Thy servant's day,
Who left for Thee the gold and mart,
Who heard Thee whisper, "Come away,"
And followed with a single heart,

Give us, amid earth's weary moil,
And wealth for which men cark and care,
'Mid fortune's pride, and need's wild toil,
And broken hearts in purple rare,

Give us Thy grace to rise above
The glare of this world's smelting fires;
Let GOD's great love put out the love
Of gold, and gain, and low desires.

p Still, like a breath from scented lime
Borne into rooms where sick men faint,
His voice comes floating thro' all time,
Thine own Evangelist and Saint.

cr Still sweetly rings the Gospel strain
Of golden store that knows not rust:
f The love of CHRIST is more than gain,
And heavenly crowns than yellow dust.

St. Michael and all Angels.

Hymn 421.

"O praise the Lord, all ye His hosts; ye servants of His that do His pleasure.'

f PRAISE to God Who reigns above,
Binding earth and heaven in lové;
All the armies of the sky
Worship His dread sovereignty

mf Seraphim His praises sing,
Cherubim on fourfold wing,
Thrones, Dominions, Princes, Powers,
Marshalled Might that never cowers.

Speeds the Archangel from His Face,
Bearing messages of grace;
Angel hosts His words fulfil,
Ruling nature by His Will.

Yet on man they joy to wait,
All that bright celestial state,
For in Man their Lord they see,
Christ, the Incarnate Deity.

dim On the Throne their Lord Who died
cr Sits in Manhood glorified;
p Where His people faint below
cr Angels count it joy to go.

mf Oh, the depths of joy Divine
Thrilling through those Orders nine,
When the lost are found again,
When the banished come to reign!

Now in faith, in hope, in love,
We will join the choirs above,
f Praising, with the heavenly host,
Father, Son, and Holy Ghost.

St. Michael and all Angels.

Hymn 422.

St. Michael and all Angels.

"There was war in heaven; Michael and his angels fought against the dragon; and the dragon fought and his angels."

f CHRIST, in highest heaven enthronèd,
  Equal of the FATHER's Might,
By pure spirits, trembling, ownèd,
  GOD of GOD, and LIGHT of LIGHT,
Thee 'mid Angel hosts we sing,
Thee their Maker and their King.

mf All who circling round adore Thee,
  All who bow before Thy Throne,
Burn with flaming zeal before Thee,
  Thy behests to carry down;
To and fro, 'twixt earth and heaven,
Speed they each on errands given.

f First of all those legions glorious,
  Michael waves his sword of flame,
Who of old in war victorious
  Did the Dragon's fierceness tame;
Who with might invincible
Thrust the rebel down to hell.

mf Strong to aid the sick and dying,
  Called from heaven they swiftly fly,
Grace Divine and strength supplying
p In their mortal agony:
Souls released from bondage here
Safe to Paradise they bear.

f To the FATHER praise be given
  By the unfallen Angel-host,
Who in His great war have striven
  With the legions of the lost;
Equal praise in highest heaven
To the SON and HOLY GHOST.

St. Michael and all Angels.

Hymn 423.

St. Michael and all Angels.

"When the morning stars sang together, and all the sons of God shouted for joy."

f STARS of the morning, so gloriously bright,
Filled with celestial virtue and light,
These that, where night never followeth day,
p Raise the "Trisagion"* ever and aye:

mf These are Thy ministers, these dost Thou own,
Lord God of Sabaoth, nearest Thy Throne;
These are Thy messengers, these dost Thou send,
Help of the helpless ones! man to defend.

These keep the guard amidst Salem's dear bowers,
Thrones, Principalities, Virtues, and Powers,
Where, with the Living Ones, mystical Four,
Cherubim, Seraphim *(p)* bow and adore.

mf Then, when the earth was first poised in mid space,
Then, when the planets first sped on their race,
Then, when were ended the six days' employ,
f Then all the Sons of God shouted for joy.

mf Still let them succour us; still let them fight,
Lord of Angelic hosts, battling for right;
Till, where their anthems they ceaselessly pour,
We with the Angels may *(p)* bow and adore.

*In Greek, from which this Hymn is translated, "Trisagion" is the same as the Latin "Tersanctus" and the English "Thrice-Holy."

St. Michael and all Angels.

Hymn 424.

"Are they not all ministering spirits, sent forth to minister for them who shall be heirs of salvation?"

mf THEY come, God's messengers of love,
They come from realms of peace above,
From homes of never-fading light,
From blissful mansions ever bright.

They come to watch around us here,
To soothe our sorrow, calm our fear:
Ye heavenly guides, speed not away,
God willeth you with us to stay.

p But chiefly at its journey's end
'Tis yours the spirit to befriend,
And whisper to the faithful heart,
rall pp "O Christian soul, in peace depart."

p Blest Jesu, Thou Whose groans and tears
Have sanctified frail nature's fears,
To earth in bitter sorrow weighed
Thou didst not scorn Thine Angel's aid;

cr An Angel guard to us supply,
When on the bed of death we lie;
And by Thine own Almighty power
p O shield us in the last dread hour.

f To God the Father, God the Son,
And God the Spirit, Three in One,
From all above and all below
Let joyful praise unceasing flow.

These Hymns on the ministry of Angels may be sung, if desired, at other times.

St. Luke the Evangelist.

Hymn 425.

"The brother, whose praise is in the gospel."

f WHAT thanks and praise to Thee we owe,
O Priest and Sacrifice Divine,
For Thy dear Saint through whom we know
So many a gracious Word of Thine;

mf Whom Thou didst choose to tell the tale
Of all Thy Manhood's toils and tears,
And for a moment lift the veil
That hides Thy Boyhood's spotless years.

How many a soul with guilt oppressed
cr Has learned to hear the joyful sound
In that sweet tale of sin confessed,
The FATHER's love, the lost and found!

p How many a child of sin and shame
cr Has refuge found from guilty fears
Through her, who to the Saviour came
With costly ointments and with tears!

mf What countless worshippers have sung,
In lowly fane or lofty choir,
The song that loosed the silent tongue
Of him who was the Baptist's sire!

cr And still the Church through all her days
Uplifts the strains that never cease,
The Blessèd Virgin's hymn of praise,
p The aged Simeon's words of peace.

f O happy Saint! whose sacred page,
So rich in words of truth and love,
Pours on the Church from age to age
mf This healing unction from above;

The witness of the Saviour's life,
The great Apostle's chosen friend
p Through weary years of toil and strife,
cr And still found faithful to the end.

mf So grant us, LORD, like him to live,
Beloved by man, approved by Thee,
Till Thou at last the summons give,
And we, with him, Thy face shall see.

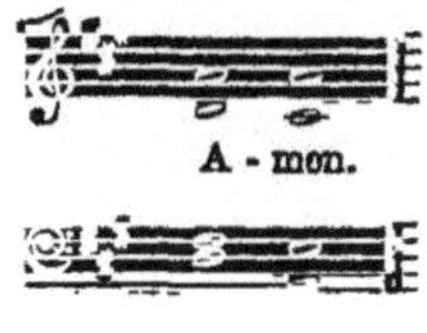

St. Simon and St. Jude, Apostles.

Hymn 426.

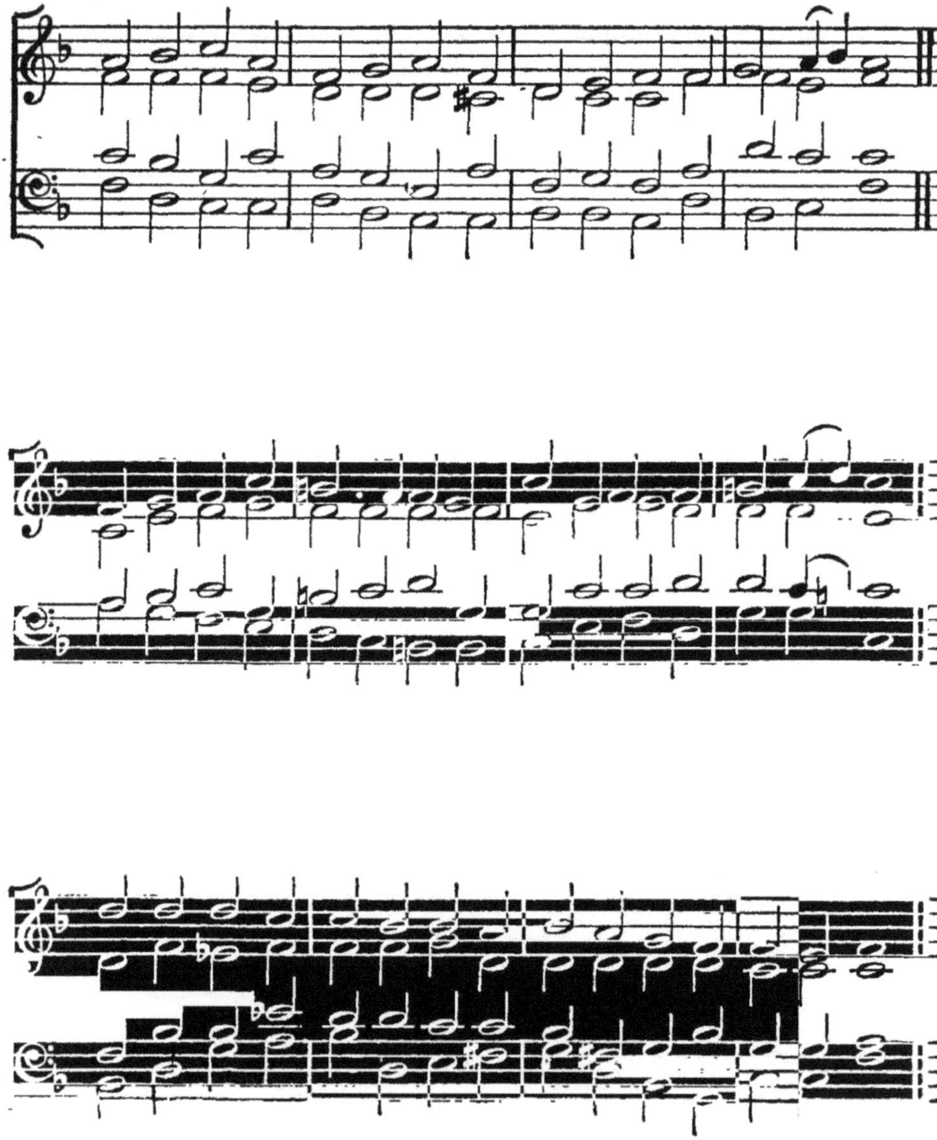

St. Simon and St. Jude, Apostles.

"Just and true are Thy ways, Thou King of Saints."

mf THOU Who sentest Thine Apostles
  Two and two before Thy Face,
Partners in the night of toiling,
  Heirs together of Thy grace,
Throned at length, their labours ended,
  Each in his appointed place;

f Praise to Thee for those Thy champions
  Whom our hymns to-day proclaim;
mf One, whose zeal by Thee enlightened
  Burned anew with nobler flame;
One, the kinsman of Thy Childhood,
  Brought at last to know Thy Name.

f Praise to Thee! Thy fire within them
  Spake in love, and wrought in power;
Seen in mighty signs and wonders
  In Thy Church's morning hour;
Heard in tones of sternest warning
  When the storms began to lower.

p Once again those storms are breaking;
  Hearts are failing, love grows cold;
Faith is darkened, sin abounding;
  Grievous wolves assail Thy fold:
cr Save us, LORD, our One Salvation;
  Save the Faith revealed of old.

mf Call the erring by Thy pity;
  Warn the tempted by Thy fear;
Keep us true to Thine allegiance,
  Counting life itself less dear,
cr Standing firmer, holding faster,
dim As we see the end draw near.

mf Till, with holy Jude and Simon
  And the thousand faithful more,
We, the good confession witnessed
  And the lifelong conflict o'er,
cr On the sea of fire and crystal
  Stand, and wonder, *(p)* and adore.

f GOD the FATHER, great and wondrous
  In Thy works, to Thee be praise;
KING of Saints, to Thee be glory,
  Just and true in all Thy ways;
Praise to Thee, from Both proceeding,
  HOLY GHOST, through endless days.

All Saints' Day.

Hymn 427.

All Saints' Day.

"*What are these which are arrayed in white robes? and whence came they?*"

mf WHO are these like stars appearing,
These, before God's Throne who stand?
Each a golden crown is wearing,
Who are all this glorious band?
Alleluia, hark! they sing,
f Praising loud their heavenly King.

mf Who are these in dazzling brightness,
Clothed in God's own righteousness,
These, whose robes of purest whiteness
Shall their lustre still possess,
Still untouched by time's rude hand?
Whence came all this glorious band?

f These are they who have contended
For their Saviour's honour long,
Wrestling on till life was ended,
Following not the sinful throng;
These, who well the fight sustained,
Triumph by the Lamb have gained.

p These are they whose hearts were riven,
Sore with woe and anguish tried,
Who in prayer full oft have striven
With the God they glorified;
cr Now, their painful conflict o'er,
God has bid them weep no more.

mf These, the Almighty contemplating,
Did as priests before Him stand,
Soul and body always waiting
Day and night at His command:
f Now in God's most holy place
Blest they stand before His Face.

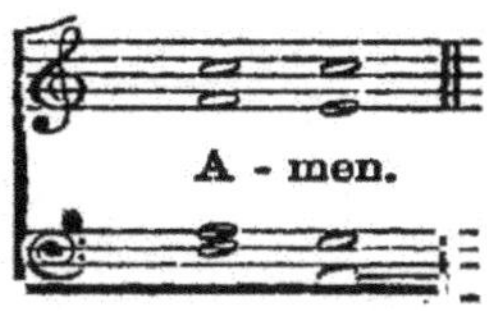

All Saints' Day.

Hymn 428.

All Saints' Day.

"That they may rest from their labours."

mf THE Saints of GOD! their conflict past,
And life's long battle won at last,
No more they need the shield or sword,—
They cast them down before their LORD:
cr O happy Saints! for ever blest,
p At JESUS' feet how safe your rest!

mf The Saints of GOD! their wanderings done,
No more their weary course they run,
No more they faint, no more they fall,
No foes oppress, no fears appal:
cr O happy Saints! for ever blest,
p In that dear home how sweet your rest!

mf The Saints of GOD! life's voyage o'er,
Safe landed on that blissful shore,
No stormy tempests now they dread,
No roaring billows lift their head:
cr O happy Saints! for ever blest,
p In that calm haven of your rest!

The Saints of GOD their vigil keep
While yet their mortal bodies sleep,
cr Till from the dust they too shall rise
And soar triumphant to the skies;
f O happy Saints! rejoice and sing;
He quickly comes, your LORD and King.

mf O GOD of Saints, to Thee we cry;
O SAVIOUR, plead for us on high;
O HOLY GHOST, our Guide and Friend,
p Grant us Thy grace till life shall end;
cr That with all Saints our rest may be
f In that bright Paradise with Thee.

All Saints' Day.

Hymn 429.

"And the city had no need of the sun, neither of the moon, to shine in it; for the glory of God did lighten it, and the Lamb is the Light thereof."

mf O HEAVENLY Jerusalem,
Of everlasting halls,
cr Thrice blessèd are the people
dim Thou storest in thy walls.

f Thou art the golden mansion,
Where Saints for ever sing,
The seat of God's own chosen,
The palace of the King.

p There God for ever sitteth,
cr Himself of all the Crown;
The Lamb, the Light that shineth,
And never goeth down.

p Nought to this seat approacheth
Their sweet peace to molest;
f They sing their God for ever,
Nor day nor night they rest.

mf Sure hope doth thither lead us;
Our longings thither tend;
cr May short-lived toil ne'er daunt us
For joys that cannot end.

f To Christ the Sun that lightens
His Church above, below,
To Father, and to Spirit
All things created bow.

The Hymns for this Festival may be used on other days.
The following Hymns are suitable for this Festival:

222 Ten thousand times ten thousand.
228 Jerusalem the golden.
233 Jerusalem on high.
235 Oh, what the joy and the glory must be.
435 Lo! round the Throne, a glorious band.
436 Hark! the sound of holy voices.
438 How bright those glorious spirits shine!
447 Soldiers, who are Christ's below.

Feasts of Apostles.

Hymn 430.

To be sung in Unison.

"And the wall of the city had twelve foundations, and in them the names of the twelve Apostles of the Lamb."

THE eternal gifts of CHRIST the King,
The Apostles' glory, let us sing;
And all, with hearts of gladness, raise
Due hymns of thankful love and praise.

For they the Churches' princes are,
Triumphant leaders in the war,
In heavenly courts a warrior band,
True lights to lighten every land.

mf Theirs is the steadfast faith of saints,
And hope that never yields nor faints,
And love of CHRIST in perfect glow
That lays the prince of this world low.

In them the FATHER's glory shone,
In them the Will of GOD the SON,
In them exults the HOLY GHOST,
cr Through them rejoice the heavenly host.

p To Thee, Redeemer, now we cry,
That Thou wouldst join to them on high
Thy servants, who this grace implore,
mf For ever and for evermore.

Feasts of Apostles.

Hymn 431.

Feasts of Apostles.

"Their sound went into all the earth, and their words unto the ends of the world."

mf DISPOSER Supreme,
And Judge of the earth,
Who choosest for Thine
The weak and the poor;
To frail earthen vessels
And things of no worth
Entrusting Thy riches
Which aye shall endure;

p Those vessels soon fail,
Though full of Thy light,
And at Thy decree
Are broken and gone;
cr Thence brightly appeareth
Thy truth in its might,
As through the clouds riven
The lightnings have shone.

f Like clouds are they borne
To do Thy great Will,
And swift as the winds
About the world go;
The WORD with His wisdom
Their spirits doth fill,
They thunder, they lighten,
The waters o'erflow.

Their sound goeth forth,
"CHRIST JESUS the LORD;"
Then Satan doth fear,
His citadels fall:
As when the dread trumpets
Went forth at Thy Word,
And one long blast shattered
The Canaanite's wall.

O loud be their trump,
And stirring their sound,
mf To rouse us, O LORD,
From slumber of sin;
The lights Thou hast kindled
In darkness around,
O may they illumine
Our spirits within.

f All honour and praise,
Dominion and might,
To GOD, THREE in ONE,
Eternally be,
Who round us hath shed
His own marvellous light,
And called us from darkness
His glory to see.

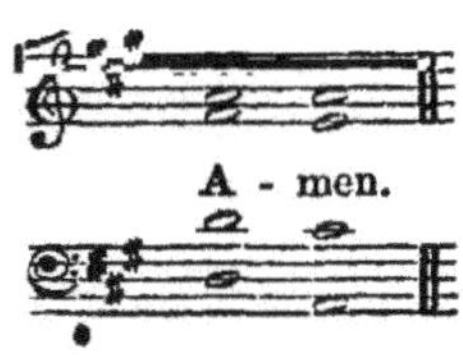

Feasts of Apostles.

Hymn 432.

" Ye also shall sit upon twelve thrones, judging the twelve tribes of Israel."

mf CAPTAINS of the saintly band,
Lights who lighten every land,
Princes who with JESUS dwell,
Judges of His Israel,

On the nations sunk in night
Ye have shed the Gospel light;
cr Sin and error flee away,
Truth reveals the promised day.

mf Not by warrior's spear and sword,
Not by art of human word,
p Preaching but the Cross of shame,
cr Rebel hearts for CHRIST ye tame.

p Earth, that long in sin and pain
Groaned in Satan's deadly chain,
f Now to serve its GOD is free
In the law of liberty.

mf Distant lands with one acclaim
Tell the honour of your name,
Who, wherever man has trod,
Teach the mysteries of GOD.

f Glory to the THREE in ONE
While eternal ages run,
Who from deepest shades of night
Called us to His glorious light.

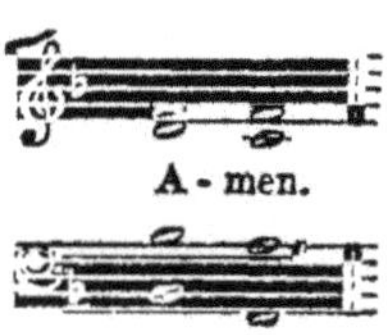

Feasts of Evangelists.

Hymn 433.

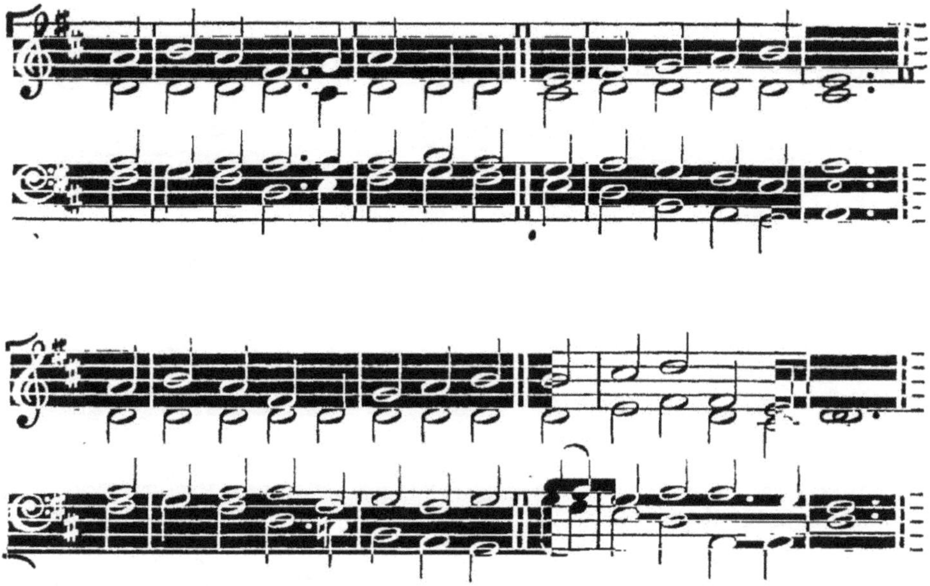

"Behold upon the mountains the feet of him that bringeth good tidings, that publisheth peace."

mf BEHOLD the messengers of CHRIST,
Who bear to every place
The unveiled mysteries of GOD,
The Gospel of His grace.

Although in space and time apart,
One SPIRIT ruled them all;
And in their sacred pages still
We hear that SPIRIT'S call.

p The things through mists and shadows dim
By holy prophets seen,
cr In the full light of day they saw
With not a cloud between.

p What CHRIST, True Man, divinely wrought,
What GOD in Manhood bore,
mf They wrote, as GOD inspired, in words
That live for evermore.

f To GOD, the Blessèd THREE in ONE,
Be glory, praise, and might,
Who called us from the shades of death
To His own glorious light.

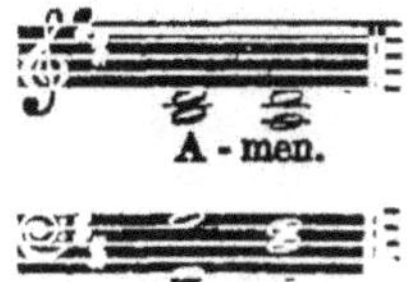

Feasts of Evangelists.

Hymn 434.

"And a river went out of Eden to water the garden; and from thence it was parted, and became into four heads."

mf COME, pure hearts, in sweetest measures
Sing of those who spread the treasures
In the holy Gospels shrined;
Blessèd tidings of salvation,
p Peace on earth, their proclamation,
cr Love from GOD to lost mankind.

mf See the Rivers four that gladden
With their streams the better Eden
Planted by our LORD most dear;
f CHRIST the Fountain, *(mf)* these the waters;
f Drink, O Sion's sons and daughters,
Drink and find salvation here.

mf O that we Thy truth confessing,
And Thy holy Word possessing,
JESU, may Thy love adore;
Unto Thee our voices raising,
cr Thee with all Thy ransomed praising
Ever and for evermore.

The Hymn No. 126, Parts 2 and 3, may be used on the Festivals of Apostles or Evangelists between Easterday and Trinity Sunday.

Feasts of Martyrs and other Holy Days.

Hymn 435.

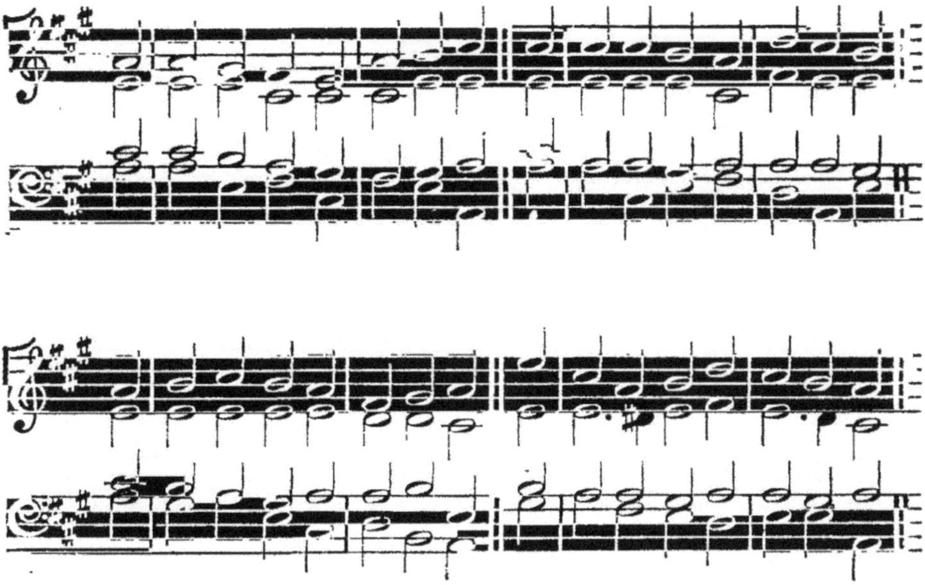

"Therefore are they before the throne of God, and serve Him day and night in His temple."

f LO! round the Throne, a glorious band,
The Saints in countless myriads stand,
Of every tongue redeemed to GOD,
dim Arrayed in garments washed in Blood.

Through tribulation great they came;
cr They bore the cross, despised the shame;
From all their labours now they rest,
In GOD's eternal glory blest.

mf They see their Saviour face to face,
And sing the triumphs of His grace;
f Him day and night they ceaseless praise,
To Him the loud thanksgiving raise:

ff "Worthy the LAMB, for sinners slain,
Through endless years to live and reign;
p Thou hast redeemed us by Thy Blood,
f And made us kings and priests to GOD."

mf O may we tread the sacred road
cr That Saints and holy Martyrs trod;
Wage to the end the glorious strife,
f And win, like them, a crown of life.

Feasts of Martyrs and other Holy Days.

Hymn 436. (First Tune.)

Feasts of Martyrs and other Holy Days.

"After this I beheld, and lo, a great multitude, which no man could number, of all nations and kindreds and people and tongues, stood before the throne and before the Lamb, clothed with white robes, and palms in their hands."

f HARK! the sound of holy voices, chanting at the crystal sea
(p) Alleluia, *(f)* Alleluia, *(ff)* Alleluia, LORD, to Thee:
p Multitude, which none can number, *(cr)* like the stars in glory stands,
f Clothed in white apparel, holding palms of victory in their hands.

mf Patriarch, and holy Prophet, who prepared the way of CHRIST,
King, Apostle, Saint, Confessor, Martyr, and Evangelist,
p Saintly Maiden, godly Matron, *(cr)* widows who have watched to prayer,
f Joined in holy concert, singing to the LORD of all, are there.

p They have come from tribulation, and have washed their robes in Blood,
Washed them in the Blood of JESUS; *(cr)* tried they were, and firm they stood;
p Mocked, imprisoned, stoned, tormented, sawn asunder, slain with sword,
cr They have conquered death and Satan *(f)* by the might of CHRIST the LORD.

f Unis. Marching with Thy Cross their banner, they have triumphed following
Thee, the Captain of salvation, Thee their Saviour and their King;
dim Harm. Gladly, LORD, with Thee they suffered; gladly, LORD, with Thee they died,
And by death *(cr)* to life immortal they were born, and glorified.

ff Unis. Now they reign in heavenly glory, now they walk in golden light,
Now they drink, as from a river, holy bliss and infinite;
p Harm. Love and peace they taste for ever, *(cr)* and all truth and knowledge see
In the Beatific Vision of the Blessèd TRINITY.

f GOD of GOD, the One-begotten, LIGHT of LIGHT, Emmanuel,
In Whose Body joined together all the Saints for ever dwell,
p Pour upon us of Thy fulness, *(cr)* that we may for evermore
GOD the FATHER, GOD the SON, and GOD the HOLY GHOST adore.

Feasts of Martyrs and other Holy Days.

Hymn 436. (Second Tune.)

Hymn 436. (Third Tune.)

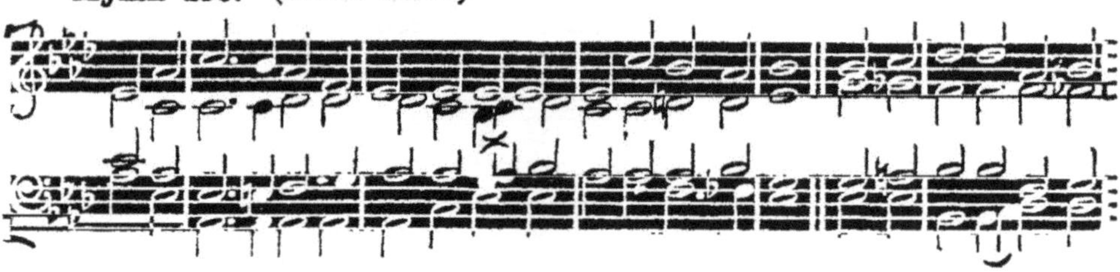

Feasts of Martyrs' and other Holy Days.

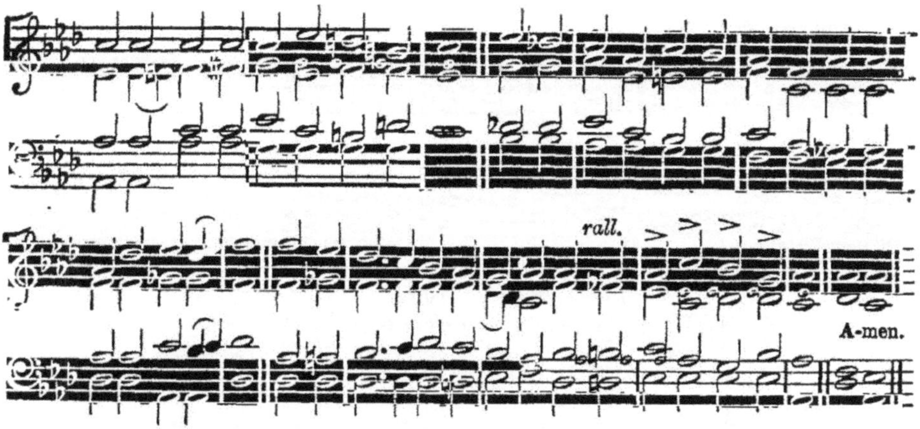

"After this I beheld, and lo, a great multitude, which no man could number, of all nations and kindreds and people and tongues, stood before the throne and before the Lamb, clothed with white robes, and palms in their hands."

f HARK! the sound of holy voices, chanting at the crystal sea
(p) Alleluia, *(f)* Alleluia, *(ff)* Alleluia, LORD, to Thee:
p Multitude, which none can number, *(cr)* like the stars in glory stands,
f Clothed in white apparel, holding palms of victory in their hands.

mf Patriarch, and holy Prophet, who prepared the way of CHRIST,
King, Apostle, Saint, Confessor, Martyr, and Evangelist,
p Saintly Maiden, godly Matron, *(cr)* widows who have watched to prayer,
f Joined in holy concert, singing to the LORD of all, are there.

p They have come from tribulation, and have washed their robes in Blood,
Washed them in the Blood of JESUS; *(cr)* tried they were, and firm they stood;
p Mocked, imprisoned, stoned, tormented, sawn asunder, slain with sword,
cr They have conquered death and Satan *(f)* by the might of CHRIST the LORD.

f Unis. Marching with Thy Cross their banner, they have triumphed following
Thee, the Captain of salvation, Thee their Saviour and their King;
'im Harm. Gladly, LORD, with Thee they suffered; gladly, LORD, with Thee they died,
And by death *(cr)* to life immortal they were born, and glorified.

ff Unis. Now they reign in heavenly glory, now they walk in golden light,
Now they drink, as from a river, holy bliss and infinite;
p Harm. Love and peace they taste for ever, *(cr)* and all truth and knowledge see
In the Beatific Vision of the Blessèd TRINITY.

f GOD of GOD, the One-begotten, LIGHT of LIGHT, Emmanuel,
In Whose Body joined together all the Saints for ever dwell,
p Pour upon us of Thy fulness, *(cr)* that we may for evermore
GOD the FATHER, GOD the SON, and GOD the HOLY GHOST adore.

Feasts of Martyrs and other Holy Days.

Hymn 437.

"Compassed about with so great a cloud of witnesses."

f FOR all the Saints who from their lábours rest,
Who Thee by faith before the wórld confessed,
Thy Name, O Jesu, be for éver blest.
Alleluia!

Thou wast their Rock, their Fortress, ánd their Might;
Thou, Lord, their Captain in the wéll-fought fight;
Thou in the darkness drear their óne true Light.
Alleluia!

O may Thy soldiers, faithful, trúe, and bold,
Fight as the Saints who nobly fóught of old,
And win, with them, the victor's crówn of gold
Alleluia!

mf O blest communion! fellowshíp Divine!
We feebly struggle, they in glóry shine;
cr Yet all are one in Thee, for áll are Thine.
Alleluia!

p And when the strife is fierce, the wárfare long,
Steals on the ear the distant tríumph-song,
cr And hearts are brave again, and árms are strong.
Alleluia!

mf The golden evening brightens ín the west;
Soon, soon to faithful warriors cómes their rest;
p Sweet is the calm of Paradíse the blest.
Alleluia!

f But lo! there breaks a yet more glórious day;
The Saints triumphant rise in bríght array:
The King of glory passes ón His way.
Alleluia!

ff From earth's wide bounds, from ocean's fárthest coast,
Through gates of pearl streams in the cóuntless host,
Singing to Father, Son, and Hóly Ghost.
Alleluia!

Feasts of Martyrs and other Holy Days.

Hymn 438.

"These are they which came out of great tribulation, and have washed their robes, and made them white in the Blood of the Lamb."

f HOW bright those glorious spirits shine!
mf Whence all their white array?
How came they to the blissful seats
Of everlasting day?

p Lo! these are they from sufferings great
Who came to realms of light;
cr And in the Blood of CHRIST have washed
Those robes that shine so bright.

f Now with triumphal palms they stand
Before the Throne on high,
And serve the GOD they love amidst
The glories of the sky.

mf Hunger and thirst are felt no more,
Nor sun with scorching ray;
cr GOD is their Sun, Whose cheering beams
Diffuse eternal day.

mf The LAMB, Which dwells amidst the Throne,
Shall o'er them still preside,
p Feed them with nourishment Divine,
cr And all their footsteps guide.

p 'Midst pastures green He'll lead His flock,
Where living streams appear;
cr And GOD the LORD from every eye
Shall wipe off every tear.

f To FATHER, SON, and HOLY GHOST,
The GOD Whom we adore,
Be glory, as it was, is now,
And shall be evermore.

Feasts of Martyrs and other Holy Days.

Hymn 439. (First Tune.)

This Tune may also be sung in Common Time if preferred, by making the Semibreves, throughout, into Minims.

Feasts of Martyrs and other Holy Days

"Fight the good fight of faith, lay hold on eternal life."

f THE SON of GOD goes forth to war,
   A Kingly crown to gain,
His blood-red banner streams afar;
   Who follows in His train?
mf Who best can drink his cup of woe,
f   Triumphant over pain,
p Who patient bears his cross below,
f   He follows in His train.

mf The Martyr first, whose eagle eye
   Could pierce beyond the grave,
Who saw his Master in the sky,
cr   And called on Him to save.
dim Like Him, with pardon on his tongue
   In midst of mortal pain,
mf He prayed for them that did the wrong;
f   Who follows in his train?

A glorious band, the chosen few
   On whom the SPIRIT came,
Twelve valiant Saints, their hope they knew,
   And mocked the cross and flame.
They met the tyrant's brandished steel,
   The lion's gory mane,
p They bowed their necks, the death to feel;
f   Who follows in their train?

A noble army, men and boys,
   The matron and the maid,
Around the Saviour's Throne rejoice
   In robes of light arrayed.
They climbed the steep ascent of heaven
mf   Through peril, toil, and pain;
p O GOD, to us may grace be given
   To follow in their train.

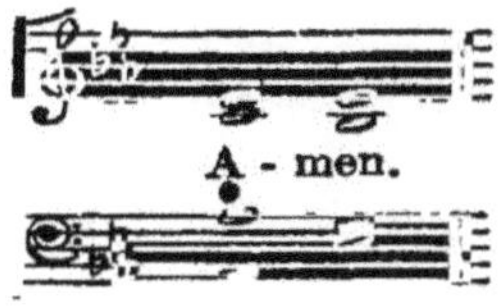

Hymn 439. (Second Tune.)

"Fight the good fight of faith, lay hold on eternal life."

f THE Son of God goes forth to war,
A Kingly crown to gain,
His blood-red banner streams afar;
Who follows in His train?

mf Who best can drink his cup of woe,
f Triumphant over pain,
p Who patient bears his cross below,
f He follows in His train.

mf The Martyr first, whose eagle eye
Could pierce beyond the grave,
Who saw his Master in the sky,
cr And called on Him to save.

dim Like Him, with pardon on his tongue
In midst of mortal pain,
mf He prayed for them that did the wrong;
f Who follows in his train?

A glorious band, the chosen few
On whom the Spirit came,
Twelve valiant Saints, their hope they knew,
And mocked the cross and flame.

They met the tyrant's brandished steel,
The lion's gory mane,
p They bowed their necks, the death to feel
f Who follows in their train?

A noble army, men and boys,
The matron and the maid,
Around the Saviour's Throne rejoice
In robes of light arrayed.

They climbed the steep ascent of heaven
mf Through peril, toil, and pain;
p O God, to us may grace be given
To follow in their train.

Feasts of Martyrs' and other Holy Days.

Hymn 440. (First Tune.)

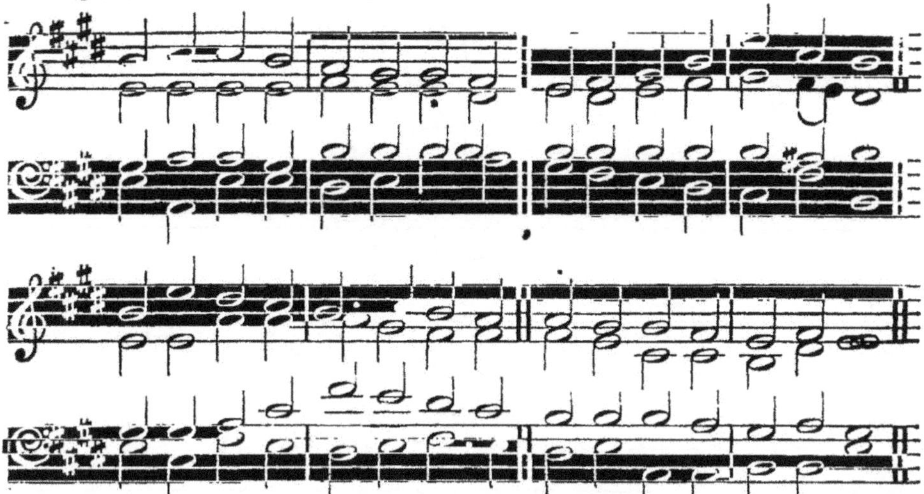

"They were stoned, they were sawn asunder, were tempted, were slain with the sword; . . . being destitute, afflicted, tormented; of whom the world was not worthy."

mf BLESSÈD feasts of blessèd Martyrs,
Holy days of holy men,
With affection's recollections
Greet we your return again.

f Worthy deeds they wrought and wonders,
Worthy of the Name they bore;
We with meetest praise and sweetest
Honour them for evermore.

mf Faith prevailing, hope unfailing,
Jesus loved with single heart—
f Thus they glorious and victorious
Bravely bore the Martyr's part.

mf Racked with torture, haled to slaughter,
Fire, and axe, and murderous sword,
f Chains and prison, foes' derision
They endured for Christ the Lord.

p So they passed through pain and sorrow,
Till they sank in death to rest;
cr Earth's rejected, God's elected,
Gained a portion with the blest.

mf By contempt of worldly pleasures,
And by deeds of valour done,
f They have reached the land of Angels,
And with them are knit in one.

Made co-heirs with Christ in glory,
His celestial bliss they share:
p May they now before Him bending
Help us onward by their prayer;

That, this weary life completed,
And its fleeting trials past,
f We may win eternal glory
In our Father's home at last.

Feasts of Martyrs and other Holy Days.

Hymn 440. (Second Tune.)

Feasts of Martyrs and other Holy Days.

"They were stoned, they were sawn asunder, were tempted, were slain with the sword; . . . being destitute, afflicted, tormented; of whom the world was not worthy."

mf BLESSÈD feasts of blessèd Martyrs,
Holy days of holy men,
With affection's recollections
Greet we your return again.
f Worthy deeds they wrought and wonders,
Worthy of the Name they bore;
We with meetest praise and sweetest
Honour them for evermore.

mf Faith prevailing, hope unfailing,
Jesus loved with single heart—
f Thus they glorious and victorious
Bravely bore the Martyr's part.
mf Racked with torture, haled to slaughter,
Fire, and axe, and murderous sword,
f Chains and prison, foes' derision
They endured for Christ the Lord.

p So they passed through pain and sorrow,
Till they sank in death to rest;
cr Earth's rejected, God's elected,
Gained a portion with the blest.
mf By contempt of worldly pleasures,
And by deeds of valour done,
f They have reached the land of Angels,
And with them are knit in one.

Made co-heirs with Christ in glory,
His celestial bliss they share:
p May they now before Him bending
Help us onward by their prayer;
That, this weary life completed,
And its fleeting trials past,
f We may win eternal glory
In our Father's home at last.

Feasts of Martyrs and other Holy Days.

Hymn 441.

Feasts of Martyrs and other Holy Days.

Blessed are they which are persecuted for righteousness' sake; for theirs is the kingdom of heaven.

f LET our Choir new anthems raise,
  Wake the song of gladness;
GOD Himself to joy and praise
  Turns the Martyrs' sadness:
Bright the day that won their crown,
  Opened heaven's bright portal,
dim As they laid the mortal down
cr To put on the immortal.

mf Never flinched they from the flame,
  From the torture never;
Vain the foeman's sharpest aim,
  Satan's best endeavour:
cr For by faith they saw the land
  Decked in all its glory,
f Where triumphant now they stand
  With the victor's story.

Up and follow, Christian men!
  Press through toil and sorrow;
Spurn the night of fear, and then,
  Oh, the glorious morrow!
mf Who will venture on the strife?
f Blest who first begin it;
mf Who will grasp the land of life?
ff Warriors, up and win it!

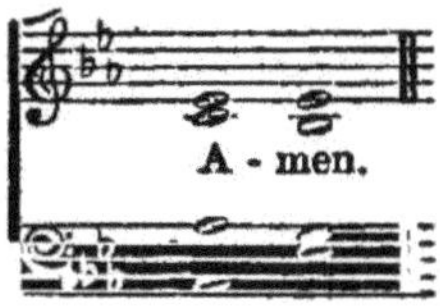

Feasts of Martyrs and other Holy Days.

Hymn 442.

"Blessed is the man that endureth temptation, for when he is tried he shall receive the crown of life."

mf O GOD, Thy soldiers' great Reward,
Their Portion, Crown, and faithful LORD,
From all transgressions set us free
Who sing Thy Martyr's victory.

By wisdom taught he learned to know
The vanity of all below,
The fleeting joys of earth disdained,
And everlasting glory gained.

Right manfully his cross he bore,
And ran his race of torments sore;
dim For Thee he poured his life away,
cr With Thee he lives in endless day.

p We therefore pray Thee, LORD of Love,
Regard us from Thy Throne above;
cr On this Thy Martyr's triumph-day
p Wash every stain of sin away.

f All praise to GOD the FATHER be,
All praise, Eternal SON, to Thee,
Whom with the SPIRIT we adore
For ever and for evermore.

Feasts of Martyrs' and other Holy Days.

Hymn 443.

"Be thou faithful unto death, and I will give thee a crown of life."

p FOR man the Saviour shed
His all-atoning Blood,
cr And oh, shall ransomed man refuse
To suffer for his God?

mf Ashamed who now can be
To own the Crucified?
cr Nay, rather be our glory this,
To die for Him Who died.

mf So felt Thy Martyr, Lord;
By Thy right hand sustained,
He waged for Thee the battle's strife,
And threatened death disdained.

Upon the golden crown
Gazing with eager breath,
He fought as one who fain would die,
And, dying, conquer death.

Alone he stood unmoved
Amid his cruel foes;
f Oh, wondrous was the might that then
Above his torturers rose!

p Lord, give us grace to bear
Like him our cross of shame,
To do and suffer what Thou wilt,
For love of Thy dear Name.

f Jesu, the King of Saints,
We praise Thee and adore,
Who art with God the Father One
And Spirit evermore.

Hymn 444.

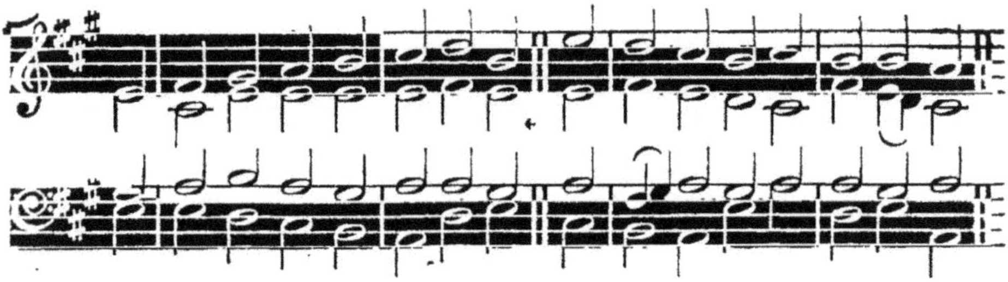

"Of whom the world was not worthy."

f YE servants of our glorious King,
To Him your thankful praises bring;
And tell the deeds that grace has done,
The triumphs by His Martyrs won.

mf Since they were faithful to the last,
Their holy struggles now are past;
The bitterness of death is o'er,
f And theirs is bliss for evermore.

p The flame might scorch, the knife lay bare,
And cruel beasts their members tear;
cr No powers of earth, no powers of hell
The souls that loved their LORD could quell.

f For ever broken is the chain
That sought to bind them, but in vain:
mf O let us strive like them to win
Our freedom from the bonds of sin.

p O Saviour, may our portion be
With those who gave themselves to Thee,
f Through all eternity to sing
All praise to Thee the Martyrs' King.

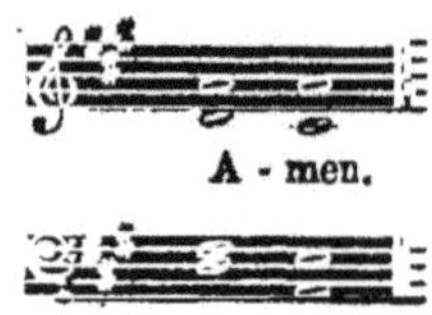

Feasts of Martyrs and other Holy Days.

Hymn 445.

"Clothed with white robes, and palms in their hands."

PALMS of glory, raiment bright,
Crowns that never fade away,
Gird and deck the Saints in light,
Priests, and kings, and conquerors they.

mf Yet the conquerors bring their palms
To the LAMB amidst the Throne,
cr And proclaim in joyful psalms
Victory through His Cross alone.

f Kings their crowns for harps resign,
Crying, as they strike the chords,
cr "Take the Kingdom, it is Thine,
King of kings, and LORD of lords."

p Round the Altar Priests confess,
If their robes are white as snow,
'Twas the Saviour's Righteousness,
And His Blood, that made them so.

mf They were mortal too like us;
O, when we like them must die,
cr May our souls translated thus
Triumph, reign, and shine on high.

2 T.

Feasts of Martyrs and other Holy Days.

Hymn 446.

"I reckon that the sufferings of this present time are not worthy to be compared with the glory which shall be revealed in us."

mf OH! what, if we are CHRIST'S,
Is earthly shame or loss?
cr Bright shall the crown of glory be
dim When we have borne the cross.

Keen was the trial once,
Bitter the cup of woe,
When martyred Saints, baptized in blood,
CHRIST'S sufferings shared below:

f Bright is their glory now,
Boundless their joy above,
Where, on the bosom of their GOD,
They rest in perfect love.

mf LORD, may that grace be ours,
Like them in faith to bear
p All that of sorrow, grief, or pain
May be our portion here;

mf Enough if Thou at last
The word of blessing give,
And let us rest beneath Thy feet,
Where Saints and Angels live.

f All glory, LORD, to Thee,
Whom heaven and earth adore;
To FATHER, SON, and HOLY GHOST,
ONE GOD for evermore.

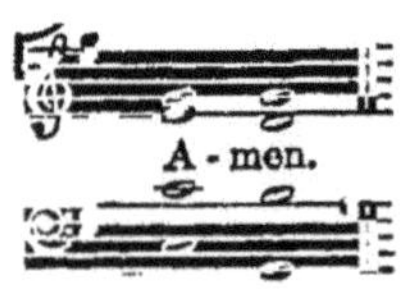

Feasts of Martyrs and other Holy Days.

Hymn 447.

"To him that overcometh."

f SOLDIERS, who are CHRIST'S below,
Strong in faith resist the foe:
Boundless is the pledged reward
Unto them who serve the LORD.

mf 'Tis no palm of fading leaves
That the conqueror's hand receives;
Joys are his, serene and pure,
Light that ever shall endure.

For the souls that overcome
Waits the beauteous heavenly home,
cr Where the Blessèd evermore
Tread, on high, the starry floor.

p Passing soon and little worth
Are the things that tempt on earth;
mf Heavenward lift thy soul's regard;
GOD Himself is thy Reward.

f FATHER, Who the crown dost give,
SAVIOUR, by Whose death we live,
SPIRIT, Who our hearts dost raise,
THREE in ONE, Thy Name we praise

Feasts of Martyrs and other Holy Days.

Hymn 448.

"And they glorified God in me."

mf FOR Thy dear Saint, O Lord,
Who strove in Thee to live,
Who followed Thee, obeyed, adored,
Our grateful hymn receive.

p For Thy dear Saint, O Lord,
Who strove in Thee to die,
cr And found in Thee a full reward,
Accept our thankful cry.

mf Thine earthly members fit
To join Thy Saints above,
In one communion ever knit,
One fellowship of love.

Jesu, Thy Name we bless,
And humbly pray that we
May follow them in holiness,
Who lived and died for Thee.

f All might, all praise, be Thine,
Father, co-equal Son,
And Spirit, Bond of love Divine,
While endless ages run.

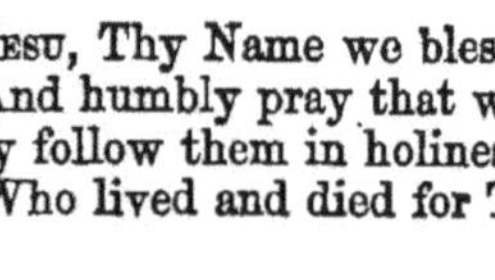

Feasts of Martyrs and other Holy Days.

Hymn 449.

"Hail, thou that art highly favoured, the Lord is with thee; blessed art thou among women."

For the B. V. Mary.

mf THE God, Whom earth, and sea, and sky
Adore, and laud, and magnify,
Whose might they own, Whose praise they swell,
p In Mary's womb vouchsafed to dwell.

mf The Lord, Whom sun and moon obey,
Whom all things serve from day to day,
p Was by the Holy Ghost conceived
Of her who through His grace believed.

mf How blest that Mother, in whose shrine
The world's Creator, Lord Divine,
Whose hand contains the earth and sky,
p Once deigned, as in His ark, to lie;

f Blest in the message Gabriel brought,
Blest by the work the Spirit wrought;
From whom the great Desire of earth
p Took human flesh and human birth.

f O Lord, the Virgin-born, to Thee
Eternal praise and glory be,
Whom with the Father we adore
And Holy Ghost for evermore.

Feasts of Martyrs and other Holy Days.

Hymn 450.

FOR THE B. V. MARY. *"Mary, the Mother of Jesus."*

mf SHALL we not love thee, Mother dear,
  Whom JESUS loves so well?
And, to His glory, year by year,
  Thy joy and honour tell?

Bound with the curse of sin and shame
  We helpless sinners lay,
cr Until in tender love He came
  To bear the curse away.

mf And thee He chose from whom to take
  True flesh His Flesh to be;
p In It to suffer for our sake,
f By It to make us free.

Thy Babe He lay upon thy breast,
  To thee He cried for food;
Thy gentle nursing soothed to rest
  Th' Incarnate SON of GOD.

mf O wondrous depth of grace Divine
  That He should bend so low!
cr And, Mary, oh, what joy 'twas thine
  In His dear love to know;

f Joy to be Mother of the LORD,
  And thine the truer bliss,
In every thought, and deed, and word
  To be for ever His.

mf And as He loves thee, Mother dear,
  We too will love thee well;
cr And, to His glory, year by year,
  Thy joy and honour tell.

f JESU, the Virgin's Holy Son,
  We praise Thee and adore,
WHO art with GOD the FATHER ONE
  And SPIRIT evermore.

Feasts of Martyrs and other Holy Days.

Hymn 451.

"Whosoever therefore shall confess Me before men, him will I confess also before My Father which is in heaven."

For a Confessor.

mf NOT by the Martyr's death alone
The Saint his crown in heaven has won,
There is a triumph robe on high
For bloodless fields of victory.

What though he was not called to feel
The cross, or flame, or torturing wheel,
cr Yet daily to the world he died;
His flesh, through grace, he crucified.

p What though nor chains, nor scourges sore,
Nor cruel beasts his members tore,
cr Enough if perfect love arise
To Christ a grateful sacrifice.

p Lord, grant us so to Thee to turn
That we through life to die may learn,
cr And thus, when life's brief day is o'er,
May live with Thee for evermore.

mf O Fount of sanctity and love,
O perfect Rest of Saints above,
f All praise, all glory be to Thee
Both now and through eternity.

Feasts of Martyrs and other Holy Days.

Hymn 452.

"If a man desire the office of a bishop, he desireth a good work."

FOR A BISHOP.

mf O THOU Whose all-redeeming might
Crowns every Chief in faith's true fight,
On this commemoration day
Hear us, good JESU, while we pray.

In faithful strife for Thy dear Name
Thy servant earned the saintly fame,
Which pious hearts with praise revere
In constant memory year by year.

p Earth's fleeting joys he counted nought,
cr For higher, truer joys he sought,
f And now, with Angels round Thy Throne,
Unfading treasures are his own.

p O grant that we, most gracious GOD,
May follow in the steps he trod;
cr And, freed from every stain of sin,
As he hath won may also win.

f To Thee, O CHRIST, our loving King,
All glory, praise, and thanks we bring·
Whom with the FATHER we adore
And HOLY GHOST for evermore.

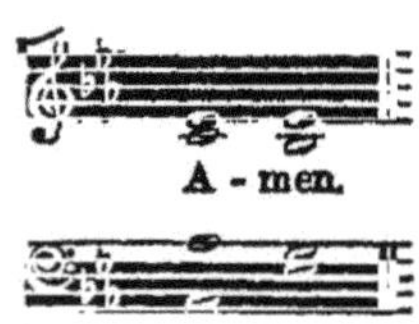

Feasts of Martyrs and other Holy Days.

Hymn 453.

"The memory of the just is blessed."

For a Bishop.

mf O SHEPHERD of the sheep,
High Priest of things to come,
Who didst in grace Thy servant keep,
p And take him safely home.

f Accept our song of praise
For all his holy care,
His zeal unquenched through length of days,
The trials that he bare.

mf Chief of Thy faithful band,
He held himself the least,
Though Thy dread keys were in his hand,
O everlasting Priest.

f So, trusting in Thy might,
He won a fair renown;
So, waxing valiant in the fight,
He trod the lion down.

p Then rendered up to Thee
The charge Thy love had given,
And passed away *(cr)* Thy Face to see
Revealed in highest heaven.

mf On all our Bishops pour
The Spirit of Thy grace;
That, as he won the palm of yore,
So they may run their race;

That, when this life is done,
They may with him adore
cr The ever Blessèd Three in One,
In bliss for evermore.

Feasts of Martyrs and other Holy Days.

Hymn 454.

Feasts of Martyrs and other Holy Days.

"He gave some . . . . Pastors and Teachers."

FOR A DOCTOR.

mf JESU, for the beacon-light
By Thy holy Doctors given,
p When the mists of error's night
Gathered o'er the path to heaven,
mf For the witness that they bare
cr To the truth they learned of Thee,
f For the glory that they share,
Let our praise accepted be.

mf In Jerusalem below
They were workmen at Thy call,
cr Each with one hand met the foe,
With the other built the wall;
f Watchmen on the mountain set,
Scribes instructed in Thy Word,
dim Fishers with the Gospel net
cr Drawing souls to Thee their LORD.

mf Like Thy learnèd sons of yore,
JESU, may Thy Pastors still
cr Know and teach Thy sacred lore
With brave heart and patient skill;
p In these latter days of strife
cr Keep, O keep them true to Thee,
f Till beside the well of life
Light in Thine own Light they see.

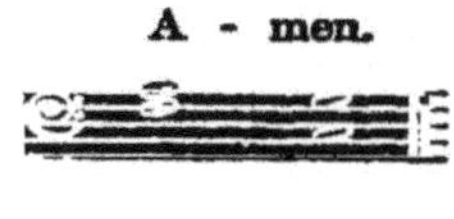

Feasts of Martyrs and other Holy Days.

Hymn 455. (First Tune.)

To be sung in Unison.

Feasts of Martyrs' and other Holy Days.

Hymn 455. (Second Tune.)

"Thy Name is as ointment poured forth, therefore do the virgins love Thee."

For a Virgin.

mf JESU, the Virgins' Crown, do Thou
Accept us as in prayer we bow,
Born of that Virgin whom alone
The Mother and the Maid we own.

Amongst the lilies Thou dost feed
And thither choirs of Virgins lead;
Adorning all Thy chosen brides
With glorious gifts Thy love provides.

And whither, Lord, Thy footsteps wend,
The Virgins still with praise attend;
For Thee they pour their sweetest song,
And after Thee rejoicing throng.

p O gracious Lord, we Thee implore
Thy grace on every sense to pour;
From all pollution keep us free,
And make us pure in heart for Thee.

f All praise to God the Father be,
All praise, Eternal Son, to Thee,
Whom with the Spirit we adore
For ever and for evermore.

Feasts of Martyrs and other Holy Days.

Hymn 456.

FOR A VIRGIN.

"My Beloved is mine, and I am His."

p O LAMB of GOD, Whose love Divine
Draws Virgin-souls to follow Thee,
cr And bids them earthly joys resign
If so they may Thy beauty see;

mf The Saint of whom we sing to-day
Was faithful to Thy loving call,
And, casting other hopes away,
Took Thee to be her GOD, her All.

To Thee she yielded up her will,
Her heart was drawn to Thine above;
Content if Thou wouldst deign to fill
Thine handmaid with Thy perfect love.

p Beneath Thy Cross she loved to stand,
Like Mary in Thy dying hour,
That blessings from Thy piercèd Hand
cr Might clothe her with undying power;

mf With power to win the crown of light
For Virgin-souls laid up on high,
And ready keep her lamp at night
To hail the Bridegroom drawing nigh.

p And surely Thou at last didst come
To end the sorrows of Thy bride,
pp And bear her to Thy peaceful home
cr With Thee for ever to abide.

f All glory, JESU, for the grace
That drew Thy Saint to follow Thee;
p Grant us too in Thy love a place
Both now and through eternity

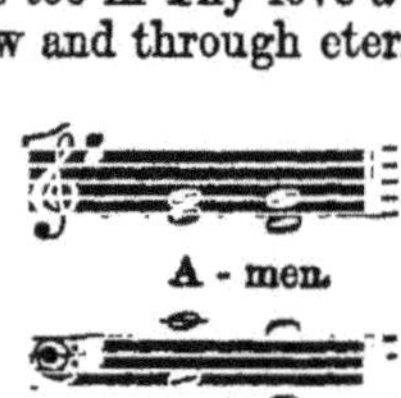

Hymn 457.

" Who can find a virtuous woman? for her price is far above rubies: the heart of her husband doth safely trust in her."

FOR A HOLY MATRON.

f HOW blest the matron, who, endued
With holy zeal and fortitude,
Has won through grace a saintly fame,
And owns a dear and honoured name.

Such holy love inflamed her breast
She would not seek on earth her rest,
But, strong in faith and patience, trod
The narrow way that leads to GOD.

She learned, through fasting, to control
The flesh that weigheth down the soul,
And then, by prayer's sweet food sustained,
To seek the joys she now has gained.

mf O CHRIST, from Whom all virtue springs,
Who only doest wondrous things,
To Thee, the King of Saints, we pray,
Accept and bless Thy flock to-day.

f All praise to GOD the FATHER be,
All praise, Eternal SON, to Thee,
Whom with the SPIRIT we adore
For ever and for evermore.

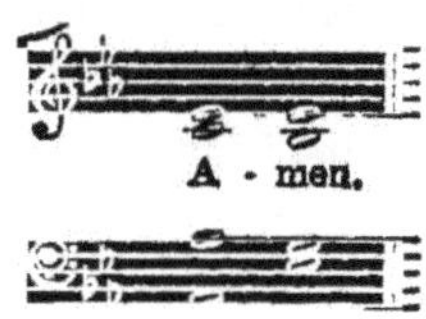

Hymn 458.

"I John, who also am your brother and companion in tribulation, and in the kingdom and patience of Jesus Christ, was in the isle that is called Patmos, for the Word of God, and for the testimony of Jesus Christ."

St. John before the Latin Gate.

mf AN exile for the faith
  Of his Incarnate Lord,
Beyond the stars, beyond all space,
cr His soul in vision soared:

mf There saw in glory Him
  Who liveth, and was dead,
There Judah's Lion, and the Lamb
p That for our ransom bled:

mf There of the Kingdom learned
  The mysteries sublime;
p How, sown in Martyrs' blood, the faith
cr Should spread from clime to clime.

p Lord, give us grace, like him,
  In Thee to live and die;
cr To spurn the fleeting things of earth,
  And seek for joys on high.

f Jesu, our risen Lord,
  We praise Thee and adore,
Who art with God the Father One
  And Spirit evermore.

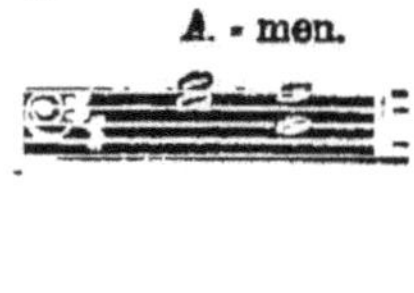

Hymn 459.

"Mary Magdalene, out of whom He had cast seven devils."

St. Mary Magdalene.

f SON of the Highest, deign to cast
  On us a pitying eye,
Thou Who repentant Magdalene
  Didst call to joys on high.

f Thy long-lost coin is stored at length
  In treasure-house Divine,
The jewel from pollution cleansed
  Doth now the stars outshine.

Jesu, the balm of every wound,
  The sinner's only stay,
Grant us, like Magdalene, to weep
  In this Thy mercy's day.

cr Absolve us by Thy gracious Word,
  Fulfil us with Thy love,
And guide us through the storms of life
  To perfect rest above.

f All praise, all glory be to Thee,
  O everlasting Lord,
Whose mercy doth our souls forgive,
  Whose bounty doth reward.

Feasts of Martyrs and other Holy Days.

Hymn 460.

Feasts of Martyrs and other Holy Days.

"His Face did shine as the sun, and His raiment was white as the light."

THE TRANSFIGURATION OF OUR LORD.

f IN days of old on Sinai
The LORD Almighty came
cr In majesty of terror,
In thunder-cloud and flame:
mf On Tabor, with the glory
Of sunniest light for vest,
The excellence of beauty
In JESUS was expressed.

p All light created paled there,
And did Him worship meet;
The sun itself adored Him,
And bowed before His feet;
cr While Moses and Elias,
Upon the Holy Mount,
The co-eternal glory
Of CHRIST our GOD recount.

p O holy, wondrous vision!
cr But what when, this life past,
The beauty of Mount Tabor
Shall end in heaven at last?
f But what when all the glory
Of uncreated light
Shall be the promised guerdon
Of them that win the fight?

Feasts of Martyrs and other Holy Days.

Hymn 461.

"Lord, it is good for us to be here."

THE TRANSFIGURATION OF OUR LORD.

mf FOR ever we would gaze on Thee,
O LORD, upon the Mount;
With Moses and Elias see
f That light from Light's own Fount;

mf For ever with the chosen three
Would stand upon that height,
And in that blessèd company
Be plunged in pure delight.

For ever would we train the ear
To that celestial Voice;
cr In Thee, the SON of GOD, so near,
For evermore rejoice.

mf Here would we pitch our constant tent,
For ever here abide;
And dwell in peace and full content,
Dear Master, at Thy side.

p But no! not yet to man 'tis given
To rest upon that height;
'Tis but a passing glimpse of heaven;
We must descend and fight.

mf Beneath the Mount is toil and pain;
cr O CHRIST, Thy strength impart;
f Till we, transfigured too, shall reign
For ever where Thou art.

Feasts of Martyrs and other Holy Days.

Hymn 462.

"And Herod sent and beheaded John in the prison."

THE BEHEADING OF ST. JOHN BAPTIST.

mf HERALD, in the wilderness
Breaking up the road,
Sinking mountains, raising plains,
For the path of GOD;

Prophet, to the multitudes
Calling to repent,
In the way of righteousness
Unto Israel sent;

Messenger, GOD's chosen One
Foremost to proclaim,
Proffered titles passing by,
Pointing to the LAMB;

Captive, for the word of truth
Boldly witnessing;
dim Then in Herod's dungeon-cave
Faint and languishing;

p Martyr, sacrificed to sin
At that feast of shame;
cr As his life foreshewed the LORD,
In his death the same—

p Holy JESUS, when He heard,
Went apart to pray:
cr Thus may we our lesson take
From His Saint to-day.

 2 M

Litany of the Four Last Things.

Hymn 463.

mf GOD the FATHER, God the SON,
GOD the SPIRIT, THREE in ONE,
Hear us from Thy heavenly Throne,
p Spare us, Holy TRINITY.

mf JESU, Life of those who die,
Advocate with GOD on high,
Hope of immortality,
Hear us, Holy JESU.

Thou Whose Death to mortals gave
Power to triumph o'er the grave,
Living now from death to save,
Hear us, Holy JESU.

p Thou before Whose great white Throne
All our doings must be shown,
Pleading now for us Thine own,
Hear us, Holy JESU.

Thou Whose Death was borne that we,
From the power of Satan free,
Might not die eternally,
Hear us, Holy JESU.

mf Thou Who dost a place prepare,
That in heavenly mansions fair
Sinners may Thy glory share,
Hear us, Holy JESU.

Litany of the Four Last Things.

DEATH.

p We are dying day by day;
Soon from earth we pass away;
LORD of life, to Thee we pray:
Hear us, Holy JESU.

Ere we hear the Angel's call,
And the shadows round us fall,
cr Be our Saviour, be our All:
Hear us, Holy JESU.

mf Wean our hearts from things below,
Make us all Thy love to know,
Guard us from our ghostly foe:
Hear us, Holy JESU.

p Shelter us with Angel's wing,
To our souls Thy pardon bring;
So shall death have lost its sting:
Hear us, Holy JESU.

In the gloom Thy light provide;
Safely through the valley guide;
Thee we trust, for Thou hast died
Hear us, Holy JESU.

Litany of the Four Last Things.

JUDGMENT.

JUDGMENT.

p When Thy summons we obey
On the dreadful Judgment Day,
Let not fear our soul dismay:
Hear us, Holy JESU.

While the lost in terror fly,
cr May we see with joyful eye
Our Redemption drawing nigh:
Hear us, Holy JESU.

mf May we see Thee on Thy Throne
As the Saviour we have known,
And have followed as our own:
Hear us, Holy JESU.

May we then, among the blest
Who Thy Name on earth confessed,
Hear Thee calling us to rest:
Hear us, Holy JESU.

HELL.

Litany of the Four Last Things.

HELL.

p From the awful place of doom,
Where in rayless outer gloom
Dead souls lie as in a tomb,
Save us, Holy JESU.

From the black, the dull despair
Ruined men and angels share,
From the dread companions there,
Save us, Holy JESU.

From the unknown agonies
Of the soul that helpless lies,
From the worm that never dies,
Save us, Holy JESU.

From the lusts that none can tame,
From the fierce mysterious flame,
From the everlasting shame,
Save us, Holy JESU.

HEAVEN.

HEAVEN.

f Where Thy Saints in glory reign,
Free from sorrow, free from pain,
Pure from every guilty stain,
Bring us, Holy JESU.

mf Where the captives find release,
Where all foes from troubling cease,
Where the weary rest in peace,
Bring us, Holy JESU.

cr Where the pleasures never cloy,
Where in Angels' holy joy
Thy redeemed their powers employ,
Bring us, Holy JESU.

Where in wondrous light are shown
All Thy dealings with Thine own,
Who shall know as they are known,
Bring us, Holy JESU.

f Where, with loved ones gone before,
We may love Thee and adore
In Thy Presence evermore,
Bring us, Holy JESU.

Litany of the Incarnate Word.

Hymn 464. (First Tune.)

Hymn 464. (Second Tune.)

Litany of the Incarnate Word.

mf GOD the FATHER, GOD the SON,
GOD the SPIRIT, THREE in ONE,
Hear us from Thy heavenly Throne,
p Spare us, Holy TRINITY.

mf SON of GOD, for man decreed
To be born the woman's Seed,
Very GOD and Man indeed,
Hear us, Holy JESU.

Thou Whose Wisdom all things planned,
Held by Whose Almighty hand
All things in their order stand,
Hear us, Holy JESU.

GOD with us, Emmanuel,
Coming here as Man to dwell,
Saving us when Adam fell,
Hear us, Holy JESU.

SAVIOUR, full of truth and grace,
Leaving Thine eternal place
To restore our fallen race,
Hear us, Holy JESU.

Image of the GOD unseen,
Still what Thou hadst ever been,
Though in form of Infant mean,
Hear us, Holy JESU.

WORD, by Whom the worlds were made,
In a lowly manger laid,
Taught on earth an humble trade,
Hear us, Holy JESU.

p JESU, led by love to share
All the forms of grief and care,
That we sinful mortals bear,
Hear us, Holy JESU.

mf Good Physician, come to cure
All the ills that men endure,
And to make our nature pure,
Hear us, Holy JESU.

p Man of Sorrows, weak and worn
With Thy woes for sinners borne,
Lest we should for ever mourn,
Hear us, Holy JESU.

mf Shepherd, Who Thy watch dost keep,
Guarding still Thy chosen sheep
From the spoiler's malice deep,
Hear us, Holy JESU.

p LAMB, from earth's foundation slain,
By Whose bitter stripes of pain
We are freed from guilty stain,
Hear us, Holy JESU.

mf Only Victim we can plead,
Our High Priest to intercede,
Advocate in all our need,
Hear us, Holy JESU.

Standing now before the Throne,
Pleading that which can alone
For the sin of man atone,
Hear us, Holy JESU.

Only Hope of those who pray,
Only Help while here we stay,
Life of those who pass away,
Hear us, Holy JESU.

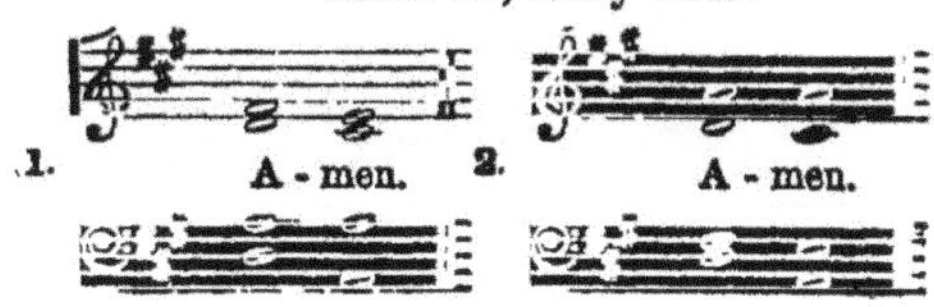

Litanies of Penitence.

Hymn 465. (First Tune.) Parts 1 and 3.

Hymn 465. (Second Tune.) Parts 1 and 3.

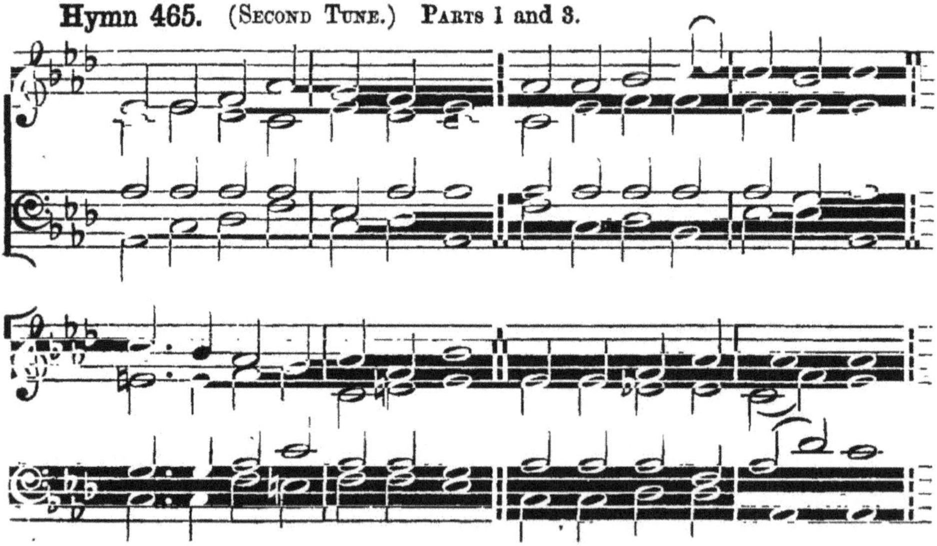

For the music of Part 2 see next music page.

Litanies of Penitence.

No. 1. Part 1.

mf GOD the Father, God the Son,
God the Spirit, Three in One,
Hear us from Thy heavenly Throne,
p Spare us, Holy Trinity.

Father, hear Thy children's call:
Humbly at Thy feet we fall,
Prodigals, confessing all:
We beseech Thee, hear us.

Christ, beneath Thy Cross we blame
All our life of sin and shame,
Penitent we breathe Thy Name:
We beseech Thee, hear us.

Holy Spirit, grieved and tried,
Oft forgotten and defied,
Now we mourn our stubborn pride:
We beseech Thee, hear us.

mf Love, that caused us first to be,
p Love, that bled upon the Tree,
cr Love, that draws us lovingly:
We beseech Thee, hear us.

p We Thy call have disobeyed,
Into paths of sin have strayed,
And repentance have delayed:
We beseech Thee, hear us.

Sick, we come to Thee for cure,
Guilty, seek Thy mercy sure,
Evil, long to be made pure:
We beseech Thee, hear us.

Blind, we pray that we may see,
Bound, we pray to be made free,
Stained, we pray for sanctity:
We beseech Thee, hear us.

mf Thou Who hear'st each contrite sigh,
Bidding sinful souls draw nigh,
Willing not that one should die,
We beseech Thee, hear us.

Part 3.*

p Teach us what Thy love has borne,
That with loving sorrow torn
Truly contrite we may mourn:
We beseech Thee, hear us.

mf Gifts of light and grace bestow,
Help us to resist the foe,
Fearing what alone is woe:
We beseech Thee, hear us.

Let not sin within us reign,
May we gladly suffer pain,
If it purge away our stain:
We beseech Thee, hear us.

May we to all evil die,
Fleshly longings crucify,
Fix our hearts and thoughts on high:
We beseech Thee, hear us.

Grant us faith to know Thee near,
Hail Thy grace, Thy judgment fear,
And through trial persevere:
We beseech Thee, hear us.

Grant us hope from earth to rise,
And to strain with eager eyes
Towards the promised heavenly prize:
We beseech Thee, hear us.

Grant us love Thy love to own,
Love to live for Thee alone,
And the power of grace make known:
We beseech Thee, hear us.

All our weak endeavours bless,
As we ever onward press,
Till we perfect holiness:
We beseech Thee, hear us.

cr Lead us daily nearer Thee,
Till at last Thy Face we see,
Crowned with Thine own purity:
We beseech Thee, hear us.

* *For the words of Part 2 see next word page.*

Litanies of Penitence.

Hymn 465. (First Tune.) Part 2.

Hymn 465. (Second Tune.) Part 2.

Litanies of Penitence.

PART 2.*

mf By the gracious saving call
Spoken tenderly to all
Who have shared in Adam's fall,
We beseech Thee, hear us.

p By the nature JESUS wore,
By the Stripes and Death He bore,
or By His Life for evermore,
We beseech Thee, hear us.

mf By the love that longs to bless,
Pitying our sore distress,
Leading us to holiness,
We beseech Thee, hear us.

By the love so calm and strong,
Patient still to suffer wrong
And our day of grace prolong,
We beseech Thee, hear us.

By the love that speaks within,
Calling us to flee from sin
And the joy of goodness win,
We beseech Thee, hear us.

By the love that bids Thee spare,
or By the heaven Thou dost prepare,
By Thy promises to prayer,
We beseech Thee, hear us.

* *For the words and music of Part 3 see the two preceding pages.*

Litanies of Penitence.

Hymn 466. (First Tune.)

Hymn 466. (Second Tune.)

Litanies of Penitence.

No. 2.

mf GOD the FATHER, GOD the SON,
GOD the SPIRIT, THREE in ONE,
Hear us from Thy heavenly Throne,
p Spare us, Holy TRINITY.

Thou Who leaving Crown and Throne
Camest here, an outcast lone,
That Thou mightest save Thine own,
Hear us, Holy JESU.

mf Thou with sinners wont to eat,
Who with loving Words didst greet
Mary weeping at Thy Feet,
Hear us, Holy JESU.

Thou Whose saddened look did chide
Peter when he thrice denied,
Till with bitter tears he cried,
Hear us, Holy JESU.

Thou Who hanging on the Tree
To the thief saidst, "Thou shalt be
To-day in Paradise with Me,"
Hear us, Holy JESU.

p Thou, despised, denied, refused,
And for man's transgressions bruised,
Sinless, yet of sin accused,
Hear us, Holy JESU.

mf Thou Who on the Cross didst reign,
Dying there in bitter pain,
Cleansing with Thy Blood our stain,
Hear us, Holy JESU.

Shepherd of the straying sheep,
Comforter of them that weep,
Hear us crying from the deep,
Hear us, Holy JESU.

That in Thy pure innocence
We may wash our souls' offence,
And find truest penitence,
We beseech Thee, JESU.

That we give to sin no place,
That we never quench Thy grace,
That we ever seek Thy Face,
We beseech Thee, JESU.

That denying evil lust,
Living godly, meek, and jus
In Thee only we may trust,
We beseech Thee, JESU.

That to sin for ever dead
We may live to Thee instead,
And the narrow pathway tread,
We beseech Thee, JESU.

f When shall end the battle sore,
When our pilgrimage is o'er,
p Grant Thy peace for evermore,
We beseech Thee, JESU.

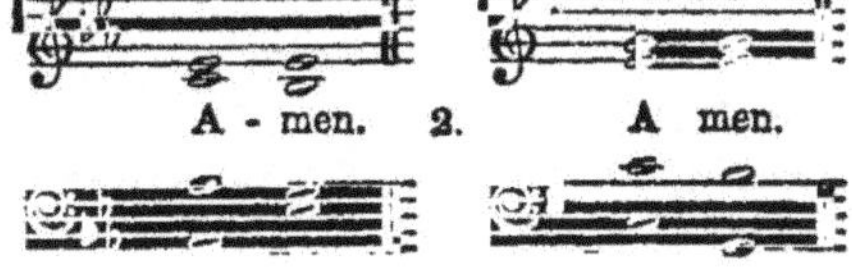

Litany of the Passion.

Hymn 467. (First Tune.)

Hymn 467. (Second Tune.)

Litany of the Passion.

mf GOD the FATHER, GOD the SON,
GOD the SPIRIT, THREE in ONE,
Hear us from Thy heavenly Throne,
p Spare us, Holy TRINITY.

JESU, Who for us didst bear
Scorn and sorrow, toil and care,
Hearken to our lowly prayer;
Hear us, Holy JESU.

pp By that hour of Agony,
Spent while Thine Apostles three
Slumbered in Gethsemane,
Hear us, Holy JESU.

cr By the prayer Thou thrice didst pray
That the cup might pass away,
So Thou mightest still obey,
Hear us, Holy JESU.

p By the kiss of treachery
To Thy foes betraying Thee,
By Thy harsh captivity,
Hear us, Holy JESU.

By the scourging Thou hast borne,
By the purple robe of scorn,
By the reed and crown of thorn,
Hear us, Holy JESU.

By the insult of the Jews,
When Barabbas they would choose
And did Thee their King refuse,
Hear us, Holy JESU.

By Thy going forth to die,
When they raised the wicked cry,
"Crucify Him, crucify!"
Hear us, Holy JESU.

By the Cross which Thou didst bear,
By the cup they bade Thee share,
Mingled gall and vinegar,
Hear us, Holy JESU.

By Thy nailing to the Tree,
By the title over Thee,
By the gloom of Calvary,
Hear us, Holy JESU.

By the parting of Thy clothes,
By the mocking of Thy foes,
As they watched Thy dying woes,
Hear us, Holy JESU.

By Thy seven Words then said,
pp By the bowing of Thy Head,
By Thy numbering with the dead,
Hear us, Holy JESU.

mf When temptation sore is rife,
When we faint amidst the strife,
Thou, Whose death hath been our life,
Save us, Holy JESU.

While on stormy seas we toss,
Let us count all things as loss
But Thee only on Thy Cross:
Save us, Holy JESU.

So, with hope in Thee made fast,
p When death's bitterness is past
cr We may see Thy Face at last:
Save us, Holy JESU.

Litany for the Rogation Days.

Hymn 468.

This Litany may also be sung in any time of special supplication.

Litany for the Rogation Days.

Jesu! Jesu!
By Thy Fasting and Temptation,
By Thy nights of supplication,
We beseech Thee, we beseech Thee,
From every ill defend us,
Thy grace and mercy send us.

Jesu! Jesu!
By Thy works of sweet compassion,
By Thy Cross and bitter Passion,
We beseech Thee, we beseech Thee,
From every ill defend us,
Thy grace and mercy send us.

Jesu! Jesu!
By Thy Blood for sinners flowing,
By Thy Death true life bestowing,
We beseech Thee, we beseech Thee,
From every ill defend us,
Thy grace and mercy send us.

p Jesu! Jesu!
f By Thy glorious Resurrection,
Earnest of our own perfection,
p We beseech Thee, we beseech Thee,
mf From every ill defend us,
Thy grace and mercy send us.

p Jesu! Jesu!
f To the Father's Throne ascended,
All Thy pain and sorrows ended,
p We beseech Thee, we beseech Thee,
mf From every ill defend us,
Thy grace and mercy send us.

p Jesu! Jesu!
mf Advocate for sinners pleading,
With the Father interceding,
p We beseech Thee, we beseech Thee,
mf From every ill defend us,
Thy grace and mercy send us.

Litany of Jesus Glorified.

Hymn 469. (First Tune.)

Hymn 469. (Second Tune.)

Litany of Jesus Glorified.

mf GOD the FATHER, throned on high,
SAVIOUR, Who didst come to die,
SPIRIT, Who dost sanctify,
p Save us, Holy TRINITY.

mf JESU, Prince of life and light,
Dwelling now in glory bright,
Ruling all things by Thy might,
p Hear us, Holy JESU.

Thou Whose Death did death destroy,
cr Who through pain didst pass to joy
Endless and without alloy,
Hear us, Holy JESU.

f Thou Who didst to heaven ascend
Still to be the sinner's Friend,
Still Thy people to defend,
Hear us, Holy JESU.

JESU, raised to GOD's right hand,
Round Whose Throne the Angel band
Waits Thy Word of dread command,
Hear us, Holy JESU.

Thou Who dost the sceptre bear
And in heaven a place prepare
That we may be with Thee there,
Hear us, Holy JESU.

Thou Who must in glory reign,
Conqueror of sin and pain,
Till no enemy remain,
Hear us, Holy JESU.

f JESU, Who art glorified
In the very Flesh that died,
With the piercèd Hands and Side,
Hear us, Holy JESU.

f JESU, though enthroned on high,
Still for our infirmity
Touched with human sympathy,
Hear us, Holy JESU.

JESU, in our time of need
Our High Priest to intercede,
Living still Thy Death to plead,
Hear us, Holy JESU.

JESU, able to bestow
On Thy struggling Church below
More than we can ask or know,
Hear us, Holy JESU.

JESU, Who to heaven upborne
Didst not leave Thy Church to mourn,
p Orphaned, comfortless, forlorn,
Hear us, Holy JESU.

mf Thou Who, still our Saviour Friend.
Didst the HOLY SPIRIT send
To be with us to the end,
Hear us, Holy JESU.

p JESU, Who Thy Flesh and Blood,
Offered once upon the Rood,
Givest for Thy children's Food,
Hear us, Holy JESU.

mf Only Balm for souls distressed,
Happiness of all the blessed,
Peace of those who long for rest,
Hear us, Holy JESU.

f Thou Who, as Thou once didst rise,
Shalt be seen by human eyes
Coming through the parted skies,
Hear us, Holy JESU.

p Thou Who then on quick and dead,
All for whom Thy Blood was shed,
Shalt pronounce the judgment dread,
Hear us, Holy JESU.

mf JESU, GOD's Incarnate SON,
By Thy work for sinners done,
By the gifts for sinners won,
Hear us, Holy JESU.

That while pilgrims toiling here
We Thy Name may love and fear,
And to death may persevere,
Hear us, Holy JESU.

cr That when earthly toil is o'er
We, in rest for evermore,
May behold Thee and adore,
Hear us, Holy JESU.

Litany of the Holy Ghost.

Hymn 470. (First Tune.)

Hymn 470. (Second Tune.)

Litany of the Holy Ghost.

mf GOD the FATHER, GOD the SON,
GOD the SPIRIT, THREE in ONE,
Hear us from Thy heavenly Throne,
p Spare us, Holy TRINITY.

mf HOLY SPIRIT, heavenly Dove,
Dew descending from above,
Breath of life, and Fire of love,
p Hear us, Holy SPIRIT.

Source of strength, of knowledge clear,
Wisdom, godliness sincere,
Understanding, counsel, fear,
Hear us, Holy SPIRIT.

Source of meekness, love, and peace,
Patience, pureness, faith's increase,
Hope and joy that cannot cease,
Hear us, Holy SPIRIT.

SPIRIT guiding us aright,
SPIRIT making darkness light,
cr SPIRIT of resistless might,
Hear us, Holy SPIRIT.

p Thou by Whom the Virgin bore
Him Whom heaven and earth adore,
Sent our nature to restore,
Hear us, Holy SPIRIT.

mf Thou Whom JESUS from His Throne
Gave to cheer and help His own,
That they might not be alone,
Hear us, Holy SPIRIT.

COMFORTER, to Whom we owe
All that we rejoice to know
Of our Saviour's work below,
Hear us, Holy SPIRIT.

Thou Whose sound Apostles heard,
Thou Whose power their spirit stirred,
Giving them the living Word,
Hear us, Holy SPIRIT.

Thou Whose grace the Church doth fill,
Shewing her GOD'S perfect Will,
Making JESUS present still,
Hear us, Holy SPIRIT.

Coming with Thy power to save,
Moving on Baptismal wave,
Raising us from sin's dark grave,
Hear us, Holy SPIRIT.

p All our evil passions kill,
Bend aright our stubborn will,
Though we grieve Thee, patient still;
Hear us, Holy SPIRIT.

mf Come to raise us when we fall,
And, when snares our souls enthral,
Lead us back with gentle call;
Hear us, Holy SPIRIT.

Come to strengthen all the weak,
Give Thy courage to the meek,
Teach our faltering tongues to speak;
Hear us, Holy SPIRIT.

Come to aid the souls who yearn
More of truth Divine to learn,
And with deeper love to burn;
Hear us, Holy SPIRIT

Keep us in the narrow way,
Warn us when we go astray,
Plead within us when we pray;
Hear us, Holy SPIRIT.

cr Holy, loving, as Thou art,
All Thy sevenfold gifts impart,
Nevermore from us depart;
Hear us, Holy SPIRIT.

Litany of the Church.

Hymn 471. (First Tune.)

Hymn 471. (Second Tune.)

Litany of the Church.

mf GOD the FATHER, GÓD the SON,
GOD the SPIRIT, THRÉE in ONE,
Hear us from Thy héavenly Throne,
p Spare us, Holy TRÍNITY.

mf JESU, with Thy Chúrch abide,
Be her Saviour, LÓRD, and Guide,
While on earth her fáith is tried:
We beseech Thee, héar us.

Arms of love aróund her throw,
Shield her safe from évery foe,
dim Comfort her in tíme of woe:
We beseech Thee, héar us.

mf Keep her life and dóctrine pure,
Grant her patience tó endure,
Trusting in Thy prómise sure:
We beseech Thee, héar us.

May her voice be éver clear,
Warning of a júdgment near,
Telling of a Sáviour dear:
We beseech Thee, héar us.

All her fettered pówers release,
Bid our strife and énvy cease,
Grant the heavenly gíft of peace:
We beseech Thee, héar us.

All that she has lóst restore,
May her strength and zéal be more
Than in brightest dáys of yore:
We beseech Thee, héar us.

May she one in dóctrine be,
One in truth and chárity,
Winning all to fáith in Thee:
We beseech Thee, héar us.

May she guide the póor and blind,
Seek the lost untíl she find,
And the broken-héarted bind:
We beseech Thee, héar us.

Save her love from grówing cold,
Make her watchmen stróng and bold,
Fence her round, Thy péaceful fold:
We beseech Thee, héar us.

May her Priests Thy péople feed,
Shepherds of the flóck indeed,
Ready, where Thou cáll'st, to lead:
We beseech Thee, héar us.

p Judge her not for wórk undone,
Judge her not for fíelds unwon,
cr Bless her works in Thée begun:
We beseech Thee, héar us.

p For the past give déeper shame,
cr Make her jealous fór Thy Name,
Kindle zeal's most hóly flame:
We beseech Thee, héar us.

f Raise her to her cálling high,
Let the nations fár and nigh
Hear Thy heralds' wárning cry:
We beseech Thee, héar us.

May her lamp of trúth be bright,
Bid her bear alóft its light
Through the realms of héathen night.
We beseech Thee, héar us.

mf May her scattered chíldren be
From reproach of évil free,
Blameless witnessés for Thee:
We beseech Thee, héar us.

Arm her soldiers wíth the cross,
Brave to suffer tóil or loss,
Counting earthly gáin but dross:
We beseech Thee, héar us.

cr May she holy tríumphs win,
Overthrow the hósts of sin,
Gather all the nátions in:
We beseech Thee, héar us.

f May she soon all glórious be,
Spotless and from wrínkle free,
Pure, and bright, and wórthy Thee:
We beseech Thee, héar us.

Fit her all Thy jóy to share
In the home Thou dóst prepare,
And be ever bléssèd there:
We beseech Thee, héar us.

Litany of the Blessed Sacrament
of the Body and Blood of Christ.

Hymn 472. (First Tune.) Parts 1 and 3.

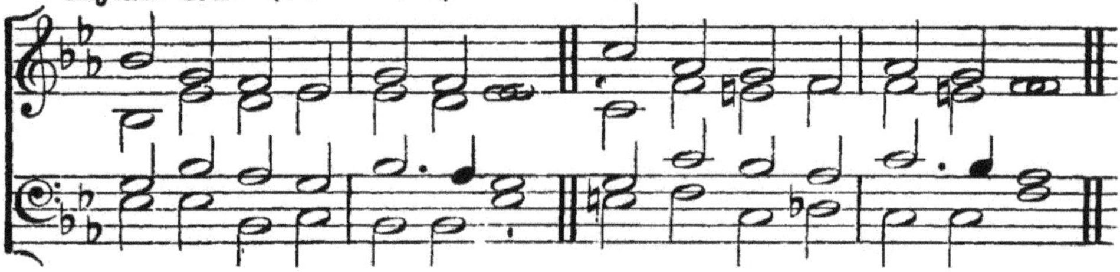

Part 2.

Hymn 472. (Second Tune.)

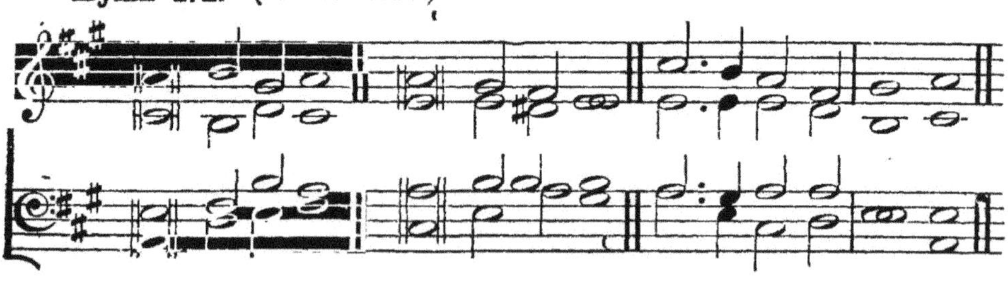

Litany of the Blessed Sacrament
of the Body and Blood of Christ.

mf GOD the FATHER, Gód the SON,
God the SPIRIT, THRÉE in ONE,
p Spare us, Holy TRINITY.

f GOD of GOD, and Líght of Light,
King of glory, LÓRD of might,
Hear us, Holy JESU.

p Very Man, Who fór our sake
Didst true Flesh of Máry take,
Hear us, Holy JESU.

mf Shepherd, Whom the FÁTHER gave
His lost sheep to fínd and save,
Hear us, Holy JESU.

Priest and Victim, Whóm of old
Type and prophecý foretold,
Hear us, Holy JESU.

King of Salem, Príest Divine,
Bringing forth Thy Bréad and Wine,
Hear us, Holy JESU.

Paschal Lamb, Whose sprínkled Blood
Saves the Israél of GOD,
Hear us, Holy JESU.

Manna, found at dáwn of day,
Pilgrim's Food in désert-way,
Hear us, Holy JESU.

Offering pure, in évery place
Pledge and means of héavenly grace,
Hear us, Holy JESU.

PART 2.

p By the mercy, thát of yore
Shadowed forth Thy gífts in store,
Save us, Holy JESU.

cr By the love, on thát last night
That ordained the bétter rite,
Save us, Holy JESU.

p By the Death, that cóuld alone
For the whole world's sín atone,
Save us, Holy JESU.

By the Wounds, that éver plead
For our help in tíme of need,
Save us, Holy JESU.

PART 3.

That we may remémber still
Kedron's brook and Cálvary's hill,
Grant us, Holy JESU.

mf That our thankful héarts may glow
As Thy precious Déath we show,
Grant us, Holy JESU.

That, with humble cóntrite fear,
We may joy to féel Thee near,
Grant us, Holy JESU.

cr That in faith we máy adore,
Praise, and love Thee móre and more
Grant us, Holy JESU.

p That Thy Sacred Flésh and Blood
Be our true life-gíving Food,
Grant us, Holy JESU.

mf That in all our wórds and ways
We may daily shéw Thy praise,
Grant us, Holy JESU.

cr That, as death's dark vále we tread,
Thou mayst be our stréngthening Bread,
Grant us, Holy JESU.

mf That, unworthy thóugh we be,
We may ever dwéll with Thee,
Grant us, Holy JESU.

Litany for Children.

Hymn 473. (First Tune.)

Hymn 473. (Second Tune.)

Litany* for Children.

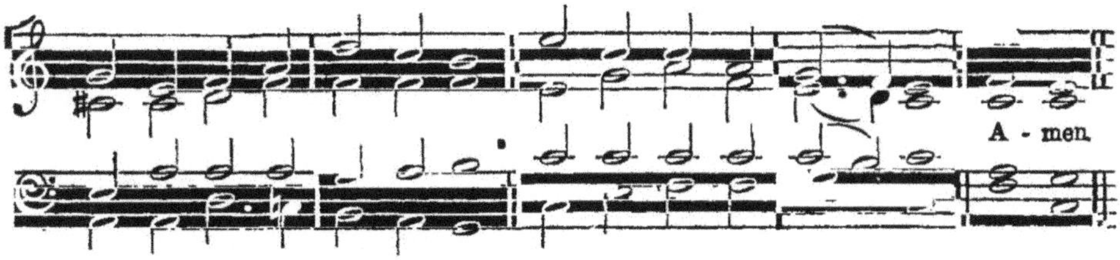

mf GOD the FATHER, GOD the SON,
GOD the SPIRIT, THREE in ONE,
Hear us from Thy heavenly Throne,
p Spare us, Holy TRINITY.

Jesu, Saviour ever mild,
Born for us a little Child
Of the Virgin undefiled,
Hear us, Holy Jesu.

Jesu, by the Mother-Maid
In Thy swaddling-clothes arrayed,
And within a manger laid,
Hear us, Holy Jesu.

Jesu, at Whose Infant Feet
Shepherds, coming Thee to greet,
Knelt to pay their worship meet,
Hear us, Holy Jesu.

mf Jesu, unto Whom of yore
Wise men, hastening to adore,
Gold and myrrh and incense bore,
Hear us, Holy Jesu.

Jesu, to Thy Temple brought,
Whom, by Thy good SPIRIT taught,
Simeon and Anna sought,
Hear us, Holy Jesu.

Jesu, Who didst deign to flee
From King Herod's cruelty
In Thy earliest Infancy,
Hear us, Holy Jesu.

cr Jesu, Whom Thy Mother found
'Midst the doctors sitting round,
Marvelling at Thy Words profound,
Hear us, Holy Jesu.

PART 2.

p From all pride and vain conceit,
From all spite and angry heat,
From all lying and deceit,
Save us, Holy Jesu.

From all sloth and idleness,
From not caring for distress,
From all lust and greediness,
Save us, Holy Jesu.

From refusing to obey,
From the love of our own way,
From forgetfulness to pray,
Save us, Holy Jesu.

PART 3.

mf By Thy Birth and early years,
By Thine Infant wants and fears,
By Thy sorrows and Thy tears,
Save us, Holy Jesu.

By Thy Pattern bright and pure,
By the pains Thou didst endure
Our salvation to procure,
Save us, Holy Jesu.

p By Thy Wounds and thorn-crowned [Head,
By Thy Blood for sinners shed,
mf By Thy Rising from the dead,
Save us, Holy Jesu.

By the Name we bow before,
Human Name, which evermore
All the hosts of heaven adore,
Save us, Holy Jesu.

f By Thine own unconquered might,
By Thy glory in the height,
By Thy mercies infinite,
Save us, Holy Jesu.

LONDON:
WILLIAM CLOWES AND SONS, LIMITED, TYPE MUSIC AND GENERAL PRINTERS,
STAMFORD STREET AND CHARING CROSS.

Milton Keynes UK
Ingram Content Group UK Ltd.
UKHW040922180224
437992UK00003B/42

9 783382 831325